C000110897

The Black Rose Series

By

LM Morgan

VOLUME 2

Book 3 - Forever Darkness
Pg.5

Book 4 – Destined for Darkness
Pg.177

IBSN: 9798478905576

An important message from the author.

Before you read this book, please be ready to delve into a dark and taboo world of demons and angels who can and will do as they please. This series, especially the first novel, will immerse you in a world filled with dark places and even darker beings. They are not human, and do not act the way you and I act or think the way you and I think. Please be ready for some controversial themes and for me to push the boundaries.

I tell you this not just because there are adult scenes or a few taboo subjects, but because I mean it, and would hate to give you any false expectations about happy endings and softly, softly romance. This series is not for everyone, and I know that, so please decide if you're ready before diving in.

If you're on the fence or have heard the rumours of the depravities and darkness that await you, please assume they are all true. I can understand how some readers were upset and discouraged by the thought of some of the darker themes, but urge you to trust me…

PLEASE NOTE

This story depicts explicit sexual relationships between consenting adults, including romantic suspense, elements of forced consent, instances of domestic violence and incest. This series is very dark, and may not be suitable for those under the age of eighteen.

Cover art by LM Morgan
Cover photograph courtesy of Deposit Photos

Forever Darkness

Book# 3 the Black Rose series

By

LM Morgan

2021 Revised Edition

PROLOGUE

The Black Prince of Hell and heir to the dark throne, Blake Rose had lived his many years of existence being cold-hearted, closed off and even downright cruel. His powerful father, Lucifer, had been both inspiring and devastating to his upbringing and Blake had lived his long and lonely life burdened and miserable thanks to Lucifer's teachings. That was, until he met Tilly. The human girl had been foolish, clumsy, and unwittingly rude when he had first laid eyes on her, but he had been immediately mesmerised by the stunning woman and chose to mark her as his follower, the first in his many years of existence.

Tilly had then gone on to push every one of Blake's buttons, forcing her way into his heart, and he eventually relinquished his tight hold on the miserable walls he had built around himself. He hadn't made it easy on her and yet Tilly had stuck with him through the good and the bad. She had taken the pleasure and the pain in adherence to her dark promises to follow and to love Blake, regardless of how much he might hurt her along the way, and she had gone on to win his heart forever. Now though, Tilly lay dying up on Earth, stabbed and unconscious thanks to the white witch, Beatrice, and her sinister methods to get her masters' terrible message to the Dark Queen and new Devil, Cate Rose.

Cate had overthrown her husband Lucifer and taken the throne many years ago to keep her family safe. She would do it again in a heartbeat and her children all knew that it was a very necessary tactic in the preservation of both their lives and her powerful reign. Together Cate and Lucifer had been strong and powerful, their union producing not only their twins Blake and Luna, but also a thriving underworld with the omnipotent duo at the helm. When an angel named Uriel had torn them apart, they just could not find their way back to each other, and the problems began.

However, Cate had already fallen in love with a human man, Harry, who deserved her love and respect far more than either of the powerful beings that had sought to own her heart. While fighting one another, Lucifer and Uriel had failed to notice her heart slip away and belong to Harry, and when the time came for her to decide, she surprised them all by choosing the kind, human man rather than either of the powerful beings. Harry was the other half of Cate's heart, her soulmate, and the man she entrusted to keep hers and Uriel's secret child safe from either light or dark influence. Cate knew when the time came that she had to take her child of half light and darkness, Lottie, back to Hell with her and so Harry had then performed an ancient ritual to become a demon and take his place in Hell alongside his new family. The lovers were married as soon as he made his way to the top of the demonic hierarchy, as a level one demon he was finally worthy of her hand in marriage and the pair of them knew without a shadow of a doubt that they would love each other tirelessly for all eternity. And for more than fifty years, they had.

Uriel was a bitter, twisted, and unsatisfied angel, though, watching the Earth from his heavenly realm. Cate had hidden their daughter away from his reach as soon as she came of age and had dealt with his threats ever since, but now he had upped the ante. He had not only instigated an attack on Blake's lover, a move that Cate truly believed was a fluke but regardless, Tilly was dying, and it was all at the hands of her ex. Cate knew she needed to act, to follow through with the promises she had made to the young girl, all the while carrying the weight of his threat on her already heavily laden shoulders.

Uriel would be dealt with soon, no matter what it took she would make sure that no one else in her care was hurt thanks to him ever again, but first the larger matter at hand was Tilly and her soul's slow descent to Hell. Cate could feel her dying, sense her soul clinging on just barely to her human shell and so she knew what had to be done.

For the sake of her only son Cate had placed Tilly above all other human's she had known in her lengthy existence, and she was willing to bend the rules to her advantage for her now, just as she had with Harry when she chose to turn him into a demon for entirely selfish reasons. She had never looked back since and knew that she would feel the same about her decision to save Tilly now, she just had to hold on a few days until the full moon rose on Earth and then everything would be irrevocably changed for the young girl. Tilly would be darkly blessed with an immortal life, and an eternity at Blake's side. Life as this once so lowly human knew it would never be the same again.

CHAPTER ONE

Cate's high priestess and most trusted dark witch, Alma, worked tirelessly on Tilly's broken and battered body for days trying to save her life. The Black Prince of Hell, Blake, had issued strict orders for the powerful witch to do whatever it took to save his lover's life, and she was determined not to let him down. Tilly's consciousness returned to her not long after her half-dead body was delivered to the edge of the London penthouse's protective dark threshold by the sickeningly satisfied white witch a few hours after her attack, keeping the human woman's soul firmly where it needed to be, but Alma could not be sure for how long.

Beatrice's enchanted dagger had somehow poisoned Tilly's entire body as well as the wound itself, penetrating her tender stomach. The ancient white magic was now fighting against all of Alma's attempts to help and while the powerful witch refused to believe she could do nothing to save her, no matter what she tried, Tilly just would not get better. She would sometimes stir, vaguely aware that she was still alive, but then the pain and darkness would overwhelm her senses and pull her under again quickly, her sub-consciousness forcing her into strange and terrifying dreams that neither she nor Blake could control.

He teleported to her side as soon as the moon was full again a few nights later and immediately fell to his knees at her bedside. He could sense the death creeping into his lover the instant he laid eyes on her. Tilly's stab wound was hardly healing despite Alma's best potions and spells, and she was barely conscious now at all, only just about hanging on to her human life. Her dark-blonde hair was matted to her head with sweat and tears, ruffled up thanks to her fretful sleep, but she still looked beautiful to him. Blake hated seeing her this way, but he wouldn't be anywhere else than with her. Tilly had loved him at his worst no matter how hard he had made it on her, and Blake was finally able to understand what it meant to truly love another with every inch of himself. He felt her pain and anguish like it was his own and knew his heart could not survive losing her now.

"I should've always known I'd be the death of you, Tilly," Blake whispered, staring at her for a moment forlornly before he forcefully shook himself free of the guilt that threatened to overwhelm him and looked over at Alma. "Go to my mother, ask her, beg her to come and see for herself how bad she is. She promised me she would help, but I need to save Tilly, now. Ask for her permission to have someone turn her, please?" he bellowed at the witch, tears streaming uncontrollably from his eyes as he took in the pale girl before him, the girl that he loved so very much and would do just about anything to save.

Blake took Tilly's hand and kissed it before he then raised his index finger to his mouth and bit down on it. He leaned forward, dropping some of his blood into her dry lips in an effort to stave off death for just a little while longer, sharing his strength with her willingly, desperately.

Tilly's deep blue eyes fluttered open after a few minutes, and she smiled when she saw Blake standing over her. Despite her agony and despair, her heart fluttered in her chest at seeing him again, away from her nightmares and away from that all-consuming darkness he had found her soul in down in Hell.

"Some things are worth dying for, Blake," she whispered back to him before she winced in pain again. His shared power had helped her, but it was just a short-term solution and Tilly soon began coughing up blood and became woozy again, hardly able to stay awake.

Blake's mother, Cate, arrived at the penthouse just minutes later and gasped as she took in the bloody, dreadful sight before her. Despite the recent demands from Uriel hanging over her head she focussed now on the girl she had promised to take care of, the girl who had been the one thing in all of Blake's existence that had ever mattered to him, and she knew Tilly had to be saved. Cate could sense her son's fear and desperation and knew that there was only one thing they could do to rescue her soul from the bottom of the hellish heap. Her son looked terrible, his mind and emotions in a fraught tangle he had never known, and she knew then that Blake was finally ready to give himself to another.

"Sire her Blake, you have my blessing, she will become the only demon with royal blood in her veins and that will make her worthy of a place at your side, worthy of being your future Queen," Cate told him, patting her son's shoulder and giving him a kind smile when he looked up into her matching green eyes in shock. The demon Berith was then summoned to her side to be witness to the demonic ceremony, and he gasped when he saw Tilly laying half dead on the bed. Despite his now unwavering loyalty to his Queen and his continually proven trustworthiness with her family, Berith could not help but panic at seeing Blake's lover in such a bad way. He had been proving himself constantly to Cate ever since he revealed her secrets to Lucifer all those years before, but she had granted him her mercy and had asked him to become a demonic sire to Harry, kick-starting his rise in her favour thanks to his loyalty to her now and his proven trustworthiness. Berith knew he should've tried harder to find Tilly when she was pulled from his grip thanks to Beatrice's trap when they teleported overhead, he should not have stopped until he tracked her down, but he had failed, and now he stood beneath his Dark Queen's questioning gaze and his stomach dropped.

"I don't know what happened, your Majesty. We were teleporting, and it was as if she was just ripped from my grasp on our way back to London. I had no control and then I couldn't find her. I went straight to Blake, but he couldn't sense her either," Berith tried to explain but Cate raised a hand to silence him.

"It doesn't matter now, what's done is done," she told the demon, her voice calm and steady, but her eyes did not leave Tilly's frail form.

"Do you need me to sire her?" he then asked, assuming that it must be the reason for her calling him to the penthouse, but Cate shook her head.

"No, I've decided to let Blake do it," she replied. "I just need a demonic witness," she then added. Berith nodded and stepped to the side, understanding his place in the ritual and staying silent now as the others continued to prepare the room.

Alma got straight to work, quickly drawing out a pentagram on the floor and then rushing to the kitchen for the required instruments for the primeval ritual. Blake then lifted his lover off the bed and carried Tilly over to the floor, where he sat down inside the powerful symbol with her before him. Blake then quickly slit his wrist using the tip of his index finger, allowing some of his strong blood to pour into the cup that Alma had placed beside him. He then reached down and grabbed Tilly's limp arm as she sat in front of him inside the pentagram, cutting her pale skin with his fingertip too and then sucking down just enough of her blood to complete the ritual adequately, careful not to drain her too much in case she lost consciousness again.

Alma stepped forward, ready to proceed with the ritual, and she spoke quietly to Tilly, drawing the frail woman's attention as she spoke the evocative words.

"Before the almighty Dark Queen, and in the presence of demons and witches, do you renounce all other allegiances and pledge your soul to your Mistress, Her Infernal Majesty, Hecate?" Alma asked Tilly, leaning closer, needing to hear her answer.

"Yes," she replied, panting and woozy but clear of mind as she spoke the words and she meant them with every inch of her being. Alma nodded, reached down and then lifted the cup of Blake's blood to Tilly's lips.

"Then drink of your master, share his blood and become his demonic sire," she told Tilly, having to tilt back her head to help her as she gulped down the thick liquid as quickly as she could manage it.

"So mote it be, hail to the Dark Queen. Hail Satan," Alma said, and Tilly repeated the words as loud as she could, completing the ancient ritual at last. She didn't even have time to think about what she had just done, there had been no time to dwell on the life-changing ceremony that she had performed, but she knew it was right and could already feel her body strengthening thanks to her lover's bloody offering.

She felt Blake holding tightly onto her hand and did her best to hold him back, shuffling closer towards him inside the black pentagram. A strange yet incredible heaviness then seemed to fill her body within just a few seconds, reviving her weak soul instantly before a black mist then rose around them and seemed to surround the pair as they sat inside the ancient symbol. The mist clung to every inch of her body, sinking into her skin, into her soul, and Tilly could feel her body healing, repairing, and strengthening from somewhere deep within, thanks to the strange fog.

Tilly also felt a new sensation resonating from somewhere inside, her master's powerful force as it flowed through her and created a new, dark flame deep within that combined with her new power to deliver her with immortality, true demonic prowess, incredible strength, and heightened senses. As the strength and power flowed through her, Tilly welcomed it, opening herself up to this precious gift and she mentally thanked both Blake and her Dark Queen for it with a silent prayer. When the black mist finally subsided, she felt wonderful, free of pain, and strangely more alive than ever. Tilly then looked up into Blake's warm green eyes and smiled, relishing in the happy smile he gave her in return.

He wrapped his strong arms around her and then pulled Tilly up so that they were standing side by side in the pentagram. She looked over at the Queen and bowed to her, sensing for the first time Cate's dark and powerful true form, and she loved her fiercely, but also feared and respected her mistress more than ever, too.

Cate released Tilly from her bow and looked down at her, a satisfied and happy smile on her face as the new demon gazed up in true awe at her beautiful mistress. Cate was beautiful, as ever, but she resonated with a dark magnificence that Tilly had not previously seen in her, an ancient and omnipotent grace that flowed from within the powerful Queen. She no longer looked human-like, as Tilly had always seen her before. The new demon could see her real form now, but she was not afraid. Cate still had her stunning features, the deep green eyes and dark curls that each of her children too possessed, all of them being her image, thanks to their fathers' non-human offerings towards their conception.

Tilly then turned to her master and threw her arms around his neck, kissing Blake with every ounce of strength she had, desperately, deeply, and so grateful for his dark gift of life. Their mouths devoured one another's, Tilly's hands gripping his neck and running up through his dark curls in a desperately passionate need to feel him. When they finally broke away from their deep kiss, Cate, Alma, and Berith were gone. All that remained was the debris of their ritual and the bloody bed where Tilly had been laying not long before, almost dead. And yet now she was very much alive, transformed forever and eternally grateful for her demonic gift of immortality, and her second chance at life.

"The witches will take care of all of this," Blake said, grinning down at her as he offered Tilly his hand. She took it and stepped even closer, smiling up at him as she took him in, sensing his true dark form for the first time, too. The shadows clung to him in an unnatural way, but she could sense his power over them. They were drawn to him, just as she was. She wasn't even the slightest bit afraid of what she saw inside of Blake now and loved how she felt in his ominous presence.

"Thank you for saving me," she said, perpetually grateful for his forceful rejection of her soul from Hell when it had left her broken form and descended, glad that she had still been able to go back to her body, and incredibly happy that he had been the one to sire her, cementing their bond even more. "What do I have to do now?" she then asked him, remembering how her friend and fellow new demon, Lucas, had been required to go to Hell and complete his initiations not long after being turned.

"We can wait until the moon wanes, my love, and then you must come to Hell with me and begin your training and initiation into the demonic world. You could potentially have a long road ahead if you do not progress up the classification's during your two attempts Tilly, but I will watch over you until you do and when it ends, it will end at my side, forever," Blake replied, scooping her into his arms and carrying her out to one of the guest bedrooms away from the blood-stained master suite. He took her straight into the bathroom where he ripped off her bloody clothes and Tilly eagerly followed his lead, stripping Blake off too and joining him in a luxuriously hot shower before falling onto the bed and straddling him with her strong thighs.

"I love you so much," Tilly told Blake as she positioned herself over his hard, ready length, eager to have him but holding back slightly, teasing him as a cheeky grin claimed her sexy red lips.

"I love you, too," he replied, pulling her down onto him forcefully and gasping as her deep inner muscles tensed around him wonderfully. She cried out, her new, strong, powerful body able to react to him in a way she had not anticipated. It was as though every one of her senses was heightened and every pleasurable tingle was ten times stronger than it had once been. She pulled up and down on him, fast and hard, not stopping for even an instant and relishing in every fantastic sensation as she built her climax, reaching it effortlessly as they moved together with such strong synchronicity and powerful love.

They did not leave the bed at all for the next two days, only stopping their lovemaking when the moon was close to waning again, but this time he would not be leaving her there alone like so many times before and she would not have to wait another month to be with her beloved master.

"So, are you ready to go and see your new home?" Blake asked, and Tilly smiled and nodded.

"Hell yes," she replied with a wicked grin, and then took his outstretched hand. She could then quickly feel the tell-tale sensation of being teleported away, however this time it was different, instead of the usual pull of travelling across the Earth. This time they were heading downwards towards Hell.

CHAPTER TWO

Blake and Tilly arrived at the gates of Hell just a few minutes before the moon waned up on Earth, and immediately the stifling heat and lack of air down there hit her lungs like pins stabbing at her from the inside and Tilly struggled for a few minutes, coughing and wobbling until eventually regaining her composure after a while, her human instincts taking a moment to give in to her new demonic senses. She then looked up at the dark gates before her, seeing through them and up to the huge, ominous castle that dominated the red sky above them. It all reminded Tilly of her most gothic fantasies come to life, the huge citadel towering over them from the centre of a vast city inhabited by demons and other dark creatures, while the royal family lived inside their huge home. She imagined it all so clearly in her head, knowing their lavish tastes from the way their penthouses were decorated and she couldn't wait to see inside. Blake watched her with a satisfied smile, he had always assumed that he wouldn't be able to bring Tilly here for a long time, that their love would be bound by the moon for many more years to come, and yet here she now was. A new demon, his demon, and he was determined to have her by his side as soon as he could.

He took her hand and led Tilly inside the city walls before teleporting her away again, wasting no time in getting her ready for her initiations. The grand tour and introductions could wait. They arrived in a small room within seconds. It was basically furnished with just a small bed and desk that was covered in old books and notepads, seemingly set out in readiness for its next demonic student. Tilly looked up at her lover and master, unsure what she needed to do next or what the proper process was behind the classifications, but no matter what, she was determined not to let him down.

"You'll be fine, my love, but I need you to stay here for now and read, practise, learn, hone your skills and, most important of all, be ready to complete your initiation," he told her. "It doesn't matter to you this time around as you are a new demon, so have no classification yet anyway, but your goal is to get as high up the levels as possible on your first time in the initiation hall. Then, if you have to come back, you start the tasks again at the beginning, but you would not go back a level even if you failed next time. So, for example, if you make it to level three this round, but next time you are wiped out at the level four stage, you still go home as a level three demon Tilly. The goal is to improve and then proceed higher."

"That's good to hear," she mumbled, feeling a little overwhelmed, but her mind was still clearer than ever before, and she knew she had to give it her best shot.

"You have just a few days to read these texts, learn them as best you can, practice the methods and harness your powers. Do not sleep, rest or take any breaks, think of this as the most important exam you will ever have to take," Blake then said as he peered down at her, his expression dark and stern, and Tilly could tell that he was worried about her.

"I will, I won't let you down, Blake, I promise," she replied, kissing his lips gently, and she was shocked to feel him tense up slightly at her touch.

"There's something else you need to consider here, regardless of our public bond when you were human, we cannot show our love in front of the other demons while in Hell, Tilly," he told her, looking at her even more intensely now. "You must not say my name unless we are alone, at least not until you make it to level one. Formality is crucial right now. There are beings here that are thousands of years old, and they expect absolute adherence to my mother's rules, even if she herself is lenient when we are alone. You were once my human follower, bound only to me by my mark, but now you are a demon who will be expected to stay within the boundaries of your classification. There is no room for error or clumsiness now, Tilly," Blake added, his green eyes warm and full of love as he spoke. "Also, I cannot do you any favours or allow you any leniency from me during your assessments in the initiation hall. The other council members know you are my progeny and will be watching me to make sure that I remain impartial, I absolutely cannot be thought of as having helped you to climb higher than they think you should have," he added, his expression becoming fierce as he even contemplated his council questioning his judgement, but she understood his reasons.

"Your blood runs through my veins now Blake, there's no way that I can fail," she replied, her own face serious now too and she meant it. Tilly didn't know if it was faith, love, or sheer determination, but somehow, she had never been surer of anything in her life. She would succeed. Anything less than becoming a level one demon would be a failure in her eyes. Blake stared down at her, relaxing immediately thanks to her encouraging words and determined thoughts.

"Good girl. Now, I must leave you here, and I will not see you again until you are brought before the council for your testing in a few days. But, if you do fight your way to the top, we can be together Tilly, anything lower and it will take us longer until we can properly be a couple," Blake reiterated, his face serious and his tone stern again but Tilly knew just how important her reaching the coveted level one classification was to them both. She reached up and cupped his cheeks with her hands, and then kissed him again.

"I understand," she replied, looking around her and quickly realising just how much work she needed to do to make their joint wish come true. "Well, you'd better go and let me study then," she added with a smile, and he grinned back before he kissed the tip of her nose and then teleported away.

Tilly hit the books right away, poring over each one and learning about the ancient stories, rituals and information held within them as best she could. One of them outlined the most important aspect of a new demon's dark power, it stressed that first and foremost a demon must learn the techniques required to harness their new powers and control the dark flame that had flickered to life deep within them, without this dominance the demon would not be able to carry out any of their most basic abilities. She followed the book's advice and lay back on the bed and concentrated as hard as she could, focusing on drawing the darkness in from all around her, adding it to her own small flame, controlling it and then harnessing it for her own means, keeping it to use at her disposal as and when she might require it. The growing power within her felt amazing, and she repeated the exercise over and over again until she felt it flowing deep within, ready to be utilised when she commanded.

The next couple of days passed by quickly as she kept busy with a mixture of revising the texts and practising their methods, and Tilly felt confident that she was finally getting the hang of all the demonic abilities she had tried out in her tiny chambers. A hooded warlock then teleported into her room and informed her it was time for her to be tried before the Black Council. Tilly nodded and stood to greet him. She was scared, but ready and eager to get it all over with as soon as possible, so she followed him out of the room and down various hallways and stairs that eventually led into a huge hall. It was dimly lit inside and there was an intense heat in there that would've felt uncomfortable on her previously human skin, but not anymore, and Tilly was grateful that she no longer needed to care about such mortal things.

A row of seven hooded figures looked down at her from atop a set of black granite stairs. They sat side by side at a long table, ready and watching as Tilly and around forty other demons filed into the large hall. Blake was sat in the centre, she could both sense him and see his green eyes as they watched her from under his black cloak, but she didn't hold his gaze, eager not to draw too much attention to their bond despite how much she had missed him over her last few days of solitude.

After everyone was inside, he stood up from his seat, looking out at the group, when they had all come to a standstill before the council table. Each of the demons immediately knelt before him, their heads bowed in respect.

"Welcome demons, you are all here for one purpose, to succeed. Whether you were once a human soul who has fought their way to the top of the pile and are here for classification after your transition, an existing demon wishing to move higher than their allocated level or a new demon entirely who is starting from scratch, we will determine your standing in our hierarchy of demons here and now," he said as he released them, and each rose to their feet.

"I hope you are adequately prepared, for your actions during these initiations will be the only deciding factor as to which level you will be placed in. Should you wish to climb higher, you can come back and try again, but be warned that if you do not progress after two attempts you are not permitted to try again for another two-hundred years," Blake told them, taking a moment to eye each and every one of the eager demons with his well-honed, business-like and strict, yet undeniably gorgeous stare.

"Very well, let us begin. Your first test is one of skill, strength, and instinct. A truly powerful demon must be ready to take down anyone who poses as a threat, without needing to ask why or trying to reason with them first. So, your orders are simple. Turn to the demon closest to you and fight them. That's it. The first one to go down is done and will be placed in the lowest demonic classification level if necessary. Go," he commanded and sat back down in his high-backed, almost throne-like and ornately carved wooden chair. Tilly looked to her side to check out the demon closest to her, and then had to crane her neck to peer up at the huge, burly man who was standing next to her. He must have been over two feet taller than she was and very thickly set, muscular and fierce looking.

"Fucking hell," Tilly said quietly to herself, thinking how nice it would have been if Blake had given her a little bit of a clue, or at least pointed her in the direction of a more equal adversary, but she also knew that he could not risk it, she was alone in these tasks and had to give it everything she had without ever expecting favouritism, special treatment or leniency, nor could she send him a silent plea for help just in case he was tempted to give her it.

CHAPTER THREE

The huge demon smiled down at Tilly wickedly, as though impressed with his unlucky opponent, and he moved closer, his hands coming up, aiming for her throat as he came towards her. Although she hadn't had any combat training, Tilly instinctually summoned every ounce of strength she could muster and stood firm, then thrust the heel of her hand hard up into his nose, which immediately broke and then spurted with blood. Next, as he raised his hands to grab it in reflex, she sent an uppercut into the man's abdomen, winding him instantly. The demon cried out, pain and anger overwhelming him for just a moment, but the distraction didn't last long. He soon regained his heavy-set composure and pushed her back, thrusting his palms against her shoulders, sending Tilly flying back into a stone pillar behind her and he shot her another wicked grin as he gained on her again, moving fast even with his burly frame.

She took a deep breath and focussed on her darkness, having been practising hard to control it, and felt her hands begin to tingle under the weight of the invisible power that coursed through her muscles at her command, feeling heavy and strong thanks to its precious gift of strength. She shoved the man back, knocking him flying off his feet and onto the floor on his back, the wind completely knocked out of him now. Tilly then stood over him and planted a swift kick to his neck and readied herself for his next move, but this time there wasn't one. He just stayed there on the ground for a moment before disappearing before her eyes. Tilly looked up at the council table questioningly and caught a quick nod from Blake before looking around at the other demons in the hall. Those that had also won their fights stood to the side and watched as the last remaining pairs finished their one-on-one battles. Tilly joined the other victors by a side wall, catching her old friend and fellow new demon, Lucas McCulloch's eye there as she wandered over. He looked her up and down, wide-eyed, and bemused, clearly wanting to ask her what had happened and how she had come to be here, but neither dared say a word to each other, knowing that her explanations would have to wait. Lucas had been deemed worthy of his new demonic power after years of servitude to the Dark Queen and having carried out his demonic trials as a human. Tilly had been travelling back from his transition in Edinburgh when Beatrice had trapped her, but Lucas had been down in Hell preparing for his classifications, so had no idea what she had been through. She would reveal all in due time, but now they both had to concentrate, so she looked back towards the council table, focussed and ready for their next task.

"Excellent," Blake said, standing to address them again when the last demon fell and had disappeared. "The next test is simple, yet crucial. You will notice that there are two black marks on the floor of each side of the hall. You are to teleport yourself from one of them to the other, making sure to land perfectly in place, for if you cannot even teleport then how can you be ready to proceed any further?" he asked, finishing his next order before taking his seat again and watching them along with the other silent council members.

The demons all stepped towards the first black mark hesitantly in turn, and Tilly knew that for new demons things like teleportation normally had to be perfected over time, she had given it a good try in her room the day before but was still worried about just how small the mark on the other side of the hall was and how exact she had to be in her landing. The few demons that went before her all succeeded, including Lucas, and when it was her turn Tilly stood and readied herself, focussing her mind as she blocked out the other demons around her. Again, she summoned the dark power within herself and pushed off, concentrating with all her might to move between the spaces with control and clarity of mind. She almost jumped for joy as she landed, realising that she had done it perfectly and was glad to be one step closer to her lover's side. Tilly smiled over at Lucas when she re-appeared at the other side of the hall and quickly moved over to the wall to watch the other demons in their attempts. Only a few of the demons failed this task, a couple falling short of the intended arrival mark and one that was not able to do it at all. Those that failed were removed from the hall immediately and the new demons given the level nine classification.

Without any break between the formal initiation processes, they then moved on to the next task, in which human souls were brought into the hall by witches, bound and silent as they knelt before the demons.

"To strike fear into a human is a much needed mid-level demonic trait, one that can only be mastered by subduing your own conscience and embracing your fierce nature," Blake called down from the council table. "You have one chance to make them beg for mercy, off you go," he commanded, watching as the demons gazed down at the humans by their feet and he read their thoughts as they contemplated their chosen methods in which to complete this task.

Tilly moved towards her intended victim, a young girl who stared up at her with a scared expression. She stood over the girl and took in the innocent face before her, struggling to stop herself from feeling sorry for her, but also knowing full well that this girl's soul must have been tried in purgatory and deemed as deserving of a place in Hell, so she quickly decided against giving her any pity, this girl was her ticket to the next task and she would not let her still lingering human emotions get in the way of that. She knelt before her and then reached around to grab the girl by her hair, tilting her face up to meet hers and staring into her eyes so that she could try and read her, to understand, harness and call forth her darkest nightmares. Tilly summoned her power again, calling on it for guidance and then she smiled wickedly, realising she could somehow intuitively read the girl's deepest, darkest fears. Tilly's facial features changed in an instant, darkening and altering slightly for just a second or two in the darkness to resemble a face that had haunted the girl's nightmares as a child, and it was more than enough for her, she took one look and screamed loudly as she looked upon the face that filled her with instant dread.

Tilly stood again and looked down at her with a satisfied smile as the girl disappeared before her eyes, she still didn't really understand exactly how she had done it, but she had somehow known that the girl had been terrified of an evil witch that she had seen in a movie once and had flashed her with a perfect resemblance of it along with a silent promise to haunt her dreams again. Tilly knew that the royals had all mentioned her intuitive nature in the past and wondered if she still possessed that side of herself, that perhaps it was helping her now. She quickly realised that she had been the first one to finish this task, and smiled to herself, hoping that Blake was pleased with her as she wandered off to the side, watching the others as they attempted to complete the challenge, too. A few of the demons were unsuccessful and dropped out, but most of them were victorious and remained in the hall to await their orders for the next one with her.

Blake rose from his seat again after the trembling souls were taken away and those who had failed were dismissed or classified as level eight demons and then excused.

"Let us continue to our next task, to establish control over both the conscious and subconscious mind," he said. "Half of you, take the potion from one of the witches before you and lay down on the floor. You will fall asleep within seconds. The other half, sit down beside one of the sleeping demons and enter their dreams. Sounds so simple, right?" he added with a grin and then sat back down, whispering quietly with the council member to his right.

Tilly was given a potion by a dark haired witch and quickly sipped it down before lying on the hard floor. She was asleep almost instantly and after a few seconds began to dream. She was at home on the farm but saw a dark figure in the distance, coming closer before she eventually saw his face clearly in her mind, he was not meant to be a part of this fantasy, his presence was forced yet very clear in her dream, telling her that the demon beside her had succeeded in this task.

She awoke after just a few minutes and congratulated the demon on his success. He thanked Tilly and swapped places with her before he drank down his own vial and lay before her on the floor, asleep almost instantly too. She sat over him, focussing on his thoughts, staring into his face, and concentrating hard on his subconscious mind, shifting her own and pulling herself into his dreams. She appeared in a city, which sprawled out before her as though it were real and the demon was sat at a coffee shop table, staring into the eyes of the woman he clearly loved, a middle-aged human woman dressed in a business suit who was telling him they were over. He jumped when he saw Tilly watching them and tried to change the image but had no control.

"Yes, well done," said a voice in her head, and she realised it was Blake telling her she had completed the task. Tilly withdrew from the demon's mind and released him from his slumber, giving him a hand up as he groggily awoke and blushed, a moment of truth passing silently between them about his unrequited love. They both said nothing but couldn't help smiling at each other over their success as they waited at the side again, watching as a few more demons dropped out, but most were successful and carried on.

CHAPTER FOUR

The next of their tests was to charm a human in order for them to willingly sell them their soul, and a second girl was brought before her by the dark witches, this one completely human, not just a soul like the last one. Tilly summoned the same intuitive prowess that she had used to strike fear into the other girl, this time searching the human before her for her desires instead of her fears and knew exactly what she needed to lure her in with—kindness and the promise of a family the girl had never had. Tilly kneeled, gazing into her eyes warmly.

"What's your name?" she asked her, taking her chin in her hand so that the girl's brown eyes couldn't help but meet her deep blue ones.

"Arianna," she replied, trembling.

"Don't be scared Arianna. I am very pleased to meet you. My name is Tilly," she said quietly, smiling across at her as she spoke, and she could sense the girl already calming down.

"That's a strange name for a demon," the girl replied, making Tilly smile wider as their rapport began without her even having to employ any devious tactics.

"Well, I'm new and as part of my new life, I would very much like a human to become part of my following. I wonder if you would like to join me? You could finally have somewhere you truly belong, and I would keep you safe," Tilly promised, making Arianna smile as she then silently filled the girl with happiness and a calm inner peace, her conscious mind asking for the girl's soul in return for her promised place at her side.

"Yes," the girl said, lifting her hand and offering Tilly her wrist to mark.

"Very good," said a voice to her side, it was the dark haired witch again, who snapped her fingers, sending Arianna into a sudden deep sleep as though she were hypnotised, and she then indicated for Tilly to wait at the side again while the other demons continued their pursuits. She stood and stepped away, catching the deep green eyes on her and slightly curved mouth that was watching from above her as she did so.

The next test involved the witches again. This time, the demons that remained were expected to absorb a powerful curse from one of the dark witches and then dispel the magic, or else succumb to a torturous agony that would last for days. Tilly was placed before none other than her master's high priestess, Selena, who wore a smug grin as she readied herself to deliver the powerful curse to her master's lover. Tilly just smiled back at her and let down her protective walls, standing tall as the dark curse hit her, sending blinding pain throughout her entire body for a moment before she focussed on it, demanding it to obey her and leave. Her hands felt tingly and heavy again, just as they had done with the demon in the first task, and she opened her eyes to see the curse pouring out of her fingertips like a black wave, and then it was gone.

The curse left Tilly with a terrible headache in its wake, but she didn't let it show and smiled triumphantly at Selena who bowed dutifully and moved away, her grin having left her dark face now as she moved on to her next demonic target, Lucas. He too succeeded, quickly casting out the curse and regaining his strong stance within seconds, seemingly unscathed.

There were others that deflected the curse instinctually, failing the task immediately as they had not followed Blake's orders properly so were disqualified. Another couple of them failed miserably and were taken away, writhing in agony, and screaming for help that they would not get.

"You have done well," the Black Prince told the last remaining few demons once the hall was cleared again, standing now to watch over them as the initiations moved towards their intense and climactic end.

"Your next task is one of pure evil and initiative. You are each ordered to kill an innocent human and drain them of their blood. We cannot have squeamish higher-level demons in our midst now, can we? Oh, and be sure not to waste a drop," he told them, watching as some of the humans from the previous test filed back in behind the dark witches.

Tilly was ordered to stand over the same girl who had agreed to sell the new demon her soul just a short while before, Arianna. She looked down at her, and could sense that she was scared, trembling again in fear as though she somehow knew what was coming next. The very idea of taking her first human life sickened her, but Tilly knew she had no other choice, she was so close and was not going to back out now, the promise of her eternal life at Blake's side was dangling so near she could almost reach out and grab it. She thought about his orders for this task, remembering the last line and then looked around the hall trying to figure out what he had meant by not wasting a drop of their blood, looking for a goblet or bowl, but then Tilly realised that he had meant something much more sinister than just gathering the blood to be used in a ritual or spell, it was meant to empower the demons themselves and Tilly knew exactly how to ensure she followed his orders. Tilly thought then of the stories she had heard of blood-drinking vampires who lured young women into their beds before draining them of their blood. She wondered for a moment if those stories might not be so far from the truth. She knelt to look at Arianna again, staring her in the eye as she leaned closer.

"It's okay, don't scream," she told her, and Arianna was instantly mesmerised by Tilly's powerful gaze again. She nodded and sat still, looking back into Tilly's blue eyes, and she began noticeably relaxing before her. Tilly smiled and then looked around at the other demons, all of whom seemed to be thinking, planning, or looking for a vessel for the blood too and she looked back at Arianna, surer than ever that her suspicions for the blood's intended use were right. She leaned closer and whispered into her ear, tilting the girl's neck and turning her head to one side.

"Stay calm and still Arianna, don't worry, everything's going to be alright," she commanded her, brushing the girl's long brown hair from her shoulder and exposing her neck where Tilly could clearly see the throbbing vein below the skin's surface. She traced her index finger across the dark line, searing it instantly, and blood started to seep from the cut. Tilly immediately covered it with her mouth, sucking hard on the artery she had just cut open and gulping down the hot, thick liquid as it poured into her mouth, careful not to spill a drop. The blood's flow eventually started to slow down, and Tilly could feel Arianna's heartbeat slowing down too, within a couple of minutes she was dead, limp in her arms and then fell to the floor while her life force flowed through Tilly's body instead, strengthening it wonderfully. She moved away with a victorious smile and looked over at the others, Lucas had done the same as she had and was just finishing up with his own sacrificial offering, his mouth carefully licking the last remaining drop from his donor's wrist that he had slashed and then drank from.

When the challenge was over, the bodies that lay dead before the four successful demons were taken away and the demons that had failed were led out of the hall, their intended victims safe for another day and the level four demons were sent off to their new homes. Tilly felt Blake's eyes on her and instinctually gazed up at him, feeling hot and horny as he peered back at her from underneath is black hood, a cunning smile on his lips.

"Excellent. The four of you have done well to make it this far. You are now at level three of the classifications and have the privilege of calling yourselves upper-level demons. There are only two more challenges remaining, but do not be too sure of yourselves, for these are the hardest yet," he told them with a wicked grin.

CHAPTER FIVE

The demons had been cooped up in the dark hall for what felt like weeks now. Tilly was unsure just how long it had been, but she could feel the fatigue trying to creep into her as she and the other three remaining demons stood awaiting their Dark Prince's next orders. She pushed the tiredness away and called upon the blood she had taken from Arianna to fuel her further, to provide her with the strength she knew she would need for the final challenges, and it worked. Tilly would have thought she would feel guilty for having killed the girl, but instead a strange satisfaction took over in its place, a dark necessity that turned off the remorse and regret in preference of survival and need. She needed every ounce of strength she had left and so would continue to do whatever it took. It would not be long now until she could be at Blake's side.

The dark witches filed in and stood before Tilly, Lucas, and the other demons again, who were then blindfolded and moved into position so that they stood side by side, just a few feet apart from each other in the now mostly empty hall. Blake's voice then called down to them quietly from the table. He didn't need to shout now that there were so few of them left. The four of them were the last contestants that would continue to fight for their place in either the second or first level of the hierarchy of demons.

"Imagine for me now, either your greatest adversary, nemesis, fear, or any guilt-ridden moment from your past or your human lives as they once were. A moment which would once strike you down with fear or regret, for in order to carry on in these dark challenges, you must overcome such obstacles and defeat your enemies at long last. It is now time to destroy all those who have ever had any such power over you," he said, stirring each of their dark thoughts to pluck the information he required from each demon's mind.

"Good, now remove the blindfolds," he ordered, having gotten everything he needed to carry on and he then took his seat again, watching them intently. Tilly did as he commanded and looked down into the face of the man she was not at all surprised to find herself facing once again, the worst person she had ever known, the man who had tried to rape, hurt, and murder her. It was the man whose face had crept into her nightmares even after he had failed Trey. He was kneeling before her about six feet away and he smiled up at her darkly, the same smile that had haunted her thoughts for the last few months. There was an evil darkness to him now that she could sense strongly, and a yearning for more. Trey clearly wanted to become a demon too and had been torturing other human souls while in Hell to strengthen his own, so Tilly immediately summoned all that power he had accrued into herself, relieving him of it with a smug smile. His grin quickly faded, and he seemed genuinely shocked when he finally realised that she had somehow changed, that she was standing strong and powerfully over him here in Hell, not as another soul but as something far more sinister. His face dropped even more when he took in her new dark prowess and realised just how different she now was to the girl he had tried to defile not so long ago. Tilly climbed down on all fours and smiled wickedly at her old friend, making her way over to him on her hands and knees, crawling almost seductively over the hard floor and revelling in his confusion and fear.

"Oh Trey," she said as she reached him, grabbing him by the neck and commanding his eyes on hers.

"You should have just listened to my warnings when you were handcuffing me to that bed, but I guess this isn't the time or the place for an 'I told you so' is it?" she asked, giving his neck a playful stroke with her fingertip across the line where Blake had slit it using her body as his vessel.

"No," he replied, his voice dry and harsh.

"Tell me, what were you going to do to me? Rape me and then kill me? Or perhaps you would have done it the other way around and killed me first. Maybe you really do like your girls, 'out cold'?" she asked, her mouth accentuating every word, toying with him and looking down into his dark brown eyes with a curious grin. Trey just smiled back at her, his body language shifting ever so slightly, and Tilly could sense that her confident, dark prowess was turning him on. The sheer thought sickened her, and she grabbed his collar playfully, staring down into his face, commanding his eyes on hers as she sent him a mental glimpse of the torture and pain she wanted to inflict upon his soul for all eternity, an unspoken promise via a vivid and impressive shared vision she had somehow summoned. His smile dropped immediately, and Trey tried to back away, but Tilly just gripped him tighter.

She then reached her hand down to his chest, over the centre of his ribcage and in one strong yet fluid and almost lady-like movement she liberated his heart from his chest and held it up for him to see for a second before she then flung it to the ground. Next, she reached her bloody hands up and snapped his neck with a quick flick of her strong wrists and dropped Trey to the floor, a calm and steady demeanour emanating from her the entire time, much to Blake's delight.

Tilly stood then and peered up at her master, catching the slight nod from his central spot at the table and then she couldn't help but look over towards Lucas as he also discarded the dead body of his own enemy, a blonde-haired woman who looked to be in her early thirties and who's cold, dead, blue eyes were the exact same shade as his sons Brent, David, and Jackson's. Tilly knew she must have been their mother, the woman Lucas had told her about so long ago, and she was glad he had overcome the obvious guilt that had stayed with him all these years. Tears ran down Lucas's cheeks, but his strength and power were almost visible in the air around him and Tilly could sense that he too had succeeded in this awful task. Both Trey's and the woman's bodies disappeared after a few seconds, and the two demons moved to one side to watch as the other two contestants continued in their attempts at overcoming their own enemies. They stood in silence, grateful for the pause as they steadied themselves in anticipation of their final challenge. Lucas didn't say anything or even look at Tilly as they stood there together, neither of them were ready to celebrate that task being over just yet, but he leaned against her shoulder slightly, a small touch that let each other know they were supporting one another in this terrible hall.

CHAPTER SIX

The other two finalists could not seem to defeat their foes and were eventually eliminated, leaving just Lucas and Tilly to compete for both their positions in the highest demonic level and their well-earned places at their lovers' sides. Lucas had won the heart of his demonic mistress Lilith many years ago, and Tilly wished him every success. She was grateful when she realised that there was not just one space available to them in the highest demonic level today, knowing that she could not ever compete with him over the much-desired position. Lucas deserved it much more than she did, having completed the demonic trials and ritual the proper way after continually proving himself worthy of the dark gifts, while she couldn't help but feel as though she was only here by sheer luck.

Blake rose from his seat once Tilly and Lucas were led into the centre of the hall by the witches for the last time, the two of them standing about eight feet away from one another in the vast and now very empty space. However, he did not speak this time, instead he removed his black cloak and walked down the few steps to join Tilly and Lucas on the hard floor. He looked dark and dangerous, and devilishly gorgeous in his black chinos and shirt, his green eyes brighter than Tilly had ever seen them. She and Lucas both bowed before him and were released just as Lilith teleported to Blake's side, following his dark summoning from across the ancient city. He nodded at her and each stood before their demonic children with satisfied grins before then swapping places with one another, him moving sideways so that he was now facing Lucas, while Lilith moved to stand in front of Tilly. The still hooded council member to the right of Blake's now empty seat stood and took his place as the master of ceremonies.

"Your final challenge is to show ultimate respect for your elders, and it is also a simple test of your survival instincts, a way to push every one of your boundaries to the limit. You are to endure the next twelve hours in order to receive your reward. You must not yield or fight back, and you must not lose consciousness, otherwise you will have failed," he said to Tilly and Lucas, his voice stern and clear. Blake then began unbuttoning his shirt, showing off his glorious torso before discarding it and loosening up his shoulders as though readying himself for a fight. He seemed to be enjoying the attention Tilly couldn't help but give him as she gazed upon the body she longed to touch, to kiss and to be commanded by. He smiled at her and winked, but quickly turned his attention on his opponent, relishing in the look of fear that was now visibly etched on Lucas's face as he took in his omnipotent foe.

Lilith stared at Tilly and then removed her jacket too, stretching her arms out in front of her and then cracking her knuckles loudly. It was obvious to Tilly then that neither seemed to want to be restricted in any way during their part in the final challenge, and that she and Lucas were about to receive an unprecedented amount of pain and beatings at their powerful hands.

Each of them smiled wickedly at each other and then at the demons before them, Blake not even attempting to hide his eagerness to get started as he poised, animal like and nodded to the stand-in head of the table.

"Go," the hooded man called, magically starting a large clock on the table before them, which began the twelve-hour countdown. Tilly barely had time to register the beginning of the task or anticipate Lilith's first move as the ancient demon was quick and fierce as she sprinted forward and leaped onto her, knocking Tilly back onto the floor where she straddled her and then began raining down heavy and powerful blows onto Tilly's face and body. She could feel Lilith trying to grab at her chest, assuming she was aiming for her heart, and she twisted away. Lilith pounced after her, pinning her face down onto the hard floor and laying intense blows into her ribs and spine. Tilly cried out in pain, turning over and readying herself to push the powerful demon away, wanting to fight back, but she then quickly remembered that the point was not to fight, but to endure, just as Blake's stand-in had said.

Tilly closed her eyes and focussed on her power again, commanding it and strengthening it from deep within as much as she could before resonating it throughout her entire body. She urged it to spread out, healing each punch and every cut as soon as Lilith had delivered it, and somehow, she succeeded. Tilly curled up into a ball protecting her chest from Lilith's grasp, but she took each and every terrible blow that was sent her way, feeling as though she was creating a dark, shielding bubble of some kind around herself. She soon struggled to keep her protective force-field strong and so risked withdrawing the protection slightly, allowing some of the pain to creep in and focussing instead on healing any damage that might be permanent or deadly to her instead, a few cuts and bruises she could handle.

Tilly couldn't let her concentration waver for even a second as the time gradually passed, requiring every ounce of her new dark power to survive this final round. She could hear muffled cries coming from Lucas as he too received blow after blow from her master and winced as she heard him cry out loudly in pain beside her. Lilith heard it too, pausing for just a split second between her beatings, but she then seemed to be extra determined to hurt Tilly in return, and she sent a spine-shattering blow down onto her neck. The loud crack and instant pain made her almost cry out too, but she forced it away, harnessing the pain and using it to enforce her protective bubble rather than to break it.

The twelve hours passed slowly, Tilly feeling as though she had lost all sense of time in her pained yet focussed state and Lilith's immense blows immediately stopped upon hearing the bell toll the final task's end at last. Tilly was incredibly weak, but she managed to stand before the demon after just a few seconds, regaining her composure. Lilith smiled at her, surprised yet impressed at her strength, before she looked down to her own progeny. Lucas was alive. He had made it through Blake's beatings in one piece but was too weak to stand.

Blake stood before him, covered from head to toe in Lucas's blood. He too had delivered many powerful blows to the new demon and had also managed to slit his neck open with a wide, deep cut. Even though blood oozed from his wound, Lucas covered it with his hand, stemming the flow efficiently enough for it not to cause any of them concern or make him fail the task. Tilly smiled over at her powerful master, basking in his warm gaze as he swept his eyes over her bloody body with a triumphant smile. He cleaned himself up and moved over to stand next to his demonic progeny and then a sudden burst of emotion nearly floored Tilly, seeming to resonate from Blake himself as he stood beside her. She could feel his affections pouring into her from him. His love, pride, and happiness were coming through as though he had opened some kind of invisible link between the two of them. He too seemed surprised at their strange connection but smiled down at her and gave her another wink before he then climbed back up the steps to re-join his fellow council members at the huge table.

"Well done," he called down to Tilly and Lucas after he had put his cloak back on. "You have both completed all the demonic initiations to our satisfaction and have been lucky enough to reach the prestigious level one of the demonic hierarchies. You are both invited to join your masters, mentors, and friends at the dark castle later to celebrate your achievements, but in the meantime, go to your new chambers and get cleaned up. See you in a few hours," he told them, and they both bowed in thanks.

The dark council members stood and teleported away, leaving just Blake behind, who came back down to speak to them all before releasing Lucas from the great hall. He congratulated him again, smiling down at him but not apologising at all for the deep gash on his neck that Lucas still held tightly, the flow of blood finally having stopped thanks to his healing powers, but it was taking a little time. Lilith lifted Lucas to his feet effortlessly with her strong arms and bowed to Blake before she held her husband tight and teleported him away.

Tilly and Blake were then alone for only a split second before she found herself enveloped in his strong arms as he planted deep and intense kisses on her lips, his pleasure with her pouring out of him as he opened up his strange link again and Tilly lapped up his affections before he then teleported her directly to the dark castle, eager to show her to her new chambers.

CHAPTER SEVEN

Blake took Tilly to her new home in the huge castle, having chosen her a particularly spacious and lavishly furnished room with an en-suite and a perfect view across the castle towards his own chambers, their windows looking out at one another's perfectly, not that she knew that yet. He gave her a quick tour and then pulled her into the bathroom for a hot, much-needed shower thanks to both of them being filthy, and he was still coated in a thick layer of Lucas's dried blood. As the water poured over them, he pulled Tilly up into his arms, wrapping her legs around his waist as he pinned her to the wall and then slid his hard length inside her as the hot water cleansed them both. Blake kissed her feverishly, never once releasing her mouth from his as he devoured her intensely, eagerly fulfilling his dark need to make Tilly climax for him at least once before he could even begin to entertain the idea of sharing her with the crowds that awaited them in the great hall of the castle to celebrate hers and Lucas's successful classification as level one demons.

He groaned as he thrust hard and urgently in and out of her sweet, wet cleft, relishing in the feel of her deep, inner muscles as they clenched around him. Tilly cried out with pleasure for him as he pursued her, so eager for Blake's touch, his kisses, and needing his release as much as he needed hers. He was so consumed with love for her and let down some more of what remained of his protective walls, finally accepting that she would forever keep the cold-hearted boy he once was locked away. He relished in her touch and deep kisses as they came together under the still running water, the walls around them shaking slightly as they throbbed wonderfully and let the world around them fall away completely, as though they were the only two beings that existed in all the worlds, both above them and beyond.

They then towelled off and made their way into Tilly's main room where she found the closet and drawers fully stocked, and an ornately carved jewellery box containing her green stone ring Blake had kept safe for her during all the craziness of her last few days as a human and the lengthy challenge phase of her initiation into the demonic hierarchy. She slid it on and then got dressed in a long, black gown similar to the one she had been wearing in her dreams with Blake and had then gone on to wear at the party at the penthouse not too long afterwards, all of which seemed like such a long time ago now.

Looking in the mirror, Tilly couldn't help but stare at herself upon seeing her reflection, she still looked like her old self but hadn't needed any makeup or hair products now to get the very same look she had always had to work so hard to achieve to even attempt to keep up with the beautiful god-like creatures and demons she was so used to having around her up on Earth. Her blue eyes sparkled effortlessly and her cheeks were flushed thanks to her recent climactic releases while her lips were a perfect shade of red. The only thing she thought she might need was a little black eye shadow to complete her usual smoky look, and as soon as she thought of it, the dark shimmer somehow applied itself to her eyelids instantly.

"Whoa, I officially love being a demon," she whispered, making Blake laugh as he joined her in front of the large mirror and wrapped his arms around her in that way she loved, one arm across her torso and the other around her shoulder as he grabbed her chin and lifted her mouth to his. Blake was now wearing a perfect match to his outfit in her dreams too, an impeccably tailored black suit complete with matching waistcoat and shirt. He looked fantastic and Tilly swooned as he held her closer, pinning her to him tightly as they embraced.

"Before we go," he said, after finally pulling his lips away from hers. "I want to show you something." Blake added as he pulled her over to the window and pointed to the terrace on the opposite side where a dark-haired girl Tilly thought might be Luna was sat chatting with a demon she recognised instantly, Harry. The girl wandered inside as they watched them, but Harry stayed there for an extra few seconds, sensing their eyes on him. He looked up at Tilly and Blake as they watched, giving them a smile and a quick, knowing wave before tapping his finger on his wrist where a watch would have been and then ducking inside too, silently telling them it was nearly time to go to the party.

"That's the royal wing, where my family and I live. Over there is my room," Blake told her, pointing to the third window along to the right of the terrace. It was huge inside, and the curtains were wide open so that Tilly could see into it clearly, noticing his huge bed and desk inside.

"Not very private, is it?" she asked, smirking at him with one eyebrow raised, thinking how she couldn't wait to make love to him in that impressive bed.

"We don't need it to be private, no one would dare watch us Tilly, only level one demons live in this wing and none of them would ever intrude on our privacy, well except maybe you but look how quickly you were caught watching the royal terrace," he told her with a cheeky smile, making it clear that she was not to make a habit of watching their quarters from her window but he couldn't help enjoy her sordid thoughts as she peered into his most private place. "And besides, down here we aren't quite so prudish about that sort of thing, anyway. Surely you don't think we reserve the orgies just for on Earth?" Blake asked, taking her hand before she could answer and teleporting away from her new room towards the main, communal area of the dark castle and then heading for the magnificent great hall.

The vast and impressive citadel had many wings, and each either housed the upper-level demons and witches or were communal and official areas, but no matter what, access was by invite or summons only, of course. The royal wing was the largest and most decadent of them all, despite housing the fewest number of beings, but was off-limits to everybody without direct invitation from the Dark Queen herself. Most demons had never set foot inside their wing, but Tilly hoped it wouldn't be long until her almighty mistress invited her to join them there, hoping to feel like a part of their family soon, like both Cate and Blake had promised her.

"I'm so proud of you Tilly," Blake told her with a wide grin as they made their way down an ornate corridor towards the doors that led into the great hall. "I have never seen a new demon with such control and strength over their power, you excelled where many, many older and well-practised demons before you have failed miserably, I should know, I have watched them fail time after time," he added, stopping to check that they were alone in the hallway and then gathering her into another deep kiss. "I truly believe that not all demons can progress because there is a natural maximum competency to their control and use of their dark power. Each demon could try and try again in the dark hall, but they always plateau at the right level for them. You had barely any training and still went straight to level one. I think it's safe to assume your natural prowess will be strong, Tilly."

"Thank you, Blake," she replied, soaking up his affections as she peered up into his handsome face adoringly. She was proud of herself too and had taken to this demonic lifestyle quicker than even she had thought she would if she was completely honest about it. "I'm so happy," she then told him, running her hands up his lapels to his cheeks, gazing into his gorgeous green eyes as she then ran her hands up through his hair and pulled him down for one more kiss. When they finally pulled away, Tilly took his hand and let him lead her the last few feet towards the large wooden doorway. Lilith and Lucas teleported into the hallway to join them then too, Blake having summoned the pair of them for him and Tilly to make their entrance together. Lucas bowed and then put out his hand to shake the Black Prince's as he rose.

"You nearly got me back there, your Majesty," he said with a smile as Blake shook his hand firmly and then laughed, shrugging as though it was nothing, but Tilly could tell that there was a satisfied smile behind his feigned nonchalance. He had truly enjoyed letting loose on his target in the dark hall, blowing off a lot of pent up steam and revelling in administering some pain in the process, even if it was on a new demon he had truly hoped would succeed.

"Well, I couldn't be seen to go easy on you now, could I?" Blake then asked Lucas, looking him over with a wicked grin.

"Of course not," Lucas agreed with a smile, his deep blue eyes alight thanks to his new dark prowess. "Lilith warned me about the final task, that the other demons masters had to deliver the blows that would decide their fate. I was just incredibly unfortunate to have the Black Prince as my fellow contestant's master. I have to admit I didn't think that was very fair," he added with an honest smile, but bowed respectfully to his master again.

"Whoever said Hell was going to be fair?" Blake asked rhetorically, his smile widening. "Oh, and you are a level one demon now Lucas, so please, call me Blake," he added before turning his attention on Lilith to give her a quick kiss on the cheek in greeting, talking quietly with her as though knowing that the two new demons needed to share a private moment together themselves too. Lilith kissed Blake back and smiled up at him affectionately, with a pure and loving gaze that Tilly had only ever seen her look at Lucas with before, and she wondered if Lilith was finally letting down her own walls now that the pair of them were down in Hell together at last too. She hoped that perhaps the cold side she had only ever seen of the powerful demon up on Earth was nothing more than her business-like persona, and that this warm, kind smile might be a side of her she could get to know better. Lucas laughed gruffly beside her, pulling Tilly from her reverie. He then turned to her and smiled, his blue eyes looking her up and down as he moved forward and embraced her tightly.

"He's really something else. I wished I could get away with hitting him back in that last task. Didn't you feel the same about my lovely wife over there?" he asked her, and Tilly nodded and grinned. He then peered at her for a second, his expression a mixture of surprise, excitement, and confusion as he took her in. "I didn't even know that you had been turned. I saw you on Halloween morning and everything was normal. I admit I was so busy with my task preparations that I hadn't heard about your transformation, but then I clocked you from across the hall at the initiations and I must admit I was shocked to see you there. What happened?" he asked earnestly.

"I know, it's a bit of a shitty story in all honesty, Lucas," she said, looking up at Blake for his authorisation to tell him the tale of her demonic rebirth, and she caught a slight nod from him, giving Tilly permission to continue. "I was trapped and almost killed by a white witch on my way back from Edinburgh the day after Halloween," she said, her smile fading as she let herself remember the pain and the swirling darkness that had threatened to take her after Beatrice's capture.

"Whoa," he replied, his eyes wide.

"Yep, the stupid bitch stabbed me, just to send the Queen a message. So much for them being the good guys, hey?" she asked rhetorically, and he laughed dryly in response. "Alma tried to save me but nothing she did was working. I was going to die, and they could do nothing to stop it, so the Queen allowed Blake to sire me." Lucas nodded in understanding and smiled warmly at her, empathising with Tilly and accepting her explanation without any need for her reasoning or explaining herself further.

"A much better alternative to death," he then told her with a wide smile before hugging her again, and Tilly loved Lucas for his warmth and his still paternal treatment of her even after her split with his son Brent and the changes she had made to her life ever since then.

"Ready?" Blake then asked them, interrupting their quiet moment, and they pulled back from their embrace and nodded. Lucas moved across and took Lilith's hand while Tilly slid her arm into Blake's in a much more formal stance as the huge doors began to open before them. She took a deep breath and mentally prepared herself, ready to embrace her new destiny and not wanting to let Blake down.

CHAPTER EIGHT

The four of them stepped inside the castle's main hall to a huge welcome, applause, and loud cheers for both Tilly and Lucas's success. Both had done fantastically well and were instantly bombarded with questions and requests to tell their new demonic peers the stories of their trials and initiations. Lucas lapped it all up, and deservedly so thanks to his many years of servitude and loyalty to Lilith and her Queen, but Tilly just couldn't help but feel as though she had cheated the system. She felt like the others there might not respect her as much, and that they would assume that she had somehow exploited her position by Blake's side to gain ultimate power easily. Bypassing the human trials had come as a welcome relief at first, but it also left Tilly feeling as though she was not as deserving of her fellow demons praise as Lucas was. Blake read her thoughts and shook his head, a slight flicker of anger flitting across his face as she stood there, doubtful of herself.

"Do you disagree with your Queen's decision to turn you Tilly?" he asked, whispering in her ear quietly, his voice harsh and stern. She looked up into his eyes fearfully. Even with her demonic powers, she still knew not to anger him and quickly tried to appease her master.

"No, I was just feeling a little overwhelmed, Blake. It's over now. I'm sorry, I would never mean to disrespect your mother, or you," she promised. "I will spend eternity proving how much I deserve this."

"Good," he said, brushing her dark-blonde hair out of her face, calming down again quickly. "Who's the beautiful tragedy now?" he then asked, reminding Tilly of her heartfelt words to him, and winking playfully as he pulled away from her. Blake had already warned Tilly that he would have to leave her side once they were inside and he walked slowly through the crowd before joining his mother in a separate seating area above where the demons partied, the set up reminding Tilly of an old amphitheatre. He had informed her earlier that the royal family always sat away from the main crowd of demons during large events and would hold an audience with a few of them at a time rather than be bombarded with their many wants and needs in one go, as well as the sheer volume of thoughts and memories that washed over them in the company of a high volume of powerful minds. They would only interact with the demons on a more personal level away from the larger gatherings, but, as with everything, it was only if the Queen would allow it. She was very protective of her family and was the only one permitted to summon demons into their main wing of the castle. All other dealings were carried out in the communal areas where the witches and other demons could roam freely.

The whole set up reminded Tilly of the Kings and Queens of ancient England, with their royal courts and strict etiquette, but she respectfully accepted the rules, knowing that following them without question was all just another part of her life from now on, despite being disappointed that she could not be at Blake's side for the evening.

He had promised that he would watch over her from their secluded area, though, and took his place with the other members of his family as she mingled and celebrated with the crowd below. Their large box was a sectioned off area set slightly higher above the main floor of the hall where the demons and witches socialised now, but it was all clearly visible to everyone that attended, and their eyes would often wander so that they could watch the beautiful Queen as she blessed the demons with their turn at having an audience with her. Tilly couldn't help but look up now and then too, and she felt Blake's eyes on her the entire time. She also knew that he would be listening in on her thoughts and conversations as she went but couldn't help but wish she was on his arm right now rather than being there alone.

She stayed with Lucas and after chatting with a few other demons, Lilith introduced him and Tilly to the six dark council members that had watched over them beside Blake during the challenges. She smiled and shook each of their hands in turn, bowing respectfully to her master's most loyal demons.

"You are very strong Tilly," one of them, an ancient demon who introduced himself as Azazel, said to her. He was the demon who had sat beside Blake during the tasks and had called out the details of the final challenge in the Black Prince's place when he had joined her and Lucas in the dark hall for the final fight.

"Thank you, I was very determined to make it here today," she told him with a smile, taking in his ugly features and finally understanding the necessity for the hooded cloaks, although she hid her disgust behind her warm smile.

"Well, you did it, and you most certainly deserve to be here. Never before have I seen a young demon so in tune with their new powers. You called it to you, harnessed it and used your darkness completely at your own will. It was refreshing seeing you command it so effortlessly. I especially enjoyed seeing you drain that human girl. I honestly don't think I have ever seen someone charm their victim first during that round," he told her, making Tilly smile wider, revelling in his empowering words.

"I just went with what felt right, I suppose," she replied.

"Well, your instincts proved to be right. Do you mind me asking, how did you deal with that boy in the penultimate round? All I saw was you staring into his eyes and then his face as it fell, but I didn't hear you say anything more than your taunts?" Azazel asked her, genuinely intrigued by her dark prowess during the challenge.

"I can't really explain it. I showed him the torture I wanted to inflict on him, letting him see that I was not afraid to really make his life hell. Somehow, I summoned the image of my desire to my mind and then, kind of, shared it with him," she said, trying to explain the dark sharing of her imagination she had inexplicably managed to do with Trey.

The group around them suddenly went silent, the other dark council members all turning to look at her, along with the open-mouthed Azazel.

"You projected?" one of them, an olive skinned demon that had earlier introduced himself as Abadon, asked her in astonishment and Tilly nodded, assuming that it must be the name for what she had managed to do to him.

"I guess so?" she replied awkwardly.

"You truly are a dark wonder to behold Tilly. Your powerful master has given you gifts far beyond any of our predictions for a royal demonic progeny," Azazel told her with a wide grin. She couldn't help but smile back at him. She hadn't thought about it before now, but he was right. Tilly was the first demon to be sired by one of the royal family, the Black Prince too, so it really was no wonder that she had done so well during her challenges thanks to his powerful blood that now flowed through her veins.

A deep and sudden pull sparked inside of Tilly a moment later and she quickly realised she was being summoned by the Queen. She looked over and saw Lucas staring at her with a strange grin, clearly feeling it, too.

"You sense that?" he asked her with a gruff laugh, and Tilly nodded, linking her arm in his as they made their way towards the steps that led into the royal area and Cate's most loyal demon and best friend, Dylan, greeted them there. She maintained a business-like approach in public, just as they were all expected to do, but couldn't help herself and grinned over at Tilly, giving her a playful nudge as she led them towards the Queen. Blake and Luna were sat at her side, talking quietly with each other, but they silenced when they saw the two new demons approaching. Tilly and Lucas bowed before Cate immediately, falling to their knees with the highest of respect and love for their Queen.

"You may rise," she told them, then smiled warmly as they stood before her. She stood too and wandered down the few steps to stand with them, looking beautiful in a long, flowing, backless black dress that showed off her slim body wonderfully and she reached out an elegant hand with black polished nails and a huge array of black diamond rings to shake Lucas's trembling one. She read him, taking in every one of his memories and experiences in just a few seconds. Cate had always preferred to make physical contact. Reading other beings' minds was easy, but the contact made the whole encounter richer, more personal and she enjoyed knowing every inch of her immortally blessed beings: past, present, and deeper, darker thoughts. Dylan had always teased her for having trust issues, but at the same time they could all fully understand her reasons for doing so.

"Congratulations Lucas. From what I have been told, you not only succeeded wonderfully in the challenges but excelled beyond my son's expectations. Lilith has prepared you well for your transition into our dark world," Cate told him, receiving a huge smile and a gracious bow in response.

"Thank you, your Majesty. It is an honour to serve you," he replied.

"Wonderful," Cate replied, smiling beautifully at him. "I wanted to greet you in person as well as offer my sincerest congratulations today. I look forward to seeing what you are capable of in the future, Lucas," she added. "Now, you may go and join your wife. I am sure she is missing you."

Lucas took his leave, grateful that she hadn't expected more of a response from him, as he was sure his voice would falter in her presence. He bowed to the Queen before being led away again by Dylan.

Tilly had remained quiet while Cate and Lucas talked, revelling in the strange and exciting link of emotion and love that Blake had opened up to her again and smiling to herself uncontrollably as she stared at her feet. He shut it off again just in time for her to steady herself as Cate stepped closer to her and placed her palms on her cheeks, pulling her gaze up to meet hers. She smiled down at Tilly, taking in all her new and wonderful memories of herself and Blake, and also sensing their even stronger connection now thanks to his demonic gift of life. She absorbed her memories of the challenges too, pleased that her son's progeny had become so powerful so quickly and had more than handled herself in that hall, just as she hoped she would.

Blake had overseen the demonic initiation challenges for many years now and had watched the demons with intrigue as they passed or failed in their tests. He had always wanted the opportunity to deliver a beating to one of the finalists. And this time, the challenges had given him not only the satisfaction of finally doing so but also the gratification of seeing for himself just how well his newly reborn demonic lover had done while receiving her own beatings from Lilith. She encompassed and represented his dark power now, and others would judge him based on her actions and abilities in both battle and everyday duties. However, right now she had excelled in the initiations as well as having left Blake's dark council speechless at her incredible skill and prowess. Cate was more than impressed with her and smiled, kissing her cheek affectionately.

"And you, my very dear child," she said to Tilly, beaming down at her. "You have astonished me once again, and I do not impress easily. I could not be prouder of you."

Tilly blushed, genuinely taken aback by the Queen's kind words and her powerful energy as it flowed through her from Cate's touch and from her kiss. She looked up into her beautiful green eyes and smiled, mesmerised once again by Blake's likeness to her.

"Thank you so much, your Majesty," she managed to reply after a moment of silence passed between the two of them, a moment of connection and bonding. "I will continue to make you proud of me," she promised. Cate then released Tilly from her gentle grasp and led her over to where Blake and Luna sat open-mouthed and speechless in their chairs as they watched them.

"You have one minute," she told her son with a cheeky smile, knowing that the two of them were eager for a stolen moment together despite the expectations and formality they had to adhere to in the openness of the crowded event.

Blake jumped out of his seat and took Tilly's hand. He quickly led her over to the side wall, ducking behind a huge black curtain and then pulling her inside with him. It was pitch-black underneath the thick drapes but was the perfect place to steal a deep and intensely passionate kiss. Blake quickly gathered her up in his arms and pinned Tilly to the wall, his mouth commanding hers for their promised minute, and then exactly sixty seconds later he began to feel Cate summoning him back to her side. Dylan waited for them beside the opening and led Tilly back out to the main hall as Blake re-joined his mother, not a word had been spoken between them during their minute together but there was no need, their urgent kiss combined with his open link of emotion and feelings already spoke volumes, and Tilly couldn't help but smile to herself as she made her way back through the crowd.

CHAPTER NINE

Tilly looked through the mass of demons around her in the hall and then her gaze quickly settled on the smiling face of her good friend, Beelzebub. He looked casual yet still smart in his black chinos and t-shirt, which was patterned with grey skulls, and his dark eyes peered at her, taking in Tilly's impressive new prowess as she approached. She made her way over to him and then hugged Beelzebub tightly, genuinely happy to see him.

"Wow, look at you," he said, pulling back from Tilly and smiling down at her. "Darkness certainly becomes you," he added with a wink.

"Thanks, I have to admit I'm kinda loving it," she told him honestly, a shy smile crossing her lips.

"Too right," he replied, looking up at Blake for a second and giving him a respectful bow of his head as he caught his eye, knowing her master was watching her every move.

"I hear you kicked arse in the challenges too?" he asked, a satisfied look in his eye.

"According to Berith she was better than any other demon who has ever tried before her," came a voice from behind them and Leviathan appeared from the crowd, smiling warmly and then lifting Tilly into a tight hug just as Berith joined the three of them as well. He too hugged Tilly and congratulated her on completing the initiations so successfully.

"I bet you didn't even realise I was there, did you?" Berith asked, a knowing grin on his face.

"No, you can't have been?" she asked, trying to figure out how he had been there, knowing for sure that Berith had not been sat at the table with Blake and the dark council.

"One of my old follower's was attempting to progress to a higher level. He made it to level four, which was two higher than he used to be, so all in all, a successful trial. I watched you from the balcony above," he told her, looking sheepish as he admitted his presence there, but Tilly just smiled.

"Wow, I didn't even know there was a balcony there! Oh well, no point being shy about it, and that's great that he progressed. Did I meet him in the hall?" she asked, trying to picture the faces of the other demons from the initiations and Berith shook his head.

"No, but you very nearly had to fight him in the first round, luckily that other guy was just that bit closer to you, saved him the embarrassment of being knocked out so quickly," he told her, almost as if he was glad his old friend had not gone up against Tilly. She took it as a compliment and nudged his shoulder with hers playfully.

The four of them chatted together for a while, the demons asking Tilly for every gory detail of her tasks, and she regaled them with the intense stories and anecdotes from her time in the dark hall.

"Was it weird having Blake there watching you?" Leviathan asked her, and Tilly instinctively looked up at her master as she thought about her answer.

"No, not at all, if anything having him there was a constant reminder of everything I was fighting for," she told him and Leviathan nodded, seeming to understand their strong bond despite only having met Tilly a few times. Beelzebub nodded too, understanding her motives completely as he knew the two of them much more closely as a couple, having spent many nights in their company at the penthouse and, of course, having witnessed them in action at the orgy.

"So romantic, isn't it?" said a voice from behind her and Tilly turned to see Harry stood there, a huge grin on his handsome face. She smiled back up at him and happily embraced Blake's stepfather when he leaned down to greet her, wrapping his arms around her tightly. Harry gave her a kiss on the cheek too, a customary greeting for family members, which made her smile even wider. She was glad that he saw her as family now and kissed him back to show the same affection for him in return. Harry truly was a natural beauty, his kind face an unusual find amongst the demons and although he was not Blake's father, Tilly could always feel a similarity between them she knew must run deeper than through their looks or even their personalities. He had short curly hair like Blake's, but his was a light-brown colour that framed his square face in a classic style that suited him. His blue eyes always seemed so alive and happy, and Tilly thought she might finally know for sure just why. She too had followed in his footsteps and joined her soulmate in Hell, and Tilly was pretty sure that her own happiness shone through now in a way she could not hide, just like Harry. Tilly had seen the pair of them for herself at the orgy held at the penthouse by the powerful couple. She and the other attendees had been utterly enthralled and mesmerised by his and Cate's incredible connection and she knew that Blake had enjoyed seeing her succumb to his mother's lure.

"How's it going?" he asked her, breaking her moment of reflection.

"Great, amazing actually," Tilly answered honestly, making him smile brightly as he watched her relish in their attention. Lucas and Lilith passed by close to their small group and greeted each of them, their strong, happy bond so clear and free from his human restraints, and Harry caught Tilly looking at them enviably.

"I know exactly how you feel, it's hard that even after everything you've been through, you still cannot sit up there with him. They hate that they cannot come down here to be with us too, but rules are important Tilly." He said, knowing exactly what she had been thinking. "It is a burden we must bear to have the love of these powerful beings," he added, looking up at his wife with a happy, thoughtful smile.

"And the rewards will always outweigh the disadvantages," she replied, and Harry nodded.

"Exactly, just holding her hand in mine is well worth all the bullshit," he whispered, leaning closer so as not to be overheard. "And having the chance to love her children as my own has made our marriage even sweeter. He has flourished for having had you Tilly. The two of you are good for each other. You will soon get used to all of this," he promised her. "And don't forget that you have many friends here to help you along the way."

"Thank you, Harry, I really appreciate your kindness," she replied, and knew he was right, so vowed to try and fit in quickly with both her demonic friends and her new life and dark home in the underworld. She had had a very misinformed view long ago that the demons were simply glorified servants for the royal family, expected to attend to them at all times, to serve as eternal commanders of their armies and upholders of their laws. Now though, Tilly realised it was one-hundred times more powerful than that, she wanted to do all those things for Cate and her offspring, she would serve her forever, she would kill, and would die for them if they commanded her to.

Tilly felt amazing stood there amongst her peers. She also had no fatigue now so knew that there was no need for her to sleep and let her mind wander about Blake's dark council and his duties, she assumed she would too be expected to take on her own job in Hell and follow orders day or night at the behest of her master, and Tilly honestly didn't care if she was a glorified servant, she couldn't wait to get started. Blake had not long ago told her he had to issue orders and see to the new or ambitious demons. She knew now what he had meant by it all and couldn't wait to find out what her own role might be from now on.

After the party was over, the demons all teleported away to their chambers and Harry took Tilly to one side, leaning close so that he could whisper in her ear.

"Go back to your room. Blake will either come and see you there or he will ask the Queen to summon you to him. You cannot teleport into their private chambers directly without her approval," he told her, and Tilly nodded. She was so excited to see Blake again and hoped he wouldn't take long to come to her. Ever since she had turned into a demon, her body cried out for his touch even more than it had ever done before. Every sense was now heightened, every urge stronger, and she could feel herself getting horny in anticipation of being with her lover again. The fact that she was physically stronger than ever also helped Tilly's excitement grow as she no longer felt that human sensitivity following their love-making that she once would have, meaning that they could just keep on going for as long as they wanted to now.

She hugged Harry goodbye and focussed on her small chambers, quickly teleporting to them with relative ease, pleased with herself for doing it correctly on her first post-task try.

"Took you long enough," said a deep voice from the bed and Tilly looked across from the doorway to find her dark master lying naked on the bed before her, hard and ready.

CHAPTER TEN

"Oh my," Tilly said with a playful smile, taking a moment to absorb the glorious sight of the Adonis that lay before her and then licking her lips in anticipation. She pulled off her black dress and quickly discarded her underwear before joining him on her small bed and she straddled her master, leaning down over him to capture his mouth in hers. Blake lifted her up in his strong arms, positioning Tilly over his hard and ready cock, sliding the tip inside just an inch, teasing her for a second before finally letting her go and she gasped as he then pulled her down hard on him. She arched her back and lifted herself so that she was sat up on him, Blake lying flat on the bed so that he rubbed just the right spot inside that drove her into a wild, crazy frenzy of need and want for him as well as a desperate eagerness for her own sweet release.

She rode him to the cusp of her first orgasm, willing her body to give in to its climactic release but then he suddenly stopped her. He grabbed Tilly's hips and lifted her up off him, pulling out of her before he then laid her down next to him on the bed. Blake climbed up, gave his lover a sly grin, and flipped his lover over onto her stomach on the dark sheets before leaning over her and whispering into her ear.

"I seem to remember telling you a long time ago that my pleasure comes first Tilly," he said, teasing her as he then slipped himself back inside her hot, wet chasm. He thrust hard and deep as Tilly arched herself back into his strong body. She ached for her release, trembling in anticipation of her sweet, dark pleasure, and urged him to carry on. When Tilly almost reached her high again, he stopped a second time, a gruff laugh escaping Blake's lips when he flipped her over once more and she leaned up on her elbows and pouted up at him impatiently.

"It will be all the sweeter, my love," he promised her, laying Tilly back and entering her again. He slowed his deep thrusts this time, despite her powerful thighs attempting to pull Blake faster inside.

"I never knew you were such a tease," she whispered between his kisses, but laughed and relaxed beneath him as he stared down at her, his green eyes glinting at her in the darkness, and he opened up that strange link to her once more.

"You are the one who has been teasing me all night," he replied, kissing her breasts and thrusting deeper as he leaned over her. He then tilted himself back on his heels, pulling Tilly's hips up to meet his as he continued on towards his release. When he reached his wall-shaking climax, her body pulsated and reverberated with her incredible orgasm at long last, her cleft throbbing over his thick length from the deep muscles within with the most intense, and multiple, orgasm of her entire existence.

"Blake!" she cried out as she gripped at the sheets beneath her tightly and rode her high during her longest aftershocks ever while he watched her unravel with a contented smile, never once shutting off his powerful link of shared emotion.

"Told you," he murmured, kissing her softly as he lay beside her on the bed.

Tilly lay in his arms afterwards, still flushed from her epic climax and revelling in their shared afterglow. Blake enveloped her in his arms and legs, reminding Tilly of how she had slept in his warm, protective embrace that day he had come to her following Trey's assault. She snuggled into him, relishing in his touch and silent expression as well as his familiar scent as she breathed him in. Tilly closed her eyes, feeling safe and loved as she listened to the rhythmic sounds of his heart beating and lungs expanding inside his chest as he breathed slowly. It still surprised Tilly that he even had a heartbeat and breathed in and out so human-like, knowing that he didn't really need to do either to survive. She couldn't even begin to try and understand the science behind it all. She knew that she too still had her beating heart and usable lungs, despite the complete lack of oxygen in Hell and no necessity to have a functioning body anymore. Tilly hated the idea but knew that she was effectively already dead. No amount of heartbeats or breaths could do anything about that now, but she would take this afterlife over being a powerless human soul any day.

"I will give you the full biology lesson someday, my love," he said with a small laugh, reading her thoughts as usual. "But just remember that without some bodily functions, we would not be able to talk, walk, kiss or fuck. Our dark power thrives on us fulfilling such urges, so for that alone we must maintain our human shells." Blake told her, leaning down to kiss her again.

Tilly supposed that his explanation made sense. After all, she really was just a conduit for the dark power she had been blessed with now, a vessel to allow it to flourish and have power both in Hell and up into the world above. It flowed through every inch of her now and strengthened both her body and soul, as well as giving her the abilities that came with the gifts Blake had shared with her along with his blood, and Tilly was ever grateful for its dark blessings.

After a few more minutes of laying wrapped in his arms, Tilly suddenly felt that same urge she had felt earlier at the party, the summoning from her Queen, only this time so much stronger as though Cate wanted her much more urgently. Blake felt it too and climbed up out of bed to get dressed as Tilly quickly did the same. She checked herself over in the mirror to ensure she was presentable and not looking too much like she had just been fucked, and then took her master's hand, ready to follow his lead.

"You take us, follow the summoning," he told her patiently, grinning proudly at his lover. She closed her eyes and focussed on the beacon, the darkness that was calling, and she went towards it, aware of pulling Blake along with her as she moved effortlessly towards her Queen's summoning.

CHAPTER ELEVEN

Tilly and Blake arrived at the source of the powerful beacon in seconds, finding themselves in a huge living area decorated with black leather sofas and huge fur rugs, while dark, erotic art adorned the walls. It reminded Tilly of the penthouse, but on a much grander scale and even more lavishly decorated, if that was even possible. There were huge windows on each side of the room that looked out at the dark red skies and down onto the huge world around them. Her new world, Hell.

Blake smiled down at Tilly, pleased that she had managed to follow his mother's summoning so easily, and having him in tow was no easy task either, but it hadn't seemed to even faze her. He gathered her up in his arms one more time, planting a deep kiss on her lips again before pulling back to take her in, enjoying having her here in his true home at last. Tilly was so beautiful now, even more so than ever before, thanks to the omnipotent dark force that he had shared with her, and he felt himself thaw even more thanks to the loving gaze she gave him in return. He knew now with absolute certainty that she had truly melted his heart, and that he could never be without her. This young, foolish, innocent girl who had at first both offended and intrigued him as she spoke his name and then failed to bow before him at Lucas's final trial. Here she now was, in Hell by his side and full of his dark power. She had well and truly knocked down his once so high walls inside, and Blake did not care one little bit.

"Wow you two really are bad aren't you?" came a voice from across the room and Tilly looked over and bowed as Luna approached while Blake just laughed at his sister.

"Hey, you can't say anything anyway, as it's all your fault. You wanted me to open up, this is me open," he reminded her, playful as ever with his twin.

"True, I will just take that as a thank you then, even if you do make me want to vomit," she joked, leaning over to give him a kiss before planting one on Tilly's lips, too.

"Welcome home," she said to her with a broad smile, and then a young man teleported into the room and bowed before Luna and Blake respectfully.

"Your Majesties," he said, then rose to his feet and looked over at Tilly. He had dark brown hair and blue eyes that were almost the same shade as hers, but he had them hidden behind thick-rimmed glasses, which suited him but somehow made him look older. He was tall, almost as tall as Blake, and Tilly couldn't help but wonder if all the men around her were going to be at least a foot taller than she was.

"My name is Ash, Luna's chief warlock, and her boyfriend. Might I ask your name please, demon?" he asked, looking directly at Tilly with a kind smile. She jumped when she realised what he had just done and immediately answered his request.

"I'm Tilly, it's lovely to meet you Ash," she told him with a shy smile. She had completely forgotten about the rules of asking for demon's names, and when he had done so the feeling caught her completely off guard, it was a strong and powerful force inside that made her have to respond, as though her refusal would cause her pain if she tried not to answer his question.

"I'm very pleased to meet you Tilly," he said, and then gave Luna a kiss before heading over to one side where he lit the large fire.

The three of them followed Ash over to the hearth and sat down on the large sofas, chatting for a few minutes before Cate arrived with Harry and Dylan in tow. Blake and Luna stood to greet their mother, each receiving kisses while Tilly bowed before her. When she rose, she too was rewarded with a kiss from the Queen before being ushered to take a seat again. Cate had enjoyed seeing the four of them relaxing together, just like the real family she had always wanted around her.

"Found your way up here, okay then?" asked Harry as he sat down next to Tilly on the large couch.

"Yep, Blake got me to do the legwork, I think he's enjoying having me around a bit too much you know, it's making him lazy," she joked, making Harry laugh and Blake gave her a playful shake of his head. Dylan greeted her at last too and flopped down on the sofa across from them, and then quickly began telling them a story about her new warlock lover and his huge cock. Tilly immediately blushed at her candid attitude but couldn't help but laugh as Dylan told them all about their depraved exploits in the dungeon and that Alma had caught them at it and punished them by making them take a chastity potion.

"I can't do it for a whole month!" she cried, obviously disgruntled, and the others just laughed.

"Serves you right you fiend," Cate said to her as she sat down next to her husband and cuddled into him with a satisfied smile, while Blake slipped back behind Tilly to wrap her in his strong arms. She looked back into his beautiful eyes and leaned into his warm embrace, feeling safe there, like she was finally home.

A few seconds later, another figure joined them, a girl the absolute image of both Cate and Luna but slightly shorter and more fragile looking. She made eye contact with Tilly and grinned, the smile lighting up her beautiful green eyes as she came closer. Tilly quickly moved to the edge of the sofa to bow before the girl she knew must be the Unholy Princess and then stood to greet her as Lottie released her and finished her approach.

"At long last," she said, kissing Tilly's lips with her own soft ones when she reached her. She felt scared of this beautiful girl, having heard the dark stories that surrounded her existence, and yet she couldn't help but think of the white witch's message to her just a few nights ago and wonder if those stories were even true.

"I am very pleased to meet you Tilly, my name is Lottie," the girl said, taking her in for a moment before she then walked around her and leaned down to kiss her mother and siblings on their cheeks. Tilly watched as she then kissed and hugged Harry with deep affection before finally taking a seat in the single armchair next to where he and Cate still sat wrapped in each other's arms.

"I think that's the first time I have ever known you to be speechless Tilly," Blake joked with her, making everyone in the small circle laugh and then ushering her to sit back down in his loving embrace.

"Sorry, I was just thinking. I guess I need to be re-taught some of the facts about you guys, right?" she asked, and they all nodded. Cate's face grew serious, and she linked her fingers through Harry's thoughtfully. They all remained silent while she contemplated her explanation, and when she was finally ready to bare all, she stared into Tilly's eyes and gave her an almost shy smile.

"Well, I suppose I should begin by confirming to you that the way we have chosen to portray Lottie with the humans is obviously not true. One thing you will learn, or may have already picked up on, is that our power is increased by fear, respect, and submission, so the more humans fear us, the stronger we become and so on. Take the black clothing, for example. It has always been my preference to wear black, and I decided around forty years ago that all my demons, witches and followers had to wear it, too. That one simple decree empowers me tremendously as it is a consistent method for all my dark beings to show me respect, it's the same with the rule about saying Blake, Luna, and Lottie's names, but no-one can say mine of course, well except from my family," Cate told her, looking around at her kindred lovingly for a moment before carrying on.

"So, Lottie became a symbol of fear for all our human followers in order to keep her strong and out of their minds. We have always portrayed her as having had no father, but you already know that to be false, don't you?" she asked, and Tilly nodded.

Cate took a deep breath before she continued, a sadness to her beautiful eyes that Tilly could not ignore. Harry held his soulmate even tighter, his affection and love pouring out of him as he gave his powerful wife some much-needed comfort.

"Her father is in Heaven. He is an angel named Uriel, the master of the High Council of Angels, to be precise, and he is not one to be trifled with. Uriel forced me into his bed many years ago, using the twins to lure me away from the safety of the church. He and Lucifer had a big fight, which resulted in an all-out imbalance of dark and light power that lasted for many years. It left us all completely powerless and the portals between the worlds were closed for both the light and dark entities. But I won't go on too much about all of that as I know Blake has told you a little about that already hasn't he?" she asked, and Tilly nodded, remembering the tragic story Blake had told her about his childhood and the night that Cate had been kidnapped thanks to his foolish ways. She pieced his version of events together with Cate's words, understanding now that she had been kidnapped by Uriel and taken away the night that he had told her about, and then Blake had not seen her for ten years. Tilly snuggled deeper into her master's strong arms, silently letting him know how much she loved and supported him while he was forced to relive the terrible story again, thanks to her.

"I have believed for a long time that we are given our omnipotent force by a higher power than even myself and all the demons and angels combined, a ruler somewhere who controls us all and that we are at their ultimate command. Call it God, fate or even aliens I don't know, I guess I just feel it." Cate continued. "Lucifer and Uriel misused their gifts in their pursuit of even mightier power, and I believe that in doing so, it was eventually their downfall. Each had an ancient rivalry with one another, an all-consuming hatred that caused them both to do evil deeds and take selfish possession of those that they were sworn to love and protect, rather than ever put their family's needs first. I still know in my heart that I did not steal or manipulate the dark throne from Lucifer. I was given it, he just wasn't the one to hand it over to me willingly."

"Whoa," Tilly replied, trying to imagine Lucifer's dethronement, and also contemplating the potential presence of a power even greater than that of her Queen, but it all made sense somehow. Even in the short time that Tilly had been part of this dark world, she and every other follower or demon she had met knew that the darkness was to be respected and feared, but most of all they were to be thankful for it. She felt as though the Queen was not its ruler, but its vessel and her reign was its omen. Cate was to be loved and worshipped for her almighty dark force, and for those like Tilly who were given just a taste of it, that power truly was an outstanding gift, which was to be received with incredible thanks and the promise to nurture it, absorb it, and submit to it for all eternity.

"I told you she was intuitive," Cate said, smiling over to her son, who nodded and kissed the top of Tilly's head, both having read her thoughts, and she blushed.

"Thank you. Do you mind me asking, how did you manage to keep Lottie safe all this time?" Tilly asked, hoping she was not overstepping the Queen's openness.

"No, I don't mind at all," Cate said, smiling warmly at her and then looking at Harry for a second before planting a deep kiss on his lips, snuggling into him.

"Harry and my mother raised me at first," Lottie said, leaning forward to speak with Tilly herself and letting her parents continue their tender moment. "Well, until I was nine years old, that is. It was then that she sensed Lucifer was alive. She felt his beacon like we all do with her now and she had to go to it. It was the only way to keep me safe. Mum came back to Hell with him after getting back her powers one night, but he was too weak to lead so she ruled in his place for a while and they waited for him to get stronger," Lottie added, and looked to Blake and Luna, a guilty look on her face as she hesitated over the next part of the story.

CHAPTER TWELVE

"But that was not the dark power's ultimate design for her," Luna said, continuing Cate's story and giving Lottie a kind, reassuring smile. Tilly could sense their closeness, realising that Lottie was just like any other younger sibling to the powerful twins she now knew so well. They were protective, fiercely so, and would do anything to keep their little sister safe and happy. Luna and Lottie could almost be twins, their likeness to Cate phenomenal, and yet Tilly could see their unique differences beyond their looks that clearly showed their own strengths and personalities. She loved them all, she even loved Lottie already despite only just having met her and she hung on their every word as the group continued to tell Cate's woeful tale.

"The throne was already hers, she just didn't know it yet," Luna continued. "Our mother tried hard to love our father again, to learn how to forget about Lottie and Harry, but her heart belonged to him all those years despite her head telling her otherwise. She kept both him and Lottie secret from us all, she had to because she knew what would happen if they were discovered," she added, looking sad as she thought back, but she didn't dwell on thoughts of him.

Luna wouldn't let herself miss the monster who had ruined her mother's life despite him being her father. She had been luckier than Blake. Her memories of him were all wonderful, but sometimes that made it harder to hate him.

Cate watched her daughter as the thoughts of Lucifer flitted across Luna's conscious mind for a few moments before she pushed them away again. Cate thought to herself that despite all the hurt and chaos of their past, Lucifer had still done some things right. After all, he had given her Blake and Luna.

"What happened, did he try to kill you?" Tilly asked Lottie but was ashamed by her sudden outburst and looked down at her hands in apology. Blake reached up and gave her shoulder a gentle squeeze, letting her know it was okay. She was free to talk openly here, and she immediately relaxed.

"Yes," Lottie told Tilly, looking into her eyes as she spoke. "Lucifer ordered Berith to kill us both. He was the one who had found us and had brought the King proof of my existence, and when Lucifer saw Harry had raised me, he put two and two together regarding their relationship. Our mother knew she had to do something to stop him. He forced her hand, and her instincts just took over in that moment. She finally let down her own walls and opened up to her full power at last, taking Lucifer's darkness from him in the process and then claiming the dark throne for herself once and for all."

Tilly looked over at Cate wide-eyed and smiled, understanding and love pouring out of her towards the Dark Queen. She was the strongest being Tilly had ever had the fortune to meet and had truly done everything in her power to protect her children, even if that had meant putting herself in harm's way rather than them get hurt. Tilly was shocked to find out that Berith had betrayed Cate but knew that these events had happened long ago and their lives were profoundly different now to how they had been then. Even Berith was no doubt a vastly different being to the demon she now knew, and she could not be angry at him for his past.

"Thank you," Cate said, reading her thoughts, and Tilly couldn't think of the words to say in response, so she smiled happily at her, bowing her head respectfully. Tilly was in awe of this woman and of her amazing family. Blake was reading her too and pulled her tighter into his arms, his strange link of emotion opening up once again and filling her with his love and devotion despite him having remained silent this entire time.

"So, let me guess. Harry was then turned into a demon and you all came home together at last?" Tilly then asked, and Lottie nodded as she smiled over at her father. He reached across to her and took Lottie's hand in his, their bond so clear to Tilly, and neither hid their pain at being reminded of the harder times from not so long ago.

"Yes, he was the first new demon in centuries, but it just had to happen. A future without him in it was never an option. Whether as a human or a demon, Harry was and always will be my father, no matter what Uriel expects will happen if we ever meet," Lottie replied, her face stoic and determined. Tilly nodded in understanding, knowing that their bond was unbreakable, even just from seeing them the last few minutes.

Blake then reached a hand up to Tilly's neck and lifted her chin, turning her back towards him gently and then planting a soft kiss on her lips as she did. He was so tender now, so different from the dark and scary Prince she had first met, and Tilly especially loved this relaxed and happy version of him here in the company of his family.

"So, now we just need to figure out what the fuck we are gonna do about Uriel and his most recent demands," Dylan added, pulling them all out of their thoughts.

"Most recent? So, he's made other threats in the past?" Tilly asked, uncontrollably thinking back to Beatrice and her message to Cate.

"Oh yeah, it has pretty much been a constant thing ever since he returned to Heaven when Lottie was eighteen," Dylan replied nonchalantly, her eyes on Tilly but her playful smile was gone for now. "You probably never even realised that everywhere Blake goes on Earth he either has an entourage of demons with him or he stays within various protective thresholds that we have had in place for years, such as at the penthouses or the old castles and our churches. I even helped plan your day out on Halloween and then went on ahead of you guys to perform the spells and put protective markings on both the island and the cabin for his yearly visit. A witch's first and most important responsibility is to make sure that the royal family are safe. Any of them being kidnapped by the white witches or angels is not an option. I'm sorry that we failed to stop Beatrice's trap from ensnaring you on your way home the day after though, that was a new one that we had no idea about and was aimed at powerful demons and their followers as they travelled overhead, trying to specifically ensnare those who might potentially have a closer link to Cate herself. I know it doesn't make what happened to you any better, but we have taken measures to ward against those kinds of traps from now on, I promise you."

Tilly hoped Dylan was right, if Blake or any of his siblings were ever captured by the angels it was pretty clear to her that Cate would do anything in her power to keep them safe, maybe even offering herself up in exchange for them. But that was a fate worse than death for the Dark Queen too as she would then be forced away from her children and husband again. Either way, Uriel could not get his own way no matter the cost.

"Thank you. Well, I'm kinda glad that it was me she caught then," Tilly replied, taking Dylan by surprise. "I suppose even Berith could have been used as bait or worse by her if she managed to get him in her enchanted grasp. A lowly human follower was not really exciting enough to warrant much more than another threat."

"Well, aren't you a clever thing?" Dylan replied with a wide smile, genuinely surprised by Tilly's instinctive nature. "I like this girl," she added, looking at Blake.

"Me too," he replied, kissing the top of Tilly's head affectionately.

"So, back to my previous question, what's next?" Dylan then asked, looking around at the forlorn faces of her adopted family and her stomach dropped, anxiousness creeping in despite her stoic features.

"I absolutely will not send Lottie up there," Cate said, her eyes flickering with dark specks, showing her inner rage at the very thought of handing over her youngest child to Uriel.

"No way," Dylan agreed, shaking her head thoughtfully. "Do you really think he meant it about the white fire?" she then asked Cate, one eyebrow raised, and the room went silent again. Blake leaned in and spoke quietly in Tilly's ear, sensing her confusion on the terminology.

"The whole threat of them 'raining down white fire' is their way of referring to them wiping out both the humans and the Earth, as well as everything on it. All that lies south of Heaven, including Hell, would be wiped out. It's kind of their 'clean slate' concept, starting afresh if you will," he said, and Tilly paled at the sheer thought of it actually happening.

"Maybe she meant it, but why would the council agree to do it?" Cate said, pondering aloud in response to Dylan's question. "I've been thinking about it. Surely this must mean that the plan is already in place to carry it out, regardless of our action or inaction. I can't help but wonder if he just wants Lottie and Lucifer delivered to him before it happens so that they are safely up there by the time they begin their clean slate tactics," she said and the whole room went silent at her words, the realisation kicking in for all of them that perhaps Cate was right and that no matter what they were all doomed. The atmosphere around them changed dramatically, each of the powerful and dark, God-like creatures buzzing with their omnipotent, commanding power combined with their shared fear and anger.

"It must be, it's the only explanation," said Blake, rage building inside him too at his mother's morbid realisation. He took Tilly's hand in his and then twisted the ring he had given her around her slim finger absentmindedly while concentrating on calming his rage.

"Then we fight. If he wants a war, we'll give him one," Dylan said, consternation clear in her tone.

"How? I doubt even my thoughts would be safe from him, Dylan," Cate said, seemingly defeated. "He would sense us coming from a mile away."

"Then we keep thinking, we figure out a way to lure him down or we convince the council not to wipe us all out," replied Dylan solemnly, and they all nodded in thoughtful agreement while the fire sizzled loudly, piercing the tense silence with its crackling melody.

CHAPTER THIRTEEN

Cate stood at her bedroom window, looking out at the dark city below. She was so deep in thought that she barely even noticed when Harry approached and jumped as he wrapped his arms around her from behind, his palms resting gently over her stomach. She looked down at his hands, covering them with her own affectionately.

"When are we going to tell everyone about the baby?" he asked her, his thumb rubbing against Cate's already slightly swollen belly as he embraced her. In private, Harry couldn't hide his happiness, but could still understand his wife's hesitation at announcing their wonderful news.

"Soon, darling, but not until we know that Lottie is going to be safe. I don't ever want her to feel like we are trying to replace her," she answered, staring out at the red sky again as tears welled in her beautiful green eyes. Cate forced them away. She hadn't cried in years and would not let her hormones get the better of her now. One thing Cate was absolutely sure of was her trust in Harry. He was truly thrilled to be a father at long last, and she couldn't wait to hold their child in her arms. She trusted the special spark of true happiness she sensed inside of him completely and knew that he would love this baby no more than he loved all three of her older children, but that wasn't the reason why she still hadn't told them all the truth just yet. The still besotted couple had waited so long to finally have a child of their own, and although Cate knew Lottie would always be Harry's daughter, despite her angelic heritage, she couldn't help but worry she might feel resentful of the new sibling. Lottie had never given her a reason to think she would be, though, and Cate knew that it was probably just her own fear of the unknown future for her child of light and darkness, keeping her from sharing their news just yet. There was also a part of her that knew she might have to sacrifice herself in order to keep Lottie safe, that she might have to single-handedly take on Uriel and that both she and the baby could die in the process. It was a terrible thought, but one she just could not push aside and so she had held off telling her children the news to stop them from growing attached to their unborn sibling.

The witches had sensed her new flicker of life almost as soon as she had felt it too, all of whom were sworn to secrecy, of course, and Dylan repeatedly pleaded with her to tell the others their joyous news, but she refused. Cate knew deep down that she had waited all this time to further her dark brood out of uncertainty and fear for their future. Uriel's threats had progressively gotten stronger and more desperate over the years and Lucifer's anguished and pleading thoughts still called out to her from within his nightmarish prison, making Cate really feel as though she always had a devil on one shoulder and an angel on the other. Her two ex-lovers' urgent declarations of hate, fear and anger towards her were a constant burden she had to bear, and sometimes it overwhelmed her, not that she ever told that to anyone, not even Harry. Cate knew she could never stand Blake and Luna resenting their new little sibling if they ever thought he or she was meant to be Cate's replacement for her precious, littlest daughter either, and she certainly didn't want Lottie thinking that she was already getting used to the idea of losing her to Uriel. Although Lottie was genuinely happy here in Hell, Cate knew she was such a delicate child and needed lots of love and attention from all those around her. Lottie had never grown close to anyone other than her family during her time in the underworld, not ever having taken a lover and Cate had always hoped that as time went on, she would find someone with whom she shared that natural, all-consuming spark with. Cate absolutely would never betroth Lottie to anyone or command her to love another like her own master had done. Cate stood by her word with all her children that they were free to choose their lovers for themselves, and her eldest two had chosen wonderfully without any intervention from her.

"Lottie will never think that of us, Cate, you know that. I sometimes think you are so used to being afraid that you forget how to just be happy. Now, more than ever, they need some good news, my darling. This baby has waited a long time for us to be ready for another, even though most of your followers expected it years ago. He or she was conceived before Uriel's threat about the white fire as well, don't forget," Harry reminded his so powerful and yet so fragile wife and Dark Queen. She turned to face him, peering up into his gorgeous eyes, grateful for the understanding, reassurance and love she saw returned in them. He was always so level-headed, so calm, and clever, while Cate would still feel so lost and afraid at times, her memories and fears still haunting every dark corner of her mind.

"You continue to astound me, my love. You really do know me so much better than I know myself sometimes. I often wonder just how you could love something so terrible as me? I've been a mess ever since the day we met, and yet you stayed through it all. What would I ever do without you, Harry?" she asked, wrapping her arms around him tightly and snuggling into his chest, breathing in his gorgeous natural scent deeply. It still surprised Cate that he could possibly smell the same even after all these years in Hell, and him now being so far away from the human man she had known all those years ago. And yet, when she closed her eyes and took a deep breath, Cate felt as though she were transported back the almost one-hundred years to his small flat and their tiny little secluded existence on Earth together. She could still picture their small home clearly, hear the birds singing in the trees outside, smell his freshly laundered bed sheets as they lay wrapped in each other's arms under them, and she could even imagine the spring sunshine as it streamed in through the open window and shined in onto his glorious, sexy body. Thinking back to those days made her smile and as she looked up into his deep blue eyes, Cate couldn't help but fall madly in love with Harry all over again.

"Was there ever any doubt in your mind, any question of what I was willing to do or how much I would take in order to be here with you Cate?" he asked, running his strong hands through her long, dark curls and then planting a deep kiss on her red lips.

"Never," she admitted as he pulled back from his kiss, smiling again at last.

"Good, don't make me have to give you a telling off," he replied with a cheeky grin, tapping her nose playfully with the tip of his index finger.

"You can try," she told him, unbuttoning his black shirt and kissing his chest, adding a little nibble on each of his nipples for good measure. Cate then grinned up at him darkly, a wicked glint in her eye and Harry jokingly tried to pull back from her deceptively strong grasp, but she held him there tight and kissed him deeper. He immediately gave in and fell to his knees before her as he unbuttoned Cate's black jeans and slid them down her slender legs along with her lace panties, which he then discarded. He kneeled before her, his eyes on hers as he focussed his kisses along her belly for a moment and she peered down at him with a contented smile as she then ran her hands through his brown, messy hair. Cate gasped loudly as his mouth trailed lower and lower, her body responding immediately to his commanding touch. She giggled and held onto him tighter as Harry lifted her legs up around his shoulders and nestled his mouth around her swollen clitoris before he then carried her over to their bed, her pleasure and satisfaction his only goal as he devoured her aching nub and slid his fingers inside her wet opening, soon delivering his Queen her much needed release as she gripped the covers underneath her and the walls around them shook violently.

CHAPTER FOURTEEN

In the weeks that followed the night of their first meeting, Tilly grew close with Lottie, quickly becoming her best friend as well as being named as her official protector by Cate. Being in Hell permanently now, even Tilly could see that Luna and Blake's immense bond as twins was incredibly powerful. She came to realise that the two of them really were a formidable and fierce duo, and it was no wonder that they now caused such mayhem to Earth's delicate balance if they were both up there at the same time. This incredibly close connection had unfortunately always left Lottie feeling a bit left out of their tight little circle, though, and despite them wanting her to be closer she had never felt like she could really connect with her siblings the way that they had always hoped. She had spent most of her days either alone or with Harry and Cate and didn't seem to mind that quiet little life at all.

Lottie seemed to miss her life on Earth, for one thing only, the food. Tilly's experiences and hopes at becoming a top chef one day were a big talking point for the pair of them, and Lottie made her promise not to give up on her dreams. She wanted Tilly to return to Earth when all of this was over and continue pursuing her career, at least now she would have her demonic powers to use to her advantage too, just like Berith had done when it came to charming record label executives and concert crowds. Tilly agreed, knowing that she still wanted it too, but was already feeling torn when it came to deciding between the two worlds and was thankful that the Queen had taken that decision out of her hands for now.

The young Princess was extraordinarily strong thanks to her royal blood and the dark power she had willingly chosen to embrace, but she also confided in Tilly that she had always wondered if she was slightly weaker than the rest of her family because of her light side. She was at a constant internal battle with it and felt as though this war inside weakened her more and more as time passed by. Alma had created a potion a long time ago to stop her from having any adverse reactions caused by her staying in Hell for so long, after Cate's illness many years ago the high priestess had worked tirelessly to ensure that no more of their family ever struggled with staying in Hell permanently ever again. Lottie was a descendent of both half-light and half-darkness just as Cate had once been, but both sides were almost as pure as you could get, and she eventually admitted to Tilly that she had needed to take more and more of the potion as her restricted existence went on.

Cate called Blake, Luna, and Lottie to her chambers one night to finally reveal her and Harry's happy news. She could no longer hide her little bump under the baggy dresses and tops she had been wearing and didn't want to anymore. Uriel and his evil promise were still looming over them all, but they had been planning their defence and retaliation at length, and Cate was certain now that they would succeed, one way or another she would do anything it took to keep her family safe and trusted in the higher power she had always given so much credit to despite never actually having had any proof that it existed. True faith if ever there was one.

"Harry and I are going to have another baby," she told them, peering down at her almost identical children as they perched on the huge bed. All three took a moment to absorb her words. Luna's mouth dropped open in shock and both she and Blake stared up at her in surprise while Lottie smiled broadly at both of her parents. Harry had stood silently beside his wife, letting her take the lead, and he couldn't help but smile back at Lottie, seeing her face light up at the news.

"That's wonderful!" she cried, jumping up and wrapping her arms around Cate excitedly.

"Wow, I don't know what to say," Luna admitted, hugging Harry, but Cate could read her thoughts and knew that both she and her quiet brother were happy for them.

"We know the timing is terrible, but it actually happened before Uriel's threat about the white fire, and we just didn't know how to tell you all after those crazy days that followed. You all know we have wanted this for a long time. We just hope that you understand our need to have kept it to ourselves until now," Harry told them sheepishly.

"You're right, the timing is terrible," Blake said with a laugh as he stood and kissed Cate on the cheek. "But at the same time, it could not be any better," he added, smiling at them both.

"He gives us all the more reason to stay strong, focussed and determined," Lottie agreed, reaching out to hug Harry tightly as Luna joined their mother by her brother's side.

"He?" Cate asked Lottie, one eyebrow raised.

"Call it a hunch," she replied with a smile when she pulled back from her father's embrace.

Luna placed her hand over her mother's stomach, receiving a tiny kick almost the instant she did, which made her laugh. Cate read her children's happy and positive thoughts, understanding at last just how right Harry had been about them and their acceptance of their new brother or sister. Harry's knowing smile a few moments later showed Cate that he could tell she was feeling better, that he knew exactly what she was thinking. Her husband could somehow read the woman that no one in this realm could ever get close to, and yet he often knew exactly what was going through her mind.

Blake looked over at Harry too, suddenly realising that his thoughts on the subject had been closed to him somehow, that his mother had hidden them from him and his sisters.

"All in a day's work, darling. One day you'll understand," Cate said, smiling at her son, and Blake knew she was talking about the day she would finally give him the dark throne, and the ultimate power that came with it. He had often thought about what it would be like taking over Hell as the new, new Devil. He wanted it but also knew he had a lot of learning to do before it would ever happen. Letting down his horribly constructed walls was just the start. It would be centuries before he was truly ready to lead, and perhaps even longer for him to be sure that he wouldn't turn into his father on that throne.

CHAPTER FIFTEEN

"I have an idea, but I want to try it out first," Lottie said to Tilly one day as they relaxed in the royal living area together. They had been spending a lot of time with each other either there or in Lottie's chambers, usually reading, talking, or she had even been helping to develop Tilly's demonic powers with her to ensure that she mastered her new gifts quickly. The young demon had progressed amazingly in the short time and was grateful for all the help she could get, especially as it was coming from the Unholy Princess herself.

"What is it?" Tilly asked her, intrigued by her carefully worded request and eager to know more. Her official role now was to be Lottie's protector and aide, to follow any and all orders from her and keep her secrets safe. She was still Blake's demonic progeny, lover, and follower, though, and she worried about keeping secrets from him. He had told her not to worry, that despite her promises to Lottie her mind was wide open for him to read whenever he wanted, so, he had added with a smirk, she never really could keep a secret from him anyway and she blushed, remembering all the times she had mentally undressed him during their time together.

Tilly hadn't seen much of Blake recently though as he had been incredibly secretive and busy with his mother and twin sister lately, and she couldn't help but think that they were purposely using her to keep Lottie occupied so that they could discuss their plans for her in secret. She sometimes got the feeling that Lottie was wrapped in cotton wool by her family, but would quickly push away those thoughts, knowing that she was not even remotely qualified to make such assumptions when it came to the Dark Queen's choices for her children. Blake had told Tilly the wonderful news about the upcoming arrival of his new brother or sister following his summons to his mother's chambers that night, and she was incredibly happy and excited for them all. This child signified everything they were fighting for and had quickly become a symbol for their dark hopes.

"I can't tell you, but you just have to trust me, okay?" Lottie answered her, a cryptic response, but Tilly knew she had to trust the

Princess's word. She nodded and sat back on the sofa while Lottie watched her thoughtfully.

"Close your eyes and count backwards from ten," she ordered, and Tilly did as she asked, whispering the countdown quietly as she screwed her eyes closed tightly. Ten seconds later, she opened her eyes again, and Lottie was nowhere to be seen. It was as though she had vanished, but Tilly had not sensed her teleport away, nor had she heard her leave.

"Lottie?" she called out, looking around confusedly, but she received no answer from her mistress and friend. Tilly stood and walked over to the window, looking out thoughtfully at the dark skyline as she closed her eyes and focussed on the Princess, trying to locate her beacon, but there was nothing. Blake then teleported into the living area and slipped his arms around behind her, kissing Tilly's neck before she spun round and kissed his lips deeply. It felt like forever since she had last been in his strong arms.

"Have you seen Lottie?" he asked her when he finally forced himself away, and she shook her head, confused too that his little sister had seemingly disappeared on them.

"Hmm, it's strange. I cannot sense her at all," he said, looking worried.

"She said she was trying something out, but wouldn't say what," Tilly informed him, but it didn't seem to relieve his anxious expression.

"I'll be back in a few minutes," Blake told her before teleporting away again.

Tilly sat back down on the sofa and rubbed her tired eyes, and when she opened them again a couple of seconds later Lottie was back in the room with her, standing over her and looking down at Tilly with a satisfied smile on her delicate face.

"Where did you go?" she asked her, jumping up and throwing her arms around the Princess with relief.

"Nowhere exciting," Lottie replied, a wider smile on her lips now, but she refused to say any more.

Blake teleported back into the royal living area and took in the sight of his little sister, back where she ought to have been when he was here just a few minutes earlier.

"What the fuck, Lottie?" he asked her, worry clear in his tone as he peered down at her.

"I can't tell you," she replied, much to Blake's distaste. "But it's good I promise, brother."

Tilly watched them for a moment, understanding Blake's worry, but she also couldn't figure out how his sister had managed to fool him, too.

"Can't you just read her thoughts?" Tilly asked them both, surprised that Lottie had been able to keep a secret from her omnipotent brother.

"It's none of your business Tilly," he said coolly, not taking his eyes off Lottie's, but she was sure that he was hiding something from her. Blake looked over at Tilly with a disapproving look and then spoke to her more firmly this time.

"Keep out of it, do not question me about Lottie again," he ordered, and she heard his voice reverberate inside her head as well as in her ears, his words a command rather than a request and she nodded to her master, knowing that they had every reason to keep their secrets from her. She had learned her lessons when it came to keeping her thoughts and mouth in check a long time ago and did not ever want to overstep the boundaries of their relationship again.

The next few months passed them all by far too quickly. Blake was kept incredibly busy with his covert plans while Tilly kept Lottie company and helped her grow more confident and carefree thanks to their strong friendship. She and Blake got to see plenty of each other during their free time though, and it was still much more than the pair had been used to thanks to their relationship, having been controlled by the phases of the moon before her demonic rebirth. Cate hid herself away towards the end of her pregnancy, but before she did, she re-iterated her orders forbidding any of them from going to Earth until she could figure out a plan for Uriel and the angelic council. She was sure that they would have their white witches lying in wait across the Earth, eager for any captive they could take, and if they got their hands on a royal family member, they would surely be used as bait and leverage again to force her co-operation all the more quickly, a concept that brought both fear and anger to the Dark Queen.

Blake summoned Tilly to his vast, private chambers as much as he could so that they could be alone together between their duties, desperate for some time alone as much as possible. They had both been so busy trying to figure out ways to keep Lottie safe and also considering how to fight whatever it was that Uriel had planned for them come the impending Halloween, very aware that the time was passing them all by far too quickly.

"I'm sorry I have to be so secretive Tilly," he said, pulling her closer in his strong arms, their naked bodies wrapped around one another tightly, following another blissful few hours in his gigantic bed together. She peered up into his striking green eyes and smiled, knowing that there was really no need for him to explain any of this to her. He was her master, her leader, and she would follow him forever no matter what he asked of her.

"I know, but I get it, Blake. This is your family and we all need to do whatever it takes to win this. Even if that means keeping secrets sometimes," she assured him, leaning up for a kiss.

"Why is it I can read every thought that runs through that pretty little head of yours, and yet you still continue to surprise me?" he asked, looking down into her blue eyes warmly.

Tilly shrugged and smiled at her master as Blake planted another deep kiss on her lips, feeling lucky to have her by his side. He had been working hard on many theories with his mother and Dylan while Lottie was kept busy thanks to Tilly's help and he loved it they got on so well, for Lottie's sake too, as she had always been a quiet girl. When his mother had appeared in Hell one night with this young, half light and dark girl on her arm, she had shocked them all with the incredible revelations about her heritage and the intense story of her life. Lottie had been welcomed by them all without any resentment or question, and both Blake and Luna always tried to treat her the same way as they did each other, building up their bonds with her over time. It had been hard, their strong connection as twins still driving a wedge between the three of them regardless of their intentions, and Lottie had struggled to adapt to her new life, even if she would not admit it. Lottie had never had a friend outside of their family, never had a lover or accepted a coven of her own to command and busy herself with. Blake often wondered if perhaps she was content in her misery too, and that having Tilly around had helped her grow in many ways, just as it had helped him.

"Promise me something," he said, leaning up on his elbow to look down into Tilly's eyes.

"Anything," she replied with a smile.

"Promise me you'll never leave me," he asked her, an almost shy look crossing his dark face as he stared down into her deep blue eyes. Tilly reached up and cupped his cheeks with her hands, staring back into his seemingly endless green irises.

"I promise," she said, and then added, "I will never let anything or anyone come between us, and if we are ever forced apart, I will fight until my dying breath to be by your side again. You are my every reason for existing, Blake. I would never leave you."

He couldn't help the huge smile he gave Tilly after her wonderful words. She always knew just the right thing to say. Blake was sure now that the heart he had once convinced himself could never love or be loved in return was beating for her, and her alone. Tilly had come bursting into his existence and had turned his whole life upside down, and he loved her for every moment of it.

"Every time I need you, you are there Tilly, no matter how hard I have made it for you to love me." Blake said, pulling her whole body closer to his and cupping her cheeks with his palms as he spoke. "I want you to marry me," he added, kissing her before Tilly could reply, but reading her mind and knowing her answer was yes.

CHAPTER SIXTEEN

On the morning of the summer solstice the next June, Cate lay resting in bed, she peered out the window at the brighter than usual sky, sensing the ancient and powerful day ahead, and she shook the sleeping demon beside her to wake him. Harry jumped and rubbed his bleary eyes, looking his wife up and down with a worried expression.

"What's the matter?" he asked her, sitting up against the huge pillows. "Is the baby coming?"

"Nothing's the matter darling," Cate answered, taking his hand and interlocking her fingers in his. "Not yet, but today's the day," she told him, somehow knowing their child was ready. She smiled and rubbed her large bump with her other hand as Harry laughed. He kissed the back of the hand he held and slid back down on the bed, snuggling back under the sheets and burying his face in his pillow sleepily.

"Well, that's great and everything, but can you wake me up when it's actually happening?" he muttered groggily but told her silently that he didn't mean it. He was just being a grumpy old man.

Cate laughed and climbed up from the bed, her long, black nightgown flowing around her ankles as she stood and looked out at the red sun. Her water's broke within minutes with a large gush, followed almost immediately by a strong contraction but she barely made a sound, the pain was nothing to the strong Queen, but Harry realised immediately and woke up properly this time, he clambered out of the bed to go to her, falling flat on his face clumsily as he did so.

"I seem to remember you being a lot more prepared last time, my love," she said, standing over him with a wide grin as he lay on their bedroom floor, rubbing his sore head.

"Yeah, yeah," he answered playfully, getting to his feet and then helping her back to the bed as the door opened and in came Alma and Dylan. "We didn't have these two to help last time," he reminded Cate as he kissed her cheek and joined her on the bed while the witches fussed around her and lay down towels beneath her on the black sheets.

Their son was born in less than an hour, his first cries echoing around the whole castle and every demon stopped in their tracks to offer a silent prayer to their new Prince. Cate held him first, eager to soothe his cries, and he stopped instantly, peering up at her with the light blue eyes of his father. Harry kissed her lips and then his son's forehead with a pure, content smile on his face as he sat on the bed and took in the most beautiful sight he had ever seen.

"Lottie was right," he whispered, stroking the baby's brown hair.

Within minutes Cate began to heal and recover her slim figure and strength, so Alma and Dylan finished cleaning her up and then turned to leave, eager to let the three of them be alone. Dylan couldn't help but stop at the doorway, happy tears streaming down her face as she took just one more look at her best friend and her wonderful family. Cate smiled over at her, happy tears rolling uncontrollably down her own face too, as the wonderful feelings of being a mother again flooded her powerful body. She handed the baby to Harry for his first cuddle before climbing off the bed and running over to the doorway and grabbing Dylan tightly, hugging the witch and kissing her cheek affectionately before releasing her and then joining Harry and their son back on the remarkably clean bed as Dylan left and shut the door behind her.

"He looks like you," she told her husband, stroking the baby's hair gently with her hand as Harry held him close. Cate hadn't even thought about it until now, all three of her other children had been the image of her thanks to her human side when they were conceived with their omnipotent fathers, but now she was the featureless yet powerful one, and their child had gotten his looks from his ex-human father instead this time. In honesty, it caught Cate slightly off guard, but she didn't mind at all. All that mattered was his safety, just as with her other children, and she would spend an eternity loving those little blue eyes no matter whether they were on the face of her husband or of their son.

"He might have my looks, Cate, but everything else is from you. You've shared with him such power and potential. Just because we can't see your gifts does not mean they aren't there," he reminded her, sensing Cate's vulnerability, and she couldn't help but smile back at him.

"Thanks Harry," she said. "So, Daddy, what are we going to call him then?" Cate asked Harry, wanting him to be the one to choose this time, and he looked over at her, unable to hide the happy glint in his eye.

"Well, I was thinking. Every rose needs its Thorne, right?" he asked her shyly, watching his beautiful, glowing wife as she purposely pretended to think about it for a second. She had known for a while that he liked that name, and she thought it was perfect too, but had wanted to let him be the one to name the baby when the time came.

"It's perfect, Thorne it is then," she replied with a smile, summoning

Blake, Luna, and Lottie to their chambers so that they could meet their new brother.

The entire underworld soon welcomed the news of Thorne's arrival with relief and delight. They partied and celebrated for days in honour of their new prince, sending their Queen prayers filled with love and joy at his safe arrival. Tilly decided she wanted to arrange a present for Blake's new brother, and she had the idea of putting together a box full of treasures and memories that each of his family members could share with him and so she set about procuring the items required as soon as he was born. One morning she teleported off towards the witch's dungeon in search of Selena, hoping that she might have a few vials in which they could put various rolls of paper inscribed with personal messages and spells that might come in useful for the powerful prince's future. When Tilly rounded the corner to Selena's chambers, she froze, finding her door wide open and Tilly could see inside. Selena was straddling a lover, riding up and down in his lap while groaning her pleasure and unashamedly bouncing up and down in his lap. Tilly was about to leave when a lump caught in her throat when the man's face came into her view. It was Blake.

Tilly's tears streamed down her face, her mouth opening and closing over silent words of shock and spite. She wanted to storm over to them and rip Selena from his embrace, to torture them both thanks to their betrayal, but she was rooted to the spot, unable to take her eyes off the terrible sight that was playing out before her eyes. When Selena had finished, she climbed off her lover's lap and kissed him, sending Tilly's stomach lurching forward and she finally found her feet as she stumbled over to the pair of them and grabbed Selena's hair roughly. Selena stumbled back in shock, finding herself sprawled on the dark floor but Tilly ignored her for now and turned to give Blake his much-deserved mouthful, only to find that it was no longer Blake's face before her, but the face of his warlock Brendon.

"What the fuck?" Tilly asked, looking from one to the other as Selena got to her feet and righted herself, a sly grin curling at her lips.

"Never heard of a simple mirage spell?" Selena answered, sniggering at Tilly's still-shocked expression. Tilly was furious. Regardless of Selena's lover not having been Blake, the fact remained that she had persuaded Brendon to cast the mirage spell on himself to get her into bed. Tilly's mind raced, and she thought back to all the loving glances Selena had given Blake since she had known them, all the desperate attempts to push Tilly aside and have his focus again, and she sneered.

"I never took you for the sore-loser type Selena. This is desperate, even for you," she said, taking her chance to snigger now and Selena's pretty face contorted into a venomous guise of envy and hatred towards the demon.

"He always used to come to me before you came along. I was always the first one he would choose. He and I have been fucking since before you were even born Tilly and you think you can just come along and stop that? He knows I love him, and he has rewarded me for that love countless times, but now he just wants you. What's so fucking special about Tilly Mayfair, huh? All I see is a stupid little girl who has had everything handed to her on a fucking plate when the rest of us have worked our arses off for centuries for this family. Whatever you think you have with him, stop kidding yourself. Give it twenty years and he'll have forgotten all about you and I'll be there to take care of him, just like always," Selena spat, her voice high-pitched and faltering thanks to her fraught emotions. Tilly saw red. She flung herself at the witch and laid punches to her pretty face while kicking her ankles from beneath her to send her flying to the floor. Tilly then straddled Selena and continued her blows until strong hands gripped her from behind and yanked her away.

"That's enough," Blake said, his voice clear and powerful, and Tilly immediately stopped her frenzy. He had teleported into the chambers with them, having sensed their altercation and Tilly's fraught thoughts from across the underworld and while he had been interested to see how she dealt with her heartache, he knew that letting her continue to beat up his high priestess was not the right tactic. Both women stood and started to shout, to tell their master their version of the story, and he silenced them both with a snap of his fingers. Blake looked at Tilly, reading her thoughts, and he grinned at her wickedly.

"So, my darling, now that you have punished my witch for her harsh words and lack of respect for a level one demon, how do you suggest I punish you for not allowing me the opportunity to deal with my subordinate myself?" he asked, shocking her. Blake released the commandment silencing her and Tilly shook her head.

"I'm sorry Blake. Do whatever you feel you have to do, it was worth it," Tilly replied, eying her bloody foe with an unsatisfied smirk. She wanted more. Tilly wished Blake had just given her a few more minutes to exert her power over the witch, having enjoyed discovering just how much stronger she was than the high priestess. Blake looked over at Selena, watching as she winced at her injuries and nursed her bruised ego. Her thoughts were more of his disappointment in her than of Tilly's vengeful blows, Selena didn't care about the beating, all that she cared about was the humiliation of Blake finding out about her secret role-plays with Brendon and her spiteful admissions about Blake's relationship with Tilly.

"And you," he said, drawing Selena's gaze to his. "Poor Brendon will do just about anything to fuck you, won't he? I suggest you stop making him cast a mirage spell and clear your mind of thoughts of you and I ever being together, Selena. Those days are over. You and I are over. If you cannot accept that, then I will transfer you into a different coven," he said and Selena fell to her knees, silently pleading with him not to send her to another master. Her thoughts screamed of her apologies and promises, telling Blake that she would stop harbouring feelings for him and move on. "Very well," he said, sending her away with a swish of his hand and then turning to Tilly again, eying her with a devilish grin. "Jealous much?" he teased, pulling her into his embrace where he laid deep kisses on her lips and pinned her body to his with his strong arms.

"Maybe, but you cannot blame me. What's my punishment?" Tilly whispered, staring up at him lovingly, so grateful that the sight she had seen was not real and that Blake had not been cheating on her. "I'm ready to take it," she promised.

"I'm inclined to take you across my knee, but instead, I think I will issue you with an order. You are hereby confined to my chambers for the next seven days," Blake told her, smiling widely. "And you will service me in any way I do so desire for the duration of your punishment," he added with a salacious grin.

"As you command, your Majesty," Tilly replied, following his lead as Blake then teleported them to his chambers and began her wonderful and far from punishing sentence.

CHAPTER SEVENTEEN

Thorne was a grouchy baby, never seeming to settle in the arms of anyone but his family and Tilly barely saw Cate or Harry as they were so busy seeing to their newborn son. Blake summoned her to his chambers a couple of weeks after his brother's birth and she teleported to him immediately, finding her master snuggled up with his baby brother on the huge bed, his fingers playing with the delicate newborn's tiny hands as he lay beside him and spoke quietly in his ear about Tilly, telling him she was going to be his aunt. She approached quietly and smiled down at the pair of them, immediately seeing Thorne's resemblance to Harry and she smiled even wider as she thought how happy he and Cate must be.

"Hi boys," she whispered, climbing gently onto the bed beside them and then stroking the baby's head with a delicate touch. She lay opposite Blake on his bed, Thorne in-between them, and peered into her fiancé's eyes, relishing in the proud, content smile on his lips and the warm energy he gave off effortlessly as he cradled his tiny brother.

"She wanted you to meet him. You are the first person outside the family other than Dylan and Alma," Blake whispered to her, his wide smile giving away his happiness at his mother's trust in Tilly. "Well, that and I think they welcomed an hour to themselves," he added, making Tilly laugh.

"He's just perfect, isn't he?" she asked rhetorically as Thorne gripped her index finger in his tiny yet strong hand, his eyes on hers, already seeming to take her in. Lottie had already warned her he was a crier, and she half expected him to scream if she got too close, but thankfully he already seemed to trust her. Tilly wondered if perhaps his internal power was already strong and despite being just weeks old, Thorne might already be putting them to use in picking out his most trusted protectors and carers. Dylan was the only other outsider who had been able to get so close to the young Prince, which they had all taken as a sign of Cate's love for her having been passed on to him, and now Blake somehow seemed convinced of his little brother's trust in Tilly already too. He sat up and lifted Thorne off the covers and placed him in her arms without a word, she sat up as well and squealed worriedly but held the baby close, smiling as he almost immediately closed his eyes and drifted off to sleep nestled in her bosom.

"Whoa," Tilly whispered, looking over at Blake in shock. "He likes me?"

"Of course he does. I already told him how wonderful you are," he replied, grinning at her wickedly as she tried to fathom this powerful new child and the connection they already seemed to be making.

"Can he seriously already know all that stuff?" she asked, peering down at the content baby as he sucked his thumb and slept soundly.

"No, but he has a profound kind of intuition. His thoughts are nothing but pictures and blurs, but he knows what he wants and who he trusts," Blake told Tilly before leaning forward and planting a soft, deep kiss on her lips. They sat together for a little while, chatting quietly while Thorne rested in her arms and eventually Cate summoned them back to her, allowing Tilly access to her and Harry's private chambers for the first time. The three of them walked up the small hallway to their room rather than teleporting with the baby, careful to ensure of his safety at all times. She handed Thorne to Cate gently, and the sleeping Prince didn't even stir as he was passed between them.

"I knew he would like you," Cate said, laying him in a small basinet beside the bed where Harry was sleeping. Tilly smiled at the sight of the napping demon and then focussed on the Queen as she approached again.

"Thank you. I have to admit I was worried," she confessed with an awkward smile. Cate just laughed and pulled Tilly into a tight hug, cupping her cheeks with her palms as she pulled back and then mesmerised the young demon with her powerful green gaze.

"Don't be," she replied. "You are already like a daughter to me, Tilly. Blake has told me your news and I could not be more thrilled. Thorne already knows that you are his family," she added, kissing her cheek gently. She smiled widely, taken aback by Cate's lovely statement, and couldn't find the words to thank her, feeling in awe of her incredible Queen.

"We'll leave you to it," Blake then said quietly from behind Tilly as both Harry and Thorne began to wake up from their naps, and he took her hand and led her away after receiving a quick kiss from his mother too, a silent conversation seeming to have passed between them as Tilly had stood dumfounded before the Dark Queen. When they reached his room again Blake pulled her inside and shut the door behind them, pinning her to the wall and then gripping Tilly's thighs in his strong hands and pulling her off the ground, wrapping her legs around him tightly as he planted deep and passionate kisses on her eager lips.

Blake couldn't help but want to reward his lover for her incredible prowess, she had no idea just how much everyone was taken with her, remaining modest and shy despite the power she possessed to make both

Blake and all the other dark beings around them want her for their own. Even his baby brother had sensed it, her strange ability to lure them in without even knowing she was doing it, causing every one of them to desire her in one way or another. Both Luna and Lottie felt that pull to Tilly too, each having admitted on more than one occasion how they felt about her, and while Blake wanted to figure out what it might be that made her so different, but he trusted that she was his, now and forever.

He ripped Tilly's clothes from her slim body quickly, eager to taste her, wanting to possess that sweet, inviting body she hid beneath her black dress before either of them was summoned away again. Tilly cried out as Blake devoured her, writhing beneath him as he relished in her screams of pleasure as she came. He loved Tilly's pleading thoughts for more, for him. She was desperate to have his thick length inside her and ripped off his chinos before he could even begin to pursue her next climax with his mouth, throwing her fiancé back on the huge bed and then climbing on top of him, slamming his hard cock inside of her with such force that they both couldn't help but cry out as her body welcomed her omnipotent master with a deep squeeze. Blake sat up and wrapped Tilly in his arms as she moved up and down on his hard shaft, her body as desperate for him as his was for her.

He cupped her face and then brushed her messy hair out of the way while she rode him hard and peered into her eyes as she gyrated effortlessly on his lap. Tilly was mesmerised, her mind, body, and soul at his command as their bodies released together and the walls around them shook violently, their heightened passion seeming to shake them even harder than usual.

Lottie continued to use Tilly's help in perfecting whatever it was that she had been trying to figure out the day that she had disappeared the first time in the living room, and the Princess seemed incredibly pleased with her progress. So much so that she took Tilly to one side one day and asked for her help again.

"Can I try something else on you Tilly? I would need your one hundred per cent trust though," she asked her, with a serious look on her delicate face.

"Of course, anything you need Lottie I'm your girl, you know that," Tilly replied earnestly, they had been working together for a long time now, her sitting down and then closing her eyes while Lottie would seemingly disappear for a few minutes at first, having built up to her eventually being gone for hours at a time. She would finally reappear and check-in with Blake or Luna quietly, but for some reason she would never let Tilly know what she was up to. It annoyed her a little bit that they were still being so secretive, but she would just keep reminding herself that it was all about the greater picture, and clearly had something to do with whatever plans they were putting into place for Halloween.

Lottie led her to the couch and Tilly sat down, closing her eyes automatically and then silently counting back from ten before opening them again, expecting Lottie to be gone like usual, but for some reason this time she was still there.

"That's it, you can get up now," she then told her, and Tilly could not help but question the wide grin on her face as she peered up at her friend.

"What was that? I thought you were going to disappear again?" Tilly asked, but then shook her head in apology, knowing that she was not permitted to ask questions about all of this. "Sorry, I mean, what now?" she corrected herself, standing to join Lottie. She knew that the royal family's powers were far superior to her own, despite her demonic gifts having come directly from the royal line, and Tilly was sure that she most likely could not even get her head around whatever their plans or intentions were for the impending fight so was better off in her ignorance.

"Will you come somewhere with me?" Lottie then asked her but gave Tilly no further details on exactly where she was intending to take her.

"Yes, of course, but," she hesitated. "I need to tell Blake first," she added, knowing that he would not be happy if she disappeared on him.

"Don't worry, he will be fine, this needs to happen now," Lottie told her, with more urgency to her tone, and Tilly couldn't help but say yes. She nodded and took the Princess's hand, trusting her and letting her take the lead without another questioning word or glance.

She quickly felt the tell-tale pull of teleporting away, but this time they were heading upward to Earth rather than elsewhere in Hell. She thought of Blake, wondering if he was truly going to be happy with her for this or not, but Tilly knew that there was nothing she could do about it right now, she just hoped he would be glad that she was by Lottie's side rather than having let her go there alone.

They arrived on Earth within seconds and Tilly quickly scanned the area, needing a moment to take in where they had landed. It felt strange being back after so many months in Hell and being here again bought back thoughts of her family and friends that had somehow been dulled down while she was away in her new home. She didn't have long to dwell on it, though, as Lottie immediately produced a small vial from her pocket and ordered her to drink it.

"Don't ask any questions Tilly," she ordered. "Just please follow my every order now, okay?"

Tilly nodded and swigged from the small bottle, the dark liquid inside was thick but tasteless and she didn't feel any different after taking it so had no idea what it was meant to have done, but did not question Lottie about it, knowing that they had to move quickly.

"Good, now follow me," she ordered and put out her hand for Tilly to take again, which she did without any hesitation. Lottie led them down a side alley and then out onto a large main road. She had no idea where they were until they rounded a corner and she found herself staring up at one of the monumental cathedrals in the centre of London.

She could see the light power emanating from within the huge building and all around it as though it was a beacon for all the white beings, she had never seen anything like it before and knew she must only be able to see it now thanks to her demonic new form.

Lottie pressed on, drawing the two of them closer and closer, and then they reached the holy threshold, where Lottie crossed over it without any resistance. Tilly was not surprised to see that the half-light Princess could cross over with ease. Her light power, no matter how subdued, seemingly allowed her entry without any pledge of allegiance required or cunning tactics, but Tilly was hesitant to try and pass over the distinct line that surrounded the church. She let go of Lottie's hand, not wanting to be thrown back just as she had been in the field thanks to Beatrice's force field, but the Princess eyed her sternly, a silent command pulling her forward and over the line almost against her will, and Tilly was shocked that she too managed to enter the threshold without rejection.

"The potion," Lottie said quietly, answering her scattered thoughts and then pulling her onwards, leading her towards the huge wooden doors. Inside there were many human worshippers either sat praying in the pews or lighting candles for their loved ones by the white covered altar, and not a single one looked up as they entered, lost in their own thoughts directed towards the higher power above. As the pair of them made their way forward to the large altar at the end of the vast room Tilly could sense the presence of other beings all around her—witches and the light ministers, all full of white power and theirs were the only eyes on them.

Lottie sensed her foreboding, so gripped Tilly's hand even tighter, pulling her close beside her, and then they approached a small group of lower-level witches who stared open-mouthed as she came closer. They all seemed to know exactly who Lottie was. They could sense her, yet none were prepared for what to say to her as she reached them.

"Hello. My name is Lottie, I believe my father is expecting me?" she asked the witch closest to her expectantly, who stood trembling before the powerful Princess. A moment of silence passed between them as the witches continued to stare at the two of them in bemusement.

"Yes, your highness, I can take you to him, but not your demon friend," she eventually managed to reply, looking at the floor as she spoke, seemingly scared to incur her wrath.

"Absolutely not. She is my progeny and my protector. Matilda is to stay with me at all times," she commanded her, making each of the witches flinch as they received her powerful order.

"Take it or leave it. Perhaps I shall just leave a message for you to take to him instead then, but don't you think he would much prefer to see me in person at long last?" Lottie asked, pushing the witch further, forcing her decision. At that moment, three more witches joined them from a side door. These were all much more powerful and Tilly could instantly sense their strong powers as they approached.

"Well, hello again," said a fourth witch who came to join them from behind Tilly, and while she couldn't see her, she recognised the voice straight away. It was Beatrice. Rage threatened to burst out from inside of her, and she had to use every ounce of strength she could muster to regain her composure. Lottie gripped her hand tighter and made eye contact with her for just a second before addressing the new witches. In that moment she passed Tilly a silent order, a commandment not to retaliate or rise to the witch's taunts, not to do anything to Beatrice to ruin her plans, but also a promise that the time would soon come that she could have her revenge, and then Tilly would be free to rip her throat out.

"Have we met?" Lottie asked Beatrice, knowing full well who she was but playing dumb on purpose so that the witch did not get the satisfaction she craved.

"Forgive me Princess, but I actually meant your friend here," she replied, looking Tilly up and down with a knowing smile. Her bright-blonde hair shone in the sunlight, and she twirled it around her long finger as she watched Tilly squirm, seemingly enjoying the fact that she had obviously been ordered not to retaliate. Lottie snapped her fingers loudly and sealed Beatrice's lips instantly, a sly smile curling at her lips when she then reached up and touched them gently, her eyes wide in shock and fear.

"You would do better to address me and my friends in a more respectful manner in future witch," Lottie told her and then looked to the others questioningly, her green eyes boring into each of the witches, and she could sense their fear.

"Now then, I already know where Uriel is and can teleport directly there myself, but I thought I would do you the courtesy of introducing myself first and allowing one of you the honour of taking me to see him officially. Are any of you actually up to the task?" she asked, her impatience clear. She read them all, taking in all their thoughts and fears at her dominative demands before she then focussed in on the one witch among them that was in one of the high council's covens, Beatrice.

"You, take us," she ordered, much to Tilly's distaste, and Beatrice nodded, still unable to speak. Lottie reached out and took the witch's hand, and within seconds they could both feel the pull skywards as Beatrice teleported the three of them to the highest of all the astral planes and the home of the High Council of Angels, Heaven. Everything was so bright and full of light that Tilly had to blink her eyes for a few minutes to adjust to it all, when they finally cleared, she realised they were stood before a huge white castle, almost an exact likeness to the royal fortress in Hell but its opposite in colour and décor. Their black clothes stood out glaringly in contrast to the lightness all around them and Tilly couldn't help but feel a little afraid at being here, outnumbered and already feeling weakened by the incredible light power all around them.

She still had no idea what Lottie's strategy was but hoped that this was all still actually part of her master plan.

Lottie gripped her hand tightly and held Tilly even closer as Beatrice led them up the marble steps and then inside the vast castle, never once showing her own fears or worries at being here in this incredibly light and powerful city, but Tilly still sent her friend supportive and warm thoughts, assuring her she would do whatever Lottie asked of her, whether it was to fight, run, surrender, or even die.

Once they were inside, they saw many lower-level angels and white witches convened in the huge entryway, reminding Tilly of their dark setup back home with the different demonic levels and their dark witches. All of them stopped whatever they were doing and stared at the two dark strangers as they entered their light citadel, seemingly surprised, and scared to see that their evil foes had somehow gained access into their sacred home. Beatrice continued on, and Tilly was grateful for her silence as it helped lull the rage she only just about kept at bay thanks to Lottie's promise. The witch then led them up a long, spiralling staircase that shimmered brightly thanks to the thousands of diamonds that seemed to be inlaid into each step and that reflected the sunlight gloriously. They made their way upwards and then down a corridor to a huge set of doors and Beatrice ushered the Princess towards them, wordlessly telling her that Uriel was inside.

"Stay here, stand right by the door and do not move," she ordered Tilly, who nodded in agreement before giving her hand a supportive squeeze. Lottie smiled back at her but didn't say another word as she then moved over to the doors. She took a deep breath and made her way inside, and then Tilly did as she was ordered, stepping forward to keep watch, not saying a word as her friend and mistress closed the doors behind her.

CHAPTER EIGHTEEN

Lottie made her way through the huge, lightly coloured wooden doors and into a brightly lit, large room. The walls inside were all adorned with bright paintings and elaborate filigree framed mirrors that helped make the huge room look even larger. A man stood at the window that looked out onto the vast city of light below, and Lottie could tell for sure now that the castle and city around them were an exact replica to the one she knew so well from back home in Hell. Lucifer had clearly created the dark castle and the city around it to be an exact match to this place, showing his nostalgia or perhaps some deep-seated sentimentality to his angelic life from long ago.

The man turned and approached Lottie slowly. He was tall and slim with dark brown hair and deep blue eyes that sparkled in the light, truly gorgeous, yet she could see that there was a lot of pain behind those eyes too. He smiled at her, the sort of broad, genuine smile that she had only ever seen on her families faces as they looked at one another, a loving and warm look that filled the silence with promises and an unadulterated affection she couldn't help but bask in. Lottie knew without even asking him that this angel was her father, she could sense his strong light, a light that she shared, and she was unexpectedly speechless as she took him in.

She continued to watch him as he came closer, seemingly taken aback by her too, and Lottie was surprised to see that he had to hold on the walls and furniture to help him stay steady as he walked. As she watched him, she couldn't help but wonder if he was still weak from his fight with Lucifer all those years ago, still affected by the imbalance of the power that Cate had always maintained he had abused for his own selfish means.

No one but her mother knew where the fallen angel was now or what condition he was in, and it was perfectly feasible that Cate could be right about that higher power she preached of. If Uriel had still not changed his ways or stopped vying for ultimate control even after all these years, then he would not have been blessed with his full power again, and the angel who stood before Lottie now was obviously at only half his full strength, making clear his continued abuse of power and unrelenting belief him himself over all others.

"Are you the angel Uriel?" she asked him as he reached her, stopping just a foot or so away and peering into her deep green eyes as she addressed him formally.

"Yes, and you must be my darling daughter, my lost piece of light, my Lottie. After all this time, I cannot believe you are finally here," he said, stepping closer and taking her cheek in his hand while the other gripped the back of the sofa beside them to steady himself. She could immediately feel his strong light pouring into her from his touch, as though seeping through her skin at his gentle contact.

She basked in it, letting down all the walls she had built around the light part of herself and finally setting it free, welcoming and marvelling at the weightless feeling as she unburdened herself and let the power strengthen her from deep within.

"Yes, I am," she replied, feeling woozy from his strong energy and mesmerising prowess.

"You look so much like your mother," he said, staring into her deep green eyes and trying to read her. Lottie could see a tiny flicker of love or lust, or something just as strong, pass over his face as he let himself think of Cate, an almost nostalgic moment before firmly bringing himself back into the room with her, focussing on trying to read her mind again, desperate to see her thoughts and memories of her life so far.

"I cannot read you?" he eventually said, looking confused. He followed Lottie as she led him over to the couch and sat down, gazing at him softly, an innocence to her delicate features. She smiled warmly back at him as he took the seat beside her, turning towards Uriel and then taking his hand in hers, enjoying the feeling his touch brought her.

"No," she replied. "No one can read me, or ever have been able to. Not even my mother," she told him, lying ever so convincingly that she knew Cate would have been proud of her. She had been taking a potion concocted by Alma for a while now so that she could hide her thoughts from everyone, including her family, with whom she had only told the very basic details of the plan to so far. She had been planning this for a while and needed the element of surprise on her side today for it all to work the way she wanted it to.

"Strange," he replied thoughtfully, but smiled warmly at her as he continued to take her in, his expression soft and happy. "Well then, you shall just have to tell me all about yourself instead," he added, reaching up and brushing a stray curl behind her ear.

"I don't have much time, I'm afraid. I snuck away as soon as I could following your message. I wanted to see for myself if you were, um," she said, tailing off and looking down at her hands shyly.

Uriel took her chin in his hand, lifting Lottie's gaze back up to meet his own.

"See what?" he asked her calmly. "The monster that forced your mother into his bed, for I am sure that is how she has portrayed me to be?"

"Yes," Lottie replied, her voice faltering slightly over the word. "But more than that, I just needed to know. To see you with my own eyes at long last and learn for myself if what she said was true."

"And what do you see?" he asked her, desperately trying to connect with the child he felt had been cruelly kept from him all these years by her evil mother.

"Not a monster, that's for sure," Lottie told him, smiling over at her father as a tear ran down her soft cheek.

"Not everything she says is true. Give me the chance to prove it to you," he whispered, rubbing away the fallen tear with his thumb.

"I cannot deliver you, Lucifer. She will never release him. He was going to kill me, did you know that?" Lottie asked him, and Uriel shook his head, his eyes reddening with rage at the very thought of his fallen brother hurting her.

"No, but I only wanted him here so that I could finally kill him. I believe that he and I are linked. If I rid the world of him once and for all, I believe I might fully regain my powers at long last. I have remained weakened ever since our fight many years ago. My powers have returned little by little, but I am not even close to being the powerful angel that I used to be." he told her honestly.

"My mother has always taught me that everything, whether light or dark, is all about balance, yin and yang if you wish. Lucifer's tyrannical, evil reign forced your hands up here. You had to act, had to stop him, but she is not the same as he was. Surely you must know that?" Lottie asked, staring into his eyes solemnly as she spoke.

"I always knew that she would be a better leader than he was, but the power gets to everyone in the end, Lottie. You cannot trust her. I have no doubt that she will have controlled and manipulated you your entire life to get you to do her bidding, but you probably didn't even know she was doing it. She has a way of making everyone love her, making them want her, and then they will do anything to keep that love and so she exploits them for it," he told her bitterly, obviously angered by Lottie's allegiance to Cate.

"Perhaps you're right. My whole life has always been decided for me, planned by her, but at least I am alive and safe thanks to that control. That's all that really matters," she said, leaning into his shoulder and hugging the angel tightly.

"My sentiments exactly," Uriel replied, hugging her back just as tight.

CHAPTER NINETEEN

Outside the huge doors Tilly stood with her back against the ornately carved wood looking out at the light castle all around her, the building was beautiful, and she admired it all for a moment, almost forgetting that she was in Heaven, for probably the first and last time in her darkly eternal existence. There were witches and angels close by that purposely came closer to have a peek at the demonic intruder but kept their distance and did not dare speak to her. Many of them watched her intently, looking over in both fear and confused anxiety. Tilly lapped it up, feeling strong and powerful thanks to their fear despite being in enemy territory, focussing on the Princess's order to stay by the door as she relished in their trepidation. Beatrice stayed close by, waiting in hope for Lottie to release her mouth from the dark commandment when she would eventually leave Uriel's room, all the while staring at Tilly with hateful eyes.

"I don't know why you're looking at me like that," Tilly warned her after a while, desperate to see the witch suffer, but Tilly kept calm, waiting patiently for her revenge when Lottie gave her the go-ahead. "You are the one who murdered me in cold blood, don't forget," she added, looking back towards the other witches with a satisfied smile as they overheard her and gasped, muttering their disapproval. She relished in Beatrice's awkward, shameful stance as she looked everywhere but at her light peers.

Tilly grinned, pleased with herself for shaming the witch and then suddenly felt a strange heat resonate from somewhere deep within her gut, like the butterflies she used to feel in her stomach back when she was human. She let her eyes droop closed for a moment and leaned her head back against the wooden door. When she opened them again, nothing was any different, but the strange tingle she had felt had disappeared as quickly as it had come on.

Behind the door in Uriel's chambers, Lottie and her father continued to talk quietly together, trying to connect and get to know each other a little. It was hard filling in the huge blanks in such a short amount of time, so she started with her life on Earth before going to Hell with her mother and then admitted to him the hardships she had faced since being there thanks to her conflicting powers.

"Well, technically, you are more light than dark, my darling," he told her. "Your mother was half human when you were conceived, don't forget."

Lottie nodded. She had forgotten about that. For such a large part of her life, Cate had been the new Devil. She hadn't ever really thought back to the woman she was before that or considered her mother's mixed heritage before she took the throne.

"Perhaps I would fit in better up here with you then?" she asked Uriel shyly, and he smiled, genuinely happy at her request, but shook his head.

"You still bear the dark mark inside of you, Lottie. You can never stay here," he said, looking forlornly down at his daughter. "It would just not be right."

"Says who? What about if I renounced her? Or gathered more lightness?" she asked, reaching up to stroke his face gently with her soft hands, eager to keep his attention on her. "I kept my virtue all these years, and I have never committed a sin, so why can't I stay here?"

"Because I say so, my love. It wouldn't matter which of us you chose or how worthy you have been during your lifetime, you could only ever live in Hell or on Earth, Lottie, never here. That was my plan for you all along, to lead as an example to the humans, to rule them. And anyway, there's only one way to get more light," he said, tailing off as a flicker of fear crossed his handsome face at the dark prospect. Uriel peered across at his daughter, the long-lost child he felt so strongly for and yet there was a part of him that hated her. He hated the dark wickedness he sensed deep within, the side that Cate had given her, and he knew he could not ever fully trust Lottie, even if she pledged her soul to him and his angelic council. He was desperate to read her thoughts, distrustful of the fact she remained closed to him, and he vowed to himself to keep her safe. The next step, the only thing he could think to do was to lock her away, keep her prisoner on one of his astral planes like he had done with Cate and when the fight was over, she would be sent to the new Earth to rule it. Uriel envisioned it now and knew that it was the right thing to do, but that he had to convince Lottie to go along with his plans that meant wiping out her entire family. As he peered into her eyes thoughtfully, her hands still on his face and he caught her eyes flicker to his side as though looking over his shoulder at something.

"Yes, there is a way of gathering more light power, isn't there, Uriel? By stealing it from an angel, from family," whispered a soft voice from behind them, just inches from Uriel's left ear. It was a voice he knew all too well, and he was desperate to see her face after such a long time, but his daughter's tight grip on his cheeks held him firmly in place. Lottie smiled wickedly at her father, taking in his shocked expression as the realisation dawned on him. She had seen her mother approach from over Uriel's shoulder a few moments before and had known to keep his focus on her so that she could sneak up on him unnoticed, and Lottie's sinister smile made him freeze in fear, knowing that he had profoundly underestimated them both.

Cate held a dark blade in her hand at the ready and she immediately slit Uriel's throat without another word, not allowing him to even turn and look at her after Lottie dropped her hands, she could not bear to have his eyes on her ever again. Lottie quickly grabbed a glass from the table beside them and held it to his gushing artery, filling it with his powerful essence as he bled out before her, shock and fear still clear on his pale face as he eventually began losing consciousness.

"Drink it," Cate said when the blood stopped pouring from Uriel's gaping throat wound, smiling down at Lottie, and then coming around to the other side of the sofa to be with her daughter. Lottie did as her mother told her, gulping down the thick blood quickly. She could not bear to look at the limp form beside her and slumped down off the sofa and onto the floor, her heart pounding loudly in her ears.

"Now, be strong, darling. You need to call upon his power, claim and invoke it into yourself, harness it, own every ounce of his light," she told her, kneeling on the floor opposite Lottie and taking her hands in hers as she began to tremble. "Close your eyes, call to the power, surrender yourself to its hold on you. Renounce me if you have to my love, do whatever it takes to be strong, to be free at last." she said, tears welling up in the all-powerful Queen's eyes at the thought, but she knew what had to be done.

Lottie concentrated hard, looking deep inside of herself, and immediately sensing the light power there that she had just stolen from her estranged father. She took a deep breath, thinking of the higher power her mother had always told her about, calling to the lightness, promising to harness and use it wisely. Within seconds, a jolt, like lightening, hit her chest hard as though from the inside. Her heart beat faster and her hands tingled, and then her body seemed to vibrate with the intense bursts of power. The force seemed to both consume and empower her all at the same time, bringing forth an almighty awareness of the world around her and all the beings in it. Lottie's mind went into overdrive, taking in every thought and feeling of each and every light being around her and on every one of the astral plains below.

After a few minutes, she steadied her thoughts and took a deep breath. Lottie opened her eyes and found her mother's smiling face just inches away from hers. As she smiled back at Cate, her memories and thoughts came flooding into her powerful consciousness now too. Lottie took a moment to bask in them, seeing everything, every moment both good and bad as Cate allowed them to flow freely into her daughter's powerful consciousness, not hiding a single moment of her equally wonderful and tormented past from her as the light power gave Lottie the almighty gift she truly deserved. Lottie watched Cate's long and tumultuous past flash before her eyes, focussing on one specific memory of her mother as she cradled a baby Lottie in her arms and kissed Harry's lips as they laughed together and held one another tightly, so happy and in love before more began to flash through her mind. Lucifer was there too, a face to finally put to the name Lottie knew and feared so much, but a being she had never known. She watched them happy, in love and a powerful couple, but then saw him as the jealous, sinister, frail entity that ordered her death to a sneering Berith before Cate stopped him. It was all too much, overwhelming and powerfully emotive, but Lottie thanked her mother for not trying to hold it back. The stories had been told so many times and now she had seen them all for herself, knowing once and for all that Cate was not an evil dictator and she had never deceived Lottie to win her affections.

"So, now you know the entire truth my darling," Cate whispered, she was not ashamed of the things she had done to keep her family safe over the years, but she was still worried that Lottie might not understand her sordid and unusual love-life now that everything was laid bare before her, or her reasons for doing the dark things she had needed to over the years in order to survive and protect those she loved. Cate hid nothing from Lottie, though, allowing every one of her secrets to be exposed, as well as her sometimes devious methods she had used to get what she wanted along the way.

"Yes, now I know," Lottie replied, giving her hand a squeeze. "There were always going to be the bad times I had to learn about from you, but think about the good ones too, Mum. Think about Blake, Luna, and Thorne. Think about Harry. Don't dwell on the darkness for too long, otherwise you will be its slave forever, just like Lucifer was. Use us to help you overcome those burdens. Use your love for your children as a constant light in all that darkness and you will never lose your way. I get it now," she then added with a wise smile. Cate nodded, knowing that her profound words were so true, that those she loved were the answer to any doubts and fears she might ever have, and she would never forget it.

Lottie felt stronger and more powerful than ever, her body coursing with lightness and a power over anything she had ever felt before or had ever hoped to gain. She finally looked back up at her half dead father, who was still lying slumped on the white sofa.

"What do we do with him now?" she asked, and Cate produced a dark silver locket from her pocket that matched the one she had always worn and then handed it to her. It was ornately engraved with ancient symbols and runes, and Lottie noticed it fell open easily but had nothing inside it yet.

"We do the same with him as I did with my own conniving master," she told Lottie, pulling her own long necklace out of her black shirt and showing it to her. Lottie hadn't thought about it before, but she suddenly realised that Cate absolutely never removed that locket from around her neck, no matter what she was doing it was on her at her all times, and for the first time Lottie finally understood what it was. This small piece of, until now, seemingly insignificant jewellery held the answer to the question on everyone's lips, the mysterious prison that had held Lucifer captive for so long and yet no-one knew about had been right in front of them all this time. Cate shared her memories with Lottie and winked. She had imprisoned Lucifer in the locket around her neck many years ago and hadn't removed it ever since. It was a constant reminder of her tragic burden, but also of her responsibilities to her family and to her followers to keep them safe and protected under her reign. She had never told another soul that he was in there, not even Harry, but now Lottie would know, and she too would have her own reminder to keep her grounded. Lottie ran her finger over her empty locket and nodded, understanding her mother's ominous yet poignant gesture.

"This is the only way to be free of him, isn't it?" Lottie whispered, knowing that despite the lightness she had embraced, she had to do this one last darker deed to survive and to protect the ones she loved too for if she left Uriel to be free, he would recuperate and come after them even if it took him centuries.

"Yes. Hold it over his heart if you are willing to imprison him inside Lottie, only you can choose what to do now," Cate told her, and Lottie peered up into her mother's warm eyes, and then did as she was asked without even a moment's hesitation. "Good. Now repeat after me. By the power of light and dark, I take command of your mind, body and soul, Uriel. You are mine to control and shall never be free from this prison until I, and I alone, release you," Cate said, and Lottie repeated the words, focussing intently on the incantation as she spoke. She repeated them over and over again until the air around them grew thick and seemed to shine brighter around her father, rather than darkness surrounding them, like she would have expected.

"So mote it be," Cate finished, and Lottie repeated her words once again.

Beneath the locket, Uriel stirred. He woke up and started trying to speak but was powerless to stop the strange transfiguration that overtook his body. He grabbed at Lottie, reaching for the hand that held the locket over him, pleading with her silently to stop, but she remained firm, her resolve and her prowess decisively and irrevocably changed and she stared into his eyes as he started shuddering violently, vibrating uncontrollably before being sucked into the locket by some kind of irresistible force that pulled him inside despite his best efforts to stop it, shrinking him down and then the locket snapped closed, a bright white light emanating from the edges as it was then sealed tight, imprisoning Uriel inside.

Lottie placed the chain over her head and slipped the locket down inside her t-shirt and then looked up at her mother in shock for a second before smiling and hugging her tightly.

"Well done," Cate said, knowing that this had been very hard for her. "It's over, you are free now."

"No, we are both free," Lottie replied. The pair hugged each other tightly and cried in each other's arms for a while before righting themselves and heading over to the door, eager to let Tilly in on the plan at last.

CHAPTER TWENTY

Lottie and Cate emerged from the huge wooden doors a few minutes later to find Tilly still leaning against the doorway as per Lottie's instructions, but with an invisible grip around Beatrice's throat as the witch lay pinned to the sparkling marble floor by her unseen force, Tilly's face dark as she stared down at the woman in disgust. She felt as though she had put up with her long enough and had grown tired of her staring, so could not help but knock the witch around a little bit while they were waiting. Tilly jumped when she saw Cate smiling across at her from beside the glowing, transformed figure of her daughter and went to speak, eager to ask them both many questions, but Lottie immediately raised a hand to stop her.

"That witch owes you a huge debt Tilly, it is time for you to collect," commanded Lottie unflinchingly as she and Cate walked over to the top of the stairs together and started descending them side by side.

Tilly was still shocked to see the Queen here with them, but didn't hesitate and climbed down over Beatrice, straddling her just as the witch had done to Tilly in the old church the night she had held her captive. She leaned closer to the wide eyed woman, pinning her to the ground forcefully with her actual hands now and then lifted her right arm up, turning it so she could see the inside of her forearm. Tilly then immediately traced her finger along the smooth skin, marking the inside of her wrist with an inverted cross that burned red beneath her demonic touch and she then looked down at her with a truly evil smile.

"Your soul is now mine to torture for all eternity, Beatrice. Let's see just how much you can take from me, shall we?" Tilly asked her with a wicked grin, and then she reached down and thrust her hand under her ribcage, crushing her bones with ease. In one quick movement she then removed the witch's heart and threw it aside, watching the life begin to drain from her for a few seconds before then placing her bloody hand over her forehead and focussing on her dark power even more, quickly engulfing the witch in black flames. Beatrice's body burnt to ashes beneath her within seconds and Tilly stood up, immediately sensing it as her soul's ownership passed over to her without any resistance from her previous angelic master, Michael, and Tilly quickly imprisoned Beatrice's soul in her own personal crypt in the depths of Hell, knowing she had all the time in the world so would deal with her later.

She then made her way over to the stairway and climbed down them, joining her mistresses at the base of the stairs, looking out at the white faces all around them and bowing to Cate and Lottie as she reached their sides. The other light beings in the castle foyer all screamed and tried to run when they saw Cate there, but a snap of Lottie's fingers opened the portals into their light realm and then the Dark Queen quickly summoned every dark witch and demon into the heavenly city. Within seconds, every light being was covered by a dark one.

They stopped their desperate attempts to flee and remained still, trembling beneath the evil glares as they awaited their potential dark torture. Tilly looked around, smiling at her friends and she soon realised that neither Blake, Luna, Thorne nor Harry was there. A quick look at Cate confirmed her suspicions, the Queen gave her a slight shrug in response to her thoughts, but Tilly completely understood her reasons for not allowing them to come and nodded to her, smiling lovingly at both the powerful women before her as she watched them, eagerly awaiting their orders along with all the other light and dark beings all around them.

Lottie and Cate then made their way down one of the marble floored corridors and through to the council room, where Lottie effortlessly summoned the High Council of Angels' to order. The other angels appeared instantly, seemingly surprised by the new head of the council, but none said a word against her as they took their seats around the large circular table and Cate stood silently to one side.

"Welcome," Lottie said, eying each of them and quickly reading their thoughts. "My name is Lottie, and I am the child of the Dark Queen Hecate and the Angel Uriel," she informed them, more out of formality than anything else, as they all knew exactly who she was.

"Might I correct you?" the angel to her right asked, and Lottie knew he was the angel Michael.

"Of course," she replied, smiling at him as she sat in Uriel's old seat at the table.

"You are the angel Lottie now," he reminded her with a small, gracious bow of his head.

"Yes, you're right," said Lottie. "I have taken my father's place at this table, his place in Heaven and his power," she added.

"Good," replied another angel, and the others all muttered their agreements too.

"I am the angel Gabriel," he then said, introducing himself, and he bowed slightly to her too. Lottie was surprised by their reactions. She had been convinced that they would fight her on this, but not a single one of them seemed to be loyal to Uriel. She read them all, eager to know how they felt, and each one of them opened up their thoughts to her willingly. She could tell that they had all had enough of Uriel's vendettas and selfish commandments, and that they were glad she had taken his place at the head of their council.

"It is my pleasure to meet you Gabriel, and to meet you all," she said, looking each of them in the eye and addressing all six of the angels that sat before her. The council consisted of seven angels in total: Michael, Gabriel, Raphael, Sandalphon, Metatron, Camael and now Lottie. Each of them had different positions and responsibilities within the council, as well as their official duties when it came to the humans in their charge down on Earth. She watched them all for a few moments, looking at every one of the archangels around her and beginning to understand each of their places within this group she was now to head up without having to be told.

Michael was her second in command, a warrior offering courage, guidance, and protection to his charges. Gabriel was known by many as the Divine Herald. He was God's messenger, the revelatory angel to the humans below of the Council's decisions and decrees.

Raphael oversaw the health and wellbeing of the humans below, bringing peace and balance to the minds, bodies, and spirits of those who would call upon him.

Sandalphon was once a mortal man, but now he served to help other men and women ascend to Heaven. His plight was that of supporting humans with their personal progression and self-discovery. His brother, Metatron, served the council by being their scribe. He was dedicated to providing focus and dedication to both the humans that called upon him and the angels around him.

Lastly, Camael opened his mind and soul to Lottie, sending her his divine repertoire too, and she smiled. He served to bring love, joy, and beauty to the world. Camael's strength and pure heart drew Lottie in and in return for her acceptance of her peers, she saw her own angelic responsibilities laid bare for her now, too. She had taken over her father's role, to bring light to those who might need it and to illuminate the paths for any that might have lost their way.

Lottie could feel her strength and power increasing as each second passed, her gifts flourishing and expanding, as was her prowess. She finally felt the war inside her settle and disappear, being replaced by nothing but love and light that would now exist alongside her darkness.

"It is my plan to stop the feuds between the light and the dark beings, effective immediately. We are all children of a higher power, two sides of the same coin, if you will. My mother has never set out to fight you, to fight us, it was Lucifer who started the war and my father Uriel who forced her hand," Lottie told them and the angels all around her nodded in agreement, their thoughts clear and her words simply reiterating what they had suspected for a long time.

"It stops now. I will stay here and my mother will return to Hell, but this will not be the last that we see of each other. I am telling you now that she is welcome here any time at my invitation, just as I will be welcome in Hell when she wishes for me to visit. The fighting ends now." Lottie told them, consternation clear in her voice. "No more threats, no more violence," she then added, thinking of Uriel's last warning.

"You do realise that we only agreed to the white fire in the hope that you would do something like this?" the angel across the table from her, Camael asked, and Lottie nodded.

"I do now. You wanted to force our hands," she replied. "But how did you know we wouldn't come in here looking for a massacre?" she then asked him, staring into his soft brown eyes, finding herself beguiled by this angel in particular, and noticing that he was just as fascinated by her too.

"Because of her," he told Lottie, pointing to Cate awkwardly, unable to meet the Devil's gaze, but he spoke honestly and calmly regarding her. "She has always promised to be different, to think and lead in a way that Lucifer never could. She has proven it today, and so have you. I vote yes to the new balance," Camael told Lottie, smiling as her eyes lit up thanks to his endearing words.

The remaining council members all agreed too. They were ready and willing for the change, and although they were all somewhat uncomfortable and disturbed by Cate's presence in their council chamber, they understood the symbolism and meaning behind Lottie having insisted on her being there.

CHAPTER TWENTY-ONE

Out in the main hallway Tilly stood silently with the others awaiting the news from inside the council chambers as they each stood watch over the white witches and angels around them, they too seemingly following orders not to fight with the demons and dark witches in their midst. She caught the eyes of many faces she knew well—Beelzebub, Leviathan and Berith, as well as Lilith and Lucas, as they too stood in wait, each of them giving her an anxious look in return that she thought most likely reflected her own uneasy facial expression.

When Lottie and Cate finally returned, Lottie was now dressed in a beautiful white gown and glowed even more brightly than she had when Tilly had seen her leave Uriel's chambers, looking like she well and truly belonged here in this castle of light. It was clear to Tilly now that Lottie had been successful and had won over the council, and she couldn't help but feel downhearted that her friend would not be coming home with them. She hugged Lottie, feeling tears well up inside of her, both happy and sad ones as she finally sensed that the Princess's true power had been unleashed. Tilly could both see and feel that the power that had once clashed within her had now truly been commanded at long last. She was free, unchained and ready to live her life at last. No more hiding and no more hardships. Lottie was an angel now and would be a fine one at that, Tilly was sure. Both Cate and Lottie read her thoughts as she pondered over the new angel's future here in heaven, and they both smiled at her in surprise and intrigue.

"When will you ever cease to amaze me Tilly?" Lottie asked, kissing her cheek lightly, and she shrugged shyly, unsure how to respond.

"You may all go home," Cate commanded to the dark beings, but she silently ordered Tilly to remain by her side for a while longer. The dark witches and demons all followed her order and teleported away, leaving just the three of them to talk briefly while the white witches and angels quickly headed off to their chambers.

"Lottie is going to stay here Tilly, but this is not goodbye," Cate told her, smiling, but she could not hide the sadness in her eyes, struggling to say her own goodbyes too.

"Before you go home, I just wanted to say thank you for all your help. I could not have done it without you," Lottie told her, smiling and pulling Tilly into another tight hug. She could feel her light power tingling throughout her body as they embraced. The new angel already seemed so much more powerful than Tilly had ever seen her before, and she realised just how much being in Hell must have affected her all those years.

"I'm so glad you did it," she said honestly as they pulled back from their hug. "But I have to admit I'm going to miss you so much. Can we still visit each other?" she asked her, peering into those green eyes she loved so very much.

"Yes, of course, and we can see each other on Earth too don't forget," Lottie reminded her, and Tilly grinned.

"Parties at the penthouse?" Tilly replied with a smile, and Lottie nodded in agreement. They hugged once more. Then she stepped back, letting Cate have her own private moment with her daughter. She prepared herself to teleport away but then noticed a pair of deep green eyes watching them from one of the doorways and stayed for just a little bit longer. It was a woman, a lower-level angel, and she watched the three of them with a mixture of fear and of love, her face revealing her obvious inner turmoil. Tilly couldn't help but walk over to her, something driving her forward and the angel peered at her, seemingly both terrified and mesmerised by her.

"I know these eyes," Tilly whispered to the woman, and she knew she must be related to Cate in some way. Her hair was pulled back in a tight bun, but Tilly could see that it was the same shade of dark brown as her Queen and was somehow sure that it would be curly if she let it down.

"She's my mother," Cate called from behind her, confirming Tilly's suspicions, but she said no more.

"Are you afraid?" Tilly asked her, and the woman nodded. She had already sensed her fear, but also knew that as a lower-level angel she could be charmed by her strong dark power easily. Cate did nothing to stop Tilly, eager to see her mother, but she had read the angel's mind and knew that she feared her, disgusted even at what she had turned into so had no idea where to even start to explain everything to her. Tilly smiled warmly and spoke to her quietly, turning on her luring abilities to help appease the woman's fear.

"There's no need to be scared. We are all at peace now. What's your name?" she asked.

"Ella," Cate's mother replied, noticeably calming down as Tilly worked her magic.

"Well, Ella," she continued. "My name is Tilly, and I am a demon. Your daughter is my Queen, the Devil, but she is also my friend, my family, and I love her dearly. She saved my soul when a white witch called Beatrice murdered me in cold blood and has protected me in many ways since long before that day," she said, making Ella jump as she finally began realising how wrong she might possibly be about her daughter. "Now, I want to ask you, Ella, who was the good one and who was the bad one in my dark tale of demonic transformation?" Tilly then asked her, not taking her eyes off the angel's for even a second as she spoke. Ella gulped, clearly taken aback by her story, and she nodded in understanding, visibly relaxing without Tilly having to control her in any way. "Good and bad can mean different things to different people, Ella. Why don't you come and see for yourself?" she added and then took the angel's hand and led her over to where Cate and Lottie stood watching them. She and Ella moved forwards and stood before Cate, where Tilly bowed, releasing Ella's hand, and then taking a step back to let them talk.

"So it's true then, you really left me to be with the Devil?" Ella asked her estranged daughter quietly, having been informed of the story of how Lucifer had somehow given him a child. Ella knew she was a means to an end and nothing more, chosen simply because she happened to be in the right place at the right time during that particular visit to Earth. When she first began her angelic initiations following her human death, Ella had been shocked to hear the truth, and even more so when she heard her daughter had then gone on to become his wife. Ella's soul had gone to Heaven when she passed just as Cate had hoped, and she had served the angels there for over a century until she was finally chosen to proceed further, but she was told of her daughter's dark heritage first and their stories of her were truly awful, having left Ella ashamed and embarrassed of Cate for many years. She had needed to work extra hard during her classifications to prove that she was not working as a spy for her dark daughter, and she had completely disowned Cate to prove her allegiance to the High Council of Angels and finally gain their trust. It had taken Ella a long time to become even a level ten angel, the process all very similar to the initiations Tilly had been required to go through to proceed through her own classifications, and she had eventually excelled. All the tasks seemed to be the opposite of the dark challenges that Blake oversaw, each of theirs focussing on the light they now possessed, the good they could do for the humans and the darkness that they would fight forever. Ella was now a level five angel—respected at last with her own charges and responsibilities, and she had always hoped to proceed higher when she was allowed to try again.

"I was borne of his blood but not his seed. The dark flame was passed on to me. He was the Devil. But not anymore, as I am sure you know," Cate answered her, reading Ella's thoughts and memories of her time in Heaven and the biased stories she had so quickly believed with a heavy heart. It angered Cate that she had so hastily disowned her daughter, but those stories she had been told over the years were very one-sided and Cate knew it would be a long time before those lessons were retaught.

"Did you really marry him?" Ella asked, looking into Cate's eyes with a confused look on her face.

"Yes," she replied, unashamed about her past, even when it came to Lucifer. She had known all those years ago that being with him was not right, but she had been weak back then, a different person completely and had bent to his every whim, desperate to be happy, to survive.

"That's a bit messed up, don't you think?" Ella replied, thinking back to the night that Cate had disappeared without a trace. The night she had chosen to be with him rather than stay with her mother on Earth.

"Perhaps," Cate agreed, her curt answers showing her frustrations, but she still felt the need to explain herself. She wanted her mother to know the truth. "I know that us being together wasn't right. I knew it even back then, but you have no idea, Mum. I guess you never heard just how he went about seducing me, and how I could never lead my own life or make my own decisions under his rule? Even before I met him that first night he had dictated every aspect of our lives before that, I bet you never even realised that you were working for one of his companies all those years?" she asked, and Ella's mouth just dropped open in shock, her words failing her and it was clear just how misinformed she truly was, so Cate pressed on, fighting her anger but allowing her harsh words to flow freely for the first time in forever. "I actually thought I loved him, but it was all a lie, just another one of his selfish orders. There was no refusing him. Lucifer did not take no for an answer, and I would've died resisting his advances," she told her solemnly.

"I bet," Ella conceded, visibly softening as she stepped forward and took Cate's hand in hers. Cate let her, taking comfort in her mother's touch and she followed Lottie's advice from earlier, focussing on her four beloved children and her husband to help her get through the dark times.

"It wasn't until I was much older, broken and more lost than ever that I truly found who I was. I owe everything to the man who taught me how, my soulmate, husband and the man my children all think of as their father, Harry," Cate then added, and Ella found her smile at last.

"I'm sorry. I guess I have a lot to learn about the real you, the real story of how you came to be here now. But first I'm especially excited to hear about my grandchildren, and how your life is now," she added, pulling the conversation away from the terrible past, and Cate was glad. She could sense Ella's resolve softening and smiled, knowing that it would take a while, but she hoped that eventually they might be able to have a decent relationship with one another again.

"Well, you obviously know that I have Lottie here. She is my youngest daughter," she said, looking over at her quiet child with a loving smile, taking in the immense lightness that now coursed through her.

"Yes, of course. It's really wonderful to meet you, Lottie, and I have to say I'm surprised that the stories about you turned out to be true, that Uriel really did have a child with Cate. Am I right in thinking that you will be staying here now?" Ella asked her, and Lottie nodded, smiling across at her as she read her hopeful thoughts.

"Yes, and it just so happens that I need a new aide," the young angel replied. "Perhaps you could take on the role and then I can help re-write the wrongs between you and my mum while you help me get settled into my new life here in Heaven?"

"Are you serious?" Ella asked, her green eyes wide with shock, but a massive grin took over her pretty face. Such roles were only given to the level one angels, but she loved the idea of being close to her granddaughter and hoped that she would be allowed to accept the offer by the council.

"Absolutely. It's my choice after all, and with my tutelage, we can make sure you proceed up the chain to be a level one angel in no time," Lottie promised, smiling warmly into the face of her grandmother.

"Well then, yes, of course I accept," Ella said, bowing to Lottie respectfully.

"Good," Cate said, eying Lottie and sending her a silent thanks via their now open thoughts to one another. Tilly watched the three women interact for a moment, feeling happy and truly pleased for Lottie and Cate to have re-connected with another lost member of their family. Ella would be the perfect companion for the new angel and although Tilly still felt sad about no longer being the Princess's aide, she looked forward to the new future that having the balance for both the light and dark sides of the proverbial coin had promised. Within a few seconds, she felt another demon teleport up into Heaven beside her, and he immediately went over to see the new angel. Harry had come to wish his daughter well and say his goodbye's. He greeted Cate with a respectful bow and was introduced to Ella, his usual calm and handsome demeanour there, but he also looked incredibly sad, barely being able to hide his tear-filled eyes and quiet thoughtfulness. Tilly could also see that he was immensely proud of his special child though and looked at her in awe, taking in her new found lightness too, basking in her radiance and beauty. Tilly knew then that it was time to leave. She smiled over at them all and then bowed to Cate before she teleported home. When she reached her chambers, a few seconds later she immediately felt her master's beacon reappear in the depths of her soul, the strong link and almighty presence inside of her that had been shut off briefly by her heavenly visit, but had now blissfully returned deep within her consciousness, a welcome presence that signified home.

"Where the fuck have you been," came his voice from the entryway to her bedroom and Tilly spun to face him, having forgotten for a moment just how much trouble she might be in for having disappeared with Lottie without telling him first.

CHAPTER TWENTY-TWO

"Well?" Blake asked, his expression dark and dangerous but his eyes were still the deep green colour that Tilly loved more than any shade in the world so she was sure that, for now at least, he remained in control and could be appeased by her explanation as long as she was careful to say and do the right thing. She hesitated for just a moment, not sure how to answer him, but she sent him her thoughts and memories of her time with Lottie, eager to answer any doubts or dissipate any anger he may have towards her for having left Hell without his permission.

Blake stormed forward and pinned her to the wall by her throat, looking down into her blue eyes before gripping her chin tightly and pulling her face up to his. He wasn't hurting her though, and his powerful grip and closeness no longer scared Tilly as she had come to know and even love this anguished side of him, ready for him to hurt her if he needed to, her promises still well and truly being kept no matter what.

"I asked you a question Tilly," he reminded her, releasing his grip of her throat but still pinning her to the wall with such force that she was glad she no longer needed to breathe. He watched her squirm for a moment, but then the slight curl of his lip gave him away at last. Relieved, Tilly leaned up on her tiptoes and planted a deep kiss on his lips. She really had missed him while she was away with Lottie and was glad he wasn't really angry with her. It had only been a day, but she had already become accustomed to seeing her dark master so much more and never wanted to be apart from him like they used to have to be when she was human.

"I'm sorry, Blake," she whispered as his mouth moved down to plant soft yet urgent kisses on her neck. "Lottie needed me, I," she started to say, but he cut her off.

"I know," he said, pulling back to look at her. "Whom do you think came up with the plan?" he asked, a satisfied smile on his face.

Tilly laughed and shook her head.

"You fiend! And there was me thinking I was in trouble," she squealed, smiling up at him. "You are gonna have to tell me all the details now, because I am still so confused," she told him honestly, hoping that now it was all over she might be let in on the secrets that they had been hiding during their planning stages.

"Okay, but after I fuck you," he told her, lifting her thighs up around his waist and then carrying Tilly over to the bed. He pulled off her black jeans and t-shirt, followed quickly by her underwear and then his jeans and shirt too. Their need for one another was so intense, their want so urgent that Tilly couldn't wait for him to be inside of her. She ached for his touch and when he kicked off his boxers and joined her on the bed, she quickly climbed into his strong arms and slid him into her ready opening. Blake did not delay Tilly her much needed releases this time, feeling the muscles tightening around him from deep within as she reached the edge of her climax and he thrust harder into her so that she plummeted headfirst into her high all the more quickly.

Even when Blake reached his own satisfied release, they did not stop, they could not stop. Their bodies still needed one another so completely it was another few hours before they could slow their fantastic lovemaking and finally rest in one another's loving arms.

"So, now are you gonna tell me?" Tilly asked him later as she lay with her chin resting on his perfectly toned pecks, one eyebrow raised.

"I suppose so," he teased, gazing down at her adoringly. He stroked her messy blonde hair away from her eyes and behind her ear, taking in her thoughts for a moment. "Firstly, consider the fact that you are the only demon to have been made directly from royal blood Tilly, I'm sure you must have realised by now that you were given not only the normal demonic rebirth but also a purer power from my siring. A deeper, darker force that both binds you to me and empowers you more than any other regular demon?" Blake asked her, and Tilly had to think for a moment. She had realised that her powers seemed stronger during her challenges and the comments she had received from the demonic council afterwards had been very positive, but they too had seemed surprised by her stronger than average powers.

"Yeah, I suppose so. I just hadn't really thought about it in too much detail. I thought perhaps it was just me being awesome," she joked, looking up at him with a cheeky smile. His hair was all scruffy and Blake was still a little flushed following their extensive workout between the sheets, and Tilly couldn't help but think how gorgeous he was. He read her thoughts and raised an eyebrow, shaking his head slightly in mock surprise.

"Focus, my love," he told her, but didn't drop his wry smile.

"Sorry, back to business," she replied, attempting to force away the horny thoughts with a shake of her own head. Blake laughed and held her tighter in his strong arms, his emotive link forcing itself open and out of him towards her, and Tilly held him back just as tight, welcoming his love and emotion as it flowed through her. She was still surprised to feel it when this raw, pure sentiment came so openly from him now, even after knowing all his efforts to change his cold ways, and she lapped up every single moment of it.

"Well," he continued after a few minutes, going over the details again in his mind so that he could fill in the blanks at long last. "It was all thanks to Lilith's help actually, she remembered my father going missing for a few hours many years ago. They were all so worried, unable to sense or feel him, but it turned out that he had not gone missing as such. He had somehow gone into someone else's body for a while, my uncle Devin's. It was not via possession as you might expect, but an entire morphing of his whole self into his son's. They were one and the same for the time he was in there, and most importantly, Devin had no idea of it. I was intrigued by this concept and immediately asked Alma to tell me about it because she was the only other one who had dealt with him after it had happened. She discovered that if the host is strong, any of the royals can go into them and stay there as long as we need to. We do not control them. We just kind of, watch and wait. Only we can do it and it needed to be practised first, and you were the perfect choice of host I'm afraid Tilly."

Blake looked down at his beautiful demonic progeny and smiled, sensing that she was eagerly following his story, completely excited to hear the rest and astounded to finally know that Lottie had been going inside of her all that time.

"So," he continued, brushing her hair behind her ear again absentmindedly. "That's what Lottie was doing. When she would get you to close your eyes, she would go inside you and cling on, watching and waiting for as long as she could. That first time when I came looking, she wasn't supposed to have tried it yet, and I was not ready for her to disappear on me, that's why I got such a shock when she somehow managed to do it and so I came to find her. I had to check that she was okay, my fear for her getting the better of my trust. It worked better than I would have even thought. I could not sense her at all even though she was technically still in Hell with you."

"Wow, yeah, that kind of makes sense now," said Tilly, remembering his argument with Lottie that day when she had eventually reappeared.

"Well, at first the plan was that you would get captured and sneak Lottie into Heaven where she would take down Uriel somehow, but that all ended up changing after she had practised with you for a while. My mother could sense the even higher potential for the element of surprise and decided that she would be the one you would take up to Heaven inside of you instead of Lottie. It was all arranged for after Thorne was born but we couldn't tell you any of this as your thoughts would have been read by the angels as soon as you got there and they would have known Lottie's true intentions before the pair of you could even get anywhere near Uriel," he added thoughtfully, his hand still playing with her tousled hair.

"Yeah, of course. What about Lottie's thoughts, couldn't Uriel just read hers and know the truth too?" Tilly asked him, and Blake nodded.

"Yes he would have, but she had also thought of that and had been playing around with a potion for weeks to hide her thoughts from everyone, we could not be one-hundred percent sure that it would include Uriel, but she knew she had to take the risk. That same day in the living room when I told you to keep out of it, I could've kicked myself for almost letting you in on the changes in her. I needed you not to question the concept at all just in case, so I had to give you an order for you to keep out of it. You and your inquisitive mind, but of course you understand now why I had to keep you in the dark, don't you?" he asked her. Tilly nodded, she knew that if she had begun questioning them or that if she pondered over it too long, she would have been useless in getting Lottie and Cate into Heaven without their plans being found out by the angels, the element of surprise included her being shocked by the events as they unfolded too.

"Only once Lottie's thoughts were clear from all of us, even our mother, did we decide that the time was right? Mum took the potion to protect her thoughts from him too and then morphed into you before you and Lottie went up to Earth, that potion she gave you outside the church was simply to allow you access over their threshold and then Lottie's power allowed you up to Heaven with her from there. She managed to convince them you were her progeny, and they had to honour her wishes, even Beatrice, as she never actually had an answer from you as to whom your master was that night she captured you, so she believed it to have been Lottie too, adding to your alibi of sorts. Once Lottie was alone with Uriel, she just had to gain his trust, to make him believe she was there to discuss his threat and then join him in the light. She would even speak ill of our mother if that was what it took to earn his trust and make him drop his guard. When he was where she needed him, my mother silently ordered you to close your eyes and lean back against the door, that was when she left you, but not that you had any idea of course, nor could you see her as she reappeared inside the door you leaned against rather than in the hallway with you."

"Whoa, yeah. I knew something felt strange, but I had no clue, that's amazing," Tilly told him, shocked and awed by the amazing skill and power Cate had honed to become the puppet master behind the entire thing, but also by the cunning planning that had gone into all of it.

"Yeah," he agreed, understanding and revelling in her silent praise of the outcome of their arduous planning. "Well, Mum took out her much deserved revenge on him and then Lottie stole his power. She absorbed his light and replaced him in the council, overthrowing him just as my mother once did with Lucifer." Blake added, his sadness at thinking of his father very present again in his dark eyes even though he repeatedly told himself that he had finally come to terms with all of that by now. Tilly reached up and touched his cheek with her hand, a simple, warm gesture that let him know she understood his unwelcome moment of sorrow.

"He will always be your father, Blake, no matter what he did to you and your family, or how he chose to end his reign. All that matters is that your family is safe now," she whispered, hoping he would not get annoyed with her, and when he didn't seem angered by her brazen comment she carried on, eager to move on from the subject of his father but she was glad he let her speak her mind about him.

"So, is Lottie going to be the master of the angelic council in his place?" she then asked, and Blake nodded.

"Yes, but it will take her a while to find her way. I'm glad that my grandmother was there and came around to it all, even if my mother had to face some of her old demons to do it. I'm much happier knowing that Ella has agreed to take your place as Lottie's aide. It will be nice for her having family up there to help with the transition. Though I must admit I'm a bit jealous that you got to see her before me, but I'm sure it won't be long until it's my turn to meet her too," he admitted, smiling at Tilly and kissing the hand that she had used to stroke his cheek with.

"She's going to love you Blake, how could she not?" Tilly replied, leaning up and kissing his mouth tenderly. He pulled her closer and then flipped his lover over so that he now leaned up on top of her, his strong body pushing her harder into the mattress as he commanded her mouth with his. When he pulled away, Blake peered down at her, his eyes alight and happy.

"I love you so much Tilly," he said. "It's not easy having all of this damage inside of me, the scars run deep, sometimes too deep for me to handle, but loving you somehow makes it easier for me to carry the burden of it all," he told her earnestly, staring down at her with so much love he felt like his black heart might burst. Within a few seconds, he grew hard and eager for her again and she peered up into his deep green eyes and smiled up at him.

"There's no need to fix what is no longer broken Blake, you are ten times the man you were when we first met. You did that, not me," she told him, kissing him as she tilted her hips up to meet him and then welcome him inside her moist opening.

CHAPTER TWENTY-THREE

"We finally did it Tilly. There isn't going to be any more war between the light beings and us. At long last, we can all be free. Lottie has ordered an end to all of it, and the council agreed with her immediately. Peace and balance, just as my mother always wanted," Blake told her later, smiling broadly at the concept as they lay enveloped in each other's bodies, both content and basking in their shared afterglows. Tilly leaned up on her elbow and smiled back at him, relishing in his happy mood as she listened to his free-flowing thoughts.

"It's amazing, isn't it, so no more fighting or killing?" she asked, and Blake nodded. Her thoughts immediately went to Beatrice and how she had taken her life right there in Heaven under the eyes of the council and the other angels, she worried that surely her actions were not a good start to the treaty, despite Lottie's permission for her to take her revenge.

"Beatrice owed a debt to you. Light beings should never kill humans no matter where their allegiance lies or their reasoning behind doing so, and without me siring you, her actions would without a doubt have ended with your death. Even the angel Michael knew this, and let you be her judge, jury and executioner, Tilly. Her soul is now yours to do with as you wish my love, you may call upon her as a slave to do your bidding or you might prefer to imprison and torture her instead, either way you are most certainly not in trouble for taking her life." Blake informed her, not allowing her to feel guilt or remorse for having done what was right, what the balance had called for. Tilly had to admit she hadn't really thought it all through when she had marked Beatrice. A sort of instinct had taken over from somewhere deep within and she just knew that she wanted more than just the witch's life as recompense for her actions. Tilly had wanted to kill her, but also to own Beatrice after she took her life away and she just somehow sensed in that moment what to do with the white witch, so had drawn the inverted cross on her wrist. She would have to figure out what she wanted to do with the now powerless soul at some point, but she didn't even want to think about her right now. However, she had a dark sense of her now no matter how hard Tilly tried to ignore it, an awareness, and a burden. She figured she would most probably just submit Beatrice to an eternity of torture, after all, forgiveness was not on her radar yet towards her despite the witch's actions having turned Tilly's life around for the better. She wondered how it must feel to own many souls and understood now why Blake had chosen not to have any followers for all those years, having Beatrice as her first was kind of daunting and Tilly decided there and then not to take any more souls out of hate, only those she wanted as her followers or aides would be marked from now on.

Blake watched as she made her decisions and was glad to hear her mind calm and settle once more. He loved listening in on her still so human thoughts and enjoyed the chaotic and sometimes frantic workings out she had to do in order to steady herself and her emotions, for so long he had existed among such rational, calm, and organised beings that their thoughts were now just boring and contrived in comparison to hers. Tilly had been a welcome breath of fresh air to him, a beautiful dark angel who saw the tragedy his existence had become and had decided to love him, anyway.

"She wouldn't let you come, would she?" Tilly suddenly asked, pulling Blake from his reverie. She had been thinking of the moment when her fellow demons arrived in Heaven at Cate's command, yet he and his family weren't with them.

"No way," he replied with a gruff laugh. "We stayed back with Harry and Thorne, but I can understand it, for one thing, despite all of her careful planning she was still worried that she might lose Lottie if it all went wrong and then we could be captured or killed if they took us too. You know she would never allow us to put ourselves in the firing line. Plus, despite the peaceful agenda, we could never just leave Hell unattended by all the royals, so she persuaded Luna and I to stay. Harry had a harder time accepting it than we did. Unfortunately, he had to be ordered to remain behind. I've never seen him try to go against one of her commandments before. They had a huge row, but he obviously couldn't fight her and stayed back too, even though he couldn't bear it. He really does love Lottie and would do anything to protect her," he said, tailing off thoughtfully.

"He feels the same about you and Luna too, don't forget. And anyway, I don't blame her. I was glad you weren't there in all honesty. The wait was intense, and we were all very anxious in case they might not be very appreciative of our hostile takeover, we honestly had no idea how it would all turn out," Tilly replied, letting herself be truthful about just how much pressure she had felt while she was up there. "I am definitely happier down here with you. I'll take Hell over Heaven any day," she then told him, leaning in for another deep kiss.

"Good," he replied after she pulled away again and then he rose from the bed and went over to his jacket, where he removed a small box from the pocket. Blake turned and then kneeled before Tilly, looking up at her with a warm smile as she sat up on the bed and peered down at him, wide eyed and grinning uncontrollably.

"In that case, I think we need to make this official," he said, opening the small box and lifting out a huge black diamond ring. It was beautiful and sparkled brightly even in the dark gloom of the castle. Blake smiled widely as he lifted it up and took Tilly's left hand in his.

"You are everything I want, and everything I need, forever. Will you be my wife Tilly?" he asked her, his handsome face showing just how happy and fulfilled he felt at saying those words.

"Yes, of course I will," she replied as he slipped the ring down onto her finger. Tilly smiled down at her fiancé and then dived off the bed onto his lap on the floor, thankful that they were both still naked.

"So, what's my job going to be now that I've been given the sack as Lottie's aide?" Tilly asked Blake as they sat together on the sofas in the royal living area of the dark castle a few days later. Thorne was playing happily in her arms, smiling and cooing up at her as she grinned down at him, his tiny hands grabbing at her nose and lips, and he giggled as she pretended to nibble on them gently. Blake laughed. He loved seeing how much his baby brother cared for Tilly and couldn't help but think that she would make a wonderful mother herself when the time came, but he knew those plans were a long way off yet.

Cate and Harry were having some much needed alone time, each of them still feeling slightly lost now that Lottie was gone from their reach, she had always been close by to one of them and the distance was proving a bittersweet outcome of their heavenly visit for them both. They had already been receiving updates via the witches on her progress though, so knew that she was doing well in her new position and had been learning about her angelic powers with an incredible understanding and extraordinary instinct.

"Well, there is one thing I do want you to do for me Tilly," Blake replied, taking the wriggling two-month-old from her and then holding him tightly as he lay back and relaxed in his arms.

"What is it?" she asked, hoping for maybe a place on his council or perhaps being named as Thorne's protector now that Lottie was gone indefinitely.

"I want you to go and spend your days on Earth for a while. Be with your family, live the life that you should have had, your parents' days are numbered don't forget, my love. Go back to work for Andre, work your arse off and make your dreams come true. Only when I am satisfied that you have fulfilled your desires and had the life you deserved can you come back here permanently. I will, however, expect you to come home to me every night. I cannot be away from you long-term ever again. Teleporting is easy for you now though, and I will come and be up there with you during the full moons as well," he promised, his words sending Tilly's mind into a whirlwind of frenzied thoughts and worries despite his kind gesture and desires for her to fulfil her dreams.

"No, I won't, I can't! What's wrong Blake? Please, just tell me honestly why you are trying to send me away. What have I done wrong?" she begged, desperately afraid that he was having second thoughts about their engagement or that he might be sick of spending so much time with her since her demonic rebirth.

"It's not that at all Tilly, stop being dramatic," he teased, but stopped himself when he caught the angry look she shot him in return. "I want you to live some sort of semblance to the life you would have had on Earth. You will have Beelzebub, Leviathan and Berith there if you need some company, as well as your human friends, and you can teleport here during your lunch breaks from work if you really miss me that badly. You deserve to be with your friends and family before their time is up, don't forget that their time is limited Tilly. They will die and you will go on living. There is no fighting it and it is better to be a part of their short lives now rather than missing out on what was rightly yours before Beatrice took that away from you."

She stared at him, still unsure but Tilly could understand what he was saying and thinking about Andre and the restaurant again made her realise he was right, she wasn't ready to give up on those dreams just yet even after everything that had happened. She remembered her conversations with Lottie and knew that it was something she still wanted. It would be nice having some time with her friends too as she hadn't seen Renee, Gwen, or Jessica in months and although they had all been made aware of her demonic transformation, she knew from her fellow demon's reports that they had still been worried about her.

"Okay, but you promise it's not because you're sick of the sight of me?" Tilly asked him, stroking Thorne's head as he fell asleep comfortably in his big brother's arms.

"Well, I didn't want to admit it but," Blake began with a cheeky grin, but stopped when she punched his arm playfully. "No, honestly. I will miss you every second that you are there Tilly, don't ever think that I am doing this lightly. I would be up there by your side if I could, but you know that's not possible. The moon restricts me, but not you. I want you to live your dreams, the ones you showed me nearly two years ago as you slept in your little home on the farm."

"Well, one of them has already come true," she replied, laying her head on his shoulder and thinking back to the image she had shown him of the two of them in bed together, so in love and happy.

"I want to make all your dreams come true Tilly, your happiness is so important to me," he promised, leaning forward to place Thorne in his basinet and then turning to face her. He pulled his legs up onto the sofa and she slid between them instantly, instinctively knowing that he wanted to hold her close.

"The full moon rises tomorrow. We will go up together and when it wanes, I will return here alone. End of discussion," he told her, a powerful order despite both having their hesitations about being separated again.

CHAPTER TWENTY-FOUR

Blake and Tilly teleported to the London penthouse the next afternoon and were joined quickly by her excited friends. Gwen and Renee couldn't contain themselves so ran to Tilly's side and hugged her excitedly the moment they burst through the huge wooden doors with Beelzebub, squealing and chatting animatedly while their demonic master made his excuses, however unheard they were by the girls, and he joined the Black Prince in the kitchen, grateful for the peace and quiet as entertaining screaming young women was never his or Blake's idea of fun. He bowed in respect and hugged his friend, patting him on the back affectionately as he rolled his eyes towards to chaotic screams from the other room.

"I'm so glad you were in here, it's great to see you, Blake. How's that baby brother of yours?" he asked, not having seen the new arrival yet, the child who had been nicknamed the 'Prince of Shadows' for all those that were unworthy of saying Thorne's real name and Blake grinned.

"He's wonderful, full of character already and it's weird 'cos he looks like Harry rather than us," he told the demon, who grinned back.

"That's great, much better than another you running around," he told Blake with a wink.

"Yeah, yeah. He may not look like me, but I'll show him how all this doom and gloom is done, don't you worry," he retorted, slapping his friend on the back before growing serious. "Listen, I need you to do something for me. Tilly is going to stay up here for a while. I want her to live out her life like she should have. She's hoping to go back to work at the restaurant, I want you to keep her safe for me, Beelzebub," Blake commanded him, although his orders were unnecessary now due to the treaty and his sister's sworn promises to them all, but he still needed his demonic friend to keep a close eye on his fiancé, just the same.

"Of course, your Majesty. Tilly is like family, just as you are and I have always vowed to keep you all safe," Beelzebub replied, graciously accepting the coffee Blake then handed to him and then taking a sip. "We have relocated to London ourselves now too, and as it happens, Gwen has a job working in one of your uncle's law firms just down the road from Innovate," he added, grinning over at his friend and master.

"That's a happy coincidence," Blake replied with a knowing smile. His Uncle Devin could never be underestimated for his forward thinking.

The girls chatted for a while before finally being joined by their dark masters once they had calmed down. Gwen and Renee not forgetting to kneel before Blake when he reached them. He released the girls and then politely reminded them they needed to ask Tilly for her name out of respect for her demonic prowess.

"Try to fight answering them," he told her before her friends asked, wanting Tilly to see how it felt to fight the strange and ancient law, and as Gwen asked her for it, she felt the same urge to instantly blurt it out that she had before, however this time she shut her mouth tightly, desperate not to tell her. Tilly could hear her heart pounding in her ears, and it felt as though she might explode, and then the sound of her one small word began rising from her chest uncontrollably despite her strong resolve. As she finally spoke her name Blake and Beelzebub couldn't help but laugh loudly at her, their jibes making Tilly scowl, but she shook it off, eagerly trying again when Renee asked her too and she managed to last about another ten seconds longer before she finally said her name a second time.

"Yeah, yeah," she retorted at the still sniggering men. "I'm sure I will do much better when I'm ancient, like you two," she teased, earning herself two open-mouthed gasps from the human girls before her and wide grins from the powerful men.

They decided to have a quiet afternoon at the penthouse rather than holding any lavish parties like they might have done before because both Blake and Tilly were enjoying catching up with their friends far too much to allow any outsiders into their peaceful, well deserved calm space. Berith had been invited along too though and teleported in with Jessica and Jared not long after Beelzebub and the girls, having picked up Beelzebub's newest follower en-route to save his fellow demon the trouble of coming away to get his straggling follower, and then the four couples relaxed together and chatted long into the night while eating copious quantities of Chinese takeaway and polishing off almost two crates of Blake's posh whisky between them all.

Jessica had been unable to contain her shrieks of delight at seeing Tilly again after such a long time either and had hugged her tightly for a good few minutes before finally releasing her grip on her long-lost friend.

"You look fantastic Tilly, it's so strange though, you are still you, but I can tell you are different. It's like I can see the changes in you, feel them and it's wonderful! We've missed you so much," she told her, and the other two girls nodded in agreement. Tilly realised then just what Blake had meant by wanting her to come back and be with her friends and family while she still could, so much had changed in the last year, a year that she had already taken for granted now that she was immortal and she promised herself that she would follow his wishes and live each day like she was still human, as though time was a fleeting gift to be cherished, much to Blake's delight as he read her thoughts with a smile. The girls all continued to chat loudly while the men talked about their plans and Blake updated the demons on the treaty and its restrictions on them all from now on. Jared stood quietly beside them, far too terrified to join in with the powerful men's conversation, but he was pleased that he had been allowed to come along nevertheless. Jessica, Gwen, and Renee all swooned as Tilly filled them in on her and Blake's engagement, showing off her huge diamond ring proudly as her fiancé watched her, his green eyes never far away and she found herself growing hot and horny under his powerful gaze as she thought about their wonderful and very sexy time together in Hell since her transformation. Once the others began to wind down, lazing on the sofas as they sipped on their drinks and chatted quietly, Blake couldn't bear to read her heated thoughts any longer, so he stood and took Tilly's hand. He made no excuses to their guests as he led her from the living area to the master bedroom, a room which held both good and bad memories for Tilly thanks to Beatrice's attack, but it was also the place of her wonderful transition into the demonic world, so she felt happy being in there again although she was honestly grateful that it was now perfectly cleaned up and back to looking the dark and sexy room she was so used to from the days she spent there as a human.

Blake fell to his knees before his beautiful fiancé, his face tilted so that he could watch her reaction to his commanding touch. Tilly grinned and ran her hands down through his dark brown curls. They were quite long now, and she loved them that way, pulling gently as she gripped him, teasingly biting her lip as she smiled down at her lover.

"No," he told her authoritatively, taking her hands and then pulling them around behind her, invisible ropes then binding her hands together as he smiled up at her. "I am the only one allowed to do the touching," he informed her, relishing in her excited anticipation as the binds held her tightly in place. Blake unbuttoned Tilly's skinny black jeans and pulled them off, moving slowly and savouring the sight of her long, slim legs as he freed them from their dark sheaths. He then trailed kisses up and down the inside of her thighs, teasing her for a while before biting on the edge of her silk underwear and then pulling them down, using only his mouth. Once they were discarded too, his kisses climbed higher again and Tilly trembled, every one of her senses alive and eager for his mouth to caress her aching body. Blake kissed her nether lips tenderly, purposely skimming over her sensitive peak with his tongue before his kisses went higher. He rose onto his knees and then slipped his head underneath her t-shirt, his mouth trailing higher and higher before he finally found himself stuck between her cleavage and shirt, the material tight around him as he kissed her breasts eagerly and then sucked on each of her stiff nipples.

Blake's hands then went around behind Tilly and up her still bound arms, he then gripped her t-shirt and pulled it up over their heads and then down her arms behind her, the invisible ropes letting the thin cotton pass through without any resistance, yet they still held her body tightly where he wanted them. Her bra was discarded next, leaving Tilly standing naked before her lover, hot, wet, and desperate for more of his tantalising touch. With a snap of his fingers, Blake released her hands, but only for a moment before he issued his next powerful commandment.

"Lie down on the bed and grip the pillow with your hands," he ordered, and Tilly immediately adhered to the command, lying back and then gripping the top corners of the pillow beneath her as Blake stood, watching her with a devilish grin on his gorgeous face.

"Good, now, you will not remove your hands from it Tilly, not even for a second," he added, reminding her for a moment of his order for her to keep hold of the bed railing in the lodge as he delivered her his hard, emotionless thrusts. He sensed her moment of angst and immediately climbed over her, kissing the tip of her nose gently.

"This is going to be very, very different from the punishment fuck I gave you that time Tilly," he whispered, feeling her relax instantly beneath him as his words ran deep. "This is just for fun, but if you want me to stop just say so," he added, gazing down into her blue eyes sincerely and she knew he meant it, she also knew that she really did not want him to stop, absolutely not and without her even having to utter a word in response Blake smiled and kissed her, his hands reaching up and closing her fingers more tightly around the corners of the pillow.

Still fully clothed, Blake then began his deep, wet kisses once more. His tongue and lips caressing every inch of Tilly's naked body before he finally opened her thighs and then climbed between them. She cried out incoherently, almost ready to orgasm for him without having had any real sexual stimulation so far other than that of his mouth against her skin and he delighted in her almost instant climax as he finally took her swollen clitoris in his lips and then circled it with his tongue.

Tilly cried out, screaming his name and trembling, while her body writhed on the bed as the powerful wave of pleasure hit her and overpowered every one of her senses. He didn't let her rest for even a second before he delved his fingers inside her hot cleft and stroked her already tender g-spot, gripping her tightly with his free hand and pressing his mouth harder onto her throbbing nub as she wriggled beneath him. She came for him again and again, never once letting go of the pillow while Blake stayed fully clothed and devoured her greedily. When the sun rose the next morning, he finally let

Tilly come down from the last of her incredible highs and climbed over her, straddling his lover as she lay exhausted on the bed. Blake reached his hands up over her breasts and then to her arms, reaching up and then unhooking her hands from their still clenched position on the pillow's top corners and then lifting them to cup his face in her palms. He smiled down at her as she reached up and stroked her hands through his hair again, Tilly's contented thoughts filling his mind as she still flushed red and panted beneath him.

"There is a part of me that sometimes just needs you at my command entirely, Tilly. I need to own your pleasure, your body, and your mind. I want to possess every inch of you," he admitted to her, kissing her lips softly.

"I love giving you everything you need, my Prince," she whispered, smiling back at him. "Especially if it involves me having a night like that," she added, a wicked grin on her lips as she kissed him back deeply, tasting herself on his tongue but she no longer cared about anything as prudish as that, her wonderful lover having shown her a sensuous world she had never even dreamed of before meeting him.

CHAPTER TWENTY-FIVE

Later that morning, after Tilly returned the favour by sliding her mouth up and down over Blake's hard length for hours, the pair of them got dressed and, after bidding farewell to their friends at the penthouse, made their way across the city to Andre's restaurant. They pulled up outside Innovate and Tilly couldn't help but hesitate for a moment before climbing out of the black taxi, unsure how best to explain things to Andre and the other chefs there about her long absence. As far as her old boss was aware Tilly had simply up and left without a word, he knew nothing of her near death and then demonic transformation, and it was not like she could just tell him the truth about her time with the royal family and then helping her fiancé's sister take control of Heaven. Blake grabbed her hand and pulled her onwards, forcing her to take that final step and leaning in so that he could whisper in her ear safely.

"Let me do the talking first. I'll set the scene, but then it's all up to you, my love. Don't forget how charming you can be," he reminded her, giving Tilly her first hint as to how best to go about winning back Andre's trust should she be struggling the old-fashioned way. She was happy to use her demonic powers if she needed to, but Tilly wanted her old boss, and friend, to trust her and accept her back without resorting to using her demonic charms so she decided to wait and see, she would figure out later how best to go about it all.

The maître d' at the front desk was new and Tilly hadn't met her before, so she greeted the two of them warmly but informed them they were closed for another hour, assuming that they were customers.

"It's okay," Tilly replied, smiling kindly at the young woman. "I'm here to see Andre for a minute. Is he around?" she asked her, stepping towards the kitchens confidently and Blake followed her lead.

"Yes, but," the woman started to say, but Tilly was way ahead of her and walked straight across the dining area and through the swinging doors, immediately catching Andre's dark brown eyes as he looked up from the hot plate in surprise.

"Oh my God, Tilly?" he called, shooing away the maître d' and pulling her into a tight hug while smiling warmly at Blake. "What are you doing here? Where have you been?" Andre asked her, stepping back and taking a good look at her. "Seriously, where have you been Tilly, you've had us all really worried," he asked again, his expression serious. Blake stepped forward and kept his promise, looking down at the slightly chubby chef as he placed a protective arm around Tilly's shoulders.

"Do you have somewhere private we can talk Andre?" Blake asked, and he nodded, leading them out of the kitchen without a word to the interns he left standing there open-mouthed until the sous chef, Leo, immediately stepped in and took over that morning's lesson in pastry techniques.

The three of them made their way to Andre's office and Tilly sat across from him at the desk while Blake leaned against the doorframe.

"Well, I don't really know where to begin," Tilly said, looking down at her hands. "But first, I am so sorry for disappearing like I did. I know everyone must have been incredibly worried. I, um," she began, but she was already at a loss for words. Tilly realised now how unprepared she was. She had no fake story or excuses lined up and could already feel herself floundering.

"It's okay Tilly, you can tell him the truth," Blake interjected, pretending that he hadn't prepared any of this, but she knew he must have had something planned, a story or a reasoning that he knew Andre would accept, and she gratefully stayed quiet to let him continue. "She had a mental breakdown Andre, a complete relapse and she needed extensive rehabilitation, that's where she has been all this time. Do you remember us telling you I work away almost all of the time?" he asked, and Andre nodded, startled by Blake's strong words. "Well, I'm a doctor working with the government. I am part of an organisation that specialises in new, sometimes unconventional procedures that are not part of the everyday medical practices you might expect. As you can imagine, I need to keep the details private so what I am about to tell you goes no further, but I know I can trust you." Blake began, looking down into Andre's eyes seriously and the chef nodded, his mouth open in anticipation.

"Whoa, I had no idea. Okay, please go on," Andre replied, feeling grateful to be trusted with the secret information, important even and eager to hear more, all of which Blake could read from his mind and he pressed on, knowing that this was the right tactic.

"Well, I run a private clinic in the south of France that specialises in the recovery of soldiers with both physical and mental scars from their times at war, as well as victims of abuse and violence from all over the world. Tilly knew none of this when she first met me. I just told her I was based overseas as a doctor, but I couldn't give her any more information on my actual assignments there until we were together for a while." He said, and Blake looked down at Tilly lovingly as he spoke, resting a hand gently on her shoulder as she peered up at him, mesmerised and enthralled by his intricate lie too. Blake carried on, drawing Andre in more and more with every word that passed his glorious lips. "In the weeks after Trey's assault, I came to see her and I could tell that she had post-traumatic stress disorder, but she refused my help. Over the few weeks that followed, even I thought she was doing better by herself. She fooled me too, despite my years of training and experience in this very field. I suppose I didn't see it because I didn't want to. I wanted her to be better, but then eventually the walls she had built came crumbling down around her and she just lost it one night. Luckily, I was with her, and I took Tilly away with me before she could hurt herself or those around her, but time was of the essence, so I just acted out of instinct, and we left without a word to anyone. She is well now and has been wanting to continue with her life for a while, but I insisted we wait until she was absolutely ready and, well, here we are at last." Blake explained, playing the role of the dutiful boyfriend so well that even Tilly couldn't help but stare up at him in shock.

"Whoa," Andre muttered, staring at Tilly open-mouthed as Blake's incredible fake story sunk in. She played along, nodding sadly at her old boss but said nothing, letting him ponder on it before offloading his frenzied thoughts at last. "I'm so sorry Tilly, I remember I thought it was too soon when you came back, but you seemed so together, and I guess I thought it might help to keep you busy. I should have known it was too soon, but who was I to say no to you?"

"No Andre, none of this is your fault, it's Trey's, but he isn't here for me to take it out on him, so I never got the closure I needed. I have exorcised those demons now, so to speak. I'm finally free of him forever and I want to live my life," Tilly replied, silently thanking Blake for opening up the conversation for her. He had instinctively known which buttons to push so that Andre would instantly forgive her, and Tilly envied him. Reading people's minds really did come in handy sometimes.

"And when you say you want to live your life, does that mean continuing with your career?" Andre asked her, and Tilly had to stop herself from smiling. She nodded, putting on her most earnest expression as she let him make the decisions he had no idea had been planted so cunningly by her omnipotent fiancé.

"I know that this is a lot for you to take in Andre, if you would prefer some time to think about it or if you don't feel like Tilly still has a place here, we will try elsewhere. Innov-ate was always going to be her first choice though, of course," Blake told him, unashamedly buttering the talented man up a little more, but he knew it was working.

"I don't need any time to think on it at all. Tilly, you are welcome back here any time. In fact, it just so happens I have decided to open up another position for a sous chef. Would you feel okay coming back here to work for me?" he asked her, and Tilly smiled.

"Yes, absolutely!" she cried, jumping up and hugging her boss tightly. After going over the details of her phased return to work, Tilly took her new uniform from Andre and hugged him once more, genuinely grateful for his forgiveness and for him allowing her to come back.

"See you next week," she said, smiling as she stepped back. He nodded and then shook Blake's hand, peering up at him with respect and gratitude, thankful that he had taken such good care of her in her hour of need. Andre had believed everything the two of them had told him, every fabricated line but Tilly didn't have to worry about remembering all the intricate details as Blake had taken him aside after their talk and made Andre promise not to question her on it again once she was back at the restaurant.

"She does not need reminders of the terrible past. Tilly just needs progress and positivity from here onwards. Only you can know her story Andre, and I know I can trust you with our secrets," he had whispered, and Andre had nodded solemnly.

"I'll never tell a soul, and I won't ever ask her about it again. Onwards and upwards," he had replied.

"Exactly," Blake agreed.

Tilly breathed a huge sigh of relief when the two of them climbed into the back of a taxi and made their way back towards the penthouse.

"Wow, where did you come up with all that?" she asked Blake, snuggling up to him in the seat.

"We needed a story good enough to explain the time you were away and also to account for my long absences all the time, as well as covering your tracks with a feasible story that he would not continue to question you on after I've gone again. This was the perfect way. I read him and knew that he is a sensitive man, a kind man. The right story and I knew he would be putty in my hands, no charming necessary," Blake told her knowingly, smiling down and wrapping his arm around Tilly's shoulders.

"You are a very clever man, aren't you," she whispered, craning her head up to speak in his ear. Blake looked down at her, one eyebrow raised.

"Man?" he asked, and she grinned back playfully before planting soft kisses along his strong jaw.

CHAPTER TWENTY-SIX

Tilly and Blake's cab soon pulled up outside the large block of posh apartments that were underneath their luxurious part-time home, all of which were inhabited by demons or their followers and still protected by their ancient wards and thresholds against the light beings despite the new treaty between the worlds, old habits would take a while to die off. Instead of going inside, though, Blake took Tilly's hand and pulled her in the direction of the nearby gardens instead, eager for a few more minutes alone with her in the cool autumn air before they returned to their friends up in the penthouse. An early, clear night had fallen, and she followed his lead without question, staring up at the full moon above them as they walked hand in hand. After a few minutes, the buildings opened out, and the orange leaved trees took their place as the pair reached the huge park in the centre of the busy city. Tilly snuggled closer to Blake, loving their comfortable silence, and she gazed up at the stars, contemplating the world above them, a world she knew she would never be able to be a part of, and doubted she would ever see again, but where her dear friend was now calling home. Tilly hoped Lottie was happy, picturing her in her mind chatting and smiling with her grandmother as they found their way together and the Princess took her rightful place in the High Council of Angels.

"I doubt I will ever get to go there either Tilly, no matter what changes she has made, there's still a divide and there always will be. This is the closest to Heaven that I'll ever get," Blake said, indicating Earth. "There will only ever be the light and the dark. The greys won't even come into the mix despite what we all might like to happen, and I have nothing but darkness running through my veins, evil and cold. I think we will have to see Lottie here when she can, I just hope she can bring Ella with her," Blake admitted, wrapping his arm around Tilly's shoulders as they walked slowly towards the brightly lit courtyard in the centre of the massive gardens and then sat on one of the wooden benches where they relaxed and watched as the already quietening city passed them by.

"I'm sure she will come when she can, and I have no doubt that Ella will be joining her when she does. And anyway, I happen to like the darkness, I love it actually," Tilly told him, kissing his cheek gently and Blake smiled down at her.

"I know you do, not that I could ever understand how someone as pure as you could ever end up such a nyctophile," he replied, reaching down to take her face in his hands and then kissing her back.

"A nycto-what?" she asked as he pulled back, one eyebrow raised, and he laughed gruffly.

"It's somebody who loves the darkness, someone who finds comfort in it. Although thinking back I'm not actually sure when you first became such a dark little minx." he replied, staring into Tilly's beautiful face that was bathed in the bright moonlight, his own dark face shrouded in shadow, but she didn't care, she found peace there no matter what was lurking beneath and knew that he was right.

"I think it was somewhere around the time I met you," she teased, grinning at him wickedly.

They made their way back and up to the penthouse after a while and then spent the rest of the evening relaxing around the fire with their friends again for the second night running, genuinely enjoying the company of those they trusted and the relaxed atmosphere that came with their presence. Tilly had gotten changed into black shorts and one of Blake's baggy old t-shirts emblazoned with the 'Forever Darkness' logo of Berith's old band before she then lay across one of the armchairs on Blake's lap with her legs stretched out over the arm of it while he stroked her bare skin absentmindedly.

"When are you two gonna get married then?" Renee asked, slurring her words thanks to having polished off her second large glass of champagne, but she had been given permission to talk openly in just their group's company now, so no one flinched at her brazen attitude towards the powerful couple. She was sat on the floor wrapped in Jared's arms as he sat behind her, his back to the large sofa that Gwen and Beelzebub were laying on together while Berith and Jessica snuggled on one of the other armchairs. Blake didn't mind her question at all, instantly reaching down to take Tilly's hand in his so that he could run his thumb over the impressive engagement ring he had given her.

"When it feels right, we have all the time in the world, don't forget," he said, not actually looking at Renee but staring into Tilly's eyes instead as he replied.

"Well, perhaps you do," Renee grumbled quietly, but said nothing more and Tilly smiled warmly at her friend.

"I think we all know now that there is much more after death than we ever contemplated before Renee. Are any of you even going to try the demonic trials?" she asked, hoping that they might at least give it a go while they were still human. Their souls were bound for Hell no matter what, thanks to their masters' marks, but she hoped they might at least try and progress willingly before their natural time came. Attempting the trials while human would show the Dark Queen their strengths, potential and stamina well before them becoming playthings for their demonic masters' Berith and Beelzebub to command in Hell for the potential centuries it might take for them to become stronger and ready to be turned into demons.

"I am," Gwen admitted, her shy smile showing how scared she was by it, but she seemed determined all the same.

"That's great. I know it will be hard, but trust me, it's worth it. Perhaps I could be your adjudicator on one of your trials, or at least help to train you?" she said, looking up at Blake, who smiled back at her and nodded.

"I don't see why not, I think you could only oversee the first trial though, the others would need to be outsiders so that it was not deemed too easy for her," he said, and Tilly knew he was right. This was his speciality after all.

"Hmmm, virgins it is then," she replied with a cheeky grin and Blake shook his head in mock disgust but couldn't help his wide smile he gave her in return.

The next morning, Blake and Tilly teleported close to her parent's home, landing in an unseen spot near the closest village before calling a taxi to take them the rest of the way to the farm. She was nervous about introducing her mum and dad to Blake, not because she thought they might not like him, but because she knew that their quiet little life on the farm in no way even compared to Blake's incredible and immortal existence. She knew he would be kind and courteous to them, but thought that he might find them mundane, boring even, and Tilly found herself just wanting to get it all over and done with as quickly as possible. There was also the fact that she had disappeared on them for the last year too and they had decided to tell them the same story that they had told Andre, for both continuity and that it seemed the most feasible explanation for her time away.

As the cab pulled to a stop, Tilly climbed out while Blake paid the driver and stopped to look at her childhood home with both nostalgia and sorrow. Her life had changed so dramatically since she had last lived here with them, changed for the better mostly, but there were still parts that she wished she could have done differently if she was given the chance again.

Tilly took a deep breath and her senses came alive. She could hear the animals in the barns across the other side of the large house, becoming especially aware of her own horse as he stood in his stable eating hay. She took another breath and could smell the small stream that ran almost half a mile away, the scent of the fresh water making its way all the way here to her strong nose somehow. She had a refreshed and profound new outlook on life and the world around her thanks to her demonic prowess, and Tilly loved having the knowledge and power at her command, feeling stronger and fiercer than ever before. She stepped forward on the gravel towards the farm gates, eager to see her family again, but then suddenly felt Blake's hands grab her shoulders and pull her back.

"Stop!" he cried, still gripping her tightly, and she looked back at him, confused and shocked. "There is a protective threshold around this farm Tilly, a circle of light that we cannot cross," he said, looking shocked too as he explained his strange findings to her.

"What?" she asked, turning to look into his face. "No way, that's impossible Blake, this is my home."

"Put your hand forward Tilly, you will feel it for yourself. One more step and you would have been thrown back by its powerful warding," he told her, and she turned back towards the invisible line and put her hand out just as he had said to, immediately feeling the strange buzz that thrust her hand back forcefully.

"Whoa, why?" she asked quietly, not really saying it to Blake, but to herself.

"Because no demon is welcome here, I don't care if she used to be my daughter," said a voice from inside the farm wall, and Tilly's father, Robert, came into view as he stepped out and walked towards them. His face was a distorted guise of hate and fear, very far from the usual softness Tilly had only ever seen on the face of the man she had thought she knew so well, and she crumbled beneath his hard stare.

CHAPTER TWENTY-SEVEN

"Dad, what are you talking about? Why have you done this?" Tilly asked Robert softly, desperate to go to him and sort this out, and Blake had to keep a tight grip on her shoulders to stop her from forgetfully walking across the protective line and being blasted by its power.

"You chose this fate when you chose your dark new life, Tilly. I had always hoped that one day you would join our order, but instead you met that circus boy and followed him down his evil path. I told your mother he was one of them, but she wouldn't believe me and now look at you," he spat, hatred in his eyes as he peered over at her.

"He is part of a religiously dedicated and righteously rigid order created by white witches called the Warriors of Light. They are humans chosen to uphold the way of life set out by their so-called God. You cannot reason with him Tilly. Even though you know the truth, he will listen to no-one other than his guardian in the light council," Blake whispered quietly into her ear.

"You mean to tell me you knew all about Brent and his Satanic life? That you two have been lying to me all these years? At least I'm still the same person I always have been, still your daughter. Unlike my so-called parents, I have no idea who you even are. You cannot pretend as though I don't matter to you," Tilly begged him, tears running down her face uncontrollably. "You're worse than anyone I've ever met, liars, the pair of you! There's a treaty now, no more fighting or war between the dark and light beings. You must know that?"

"Yes, I do, but the proviso for the treaty is not fighting, and we are not fighting now, are we?" Robert asked her sarcastically, his tone cold and emotionless. "If you want to start something, go ahead. I wouldn't expect anything less from a couple of filthy demons. Who is this guy, anyway? I see you got rid of that circus freak quickly enough," he muttered, looking at Blake with disgust.

Tilly felt Blake tense up behind her, and now it was her turn to stop him from retaliating. She sent him pleading thoughts and took a deep breath before replying to her father's heartless words.

"This is my fiancé, and while I might just be a filthy demon, as you so eloquently put it, he is far from that. He is Blake Rose, the Black Prince and you will not speak to him that way," she said, her tone powerful and her dark strength shining through as she stood up to the man who dared try and make her feel so worthless, no longer caring that he was her father.

"You and he?" Robert asked, his face flickering with a quick burst of raw emotion that Tilly took for either guilt or sorrow.

"Yes, he saved my life when a white witch tried to kill me," Tilly told him matter-of-factly. "There is more than just the good and the bad in this world, Dad, perhaps if you open your mind you will finally see that there are two sides to every story, a balance, and until you do, then perhaps I really am dead to you."

"If you're such a misunderstood demon, tell me you've not done anything evil in order to become what you are now? Tell me your name and admit to me the truth about your disgusting transformation, who you have killed and what souls you have taken," Robert replied, sneering at her.

Tilly immediately felt the familiar urge to tell him her name, that force inside that demanded she blurt it out straight away, but this time, she fought it harder than ever. She didn't want to give him the satisfaction of having that power over her and she swallowed her words, using every ounce of strength she had to fight the ancient law and Robert's sly smile immediately faltered, realising just how assertive and powerful his child now was.

"We will go now, Robert, and we will not return unless you invite us to but know this. You will never speak to Tilly, or me, like that ever again. Have some respect for yourself and the order you have placed before the needs of your family, the order whose acceptance you consider so dear to you. Do remember though that the Warriors first law, and the one the order believes is most important of all, is that of showing courage and conviction in the face of darkness, not bitterness and rage," Blake said, immediately stepping back and giving Tilly her silent orders to join him, summoning her away with him, knowing that he had to force her to turn back from her family. She had so many questions, and he didn't even know where to begin to answer them.

Robert watched them leave from behind the protective threshold, remaining stoic and calm as he watched the fabled Black Prince wrap his arm around his only child's shoulders as he gave her comfort while they walked away. He could see that Blake was supporting her as she sobbed, his body language loving and protective, and Robert couldn't help but fall to his knees, crying and sobbing hard into his hands as the realisation finally hit him. Tilly was lost to him forever.

Bianca ran from the front door of the house and joined him on the drive, where she fell to her knees and cried too, having watched the terrible events that had unfolded between him and Tilly. They always knew that this day would come, that she would eventually return and try to lure them into her new, dark life with her. But they had been warned. Schooled in the cunning methods demons used so had remained strong. They had been extra vigilant and strengthened their protective circle, and it had worked perfectly. The demons had been kept at bay for another day, and although it pained them both to send Tilly away, they knew that they had to follow the orders from their council. Robert gave a silent prayer to their guardian, a powerful white warlock and, even more troublingly, Alma's eldest son, Mike.

CHAPTER TWENTY-EIGHT

Blake teleported Tilly away and within seconds of leaving the farm, they arrived in the master bedroom of the London penthouse, having teleported directly there this time. She immediately crumpled in a defeated heap on the bed, her dark power and strength completely forgotten thanks to her human emotion and pain taking over for a short while.

"I just don't understand," she whispered, looking up at Blake with red eyes and with a heavy heart. He stepped forward and stood in front of her, wrapping his arms around her as she leaned closer, resting her head against his stomach and gripping him tightly around his back, eager to be snuggled in his strong grasp.

Blake couldn't really answer her, his own dark past affecting his ability to empathise with her fraught emotions, but he knew that she was hurting, and that was the only thing that mattered to him. He held her silently for a few more minutes before kneeling and peering up into her eyes, brushing her dark blonde hair out of her face so that he could see her properly.

"They have been brainwashed Tilly, there's nothing we can do. The Warriors of Light are a cult, that's the only word I can think of to describe them and their methods. The white witches and warlocks find devout Christians and promise them immortality and a higher status in Heaven when they die if they carry out their orders, but it's all lies. The members commit all sorts of sins at the behest of their masters, believing that they are doing 'God's work,' but it is just a way for the light beings to get away with their darker deeds being done, their very own loophole if you will," he told her, knowing it would upset her, but Tilly needed to know the truth. Her parents were a lost cause, there was no way to save them or to infiltrate the order. His family's demons and witches had tried many times. The only option now was to stay well away, but Blake knew that convincing Tilly of that was not going to be easy. He summoned Gwen, Renee, and Jessica to the bedroom, knowing that her friends would offer Tilly an outlet and a support network that he just couldn't give her. He was grateful when the three women came bursting through the door and took over the situation, talking loudly with his fiancé to get all the facts from her and he left them to it once Tilly finally let go of him and gave him the silent go-ahead.

Tilly stayed up all night, talking it over with her friends before finally coming to the realisation herself that she would no longer have her parents in her life without Blake having had to deliver her the hard truth he had known all along. She shut herself off emotionally, casting out that last part of herself that felt the loss of her family and she felt the darkness take its place inside, her heart and soul blackening a little bit more. Blake sensed it too but didn't care. He knew she needed to say goodbye to all those parts of her humanity eventually and at least her parents had forced her hand this time rather than some terrible attack or tragedy befalling her like her dark path had done so far.

As her friends drifted off to sleep beside her, Gwen, and Renee on her right while Jessica slept soundly to her left, Tilly lay in the centre of the huge bed, her body not even the slightest bit tired even as her scattered thoughts settled at last. She was still confused by the incredible events of the day before, but she thought back to all the twists and turns her life had taken so far and found herself more disturbed by the lies and omissions from her parents rather than her father's dismissal of her now that she was a 'filthy demon' as he had so viciously called her. Tilly had been able to sense her mother's eyes on her during the exchange too, a mother who had done nothing to stop the terrible words and emotionless taunts that her father had aimed at her, a mother who had chosen her allegiance to the Warriors of Light over her daughter, and Tilly hoped that in time she could close her heart to them both completely and no longer feel the pain of their betrayal. She focussed instead on Blake, he was her family now and her estranged parents had just made the transition even easier for her to come to terms with, she was grateful that she no longer had to lie or make up excuses to keep their intrigue of her life at bay. She couldn't help but feel sorry for them though, they would live the rest of their lives in the belief that they had done the right thing, but she was sure that they would get a shock when they finally crossed over into purgatory and although Tilly hated the idea of being able to tell them an, 'I told you so,' she knew it might be inevitable.

As she lay there still locked away in her own mind, Blake joined his fiancé in the master bedroom, watching her from the doorway for a moment before he wandered over and stood at the foot of the large bed, listening in on her despairing thoughts while she lay still, not having realised he was even there. He effortlessly climbed up and leaned over her, moving forward on his hands and knees while the other girls seemed unaware of his presence. He smiled slyly as he crept higher, looking down into his lover's eyes as she jumped and her eyes came back into focus. She smiled back up at him and started to speak, but he held his index finger to his still smiling lips to silence her, and she immediately obeyed. Blake slithered back down Tilly's still relaxed body, and he silently lifted her black dress as high as he could manage without having to lift her hips up off the bed and possibly disturb her friends' slumber. She bit her lip and panted excitedly as he kissed her belly button, his mouth expertly caressing her skin before moving south and sliding her black lace panties down to her knees. He nestled himself in her barely parted thighs, using his tongue to free her already swollen clitoris from its hood before sucking on it gently at first, and then faster as he felt Tilly unravel beneath him, her hands running through his dark curls as she desperately tried to keep silent and still. As she neared her glorious climax, Blake slid two fingers inside her tight opening, sending her flying over the edge and crashing into her orgasm while he continued his pursuit, only stopping once her shudders subsided and her body relaxed beneath him. He slid her panties back up and pulled the hem of Tilly's dress back down before sliding back down the bed and standing over her with a sexy smile before he then left without having uttered a single word. Tilly grinned and exhaled happily, knowing that there was nothing to worry about, that she would not miss her family. After-all, she had everything she needed right here.

After a few minutes of calm, satisfied rest, Tilly got washed up and changed while her friends still slept soundly on the bed, and she then joined Blake and the other demons in the living room. Beelzebub, Leviathan and Berith all greeted her warmly, with knowing and understanding smiles on their faces as she helped herself to coffee and biscuits from the small table that nestled between the sofas and then sat down beside her fiancé.

"Berith has had an idea. He thinks we might be able to get your parents out of their pledge to the order, but we need to get some advice on it from my uncle first. He knows everything there is to know about the Warriors of Light, and I know he will help if I ask him. I only have a few hours until I have to go home Tilly, but if you want to we can go and see him?" Blake asked her, pulling her onto his lap and smiling as he watched her dunk her biscuit in the black nectar and then quickly eat the soggy remnants in a race against time before it broke off and ruined her drink with its mushy remains.

"No, I've decided to just let them burn. I'll see them in Hell before long and perhaps then I'll keep them for myself when that time comes. Perhaps not," she mumbled coldly, her response shocking them all, but they could also understand her reasons for saying it.

"Tilly, at least think about it," Blake replied, kissing her lips gently. "I want you to have answers and closing yourself off is not the same as having closure. Trust me, I know all about these things," he added, his green eyes peering into hers lovingly and she knew he was calling on his own experiences to try and help her do the right thing, but for now she was the one content in her misery, and she refused to help her parents.

"I know, but it's still a no," she said again, and Blake nodded, dropping the subject immediately.

Later that morning when Blake had to return to Hell because of the waning moon that grew closer, Tilly teleported home with him, pleased that she had the option of coming to Hell alongside her lover now and she stayed for one more deep kiss, uncontrollably hesitating when it came to her heading back up to Earth alone.

"I don't think I can leave you Blake," she admitted, peering up into his gorgeous face as he towered over her, so commanding and yet his hooded eyes showing her the tiny spark of vulnerability that he too felt at the prospect of her leaving. Tilly leaned up onto her tiptoes and kissed him again, her tongue delving into his mouth as his caressed hers in return, their passion and connection so incredibly strong that she couldn't help but reach her hands up to unbutton his black shirt in the hope of a little bit longer together before her isolation began again.

"No," Blake whispered, pulling back from her embrace with a solemn, yet frustrated, smile.

"No? God, you're such a tease," Tilly replied, smirking up at him.

"You can have me all night long when you have done your first proper stint at work again. I have initiations to carry out, so I am going to be busy for the next few days, anyway. You wouldn't see me even if you were to stay here," he informed her, and Tilly thought back to her time in the demonic hall fighting her way to the top level of demonic classification, knowing that he wasn't lying about being completely detained the entire time he would be needed there.

"Hmmm," she replied, taking another step back to show her forced willingness to comply with his request without needing to be ordered away. "I suppose I will let you off, but I will be home in a few days, Blake, and you had better be ready for me," she teased, blowing her fiancé a kiss before teleporting back up to the penthouse.

The next few days were incredibly busy for Tilly, her phased return to work at Innov-ate was fortunately thrown out the window by the second day thanks to her expert and unforgotten cooking skills being a much needed asset to Andre's team, so she quickly fell back into her old routine of ten or twelve-hour shifts, and Tilly enjoyed every single minute of it. Blake had been right to send her back to Earth, as he always was, and every one of the other chefs around her couldn't help but be in awe of her capable hands and quick, almost unnatural reflexes when it came to her adept practical skill and her ability to recall any recipe or technique without having to check the textbooks.

Being so busy helped Tilly stay focussed and driven on her career, keeping her mind off the terrible situation with her parents, and she had heard nothing from them since that day at the farm, not that she had expected anything, anyway.

When the next weekend arrived and Tilly's day off was finally on the horizon she teleported immediately to Blake's chambers when she finished work, being given permission from Cate to come and go as she pleased now and hoping to find him there waiting for her, but sadly he was nowhere to be seen. Within seconds Luna appeared instead, her green eyes twinkling knowingly as she took in the still so new demon with a happy and loving expression. Luna looked amazing, as usual, and wore her long dark curls loose today, which cascaded down her back beautifully over her black tube dress.

"He's still in council Tilly," she said, delivering the disappointing news as she approached and then she kissed her cheek gently.

"Any way I can get him out of it?" Tilly asked with a cheeky grin and Luna couldn't help but laugh, shaking her head as she took her hand and led the demon she already considered her sister out into the main living area of the royal suite.

"No, you naughty girl," she eventually replied with a grin. "But perhaps cuddles with your second favourite brother of mine will do this time?" she asked, and Tilly nodded in agreement as Luna pulled her over to join the rest of the family on the sofas, noticing that the chair where Lottie normally used to sit was now so glaringly empty. Tilly bowed to the Dark Queen, kissing her cheek affectionately as she stood and then she graciously accepted the bouncing, happy baby when Cate lifted Thorne into her arms.

"Someone's pleased to see you," Cate said, smiling contentedly up at her soon to be daughter-in-law, who couldn't help but smile back at her Queen.

"Hey gorgeous," she said, kissing Thorne's head gently. "Don't tell Blake, but I think you are actually my first favourite one of the Rose boys," she whispered to him, making the other's laugh, before she took a seat on the large sofa near the huge window.

"Hey, what about me?" Harry teased, feigning hurt feelings and Tilly rolled her eyes but grinned back at him, nearly having forgotten that there was another Rose boy in the room. Blake had told her a while ago that as a sign of his loyalty and devotion to Cate, Harry had taken her name when they got married and she loved the sentiment, knowing that although it wasn't the ordinary custom, it was a truly romantic and symbolic gesture.

"Shush, not in front of your wife!" she joked, and Harry quickly put his hand up to his mouth, covering it jokingly to keep up the pretence.

"Yeah, yeah," Luna retorted, flopping down on the sofa next to Tilly and cooing at her baby brother. Tilly truly loved being here, both with and without Blake, and she happily chatted with her new family for a while before handing Thorne back into his mother's loving arms and preparing to make her way back up to Earth. As she watched him smiling up at Cate from his favourite place, her arms, Tilly couldn't help but feel a strange pang come from deep within her, not of jealousy but of longing. She had never felt broody before, but this was undeniable, and she blushed as Cate and Luna both looked up at her with wide, knowing smiles. She quickly pushed away the instinctual emotions and focussed on Blake again, missing him terribly, but she could sense him far down in the depths of the castle and sent him silent thoughts of love and need for him.

"Okay, I know that he'll already know that I came back, but please can you tell him, and ask him to summon me as soon as he is free?" she asked Luna, hugging her tightly.

"Of course he will. It should only be a few more days. See you soon," Luna replied, kissing Tilly's cheek goodbye and just a few minutes later she arrived back in the empty penthouse, feeling lonely and horny and not able to do anything about either of the powerful urges.

CHAPTER TWENTY-NINE

Another insanely busy week passed Tilly by, and Blake was still unavailable thanks to his commitments chairing the demonic classification proceedings, a larger than usual group that seemed to be taking far too long, in Tilly's opinion. Jessica kept her company at work while the three demonic couples stayed with her during the quiet evenings. However, their presence only served as a reminder of Blake's glaring absence. By the next weekend Tilly still had heard nothing from her fiancé and had been informed by Luna during another of her brief homecomings that the initiations were taking longer than they had expected, the progress slower now thanks to some of the restrictions on the proceedings and changes thanks to Lottie's new requests about banning the killing of innocent humans.

"There is nothing you can do. You just have to learn to be patient. This is his job, you need to get used to it," Luna had told her, trying to be understanding, but Tilly could see she was getting frustrated with her. She had nodded and bowed to the Black Princess before bidding her farewell and teleporting back up to the empty penthouse. She then decided not to stay by herself this time, opting instead on paying Lucas a visit, she had not seen him in a long time but had been informed that he and Lilith were living back on Earth too, staying in Edinburgh with the boys while preparing for their loyal audience's long anticipated return of the Diablo Circus.

Tilly teleported straight up to Scotland, being careful to arrive in a secluded spot near their huge home in the city centre. She made her way over to the metal front door and pressed the buzzer, expecting to hear Lucas's dulcet tones come through the intercom, but then she jumped as the door swung open and his eldest son, and Tilly's ex-boyfriend, Brent answered, staring at her open-mouthed.

"Whoa, look who finally decided to pay us a visit!" he cried, looking her up and down while shaking his head in surprise. Tilly looked amazing, as usual these days thanks to her effortless good looks and sexual prowess that had come with her new dark power, wearing skinny black jeans and a thick wool jumper, her dark blonde hair pinned up in a high ponytail and her perfectly made-up face looking fresher and more delicate somehow even though she hadn't used her powers to make herself look younger. "Come on in then demon, but first, can I have you your name please?" Brent asked, eager to get the formalities over with quickly and Tilly shook her head, surprising him even more with her command of the dark power that now coursed through her veins.

"No way," she replied with a wicked grin, stepping forward and instinctively hugging her old friend without even thinking. An awkward smile passed over Brent's face as she pulled back and he stepped aside to let her in.

"How are you able to?" he started to ask, but she cut him off, blurting out her name when she could no longer bear to hold it in and then laughing loudly with him as he couldn't help but laugh back at her.

"Nice to see you Brent, how's everything going?" Tilly asked him, following her ex into the large house and through to the kitchen, where he clicked the button down to boil the kettle and grabbed two mugs from the cupboard without having to even ask. He turned back and propped a hip against the counter, gazing at her again, his deep blue eyes staring into her beautiful face warmly but he still couldn't hide that same flicker of guilt he had not been able to get over since that night two Halloweens ago at the castle when Lilith had lured her there in the hope of initiating Tilly into her following but instead Blake had ended up marking her and the two of them had been forced apart by the Black Prince's new ownership of her.

"I'm great Tilly," Brent replied, grabbing the teabags and adding the sugar, again without needing to ask how she wanted her tea.

"Really great, just a little bit great, or not actually great at all?" Tilly asked, knowing him better than he thought she did. Even after all this time, she could still see through his smile and knew that he was trying to hide some inner sadness or heartache.

"Got me," he admitted, adding the boiled water to the mugs and stirring them absentmindedly. "I've nearly finished my a-levels but Dad wants me to come away with the circus. The first show is before the term is over, so I won't get to finish my exams. He just doesn't understand. He thinks the circus is more important than school," Brent admitted, finding himself saying the words without even thinking, opening up trustingly to the girl he once loved so dearly without hesitation or question.

"He thinks it's more crucial that you all stay together?" she asked, and Brent nodded.

"He says I have all the time in the world for studies. For now, I need to focus on being strong, being ready," he replied, tailing off thoughtfully.

"Ready for the demonic trials?" Tilly guessed, grabbing her mug and taking a long swig, the heat of it not hurting her at all.

"Yep, I just don't think I'm ready yet. And Juliet is pregnant," he told her, dropping the statement in like he desperately needed her to know but hadn't quite known how to tell her that his new girlfriend was expecting his child.

"Then tell him that, but you know he is right, you could always distance-learn? Time with your family is important. I know I'm always gonna be on his side here though, all part of the territory, so I might not be the right one to ask. Congratulations on the baby, too," she said, and meant it. Looking at Brent now brought Tilly nothing but happiness and good memories, she didn't love him anymore and knew that she hadn't for a long time, but there was a fondness there that would never leave her, and she knew that he felt it too.

"Thanks, I get it, but I suppose I have just enjoyed being settled this past year. I know Juliet will come with us but it's not much of a life for her and the baby on the road, not that we're staying in motor-homes anymore," he laughed, his blue eyes alight at the memory of his old home on wheels and she laughed.

"Do what you think is right, but don't forget your vows," she replied, reminding him of his binding contract with Cate and his demonic master Lucas, who had accepted ownership of his sons' souls from Lilith following his own demonic transformation.

"I know, I guess sometimes I just like the idea of giving all the circus stuff up and finding myself again," Brent mused, staring into his mug thoughtfully.

"That makes sense too, but just remember that your duty to Lucas as your new master comes first, and he will always want what's best for you, just trust him," Tilly told him, knowing that would be her approach to it all if it were her and her own family of followers. Brent nodded, his mind still clearly in a jumble even after their talk, but Tilly knew there was nothing else to say on the subject so was willing to drop it and carry on catching up instead.

"Hey there stranger," came a voice from behind them, interrupting their conversation and Tilly turned to see Brent's youngest brother, Jackson, stood in the doorway. He had grown at least another foot since she had last seen him and looked more like their father now. His handsome features had flourished at last, and he had grown into a man.

"Hey yourself, the name's Tilly by the way, in case you didn't already know," she replied with a smile, negating the need for him to ask her, and Jackson smiled back.

"It really is true then, you're a demon now?" Jackson asked, looking down at his hands shyly.

"Yep, it's better than being dead. Well, you know what I mean," she replied, her awkward personality not having left her, which instantly made him smile again.

Tilly spent the next couple of hours catching up with Brent and Jackson while lounging with them on their huge sofas, telling her old friends the story of her near-death-experience thanks to Beatrice's attack and then her transformation at the hands of her now fiancé Blake.

"Wow, so he sired you?" Jackson asked, looking at her in awe.

"Yeah, I'm the first demon ever to be made by their bloodline. It was a sudden decision. No one had any idea, not even your father, until we saw each other during the initiations in Hell. It all happened really quickly, but I'm so happy it did," Tilly told him, feeling herself blush.

"Who would've thought it, you and him?" Brent said thoughtfully, but quickly corrected himself. "By that, I mean when he first marked you, who would've thought you two would end up here. I'm happy for you Tilly, honestly," he blurted out, obviously worried, and she wondered if he was thinking back to Lucas's demonic transition ritual and the way Blake had gotten so jealous over Brent's fond memories of her.

"Don't worry Brent, Blake and I both know that you are happy for us. Just as I am happy for you and Juliet, the past is never going to change, but our futures are ours to command. Blake is my future. He knows that," she replied with a happy smile.

"Wise words, well-spoken my dear," came another new voice from the hallway, it was Lucas, and he was grinning wickedly at them all for a moment before he joined them by the sofas, giving Tilly a tight hug before he sat leisurely in the huge armchair. "What a nice surprise, are you here at the behest of your fiancé?" he asked, and Tilly shook her head, letting him know she was not there for a formal visit.

"Nope, I just fancied catching up with some old friends," she replied, taking in the even younger, fitter demon as he lounged casually between his sons. Three men that any outsider would have taken for brothers rather than a father and his children.

"In that case, you are very welcome here, Tilly. Thanks for coming up to visit little old us," Lucas said, smiling wider at her.

"Thanks for having me, however I do think I gave poor Brent the shock of his life when he answered the door," she teased, her expression playful and being with the guys reminded her of their fun days together that now felt like a lifetime ago. "I'm back up here for a while now that the threat is over, working under Andre and then heading home during my days off. Blake is in initiations though, so I thought I'd kill some time by coming to see you lot," she added, and Lucas grinned over at her. Tilly had noticed Brent wince as she had said her master's name, she thought maybe he had forgotten about her demonic transformation for a minute and couldn't help but be thankful he still saw her the same way, as the same person she always used to be—human, clumsy and fun-natured.

"That's great, well for old time's sake, do you fancy coming to watch today's practice?" Lucas then asked, his blue eyes twinkling warmly at her. He seemed to be enjoying this nostalgic moment between them all, too. Tilly grinned and nodded, jumping up out of her seat and following him with ease after Lucas took his son's hands and teleported them straight to their new, massive indoor arena.

Brent and his brothers had not lost a single ounce of their strength or skill over their gap-year. If anything, Jackson was bigger and stronger than ever. The middle of the three McCulloch brothers, David, greeted Tilly with a happy smile and the obligatory question for her name before he hugged her tightly too, an unusual show of warmth from the normally coolest of the three boys that took her by surprise. When he looked into her blue eyes though he really looked, for the first time ever and Tilly wondered what he was thinking, but it wasn't long before he answered her.

"Wow, you really look amazing Tilly. It must be wonderful to be a demon?" he asked, letting his own want for demonic power show clearly for a minute while he was out of earshot from Lucas.

"Yeah, it's pretty damn good," she replied with a knowing smile. "One day you just might get to be one too," she added, slapping him on the back and nearly knocking the wind out of him, but he just laughed. They soon began their practice while Tilly took a seat and watched them, feeling as awed and amazed as always when they took their places on the stage and showed off their skills. She even helped Brent out like she would have done so long before, throwing batons into his fast-paced juggling act but keeping her eyes on his, their friendly smiles firmly planted on their faces as neither dared to even acknowledge anything else that might still have lingered there between them despite their relationship being a long time dead.

Juliet appeared behind Brent after a while and Tilly immediately stopped her playful banter as she threw in the last of her batons and watched her approach, a contorted fake smile on the girl's face. Brent's girlfriend was clearly not happy to see her, and Tilly wondered if he had eventually told her the truth about the two of them during their past year together.

"Brent, darling," she called, putting on her best friendly look and approaching the two of them in the training area, attempting to saunter over casually but she seemed to forget that she was in the presence of a very powerful demon who could effortlessly read her emotions and demeanour. "You were supposed to come and meet me half an hour ago," she said, her sickly sweet voice unfaltering as she spoke, but Brent's apologies went unheard as she ignored him and turned her attention on the demon before her.

"Hi, I'm Tilly, I don't know if you remember me from last Halloween?" she told her, and Juliet nodded. The fact that she remembered her told Tilly that her hunch might just be right and Juliet finally knew all about Brent's first love. "I hear congratulations are in order?" Tilly added, eager to change the subject, and looked down at the girl's slightly swollen belly.

"Urm, yeah. I guess he told you then, thanks," she replied, looking uncomfortable.

"It's okay, Tilly's just a friend. You know she's a demon now, just like Dad, and she's engaged to the Black Prince," Brent told her, looking down at his girlfriend with his best look of nonchalance.

"Oh, good. Well, in that case I won't have to tell her off for flirting with my man," Juliet replied, her bitchy grin instantly in place again and her playful bounciness coming back to her, reminding Tilly of the girl she had met that first night in the castle. Tilly had no time to play games with this girl, she had no desire to steal Brent away from her or fight her for his attention but instead of letting her off-handed comment go, she leaned forward and caught her gaze, luring her in and forcing her to keep the eye contact for a few moments.

"Listen to me Juliet, I don't know who the fuck you think you are but if you speak to me like that again you'll quickly regret it," she promised, raising a hand in front of Brent's face to quieten him. He had opened his mouth to try and defend his girlfriend, but Tilly didn't care to hear his excuses for her behaviour. Juliet trembled before her, still unable to pull her gaze away, and Tilly leaned in closer, sensing her fear and relishing in it. "Now, you make sure you show more respect for me, and for yourself next time we meet, otherwise I might just have to take this mark," she said, running her hand over Juliet's forearm where the red inverted cross rose to the surface of her skin on cue. "And replace it with my own, then I can show you what a real punishment for insubordination is," she finished, flashing Juliet a wicked grin and a mental projection of the fiery pit where Beatrice now resided, burning for her sins without any remorse from her demonic mistress. A single tear slid down the girl's face and then Tilly released her, stepping back, and smiling over at her clearly frightened ex-boyfriend, but she didn't care. This was who she had become, and these humans had to respect it.

The three of them all welcomed the distraction when Jackson then came over and handed them cans of cold cola.

"Cheers," Tilly said, clinking cans with him in a mock toast. "Here's to you all, and to the Diablo Circus. May you all have thousands of adoring fans and untold riches," she said, taking a large gulp as Jackson bowed graciously to her, a huge smile on his handsome face, seemingly oblivious to what had just gone on between the two women. "Well, I had better get going. Tomorrow is Halloween after all and I have some plans to make," she then told him with a wink. She bid farewell to Brent and Juliet, eying the girl for a second longer than was necessary to let her know she was still seething as she went.

CHAPTER THIRTY

Tilly teleported to her chambers in Hell after her evening shift at Innov-ate, unable to stay away from home anymore and, after all, Blake had told her to come back between her shifts at the restaurant, so she climbed into her bed and dozed happily, resting beneath the black sheets and snuggling into the pillow that still smelled of her fiancé with a deep sigh. When she woke up again the next morning, it was Halloween and this year it had been arranged that Luna would take her turn to spend the day on Earth with Ash by her side because Blake was still detained in the dark hall and no longer needed to monopolise those sacred days thanks to Tilly's transformation. She got herself ready and, in a moment of pure cheekiness and greed, desperately wanting to see her lover, teleported to the balcony above where the demonic tasks were still going on. She looked down and noticed Blake's head jerk upwards ever so slightly as he became aware of her presence there, but he issued her no silent orders to leave and so she watched and waited, pleased to see him after their few weeks' separation. She hoped she wouldn't be in too much trouble for being there. Today was, after all, their anniversary.

"Those that are remaining have made it to the prestigious level two classification, well done. We will now take a short recess and then the final task will begin," he ordered them, rising from his chair and he climbed down from the table without a word of explanation to his dark council. Tilly immediately felt the pull of being summoned and she teleported to his beacon, back to her chambers in the dark castle.

"What the fuck are you doing Tilly?" Blake demanded, his gorgeous face thunderous as he stared her down angrily from beneath his dark hood. He didn't even let her respond though before he stormed forward and pinned Tilly to the wall by her throat, pushing her into the stone with his almighty frame and staring down into her face, his mouth just inches away from her own. Tilly knew better than to fight, not even wanting to resist, so she submitted to him entirely, her mind and body at his every command. She knew she had been selfish, childish even, but she just needed to see him, every one of her urges overwhelming each of her powerful senses and causing her to act rashly. Blake still had his black cloak on, covering his head and shoulders completely and she couldn't see his eyes yet, but assumed that they would be swirling with the familiar black specks that showed his inner rage that threatened to bubble over.

"There was something I desperately needed in there," she replied, her voice a haughty whisper through her tightly held throat. Blake released the pressure slightly and ran his hand up to her chin, pulling her gaze up to meet his and she was surprised to see his warm, green eyes staring back at her from the shadows beneath his hood.

"Oh, and what was that?" he asked, his own voice gruff and full of desire towards her, giving him away. Tilly could tell right away that he was pleased to see her too and had missed her. She didn't need to answer, instead she kissed him deeply, hard, and intense, and he couldn't resist her. The powerful thrusts of their tongues as they collided and delved drove them both crazy, commanding one another, and then they eagerly ripped off each other's clothes. Blake's dark cloak floated down to the floor along with his shirt as she tore open the buttons and freed his incredibly muscular torso from its cotton prison and kissed his skin eagerly.

"No," he commanded, tearing off the last of Tilly's clothing and then turning her around so that he pressed her into the wall from behind. She instinctively raised her hands and placed them on the warm stone either side of her, knowing now how he loved to have her acquiescent to his every whim as he delivered his delicious ravishments, bound by nothing but her silent promise as he took ownership of her body. His hard erection pressed into her back once he removed the last of his own clothing, and she licked her lips in anticipation, groaning uncontrollably.

"You've been a very naughty girl Tilly," he groaned. "But it's a good thing I love bad girls, isn't it?" Blake whispered in her ear as he parted her naked legs and then thrust his hard cock inside in one deep, forceful thrust and she cried out thanks to the intense pleasure, her fingers digging into the brickwork while he pounded her hard and steered Tilly towards her much needed climactic release.

The walls beneath Tilly's hands soon shuddered and began to shake, mimicking her own trembling body as Blake climaxed inside of her. She relished in his powerful lovemaking for the last few moments before he pulled his hips away, her own climaxes having come fast and all-consuming as her need for him overwhelmed every one of her senses. Blake's hands slid up her bare back and along her arms where his fingers then locked around hers while she still stood pressed against the wall, waiting to be released by her dark master, and he turned her to face him, peering down into his lover's eyes as he took her in.

"Don't ever do that again Tilly, is that understood?" he commanded, his face serious again, and she nodded, desperately hoping that she was not in any real trouble with him.

"How could I not see you on today of all days? It should be a new law that we have this day together every year," she teased, running her hands up through his dark curls as their naked bodies still pressed into one another's perfectly against the warm wall.

"We'll see," he replied with a sly smile, clearly having felt the same about wanting to see Tilly on their anniversary. "You really are a naughty girl getting me out of the task hall like you did, and you know we are gonna have to answer to my mother for it?" Blake added, a cheeky grin on his lips as though he still could not quite believe her gall.

"I will take any punishment. It was totally worth it. You are worth it," she replied, her own wicked grin lighting up her beautiful face as she binned her ripped clothes and grabbed a new set from her drawers.

"So are you Tilly. When I think how different I am now than I was before I knew you, I cannot believe the difference in me. Love really has changed me. It has broken me down in such a way that I am ready to take every beating it needs to give. I crave it and I will always come back for more and more," he marvelled aloud, watching her intently. "I'm a glutton for the punishment, never satisfied, never having had enough. I could live for a further one hundred years and I would never find someone like you. Don't ever think I take you for granted," he promised, kissing her softly before getting himself dressed again too, his clothes miraculously having mended and were perfect once again.

"I could never think that, and the feeling is entirely mutual, by the way. I'd take any bruise, any beating if it meant staying by your side Blake, you're worth every scar, no matter how deep they might run. Goodbye for now my beautiful tragedy, but please don't keep me waiting so long next time," she told him, sensing as he began to teleport back to his dark hall, a broad, satisfied smile on his gorgeous face.

Within a couple of days the demonic classifications were finally over and Blake was back to his usual routine in Hell with his family, he had missed Tilly terribly during his time in the task hall, but his commitments to his council would sometimes have to come before his fiancé, unfortunate as that was so he didn't dwell on it and instead enjoyed her nightly returns to him in his chambers, a strange but seemingly normal commute now for Tilly to and from work at Innov-ate. He relished in her regular company now, finding himself more desperate than ever for her affections and attention, basking in her happy smiles and sensuous glow. He also couldn't help his mind wandering sometimes, wanting more naughtiness from his beautiful lover despite his warnings, and enjoying her new, darker, confident sexuality. She felt it too and fantasised openly while both in Hell and up on Earth.

Blake had thoroughly enjoyed their sneaky little break from his seat in the centre of the council table and hoped to see that dirty side of Tilly again in the near future, despite his mother's rather polite warning afterwards that they never be so unprofessional again and he had promised to maintain his business-like persona in the future, desperately trying to hide his cheeky smile as she had delivered her telling off.

"Good," Cate had replied, but even Harry couldn't hide his sordid thoughts as he remembered the times that they had snuck off to be together before he was able to call her his wife, making Blake shake his head in mock disgust at his mother's hypocritical reprimand, but he was grateful she had chosen not to punish either of them. If it were anyone else, they would be burning in a pit or being tortured for the misuse of their power, but for Blake and his happiness she would overlook their smitten foolishness provided they didn't repeat their mistake or carry on with any further insubordination.

"I didn't say I had never done anything like that before, I just said you two weren't allowed to do it," she retorted, unable to hide her affectionate smile at Harry and Blake just bowed courteously, a knowing smile on his lips too.

Two days before the next full moon, Tilly was working hard at the restaurant, making delicate pastries and baking them carefully to perfect crispness. She suddenly felt a pang deep in her belly, a forceful urge that meant only one thing—Blake was summoning her back to Hell. Tilly immediately panicked, worrying that something might be wrong, and she quickly made her way over to Andre.

"I'm not feeling very well. I think I might have a migraine coming on. Would you be terribly angry if I went home?" she asked, her pained expression far from forced, and he immediately beckoned for her to go.

"Of course. Take a few days if you need it," Andre replied, looking at her with a worried expression. Tilly was never ill, and he couldn't help but fret over her sudden downturn but let her go. "Call me if you need anything," he added, and she smiled, thanking him before heading off towards the cloakroom to quickly change and find a secluded spot from which to teleport from.

Tilly went straight to her lover's chambers, following Blake's beacon, where she found him lying naked on the bed, the satin sheet just barely covering his glorious body, and he grinned up at her wickedly. He looked more delectable than any food or delightful treat she had ever seen in her life. Tilly wanted nothing more than to touch and taste her darkly delicious lover and peered at him, savouring the sight of his perfectly toned abs and thickly muscled thighs.

"Touché," she whispered, immediately calming down, and she shook her head as if she were unimpressed that he had managed to get her away from work on the pretence of something more urgent than his libido.

"You can go back if you really don't want me?" Blake teased, calling her bluff and Tilly shrugged.

"Seeing as I'm already here," she replied, stripping off and joining him on the huge bed. Blake was inside her in seconds, their bodies ready as always for each other's touch. Tilly let him command her every sense, thought, breath and climax as he dominated her very willing body. Their love was so dangerously powerful now that they both surrendered willingly to its command and revelled in the emotion and enraptured adoration they felt for one another.

"I can't wait for you to be my wife, my Queen and the mother of my children, Tilly," Blake whispered as they writhed in each other's embrace and she fell for him even more, succumbing already to every order he had yet to give her, and she didn't have a care in the world.

Tilly lay deliciously exhausted in her lover's arms while lazing in his huge bed in the dark castle the next morning, her body still trembling and her cheeks flushed thanks to their all night long escapades having made the walls around them shake many times, a thought that still made her blush. Her slim body lay wrapped in his, Blake's strong arms enveloping her tightly as they rested in comfortable silence, and he stroked her hair thoughtfully.

"You remember you said Berith had an idea about my parents?" Tilly eventually asked him, breaking the silence and Blake pretended to be surprised, although he knew she had been thinking about them despite her insistence that she no longer cared.

"Of course," he replied, looking into her blue eyes intently. "I can take you tomorrow if you want? All I need is one little word," he asked, checking if she really wanted to try this potentially difficult and forever life-changing task, for he was sure that she would have to take some dark steps to change the devout followers' minds.

"Yes, I want to do it," she replied, understanding his need completely, and he nodded, ready to do whatever it took to help her.

Tilly and Blake teleported to the penthouse as soon as the moon was full and after only staying long enough for their demon and human friends to welcome them, he took her hand in his, a silent order telling Tilly that it was time to go. She got changed into her best business-like outfit, feeling as though she were off to an interview of sorts, and he led her through the front doors and down in the lift, through the vast lobby and out onto the street below where the doorman hailed them a taxi. They slipped inside and he instructed the driver to take them to the head office of Black Rose Industries in the centre of London, teleporting was not an option as his uncle Devin was a stickler for human-like appearances when it came to the business side of their lives on Earth. They arrived at his family's offices in just under half an hour, greeted by the huge building as it loomed over them, oppressive and dominative in the city sky. Blake watched Tilly as she peered up at the dark brick monument to his uncle's Earthly reign of sorts, taking it all in, and she couldn't help but wonder why he had brought her here instead of somewhere more private.

"Well, I thought that first and foremost, it was about time you actually met my uncle, and despite its seemingly normal appearance, this is the most private place in the world," he said, reading her thoughts and then taking her hand in his as he pulled her towards the side door and then punched in a code to open it.

Tilly had already heard a little bit about his aunt and uncle, the only family of sorts of the Devil herself, and that they were afforded many kindnesses by the Dark Queen, their Earthly existence granted to them thanks to their unbound relationship with the moon and Cate's desire to empower her siblings as much as possible now that her eldest son was next in line to her throne. Tilly knew Blake loved them dearly, that Devin and Serena Black had taken wonderful care of him and Luna when they were stuck in Hell without their parents all those years ago, and that they had tried hard to mend the broken boy he had become thanks to his father's punishment.

She knew they were family and Tilly had to admit that although she had been shocked to learn the truth at first, somehow she understood Lucifer's all-consuming need to love Cate despite first siring her as an heir. His was a love that eventually resulted in his demise. Everyone loved her though, and by all accounts they always had, even when she was still half-human. Although Cate was a young and quite possibly even weak girl back when Lucifer had first seduced her, Tilly guessed they would never have had much else. He was never a real man in any aspect of the world. He'd sired heirs he hadn't intended to love. Instead, he'd coveted his omnipotent presence so much that he was more of an evil entity, an eternal dark cloud that could never have been a real mentor to Cate, her other sired heir, or even to the twins he later went on to have with her when he made Cate his wife. Lucifer's selfishness and need to have control and power over everybody seemingly overshadowed even his most basic instincts to care for and nurture those he loved. Those who needed him so desperately to help and guide them. He was a tyrant and a bully, and as far as Tilly could tell, Blake was better off without him in his life.

As she had let her mind wander and become more engrossed in all the sordid revelations from Cate's past, Tilly hadn't even realised that they had come to a stop just inside the door. Blake's tall frame stood so still in the dimly lit hallway as he read her thoughts, and Tilly immediately cursed herself for thinking of it so carelessly, she hadn't been able to help herself and regretted it in an instant. She didn't dare speak a word aloud to her fiancé. She didn't need to see his face to know that he was tormented and angered by her foolish judgements and thought for sure that if she could see his eyes right now, they would be blacker than she had ever seen them.

After a few moments she instinctively let go of his hand and backed away, pressing herself into the wall as she anxiously awaited the hands that she was sure would soon be wrapped around her throat, the tight squeeze that would choke her and perhaps this time there would be even further punishments he might want to deliver for her stupidity, he had warned her so many times and Tilly was angry with herself for being so reckless. She sent him silent pleas and apologies with her thoughts, but Blake still just stood there, staring straight into the dark hallway like a statue, not having moved at all since he had clammed up.

When he finally flinched, Blake did not storm towards her with a dark look in his eye or with his hands reaching up to dominate her body and soul. Instead, he turned to her and let out a tiny sob, the closest he had ever been to truly breaking down since his father had crumbled his will so many years ago. Her thoughts had struck him deep, too deep than he was ready for and rather than be angered by it, Blake couldn't help but seem to be utterly broken by them. He fell to his knees, sobbing hard and seeming so pained and sad that Tilly couldn't help but fling herself to her knees before him too, cupping his cheeks in her hands and kissing every inch of his sad face as she cried.

"I'm so sorry, me and my stupid thoughts. Please forgive me, master?" she begged fearfully, finding herself instantly resorting to her old human-like ways as she cowered before him, both physically and mentally. Her body ached to comfort him, yet she knew she was the reason that he was hurting, and the realisation cut like a dagger to her soul.

After what felt like hours, Blake blinked and refocused his hooded green eyes at last, peering back into her blue eyes tenderly, showing his complete and raw vulnerability for the first time ever.

"Tilly," he whispered gruffly, his voice quiet and soft. "How do you do that?" he asked, his hands gripping her face gently as he peered back at her.

"I'm so sorry Blake, I didn't mean to upset you. I love you," she pleaded, hating seeing him so broken.

"I'm not upset by you, but by the truth you always seem to find so easily in the dark corners of your mind. How can you love a monster like me when you are so good, so smart, and so intuitive?" he asked, his face pale and tormented.

"In all the darkness I have known this last couple of years, Blake, I have yet to meet a true monster, least of all you," she replied, kissing his trembling lips softly.

CHAPTER THIRTY-ONE

By the time they walked through the huge, black wooden doors into Devin's office, Blake was his usual calm and collected self again, while Tilly still felt emotionally battered by the intense couple of hours they had just spent in the hallway below. She was glad he had managed to bring himself back to her again, instead of being dragged into the dark despair that had threatened to take him from her thanks to the depressive realisations she had so foolishly muddled over, and she was truly grateful that his uncle was unable to read their thoughts. Blake and Devin hugged and chatted for a moment while she watched them, and Tilly vaguely remembered Blake telling her a little while ago that Devin had not been granted permission to read minds by his almighty ex-lover, that talent only being given to her offspring. As recompense he was given his own freedom of thought to live without being listened in on by the royal children in return, the Queen still could read his thoughts if he opened them up to her, but only she could work around their invisible walls, never truly letting him or his wife be completely free, but Tilly could understand Cate's reasons behind never being able to truly trust others.

"And this must be your beautiful fiancé, Tilly?" Devin asked, reaching out to hug and kiss her, treating her like family without even having to be told that his assumptions were correct. He was handsome and exuded the same sexy, dark prowess as his nephew, while hiding something else behind his deep blue eyes, a profound knowledge beyond his fake youth and an evil glint Tilly could not help but find alluring. He had dark blonde hair not dissimilar to hers, looking nothing like his omnipotent ex-lover, but she had already known that they didn't look alike from Blake's explanation about how all of that worked, Thorne being more than enough proof of that strange fact. His tall frame matched Blake's, but he had a much slimmer body than his muscularly built nephew and Tilly thought for sure that he could not possibly be as strong as him either, having seen her fiancé in action during hers and Lucas' final classification task and she was sure that he could overcome any opponent with relative ease.

"It's wonderful to meet you, your Majesty," she replied, bowing in respect to Cate's sired brother, who smiled and relished in her unexpected courteousness.

"Please, call me Devin," he asked, stepping back to take in the couple with a cheeky, happy smile.

"Now then, young Prince. I hear from my youngest son that the two of you are extremely loved up and that you have finally lowered those mile-high walls of yours, thanks to this girl. Tell me it's all true?" Devin asked with a happy smile. Blake blushed, his coyness taking Tilly off guard, and he just shrugged, smiling across at the half-human man he had considered his mentor and father-like entity for many years before Lucifer had returned and he had moved to Earth with Serena and their children, a void that was only ever marginally filled by Harry in the years that followed their father's imprisonment.

"I guess so, I do know I'm a very different person for having her around," Blake admitted, making it Tilly's turn to blush now. "This girl has a way of getting inside my head better than anyone I know, including my mother," he added, taking her hand and rubbing his thumb over her engagement ring thoughtfully.

"Whoa, and there was me thinking you would always be too black-hearted to ever care about anyone or anything. What a welcome change in you Blake, and for that alone you have my eternal gratitude, Tilly," Devin replied, eying her intensely and she couldn't help but swoon a little under his dark gaze. She had always thought that Devin and Serena would be weaker, less commanding, and less dark than their mistress or her children, having mistakenly expected to find them almost demon-like but she realised now just how wrong she had been. Blake certainly encompassed all that she would expect the eldest child of the Devil and next in line to the dark throne to, but he could still surprise her with the all-consuming darkness he still found hard to control sometimes. It was an overwhelming force and even Blake could not regulate it when it surged within him at times, but he respected it, knowing that he would eventually take all of that and more when Cate finally passed her full darkness on to him somehow.

Tilly could see now that Devin was far from weak. He was clever, cunning, evil, and driven. He ran his domain like the king of Earth and everything he touched obeyed him. Tilly thought for sure that his followers must worship at his feet, and that everything he commanded must tremble under his incredible prowess. Blake cleared his throat, pulling Tilly from her astonished thoughts and she couldn't help but feel guilty, he had just spoken so highly of her and yet here she was focussing on the man before her rather than the one whose heart she had just been credited with for capturing for all eternity. She peered up at Blake, sending him a silent apology, but for some reason he didn't seem jealous or angered, remaining stoic and calm.

Tilly wondered if perhaps he could tell she was not swooning over Devin in a sexual way, she was simply surprised by and drawn to his commanding dark power, the same way that she had been inexplicably drawn to the Queen when she had first met her.

"Thanks Devin, who would've thought a clumsy, misinformed human would get under his skin, hey?" Tilly joked, releasing the thick tension in the air around the three of them in an instant.

They then chatted for a while, Blake laying out the details regarding Tilly's family and their allegiance to the Warriors of Light while Devin sat quietly and absorbed his words with a thoughtful expression before he finally offered his opinion.

"I fear the only option might be their death. Only then will they learn what their dark deeds have earned them in the afterlife. You would have to claim their souls and entrap them in your private cell, otherwise, they would go straight to the bottom of the shit-pile for the enjoyment of any demon that might like a go. Leyla would have happily been able to claim them before, but obviously, things have now changed. You could still lure them out of the order and relieve them of their miserable existence if I asked one of my guardians to help, however I'm not sure your little sister would be entirely happy with that," he replied, and Tilly thought it all over, hating every one of his ideas. She didn't know who this Leyla was, but Tilly knew Devin was right and any such action would not sit well with Lottie's treaty.

"Leyla is Devin's only daughter, but she is the strongest and most cunning of my cousins. She has had to curb many of her natural instincts since the treaty and has even been living back in Hell, helping out in the dungeons back home in order to let off some steam rather than use her skills up here like she used to do. She is, well was, the top assassin and bounty huntress of the Crimson Brotherhood, the best our kind has ever known, and yet now she is having to learn to ignore all her years of training to settle for being a protector of the order rather than its most effective offensive weapon. My cousins have had a hard time letting go of their darkness Tilly, Devin's other son Corey has had to be punished for his wrongdoings," Blake told Tilly, clearing up any question in her mind about his Devin's allegiance to Cate, and to Lottie's new laws. If he was willing to punish his own children for their dark deeds that went against Lottie's new balance, then surely he was a more formidable being than even she had taken him for. Devin was clearly a devout Satanist, as strong as they come, and she couldn't wait to be a part of their fiercely loyal family when she eventually took her place by Blake's side.

"Whoa. Perhaps we can just convince them to switch sides instead?" Tilly asked hopefully, looking between the two God-like men as their expressions both went blank.

"No Tilly, it's just not that easy. The only way would be to turn the witch that owns their souls, the switch of their allegiance would blacken your parents' souls enough for us to charm them into joining us, too. But it would not be easy, and we would need to call in many favours, from both sides," Devin offered, making her face drop. The lack of any other ideas made her feel sick. She then started to realise that perhaps her parents really were lost to her after all. "Times are changing, as are alliances. We can try?"

Having had some time to calm down and re-think the rash decisions she had made after her father's terrible words to her at the farm had proven Blake right, Tilly wanted desperately to save them and would settle for either their forgiveness from Heaven for their foolishness or their change in allegiance, hoping that they might eventually decide to become her first proper followers.

"What would it take, Devin?" Blake asked, having read her desperate thoughts and she couldn't help but smile. He really did put her needs first sometimes, and she truly loved him for it.

"Firstly, I would require that Tilly becomes an official client of the Crimson Brotherhood," his uncle replied, and Blake jumped up from his seat, anger exuding from him within a split-second of Devin uttering the request.

"Absolutely fucking not. She belongs to me," he replied, his eyes swirling with black specks as he stared his uncle down.

"Suit yourself, it should go without saying that she would have to pledge her soul to me just as all the others have had to before the Brotherhood will even agree to offer her help," Devin replied, remaining calm as he took his seat at the huge desk and stared at the confused girl, his features as unreadable as his mind.

"The Brotherhood won't help until she pledges? I think it's more that you won't help until you have your newest trophy," Blake snapped in reply, and Tilly caught the slight curve of Devin's mouth in response, but he did not answer. "Thank you for your time Devin, I'm sorry that we could not come to an understanding," Blake said curtly after a few minutes of tense silence, taking Tilly's hand and leading her from his uncle's office without any explanation or response from the powerful leader that sat silently behind the huge desk.

He didn't stop until they reached the street, where he then paced up and down and ran his hands through his hair thoughtfully, trying to calm down while Tilly eagerly waved down a taxi. They climbed in and she instructed the driver to take them to the penthouse, giving him the address and all the while staring fearfully at her fiancé.

***

"Fucking cheek of him!" Blake bellowed as he burst through the doors of the thankfully empty flat not long later and in his rage, threw the small table that had been inside the door across the room with an effortless flick of his hand, shattering the dark wood into a hundred tiny pieces. Tilly followed him inside but kept her distance and stayed quiet, even her thoughts were forcibly silent as she was determined not to be on the receiving end of his rage but hoped that he would be summoned away if Cate was too worried about him as she had always promised. He stormed through the flat to the bar on the other side of the living area and poured himself a large glass of whisky, not bothering with any ice this time, and then downed the lot in one big gulp before repeating the move over and over again.

Tilly hovered by the sofa in the centre of the room, her hands gripping the back of it as she stood and peered out the huge doors to the terrace and waited for Blake to calm down, not daring to question him or try to talk him down from his rage. After drinking almost a bottle's worth of the dark liquid Blake came over to her and took her chin in his hand, turning Tilly to face him and she turned her body along with her gaze, peering up into his still black-speckled eyes fearfully. She instinctively fell to her knees before him, her eyes low and her body hunched. This submissive pose turned him on instantly despite his anger and he peered down at her, a satisfied smile curling his lips ever so slightly.

"You know I love it when you're down on your knees before me Tilly," Blake growled. "Look at me," he then commanded, his request an order that forced her eyes skywards without her having any control over them.

Blake grinned down at her, his wicked, sexy smile reminding her of the night they had first met in the castle and his face when she had finally figured out how to act in his almighty presence. "Good. Now, I want you to prove to me once and for all that you are mine, Tilly. I do not like to be made a fool out of, especially by my fucking family. I need you to make me a promise now, an agreement that no matter how much I hurt you, you'll never leave me," he explained, making her gasp.

"Blake, you know I won't," she started to remind him, but he cut her off, his eyes darkening as he peered down at her.

"I mean it, Tilly. I am overcome with a need to punish you and I need you one-hundred per cent on board. I want to punish you for your unfaithful thoughts as you flushed like a cheap whore before my uncle today, and discipline you for making me feel every one of those thoughts like tiny daggers in my heart."

"I didn't," she began to respond, shaking her head. She was desperate to appease him, but the hard slap that hit her cheek quickly silenced her, sending Tilly's still hunched frame sliding across the floor with the force of his powerful hand.

"Don't lie to me Tilly, you think you can just stir me up inside with those horrendous thoughts about my father and then get away with swooning over Devin just minutes later?" he bellowed, and she knew he was right, her thoughts had gotten away with her and while she had thought he was okay with them at the time he was clearly seething but had hidden it all too well while they were still at Black Rose, teaching her yet another valuable lesson about her false sense of security with her Black Prince.

"I'm so sorry, Blake," she whispered, bowing low to him again and ignoring the sting of her cheek. "I'm sorry. Do it. I told you I'm willing to take whatever pain you think I deserve. I promise I won't leave you," she added, staring up at him again, silently submitting to his every dark whim.

"Good," he said, a sinister smile curling his lip. "What if I told you today's punishment was not a physical one, but a mental one? Can you still take it?" he asked, his gruff voice harsh, and she nodded.

"If it will absolve me in your eyes, then yes, of course. I'll do whatever you ask of me," Tilly replied, scared what mental torture Blake might be planning to inflict on her and she was not sure she would find it any easier this way at all. Without another word, he then grabbed her arm and teleported them away, landing outside the familiar building where she had spent the day just a couple of weeks before, Lucas's home in Edinburgh.

"Blake?" she asked, looking up at his dark silhouette in the pitch-black night.

"I want you to go into Brent's dreams, and kill him," he ordered her, stroking her cheek gently, his voice calm and collected. "I've had more than enough of this boy and his claim over you. Despite your best efforts to forget him, you somehow end up back here time and time again. I want him to burn and be tortured at my hands Tilly, but the only way I can get away with it is in secret. A heart attack in his sleep is believable enough. I will then claim him and seal his mouth shut so that he can never tell a soul. Do this for me now, my love, and you are forgiven."

CHAPTER THIRTY-TWO

"Blake, I," Tilly began, but he just shook his head and looked up at the dark house, not taking no for an answer, and she knew that every second she hesitated just landed her in more trouble. She knew that to win him back she had no choice, she had to do as he commanded and so she closed her eyes and focussed on the sleeping man a couple of floors above them, the man that she had once loved but who was now going to become her bargaining tool for her fiancé's forgiveness.

She worked her way inside Brent's consciousness, seeing the dream that played out in his mind as he relaxed beside his pregnant girlfriend. She watched his subconscious mind as the dream changed, turning into a nightmare thanks to her demonic presence there and he began to dream of dark alleyways while his disembodied form ran down them, fearful of the eyes he felt on him from the shadows, her eyes. Tilly's long fingers caught his shoulders from behind and pulled him to her chest, reaching around to silence Brent's screams with her palm as his nightmare played out uncontrollably in his mind. He raised his prickling arm and peered down as his red inverted cross rose to the surface of his skin and then changed to black, his body trembling as he tried to express his confusion to his captive.

"Sometimes we have to do whatever it takes in order to survive Brent, I'm sorry," she whispered in his ear, still holding him from behind and he tried to squirm away, recognising her voice but she didn't give him the opportunity to ask her what was happening. Tilly reached down with her free hand and thrust it effortlessly into his chest, removing his still beating heart from its cavity and together they watched it slow and then stop in her grasp. Tilly was then quickly forced from his consciousness by Blake's summoning, and as she left Brent's mind, she felt him slip away, his soul descending to her master's dark prison below.

"Good girl," Blake whispered as she returned to him, her hot tears streaming down her face as he took her arm and teleported them both back to London. Tilly couldn't help but fall to the floor and sob uncontrollably as the reality of what she had just done washed over her. She curled into a ball on the hard floor and screamed. She was furious at Blake for making her do it. He did not comfort her, instead he poured himself a new glass of whisky and sipped it while he watched her tortured soul darken just a little bit more thanks to her first truly evil deed, a sly smile turning the corners of his mouth.

When he had finished his glass, he poured another, and filled a glass for her too, offering it to the still floored young demon before him. Tilly took it and downed the fluid in one quick gulp before standing and gazing up at Blake angrily before she then tossed the glass across the room, where it smashed against the wall and shattered.

"Don't ever call me a good girl again," she demanded, staring into his green eyes as her own still streamed.

"Why not? Should I call you my bad girl instead?" he teased, relishing in her angry confidence.

"Call me what you want, just not that," she retorted, feeling her anger fading and slowly being replaced by her heated core taking over. This angry back and forth was making her feel strangely good, assertive, and even horny. There was a part of her that still felt like she deserved the physical punishment from him for some reason, even after already having earned her forgiveness thanks to her awful deed, and he knew it. Blake could tell that she wanted to be taken over his proverbial knee and spanked, so he gave her a reason to be naughty for him again, to earn her ravishment.

"Good girl," he said again, unashamedly teasing her and Tilly flushed with a red-hot fierce rage that took over her, causing her hand to uncontrollably fly up and slap Blake across his face.

She regretted it instantly and tried to back away, an anguished sob escaping her trembling lips as she held up her hands and uttered a silent apology. She was sure that his eyes would soon be black and that his forceful anger would not be so reasonable for the second time in one day, but instead, his lip curled and he let out a gruff laugh.

"You might wanna run," Blake said, but he gave Tilly less than a second as a head start before he stepped forward and forced her retreating steps to move her back towards the huge dining table. As she hit the wood with her back Tilly couldn't help but still stare into Blake's eyes, shocked that he was still so controlled of his rage after her foolish blow, but then he smiled widely and gave himself away, this was what he wanted too. She could tell now that there truly was a dark desire in him to control and dominate her without punishment being the reason. He wanted to enjoy it and not be consumed by the rage urging him to perform the dark acts. She watched him for a moment and then held her ground there, welcoming his powerful body when he then stepped forward, closing the last few feet between them and shoved himself into her, hard. Blake then lifted Tilly up to sit on the wooden table and wrapped her legs around his waist as his mouth pressed into hers roughly, his lips bruising hers as he forced his kisses on her, and she gushed as he took control of her body so forcefully, this was exactly what she needed too, and he knew it.

Blake ripped off her black pencil skirt and blouse, popping buttons and ripping the material in his pursuit of her nakedness, wanting to unleash the body he so desperately needed to possess entirely, and Tilly squirmed in brazen delight when she sat naked before him, panting and wet. He stepped back and looked at his lover, taking in her dark, seductive expression and delighting in her mixture of fear and lust he sensed as she stared back at him. He undressed slowly, teasing Tilly even more and she couldn't help but spread her legs, showing her body off without any fear now, knowing that this was all just a dark game he had initiated so cunningly. She hoped that exposing that intimate part of herself so confidently would quicken his striptease, and it worked. One look at her naked cleft sent Blake over the edge and he quickly discarded the last of his clothes and pounced on her, pinning Tilly to the dark wood as he pressed his hard erection into her belly and climbed over her, closing her legs and straddling her, lifting her hands above her head and locking her fingers closed tightly, needing to be in complete control. His unspoken command kept them there without ropes or chains, just her silent promise spurring her onwards and Tilly revelled in the powerful feeling it gave her despite her being the submissive one.

Blake sucked on each of her nipples, biting down on each one in turn just hard enough to drive her wild with both the pleasure and pain before he pulled her still tightly closed thighs upwards and slid his hard length up towards her wet, sweet opening, finding it easily and then delving hard within her without any resistance. They rocked together in perfect sync, Tilly relishing in the deep, tight thrusts as his long shaft rubbed her tender spot inside and Blake fucked her hard. Every thrust nearly sent Tilly crashing into her climax, but she held back, desperate to prolong the pleasure for as long as she could but it was no use, she came crashing down with her first orgasm within minutes and cried out, her body trembling beneath him as he gripped her hips and thrust even harder, bringing her another one almost instantly. Her head swam, and she welcomed his hard kisses on her tender lips again as Blake continued his relentless, pleasurable punishment and rewarded her with orgasm after sweet orgasm before finally releasing his own tension in an almighty explosion of pleasure and torment.

"Good girl," he whispered into her ear as they lay sprawled on the wood and came down from their joint highs, but this time, his taunt just made her laugh.

Just before sunrise, Blake and Tilly moved over to the sofa where he laid with her bound tightly in his strong arms, kissing her softly as they wrapped their legs around one another and lazed comfortably on the soft leather.

"You surprised me yet again Tilly," he admitted, stroking her hair out of her face. "I love having my very own bad girl in the making," he teased, making her laugh.

"Well, don't you go complaining about it. After all, we both knew whose fault it is that I'm becoming this way," she retorted, running her hand up through his curls and she pulled him closer for a deep, soft kiss.

"Do you see me complaining?" he asked, his voice a harsh whisper between kisses, and she shook her head.

The news soon reached them of Brent's untimely death. His family were distraught and while Tilly was convinced they would suspect something was awry, no-one ever said a word to either her or Blake to confirm or deny her guilty assumptions. She took the day off from Innov-ate and attended the funeral alone, feeling like a fraud the entire time, but everyone simply took her quietness as a sign of her grief. Andre had been happy to let her go, knowing just how much Brent and his family meant to her, and yet part of her had hoped that he wouldn't be able to spare her so she could have an excuse not to go.

Lucas was inconsolable, his confusion and anger affecting him so violently that he barely stayed to greet the guests or his fellow demons after the ceremony.

"He doesn't understand it," Jackson told Tilly later that evening. "Brent was his follower now. His soul should have gone to him when he died, but he is nowhere to be found."

"Purgatory perhaps?" she offered weakly, and Jackson just shrugged. He looked truly lost and alone. David was acting completely closed-off about it while Lucas was a wreck and Tilly could tell that Jackson needed some support. She wrapped her arms around him and hugged him tightly, trying to give some sincere warmth to the boy that had just lost his brother, but she still felt like a fraud, a murderer, the possibility of being caught hanging over her head every second that she was with them.

She soon felt Cate summoning her away, and assumed that she must be heading for, at the very least, a telling off for having committed such a terrible crime regardless of the order having come from Blake. She said her goodbyes and then teleported back to Hell, where Cate greeted her and hugged her tightly, kissing her cheek affectionately without a hint of anger.

"I don't know why you would think I'd be angry with you, Tilly. You did as your master commanded. No-one will ever know, and who am I to question his motives?" she told her, completely unperturbed by her murderous actions.

"But," she began, staring up into the Queen's beautiful green eyes.

"But nothing, I don't think you have any idea just how much that boy tormented Blake's thoughts, he was the last brick in his cold wall that needed to finally be knocked down and having you do it was very symbolic to him," she added, kissing her lips tenderly and Tilly immediately felt her guilt dissipate, leaving nothing but the usual warmth and love in its place.

"Thank you," she replied, smiling up at Cate through tear-blurred eyes.

"No need," the Queen replied, stroking her face affectionately. "Now, down to business. There is something I would like you to do for me Tilly," she added, her face growing serious, and Tilly immediately nodded, eager to assist her Queen with whatever she needed. Cate leaned closer, holding her gaze commandingly as she issued her with a direct and clear order, making Tilly's stomach lurch.

"I want you to say yes to Devin. Do whatever he commands of you to prove your allegiance and agree to do whatever he tasks you with in order to join the Crimson Brotherhood, but not if it involves your infidelity, of course. That is the only stipulation, otherwise anything goes. Blake will not be happy that I have asked this of you and is therefore not to know that I have issued you with this order. I will block those thoughts from him, and you will never reveal your secret mission to him. It is our little secret. You are to go to Devin while Blake is bound to Hell with the moon. I will keep him nice and busy here and then you can go and see my darling brother and come back to me with all your findings. Accept his offer no matter the cost. Is that understood?"

"Yes, your Majesty," Tilly replied, taken aback by Cate's request, but feeling the promise she had made burn into her dark soul like a wicked yet solemn vow.

CHAPTER THIRTY-THREE

Just a few days later, hundreds of demons milled around the communal hall in the dark castle, all of them various levels and speciality. For many, their presence here was a rare treat thanks to the Queen's hospitality, and she watched the crowd from the secluded box with Luna and Blake at her side. No one knew why she had decided to throw an impromptu gathering, but they were all relaxed and spirits were high as the mixed classifications mingled and chatted happily together. It still surprised Tilly that some of the lower-level beings were so at ease with their positioning in the demonic hierarchy, quite a few she had met seeming content to their place and she couldn't help but wonder if she was more ambitious than she had ever given herself credit for.

"I used up all my tries in the task hall, but in a way I'm glad I didn't get any higher," said one girl, Layne, a level six demon who smiled sweetly and pretended not to care but Tilly was sure she caught an envious glint in her eye as she chatted animatedly with the level one demon before her.

"Well, I'll try again as soon as I'm allowed to if it means I get to have his eyes on me again," a second demon girl named Maura replied, indicating with a nod in the direction of the royal area, obviously meaning Blake. Tilly's lip curled in a satisfied smirk. These girls clearly had no idea who she was, but rather than feel jealous, she revelled in their swooning glances towards her fiancé, and didn't say a word to inform them of her position. She had always known that the royal family were private when it came to their personal lives and realised now that she had perhaps taken her closeness with them for granted during the past year, forgetting that there were thousands of other demons and various other types of dark beings in this underworld too who would have given anything to get close to them.

"Oh yes! I would definitely love to have those gorgeous green eyes peering down at me again from under that sexy hood, that's the closest I've ever been to him. I heard he's seeing some ex-human girl now, though. Apparently, things were very hot at an orgy the Queen held on Earth. Fuck, I'd kill to have seen it and to have watched him in action. Another drawback of not being a level one I suppose. Where you there?" Layne asked Tilly, desperate for the gossip, and she nodded.

"Yeah, it was seriously hot," she replied, purposely keeping the two women in suspense.

"I bet I could show him a better time than any human, though, aah if only we got the chance to participate," added Maura with a dreamy sigh.

"You have to respect the bonds in an orgy," Tilly couldn't help but remind her. "That's one of the fundamental rules."

"Yeah, I know. But one look at my glorious nakedness and I'm sure he'd forget all about her," Maura replied, giggling as she fantasised about it, making Tilly finally start to feel jealous.

"Well, look who it is," came a voice from over Maura's shoulder, and Harry came sauntering through the crowd, looking relaxed and casual in his black jeans and open-buttoned shirt. The two girls' mouths dropped open in shock as he smiled over at them, introducing himself politely, while neither could seem to respond.

"Hi Harry," Tilly replied, kissing his cheek affectionately and Maura's eyes widened in shock as the realisation suddenly dawned on her.

"You're Tilly, aren't you?" she asked, and her cheeks flushed bright red as she visibly cringed at the words she had just dared to utter. Tilly nodded but did not get the chance to reply as the crowd was then silenced by Cate's unspoken command and she stood, peering down at them all lovingly, almost maternally, looking beautiful and powerful as always.

"Welcome everyone, I guess you are all wondering what you have been called here for?" she said, her voice echoing around the vast hall even though she was only speaking in her normal tone. "I have decided to give you all a free pass, an extra try in the demonic task hall in the hope that many of you may proceed higher up my ranks. So, my darling son and his council will now begin taking groups of you aside for the trials and initiations. Be patient and your time will come. Those of you that are level one demons, or are happy in your current classification, feel free to leave now," she called, her eyes sweeping over the crowd, where they lingered on Tilly for just a split-second longer than anywhere else, telling her that this was the much needed distraction for Blake that Cate had promised. He would be kept busy for weeks if not months now, giving Tilly some much needed time on Earth to join Devin's dark following and carry out Cate's strange request.

Blake managed to steal a quick moment with Tilly before she teleported back to Earth, each of them desperate to at least share a kiss before he had to go about his official business for a while.

"I'll be as quick as I can," he whispered, his hands fisting in her tangled hair as he pinned Tilly to the wall of her chambers and ravished her lips with his.

"You'd better, I don't want to have to resort to being naughty again," she teased, and then quickly backtracked when he peered down at her seriously, knowing that his mother would not stand for her breaking the rules a second time. "Just kidding," she added with a cheeky grin, reaching up to run her hands through his dark curls before kissing him softly. Blake soon felt himself being summoned away and after another quick, deep kiss, he had to leave his lover alone, where she readied herself, took a deep breath and teleported up to the penthouse. Tilly poured herself a large whisky and then quickly wrote an email to the address Cate had given her for Devin, telling him that she wanted to talk. She then downed the rest of her strong drink, clicked the send button, and then sat back, eagerly watching the screen for his reply. Within seconds he and Serena teleported into the penthouse and Tilly trembled as she bowed before them, unsure what the next few minutes would be like under their scrutiny but knowing that she would have to do whatever it took to win their trust and a place in their secret society.

She took in the beautiful couple and relished in their warm smiles, both eying her like a much desired prize. She had not met Serena before, nor hers and Devin's children, but she knew right away who she was and found herself swooning under her powerful gaze, just as she had with Devin before. For some reason the powerful couple had not attended any of the parties at the penthouse or been present during the rituals in Scotland when Cate had come to Earth to oversee Lucas' ritual, but she could tell right away that the woman before her was Serena and looked forward to getting to know her better.

Cate had explained a little more to her and Tilly knew now that the Queen's siblings had a separate life all their own up here on Earth, a dark and powerful command that they had earned over the past century along with their multi-million-pound business and their cult style following she had heard mentioned a few times over the last two years, the Crimson Brotherhood. Until their two youngest children's' seemingly recent return to Hell, Devin, Serena and their three children had all resided in their private estate nestled in the Yorkshire countryside, their home a twenty-bedroom mansion with thirty acres of land surrounding it, a lake and even a private road that lead its way from the gates where visitors had to either type in a pin or be escorted via their security guards to the premises. Their hamlet was completely secured behind those iron gates. They even had their own private security guards and systems, and their biggest adversaries, the Warriors of Light, had never once infiltrated it. Their mansion was not only their home but also the headquarters for their own special group of elite followers, some of whom were allowed to live there with them while others would only come to the huge property when it was used as a meeting ground for all their secret activity. The order had powerful dark witch and warlock guardians who worked underneath the powerful couple to recruit and give commandments to their members, always upholding their promises and empowering the order thanks to their dark deeds and willing human pawns. Cate had given Devin permission many years ago to set up and run this secret society, allowing him to bypass the usual marking and ownership methods Tilly had known in her short time in this dark world, in preference of a more refined, business-like approach to his control over the humans who craved his attention and the promised wealth and fame, and that was when the Crimson Brotherhood was formed.

The elite group of clients and followers consisted of important businessmen and women, along with politicians and celebrities, all of which owed their personal success and the success of their businesses and careers to the work of their powerful guardians and their allegiance to the secret organisation. The perks that they were afforded for selling their souls to the powerful couple were infinite, so much so that the humans involved were constantly rewarded. But, as is human nature, they were also never satisfied with the success that they had already earned, always wanting more and so they repeatedly darkened their souls in return for fame and fortune. Devin found it so very effortless to control them all, and so each of his dedicated brothers and sisters adhered to their stringent rules without question. It was all just too easy.

"It's wonderful to meet you at long last Tilly," said Serena, her American accent still clear despite her years away from her old home and practiced Briticism, hugging her affectionately before kissing her cheek. Devin kissed her too, his deep blue eyes not leaving Tilly's face as he watched her intently, only barely hiding his impatience and eagerness to know why she had reached out to them.

"Thank you for coming," she replied, indicating that they take a seat at the large sofa and the two powerful entities followed her lead. "I have had time to think about your offer Devin, and if it is still on the table, I would like to know exactly what you meant by your remark regarding me joining the Crimson Brotherhood. Blake acted impulsively and didn't give us the chance to negotiate, but after the two of us talking about it at length, he is now happy for me to do whatever it takes to free my parents from their shackles of light and has granted me permission to meet with you today to discuss our arrangement," she lied, looking into Devin's eyes as she spoke, her voice unfaltering and her intentions clear, she was willing to join them whatever the cost would be to her. Devin and Serena exchanged satisfied looks and then he leaned forward and spoke to her quietly, his grin now gone and he was all business.

"Very well, firstly I require you to relinquish Blake's mark and take mine instead, pledging your allegiance to us and our order," he said, lifting his hand up to indicate that he needed hers and she noticed that he wore a dark red ring on his finger, demonstrating that Cate had also given them permission to wear their preferred colour of red rather than just black, another sign of her affection for her family.

Tilly didn't hesitate, Cate's order was pushing her onwards, and she knew the Queen would reveal her reasons to Blake, and to Tilly, when it was time, but between now and then she would do everything that Devin asked of her, just as Cate had ordered her to. She slipped her hand in his outstretched one and leaned forward, exuding her calmness effortlessly, and Serena watched her with intrigue. She was a natural, beautiful dark goddess, just like Cate however she looked nothing like her mistress, the same as how Devin held no resemblance to her either but just as he did, Serena seemed like an alluring dark beacon, her presence here with her husband sending Tilly into a haze of dark need to fulfil their every request, to satisfy their urges by her actions and she could see just how the humans around them were easily sucked in. She had long red, coppery hair that she had left down, and it seemed to shimmer with gold tones in the sunlight that had now strewn in through the window behind her. Serena's bright blue eyes seemed warm and kind, a delightful contrast to the strong dark power that Tilly could sense flowing within in her thanks to her omnipotent heritage. She was beautiful, curvy, and altruistic, and Tilly could sense her ineffable bond with her husband as they moved in sync with one another so effortlessly.

Devin slid his hands up and down Tilly's forearm, sliding his fingertips over her skin with delicate, almost sensual strokes. He inspected her arm thoughtfully for a while, not letting her go but also not covering Blake's black cross with his own mark, either.

"It's no use," he whispered after a few minutes, looking back at Serena. "She's Blake's follower sure enough, but Cate has claimed her too, and I cannot overwrite it. Did you make a deal with her?" he asked, looking at Tilly intensely as he released her hand.

"No, but I let her mark me before I was turned into a demon. I suppose it was a deal of sorts, her protection and acceptance in exchange for me wearing her mark," she replied, suddenly worrying that they might have hit a deal-breaking snag right at the start of their negotiations.

There was a long and uncomfortable silence while Devin seemed to mull over his options. When he finally spoke, he nearly floored Tilly with his request, making her finally understand just how coveted a place in the Crimson Brotherhood was.

"So be it. Nothing can be done, and I would never go against my mistress's wishes," he said solemnly. "But, for you to become a member of our order, you are required to complete an induction task. You are required to kill my eldest son Braeden."

CHAPTER THIRTY-FOUR

Tilly stared at Devin for a minute, waiting for the punchline, but it did not come. Both he and Serena observed her reaction, serious expressions on their faces as they watched her think about their request. She opened her mouth to ask him to repeat the request, needing to hear him say it one more time, but Serena cut her off, sensing her hesitation.

"He's deadly serious Tilly, if you want our help, this is what it's gonna take. You have one week. If you succeed by then, you're in. Otherwise, we will consider this meeting as nothing more than a casual expression of your interest in our order," Serena told her. She gave Tilly a second to let it all sink in and then the two of them stood. They each shook her hand before heading out the penthouse doors without another word.

Tilly flopped back down on the sofa, her head swimming and the knot in her stomach tightening a little more. She knew Blake would never forgive her for killing his cousin, and surely Cate would not be best pleased about it either, so she called to her Dark Queen for guidance, desperate for some sign that she was doing the right thing, but she felt nothing, sensed nothing and Tilly then spent the rest of the day in complete and utter lonely turmoil.

By the next morning, Tilly had a plan. She had still had no indication from the Queen whether she had to go ahead or not so she decided to stick with Cate's original order. She would do exactly as Devin had asked of her. Tilly knew Braeden resided in the mansion at the centre of the Crimson Brotherhood headquarters with his family, and that she would not be able to get close to him without the help of an insider, so she thought of the only person she knew who was part of the order and teleported straight over to the New York penthouse. Tilly then hailed a cab and travelled over to Maximilian Dante's prestigious restaurant and made her way inside, still unsure how she might go about asking for his assistance, but she knew she had to try.

"Hello again!" Maximilian exclaimed as she greeted him, having had to charm the maître d' to gain access into the kitchens, but she had no time to waste. She grinned warmly at the commanding man, still feeling a little star-struck under his gaze, and Tilly even found herself blushing as he leaned in close and whispered in her ear. "Darkness becomes you. May I please know your name, young demon?" he asked, smiling down at her.

"Tilly, and thank you," she replied, grinning back up at the impressive human. He truly was a good-looking man for his age, his only wrinkles were laughter-lines around his eyes that were very delicate despite him being in his late fifties. Tilly wondered just how much he had done for the Crimson Brotherhood to receive his wealth, power, and fame, but part of her didn't want to know.

"Well, to what do I owe the pleasure Tilly?" he asked, taking her elbow and leading her away from the kitchen towards his private office. When they were seated at his formal desk, she finally answered him, deciding that telling the truth, although not offering him complete and total honesty, was the best approach here.

"I would very much like an invitation to the next gathering of the Crimson Brotherhood Maximilian, and I was wondering if you would be kind enough to let me come along as your guest?" she asked, watching his face turn serious as he thought it over. Maximilian was clearly a little scared at having to consider an outsider accompanying him to one of their very private affairs. It didn't matter that she was the Black Prince's fiancé. Tilly was not a member of their order and should be expected to earn an invitation, just as anyone else would have to.

"I would need to check with my guardian first. We are not allowed to bring in outsiders regardless of their position in the Queen's hierarchy. I hope you understand? And please, call me Max," he replied, looking anxious at having to try and get her a free pass.

"Perhaps I could meet with your guardian myself, express my interest and request an audience with Devin?" Tilly asked, trying to make out as though this was her initial attempt to contact the Brotherhood's powerful figurehead. Max flinched when she said Devin's name aloud, the rules seemingly the same for their omnipotent master as it was for the royals Tilly loved so dearly, despite now being allowed to say Blake's name along with his siblings, she had still never spoken Cate's name aloud, and probably never would. Tilly still had a huge amount of fear and respect for her Queen that she would never forget, and she knew never to become complacent thanks to having Blake's heart. She had an immortal existence stretched out before her and was well aware how quickly things could still change for her.

"In all honesty, I think it would be better coming from me," Max replied. "I will reach out to him and get in touch with you as soon as he gives me an answer Tilly, I'm sorry if that's not what you were hoping for but there are strict protocols in place here and I cannot risk my position in the order. I hope you appreciate that?"

"Absolutely. I would never want to jeopardise your future, Max. I will wait for your call, thank you for your help," Tilly replied, knowing that she would just have to try and be patient, but that it would be hard. After all, this initiation of sorts would be no good if it were too easy, so she said her goodbyes to the poor pawn in her game. But it had to be done, and she was sure that Max would not be in trouble for his part in assisting Tilly to complete the terrible challenge Devin had set her.

She threw herself into work over the next couple of days, checking her phone every five-minutes to check she hadn't missed Max's call and they felt like the longest two days of her life. When she finally felt the mobile phone in her pocket vibrate, Tilly could have jumped for joy and she quickly answered it, hoping to hear good things from her American assistant.

"Hi Max."

"Hey Tilly. So, I have had an answer from my guardian," he replied, making her smile widen already. "Jonah just got back to me, he's fine with you coming to the mansion on Sunday for brunch as my guest. I think he is hoping to procure you as a client, so be ready to have your ass kissed and the world handed to you on a plate," he joked, laughing gruffly, and Tilly joined in. "Would you mind coming here to collect me?" Max then asked, clearly meaning for her to teleport him to the meeting.

"Absolutely not," Tilly replied, grinning broadly. She had heard of Jonah, Devin's chief warlock, and was glad to have been given the go-ahead by someone so high up in the order. She hated she had a few more days to wait, but Sunday was the day before her week was up, and so she happily dealt with the torment of those few excruciating days. On Sunday morning Tilly lay in the huge bed of the London penthouse's master bedroom for a while, missing Blake terribly and hoping with everything she had that he would forgive her. She closed her eyes and focussed on Cate, silently calling to her and was soon filled with a strange wave of emotion that reminded Tilly of her duty, a deep sense of her powerful mistress from her dark flame within and she knew she was doing the right thing. Tilly gave herself just a few minutes of basking in her strong sense of purpose and resolve before dressing in a figure-hugging black dress and super high stiletto's and then finally making her way over to New York to collect her date.

Max waited at the penthouse for her, dressed in a perfect and crisp black tuxedo, and he looked fantastic. Considering they were going for an 'informal brunch' they both looked sophisticated and elegant, every inch the high society socialites Tilly would always have associated with members of a powerful secret society.

"We have to teleport into the nearby village and Jonah will collect us from there," Max told her, taking Tilly's hand in preparation for the long-distance commute to the small village, his face still anxious but she chose to ignore it. After all, this is what Devin had asked of her, so surely he would have anticipated her presence in their compound?

They arrived in the village in seconds, and Tilly could sense the ancient power there immediately. They waited for just a few minutes and then an elegant black vintage sports car stopped at the curb and out stepped a young, handsome, cocky-looking warlock with dark hair and almost black eyes. Max bowed before him respectfully, and Tilly put out her hand to him, knowing that as a level one demon she out-ranked even the highest-ranking warlocks.

"It's a pleasure to meet you, Jonah. My name is Tilly," she told him, smiling as he placed a soft kiss on the back of her hand.

"The pleasure is all mine," he replied, running his thumb over her engagement ring with a knowing smile, and she couldn't help but wonder if Jonah knew all about her macabre task. The three of them then climbed in the sleek car and Jonah sped towards the compound, swerving around the winding country roads effortlessly, making Tilly laugh while Max couldn't help but gasp and tense up in the back seat. Within minutes, they were inside the protective gates that surrounded Devin and Serena's home and they pulled up outside a massive old brick mansion. It was truly impressive and the buildings all around it were just as commanding, their little hamlet seeming almost like a tiny town, bustling with staff and members of the Brotherhood, who had already arrived. Tilly took it all in, noticing the relaxed colour scheme again thanks to the dark red flags and awnings that were all around them as they made their way inside the large mansion.

Tilly remained on her best behaviour the entire brunch, staying by Max's side and chatting with the many men and women of the order who delighted in having her ear for a few minutes, her reputation as both the Black Prince's fiancé and the first demon to have been sired by one of the royal family having seemingly turned her into a celebrity of sorts herself, and Tilly could tell that many of them were foolishly hoping that they might be allowed to compete for their own demonic power too someday. Devin and Serena greeted her warmly when Jonah introduced them, the omnipotent pair pretending never to have met her before and they introduced the only one of their children to still reside on Earth, Braeden. He remained quiet and almost surly as he met his cousin's intended wife, taking himself off to his chambers later that afternoon, seemingly bored of the formality of the brunch.

Tilly knew that the best chance she had to complete her task was now, while Braeden would be alone and all the other members of the order would be together in the main reception rooms of the gigantic house for a while. She made her excuses to Max, charming him to believe she had gone to chat with some of the other women for a little while so that he had no need to look for her, and then made her way down the long halls and up the narrow service stairway, following Braeden's dark shadow silently as he made his way to what she assumed must be his room. He disappeared inside and she slipped silently towards the doorway, finding it open and she then watched for a few seconds as he slid off his black jacket and sat down on his armchair, picking up a large book, which he began flicking through the pages of thoughtfully. Silent and stealthily Tilly made her way over to him and stood for a moment, looking over his shoulder at the book in his hands. He was reading an old Satanist's bible, the version that spoke of Lucifer as Hell's ruler rather than Cate and she hesitated for just a moment, wondering why he might be reading it, and if it was perhaps the reason, his parents wanted him taking care of. Tilly then leaned forward and grabbed his neck with her strong hands, choking him with a tight and relentless grip that soon caused his breath to slow and his body to start becoming limp, she twisted, eager to hear and feel his neck when it snapped beneath her grasp which would signify her success, but he had other ideas. Braeden played the victim well and gave her exactly one more second before he turned and pounced, his fists winding Tilly instantly as they collided with her chest, throwing her across the room towards the wall. She fought back, aiming for his chest now too in the hope of ripping his heart from it like she had done before, but he was quick and fast, and so Tilly soon changed tactic. She raised her hands in defeat, kneeling before him in an apologetic stance while Braeden stood over her, panting and rubbing at his sore neck with his hand. His blonde hair looked dark in the dim light, stray strands of it falling across his face alongside the shadows, but Tilly could see that he was seething, furious at her for having attacked him. Braeden watched her for a second, seemingly trying to understand her motives and so, rather than retaliate, he went straight for the softer tactic, clearly planning on questioning her instead of subduing Tilly first.

"You will rot in my father's worst torture dungeon for this insolence, demon," he told her, grabbing Tilly's arm forcibly and pulling her towards the door. But she had other ideas. With a fast, strong grip, she then turned and thrust Braeden towards the wall, pinning him to it as she dug her fingernails into the skin of his back, at the exact point over his heart, and pushed.

Braeden squirmed, only forcing her fingers deeper into his flesh and he couldn't help but cry out, the pain finally affecting the Queen's dark nephew in the way Tilly knew she needed it to. She dug a tiny bit deeper into him, eventually feeling his bone under her fingertips and knew that she had to proceed. She had to do what was required of her. Tilly wrestled with her conscience in that moment, though, because deep down she knew it was not the right thing to do. In her second instant of brief hesitation, Braeden acted, slipping sideways before turning and grabbing her and pinning Tilly to the wall in a complete reversal of their positions. Their bodies pressed against each other's, the two of them face-to-face, just centimetres apart. Braeden wrapped his hands around her neck, reminding Tilly of her powerful lover for a moment, and she couldn't help but grin.

"Looks like I didn't make the cut then," she whispered, her voice hoarse thanks to his strong grip on her and he couldn't help but smile broadly at her in response, a smile Tilly immediately took for some kind of sick satisfaction at having bested her. But then Braeden found himself staring at her lips intently, a look that worried her more than the sinister glare he had given her just a few seconds before.

"Where did you come from Tilly?" he asked, his body still pressed into hers but the grip on her throat loosening ever so slightly so that he could question her, but she didn't know how to answer him, thinking that it was obvious she was from Hell. "There is something in you, something I have never come across before. Perhaps it is simply Blake's blood in your veins, but I want whatever it is. Perhaps my father will let me keep you after all?" he pondered aloud, making Tilly feel sick but also slightly flattered at the same time.

"Why don't you give me a kiss and then we'll see what your cousin does to you for your advances?" she replied, sending Braeden a mental projection of the gory scene with Trey in his flat. He smiled, a wicked and sick grin that turned her stomach.

"Well, in that case, I suppose I should just congratulate you instead," he said, stepping back and releasing Tilly from his grip before putting out his hand for her to shake. "Matilda Mayfair, welcome to the Crimson Brotherhood."

"What?" Tilly cried, shaking her head in confusion at Braeden's words and he laughed, dropping his hand and wandering over to the armchair again where he straightened his clothes and sat down, indicating for her to join him in the opposite chair with his hand. She walked hesitantly over to him and sat down, watching him carefully in case this was a trick.

"You passed my father's acceptance test Tilly, well done. And, might I add, you did better than anyone else has ever managed. The test was just to see whether you would be willing to try and kill me, most humans only make it to my doorway, which is still a sign of their willingness to at least have a go at taking me on, while other demons will usually come on in and attempt a showdown. You, on the other hand, you truly are something else, aren't you?" he asked, staring at her again with handsome blue eyes that she couldn't help but stare back into, his blonde hair messy and dishevelled after their tussle.

"Am I?" Tilly asked, too shocked to say more.

"Yes, not only did you give it a good go, but you actually almost got me! Thanks to the Dark Queen that you hesitated Tilly, I can still feel those sharp nails of yours in my spine. No wonder you are so renowned for your skills in the demonic tasks, Blake is a very lucky man."

"Man?" she replied, mimicking her lover, and Braeden laughed, shrugging as though he had no idea what else to call his powerful cousin.

"So, how about we get down to business then?" he asked, and Tilly nodded, eager to hear what help they might be willing to offer her. "Your parents are commanded by their magical guardian, similar to our infrastructure, and we would first need to turn him for his hold over them to darken enough for us to charm them, after which they will be all yours to mark and own. The problem we have is that their guardian is a warlock named Mike, and he just so happens to be Alma's son, and Dylan's brother. We cannot kill him Tilly, turning him is the only option, and the only way to do it is for an incredibly powerful and provoking demon to seduce him," he told her, raising his eyebrow when he said the last few words of his sentence.

"What is it with you guys? Everything always boils down to sex, filthy the lot of you," Tilly joked, shaking her head.

"Why not? We are but slaves to our darkness Tilly, creatures of instinct, desire and need." Braeden replied, staring at her red lips again.

"Well, I intend to seduce with my words, not my body," she replied curtly, her expression fierce and intent.

"Okay, we will just have to see then. For now, though, I will draw up some plans and we can go over them next week again at brunch. You may go back to your friend now Tilly, I look forward to seeing you again next time," he added, looking down at his books again and she stood and turned to leave, but came face-to-face with Devin and Serena again. Before she could say a word, they both reached out and covered her eyes and forehead with their hands. A powerful wave went right through Tilly, making her feel woozy for a second before they let go. The omnipotent couple smiled widely at her once they released her from their grip, and Tilly stared back at them in shock.

"What was that?" she asked, sitting back down on the sofa and staring at the two of them as they joined their eldest son on the couch opposite her. Serena couldn't help but rub Braeden's back, her motherly instincts kicking in as she soothed the still-sore spot where Tilly's fingernails had pierced his skin.

"You did incredibly well Tilly, well done," Devin told her, smiling warmly and she could feel herself swooning slightly again, and immediately stopped it.

"We just cloaked you from Cate's reach for a moment so that we could talk in private, she won't know we have had this conversation, nor will she even be aware that we have hid you from her, so don't be worried," Serena added, but Tilly couldn't help but be petrified at the sheer thought of them having a conversation out of her mistress's vast reach.

"Well, I have to admit I'm not entirely comfortable with it, but if you believe it's necessary, then let's get this over with," Tilly replied, and the three of them smirked.

"Such a clever little thing, isn't she?" Braeden whispered, and Serena nudged him, shaking her head with a very serious look, a look that told him to stop flirting with his cousin's fiancé. It was also a look that made Tilly feel ten-times better as it told her that Blake's aunt and uncle were also mindful that she was off-limits in that department.

"I shall get right to the point then," cut in Devin, leaning forward and placing his elbows on his knees. "And you won't have to worry about feeling uncomfortable about this conversation, because as soon as it is over you won't remember a single moment of it, nor will you ever be allowed to tell another soul what was said here, not even my mistress."

CHAPTER THIRTY-FIVE

The next day after her shift at Innov-ate Tilly felt herself being summoned back to Hell by the Queen. She immediately teleported to the beacon's source in the royal chambers, finding herself in one of the smaller, more private annex rooms in Cate's vast tunnel of chambers. She bowed to her mistress, happy to see her and eager to hear her verdict on Tilly's achievement in getting into the Crimson Brotherhood.

"You may rise Tilly," Cate told her, kissing her cheek affectionately as she did and stepping back to take a good look at her. "You bear the mark of your association with the Brotherhood already, but thanks to our previous agreement and Blake's mark, you still truly belong here with us. I hoped that would be the case," she said, smiling knowingly and Tilly was glad, grateful that her dark allegiance had already been won by her lover and her mistress before Devin had even come along so could not be taken over by her new membership to his secret order.

"Well, I was worried for a minute there," she admitted, and Cate just grinned over at her and led Tilly to a small desk where they each sat on opposite sides of the dark wood.

"I always have your back Tilly, I think sometimes you forget just how much, but I cannot blame you for not being able to fathom just how far my reach goes," she replied. "So, have you had any indication on what they wanted from you?"

"No, I think it has something to do with my parents' guardian, he's Dylan's brother, Mike," Tilly told her, thinking how carefully they would need to tread with their plans for him. "Braeden is going to give me the information on Sunday."

"Yes, we do need to be careful here, and you must not say a word to Alma or Dylan until I permit you to Tilly," she ordered, and she knew it was not a request. "Are you sure they didn't ask you for anything else? Surely they want something from you in return for your family's freedom?" Cate pondered aloud, staring across at Tilly, reading her memories and mulling it over thoughtfully. She stayed quiet, letting Cate read her, and she opened her mind as much as possible, thinking back to her conversation with Braeden before how she then returned straight to the brunch where she and Max had chatted away with some of the other members of the Crimson Brotherhood for a while. She had met some of their other guardians and upper-level followers there too, one was a woman a few years older than Tilly who had clearly been through a terrible time with her husband, but she seemed strong-willed and ready for any challenges the world threw at her and Tilly had endeavoured to help her as much as she could, having clicked with her instantly.

In less than a second, the world around Tilly then seemed to slow down. Every second felt like ten as she watched her beloved Queen's entire demeanour change from her usual warm and loving manner to a cold and terrifying version of herself. With eyes as black as night, she flung the desk aside and stormed towards Tilly, her beautiful face mashed into an almost unrecognisable guise. Cate grabbed her face and peered into her eyes intensely, forcing her submission and fear to come pouring out of her. She opened her mouth to try and speak but couldn't find the words, her voice and breath completely escaping her.

"There's something you are not telling me Tilly," Cate said, her voice deep and growling, full of evil and malice. "I command you tell me," she boomed, letting go of her face as the Queen's powerful outburst sent Tilly flying back in her chair and she toppled to the ground. Cate then stood over the trembling demon and straddled her, staring into her very soul as she tried to get around the enchanted walls Devin and Serena had placed around her memory of the conversation in the mansion. Tilly tried desperately to think back, so sure she wasn't hiding a thing from her powerful mistress. If she could have remembered anything else, she would have told her every last detail, desperate to have the Cate she knew and loved back again, but that, it seemed, was exactly the reason why Tilly couldn't remember Devin and Serena's presence there in Braeden's chambers or their orders, they knew she would be too weak to resist her Queen all by herself.

"I'm not hiding anything, you have to believe me," Tilly cried, tears rushing down her temples.

"Tell me!" Cate bellowed, the sound of her deep, ominous voice echoing off the walls around them as well as inside Tilly's head as she racked her brains to try and answer her. She wanted to remember, wanted to answer, but her mind was just completely blank.

"I can't, I'm so sorry. I just, I don't even know what you want from me. Please Cate!" she begged, her head pounding, and her stomach dropped as she realised she had dared to say the almighty Queen's name. The mistake rolled off her mistress though, her only desire now was to break down the walls inside Tilly's mind and so instead of punishing her for the usually death-warranted lapse in courteousness Cate just smiled at her, reaching down to stroke her cheek in what would normally be an affectionate way, but now it was menacing, disturbing and evil.

"In that case, my darling, it looks like I will have to force it out of you. I'm sure you can understand?" she asked, no hint of regret on her shrouded face. "Now, I want you to be a good girl and take it like I know you can, like I know Blake will be proud of you for. I will even do you the courtesy of asking for your permission to get inside your head and break down your memories Tilly, say yes and I will make it as quick and painless as possible for you, fight and it will be one hundred times worse," Cate promised, and Tilly knew that there was never going to be any other option anyway, she could never fight her formidable mistress. Tilly peered up at her Dark Queen, who still straddled her on the floor of the now devastated small room and a desperate sob escaped her lips uncontrollably. For some reason, the first thing she thought about was her commitment to her boss, Andre, up on Earth and how she couldn't explain leaving unannounced again, and Cate rolled her still blackened eyes.

"He will believe he's sent you to New York on a short-term placement with Maximilian Dante. You will not be missed, and you will not have to explain yourself when you return," Cate told her, growing impatient. Tilly nodded, but before she could respond, she thought of Blake, how she was desperate to see him, to kiss him. But a slight shake of Cate's head answered that silent plea without any need for her to explain. She thought of him down in the dark hall, working hard and completely unaware of what was happening above him, but she knew he needed her to be strong, that their future together depended on his mother's love of her and as soon as that realisation hit, Tilly needed to think of nothing else to ready herself for what was to come.

"Yes, do it," she told her Queen, ready to take her beatings. Her trust was worth the pain and Blake was certainly worth all the agony and torment Tilly could possibly endure. Cate grinned and nodded.

"Right answer," she replied.

In less than a second Cate had transported the two of them downwards, further down into the depths of the dark castle than Tilly had ever been before, and then they finally stopped in a pitch-black, stifling hot dungeon. Cate climbed off her and helped Tilly to stand, peering down at her with still jet-black eyes and a cold, emotionless stare. She hoped that her Queen's rage at her sibling's secrecy was the only thing making her look at her this way, she had never wanted to go against Cate, nor would she ever have been willing to hide anything from her and she sent her such thoughts as she peered back at her, pleading and desperately trying to open herself up to her Mistress's probing power.

Quick as a flash, Cate then grabbed Tilly and held her close, embracing her tightly for a few minutes and they both sobbed, even the usually so steady Queen let out a tear, and Tilly knew then that it was hard for her too.

"You will be rewarded when this is all over. I promise you now that you and Blake will be married immediately as your recompense for your service and unwavering loyalty to me. I cannot go any longer without calling you my daughter. I love you as my own Tilly and I am truly sorry for what I have got to put you through now," she whispered, kissing her cheek again before stepping back.

As Cate continued her slow retreat, Tilly soon found that she could barely see her in the darkness anymore. Her eyes had gone back to being the shade of green Tilly loved so very much and soon they were the only things she could see in the overwhelming blackness that now surrounded Cate. Tilly heard a loud 'click' of Cate's fingers from a few feet away and then she immediately fell to her knees, overwhelmed by a tormenting, consuming pain that reverberated throughout her entire being. She screamed loudly, her body writhing in agony as she fought to resist the pain, her natural instinct to fight back kicking in but she forced herself to stop, knowing that resisting would only make it harder on herself, that the pain would last longer if she battled against it. For now, she knew she had to endure, and Tilly was grateful for having been through the final demonic task because it had given her a welcome bit of practice in doing so.

Cate watched for hours, wincing as the girl that had become so loved and respected thanks to having won the heart of her son let out a blood-curdling scream and then eventually fell unconscious, the pain finally having taken its toll on her and it had claimed her body, for now. She truly hated every moment of this torture. This was not a satisfying or deserved pain and although Cate knew it had to be done, she had to summon extra dark power to strengthen herself in order to see it through. As she lay back on the cold floor, Tilly's limp body rose a few feet as though she were levitating and then the sound of bones breaking found its way into her dreamlike state, jolting Tilly awake as the final splintering of her spine almost snapped her in two while invisible hands pulled and twisted her body against every natural curve.

Tilly drifted in and out of consciousness, crying out and begging her Queen to stop each time she was lucid, and the painful turmoil overwhelmed her again. Cate didn't listen, and her torture did not lessen. She kept Tilly locked away for over a week of relentless torture before she finally felt the dark spell Devin and Serena had cast on her waning from deep within her psyche. The demon cried out incoherently as she was then whipped and beaten by hooded figures while Cate watched on, her mind focussing completely on Tilly's vulnerable barriers. Eventually she began to feel them shatter under the weight of her heavy burden, and falter thanks to the omnipotent woman's command of the death that had begun creeping into the poor girl's body and soul. Pain was the only way, Cate had learned that lesson long ago when she had spent those years in these dungeons herself and although she knew it was working, that it would be over soon, she couldn't help but be furious with her siblings for trying to keep secrets from her.

Cate eventually felt a change in Tilly. Her mind emptying as though her immortal existence teetered on a knife's edge and death was ready to take her. Only then did the omnipotent Dark Queen feel the spell Devin had seemingly cast begin to dissipate from within. Cate raised her hand, signalling for her macabre helpers to stop, and she then dismissed them before stepping closer and looking down at the broken demon before her. Tilly's mouth began to move over strange sounds, ancient and powerful words that Cate had never heard with her own ears before, but thanks to her almighty omnipotence, she could understand every word of the divine language. Cate had only ever heard this dialect through the memories Lucifer had been forced to share with her when she took the throne. Enochian words hadn't been uttered in centuries, but the ancient words were still clear as Tilly uttered the pleas. Her dark power was calling out to her directly from within Tilly's soul, begging its powerful Queen not to let it die within its demonic host. This primeval power spoke to her in a deep, harsh tone that let Cate know the time of action really had come.

"Galvah," Tilly then said in a deep voice that once again was not her own, peering up at Cate blankly. The force within spoke directly to Cate and called its mistress, 'Galvah,' the fourth divine supreme being alongside the holy trinity. That one strange, small word surprised but also enraptured Cate because it meant that the dark power which both commanded and served her considered her to be worthy of divine supremacy she had only dared to dream she held before. The ancient power spoke again, Tilly's mouth moving over the angelic language, acting as its conduit, and Cate understood every word. "Mother. This demon will perish in this inferno. She will die thanks to the faith and obedience she has placed in you. Go no further or else answer for your sins."

"I understand. I would never let her die. I will never abuse the trust and loyalty of my demons. You know my agenda and the time has come to set her free from the magical restrictions Devin placed inside her mind. Send Tilly back to me, I am done punishing her," Cate replied, speaking directly to the powerful source of dark force within Tilly, and she nodded.

"So mote it be," it said, her head dropping down so that her chin bobbed against her chest for a few seconds before Tilly began shuddering for a few seconds until rousing again.

"Tell me the truth," Cate ordered, and Tilly looked up at her pleadingly, managing to just about stay conscious, but her mind was racing thanks to her confusion and fear. She was still kneeling before her Queen, broken and a huge part of her was just desperate for death now, not caring for anything or anyone that might want her to remain in this tumultuous existence for she was now so broken she could never imagine this eternal life ever meaning anything to her again. Cate could read every one of these thoughts, hating them with a vengeance, but she pressed on, knowing that she was nearly ready to give her the answers she needed. Tilly coughed and sputtered, desperately trying to gather some more of her dark power to heal herself, but Cate stopped it from returning to her somehow, calling all of it into her omnipotent form temporarily instead. Thick, dark blood then spewed from Tilly's throat as her body still tried to resist Cate's command, desperately attempting not to say the words as her inner orders fought one another in a riotous battle.

"No!" Tilly cried, choking on her last attempt to resist Cate's request.

"What are they hiding from me Tilly, what do they want you to do?" Cate then bellowed, and Tilly finally spoke her answer, free from the magical binds within.

"They want Lucifer," she finally managed to reply through the blood-garbled coughs. "They want me to find out where he is and find a way to free him," Tilly added, blurting out the words with her mouth full of blood, her teeth and face covered in it. The answer to her torturous questioning brought the all-powerful Dark Queen to her knees.

"Why, do they want him to have his throne back?" Cate whispered, her voice panicked, and her body curled into a protective ball as she kneeled beside Tilly. She felt weakened, sickened by the words, and her body trembled uncontrollably. Their strange motives made Cate feel just like the young, naïve woman she had been so very long ago whom had suffered at her master's hands, the once tortured and broken soul by him and his dark designs, and she hated it.

Tilly's mind suddenly sprang open, the memory of her time in that chamber with Devin, Serena and Braeden coming back to her with a thud. She recalled their words to her, how they wanted to find out where Cate had imprisoned Lucifer, or if he were even still alive. They had tried asking her so very many times and their omnipotent mistress had vehemently refused, having finally told Devin to leave the matter forever years ago. Tilly now remembered sitting across from them, confused as to why they wanted access to the tyrannical dictator that Cate had done them all a favour by removing from his throne and their lives. Tilly too had asked them why they wanted him, inquired as to what their reasons were, and she relayed Devin's answer to her Queen now while the pain and torment within still raged like two monsters in a sea of guilt, fear, and love.

"No, it's because Devin wants to steal Lucifer's angelic essence from him. He wants to become an all-powerful King of Earth. He wants to rule the humans, but he needs to become a being of half-darkness and half-light to do it. He knew what Lottie was capable of if she had only pursued that power, but now he wants it for himself, he wants his own throne." Tilly replied, still coughing and trembling uncontrollably. "You took Lucifer's darkness from him. Devin just wants what you left behind. He wants your master to die at his hands once and for all," she added before she choked on her own blood and fell to her knees, gasping for breath, but she was glad that the terrible truth had come out at last.

The realisation dawned on Cate in an instant, and she finally connected the dots. The powerful Queen stopped her frenzied thoughts. So, this was why Devin had been so secretive. He had been surrounding himself for years with willing followers who had lightness inside of them, secretly coveting that light power and harnessing it for himself. That was how he and Serena had cloaked Tilly's memory. They had somehow learned how to use that light power for their own means, and now he wanted more.

"That's why he wanted you to join them as well Tilly, you're the first demon with light inside of you. A much desired prize for the Crimson Brotherhood," she whispered, stroking the broken demon's face gently.

"Me?" Tilly managed to ask, completely lost and struggling to stay lucid.

"Yes, I'm surprised you weren't told about your heritage, but I guess no one else has figured out that the special little spark inside of you but me and my siblings. Blake and Luna both sense it, but they are so far removed from the light power they have no idea what it was that they were drawn to inside of you. You are the descendant of a very powerful warlock, and his mother was once the high priestess of Heaven. Mike is your parent's guardian in the Warriors of Light, and why he chose them as his followers. He is your great-grandfather Tilly," she finished, her words flowing through the scared demon like a wave of fire. Cate then leaned down and kissed Tilly's lips, healing her wounds instantly, but her mind and soul were still weak and would remain so for a while thanks to her tremendous beatings. Cate let her go and then Tilly fell back and laid her head back on the blood-stained floor, desperately trying to make sense of it all and wondering what the next step would be in her dark mistress's plan, but she just sat silently beside her, completely lost in her own frenzied thoughts for a while.

Cate eventually teleported the two of them back to her private chambers without another word, carrying Tilly in her arms, her face solemn as she pieced together the possibilities for Lucifer's ultimate, final death with the help of her siblings, even if that meant giving Devin the earthly throne he desired so forcefully.

"Maybe," she wondered aloud, laying Tilly down on the bed to rest before taking a seat in the huge armchair by her side while she mulled over every possible plan and its outcome, twiddling the locket housing her master's broken form between her fingers as she contemplated her freedom from Lucifer at long last. "Yes, maybe," she whispered to herself, still lost in her thoughts, a sinister smile creeping into her beautiful red lips as her soon-to-be daughter-in-law slept soundly beside her.

Down in the initiation hall, Blake just could not shake the deep-seated feeling of dread he had inside. He knew it was affecting his concentration, but his second in command, Azazel, read his distant body language and took the lead with many of the challenges without ever needing to be asked. Eventually Blake could take it no longer and he called for a quick recess, teleporting up to his chambers and summoning Tilly to his side, but she didn't come. He suddenly felt very fraught when he quickly realised that he could not properly sense his fiancé either in this realm or the one above. Looking around at his empty room, Blake felt lost and afraid, fearing the worst. He then felt the pull of his mother's summoning and followed her beacon immediately, teleporting to her side in the small chamber behind her bedroom.

"What the fuck happened to her?" Blake asked, seeing Tilly lying unconscious in the bed. He ran to her, gripping her hand in his, and he could immediately sense the death that was trying to take her away again, this time seemingly stronger than the last. "Who did this?" he begged, staring up at his still silent mother and she could read that his mind was all over the place. Blake was ready to strike down whoever had hurt his lover so violently. His vengeance knew no bounds, but Cate knew that the time had come for her to finally be honest about her oppressive methods to withdraw information from his fiancé's mind.

"I did this. I almost killed her because I needed some information that was hidden inside her consciousness. Tilly gave me permission to find it. She knew what I was going to do, and she still said yes. She will recover, and I made her a deal for when she does. You two have my blessing to be married as soon as you want to be," Cate told him, trying to appease her own guilt and the fraught emotions she felt resonating from deep within her son. She read him, knowing that he was glad to have permission to make Tilly his wife, but Cate also hated the spiteful thoughts Blake didn't even try to hide from her. It was the first time in her entire reign as Queen that he had thought of her this way, that he had second-guessed her actions and while she wanted nothing more than to beg his forgiveness, Cate simply teleported away before Blake could articulate any of the terrible things he so desperately wanted to. She needed her husband's arms to hold her and his wise words to help her deal with the information Tilly had given her and to help her make the choice between killing Devin for his treachery or giving him what he wanted. Cate had kept Lucifer locked away for all this time in the hope that he would repent or at least relinquish his hatred for her and the new family she had given him, but he was so consumed by his evil hatred that she knew that there would never come a time or a place in which her children would be safe from him. Lucifer could never be a part of their new life, but she had never been strong enough to finish him off herself. She had kept him alive, albeit left alone and unloved in his prison, because somewhere, somehow, there was still a part of her that loved him and to end his existence would be to end part of herself and Cate just couldn't bring herself to do it.

No matter what, Cate knew now that this would have to end at last and the matter would finally have to be put to rest. Either way Lucifer would have to die, whether at her hands or Devin's, there was no other choice. She just had to figure out how best to go about it and whether Devin was worthy enough to receive the gift of his ancient angelic essence when Lucifer was vanquished at long last.

The end.

Destined for Darkness

Book #4 in the Black Rose series

By
LM Morgan

2021 Revised Edition

PROLOGUE

The Dark Queen of Hell, its ruler and mistress, Cate Rose sat beside the bed and watched her soon to be daughter-in-law sleeping so soundly it was as though the young demon were truly in a deep, peaceful slumber, but Cate knew she was far from it. Tilly had just endured weeks of suffering and torture at her Queen's hands in order to break down the magical walls put inside her head by Cate's trusted ex, Devin Black. When the poor girl had caved, her resolve and ability to resist Cate's powerful command crumbled along with Tilly's body and mind. Nevertheless, it had been worth it. The information carefully hidden away in the recesses of Tilly's mind had honestly shaken the usually so calm and collected Dark Queen to her core.

Devin wanted their master's primeval angelic essence for himself, he wanted to take it and end Lucifer's dark life once and for all, becoming a powerful being of half-light and half-darkness in order to take full control of Earth as its leader and King.

Part of her wanted to grant him this power. The wars were over and balance had been restored at last. Devin had earned his place atop a throne of his own after the years of servitude to his sibling's reign, while overseeing the cunning and clever secret society of humans called the Crimson Brotherhood on Earth. The order had been set up as a way to claim human souls in preparation for an afterlife of service in the depths of Hell, but it had now grown beyond their expectations. The order had become both a lucrative business and a source of control over the humans inducted into the cleverly constructed web of secrecy, intrigue, acumen and deliverance. The guardians of the dark cult took their orders from Devin and Serena Black, heads of both Black Rose industries and the Crimson Brotherhood, and siblings of sorts to the Dark Queen. Their guardians were powerful, clever and utilised any means at their disposal to procure souls. The cunning masters would make deals with their human underlings and deliver on their incredible promises over time in order to keep to their end of the bargain. When their time was up, their guardian would either demand dark favours from the pitiful humans, offering them more time before descending for their lengthy enslavement, or hunting them down and carrying out the retrieval of the promised prize when their contract was null. With each soul added to their list, the Black family's omnipotent power grew, as did the Dark Queen's, so there was no denying that they had worked hard to add as many new clients to their order as possible and deserved to be rewarded.

Thinking back over the last few years reminded Cate just how many changes Devin and Serena, along with their children, had been forced to make in order to adhere to hers and Lottie's new balanced reign. The powerful couple had made many sacrifices along the way and as Cate watched Tilly sleep, the past replayed in her mind, haunting her as she pondered how best to proceed with her sibling's request.

CHAPTER ONE

Five years earlier - Earth

"Why did I wear these bloody shoes?" Melody asked herself for the hundredth time as she rode the packed tube train heading for home on a busy Friday afternoon in London, England. As the train then pulled to a stop she followed the swarm of people out onto the platform heading for the welcome, 'way out', above, but then her heel got stuck on a jagged rock, halting her progress and sending Melody plummeting to the ground, where the people around her soon turned into bumbling idiots, clambering around her in an attempt to free themselves from her foolish form rather than actually help. She quickly felt herself starting to panic, tears stinging at her eyes as she tugged at her heel and tried to stand.

Strong arms then appeared through the swarm, grabbing her elbows from behind and pulling her up to stand before sliding her effortlessly through the crowd towards an empty spot near the billboards. When she finally got a look at her surprise, protective saviour, Melody couldn't help the spark that instantly ignited inside of her. He was spectacularly gorgeous. Tall, slim and blonde with just a hint of red running through his short, stylishly coiffed hair and with the deepest blue eyes she had ever seen.

"Thank you so much," she managed to say, feeling herself blush beneath his intense stare, and he smiled back at her with a sheepish grin.

"No problem, how could I not help a damsel in distress?" he answered, joking with her as though he somehow knew she might need some help to stop the tears that still pricked at her eyes. "Are you okay?"

'I am now,' Melody thought, forgetting all about her sore ankle, but just nodded and smiled weakly back at the model-like man who still held her close, still protecting her despite the crowd being long gone. "Do you have another train to catch?" he then asked, an almost shy smile on his lips now too and she shook her head, still finding it hard to speak thanks to her stunning rescuer and he smiled. "Good, then how about we get a coffee so I can make sure you're okay? And maybe I can finally get more than four words out of you," he said, taking Melody's hand in his and guiding her up the stairs towards the exit, walking slowly and carefully to make sure she wasn't putting too much strain on her sore foot.

Melody watched the man as he guided her, unsure just why he was taking such an interest in her, but she let herself enjoy the attention. She was not a shy girl but had never been overly confident with men either, only ever having had a few semi-serious boyfriends in the past, all of whom had had to make the first move as she was far too reclusive to go out meeting new people and picking up men in bars like her friends would do most weekends.

As they walked, she enjoyed the closeness that had seemingly happened between them both so effortlessly and natural. Holding onto his strong arm brought her both comfort and a sort of giddiness that she mentally wanted to kick her own arse for. They soon made it to the top of the stairs and took the few tentative steps towards the coffee stall, Melody taking a seat while her gorgeous saviour ordered them two cappuccinos, guessing what she might like without him even needing to ask.

"So," he said as he brought the two frothy drinks over and pushed one towards her. "My name is Corey, pleased to meet you," he added, smiling sexily across at her as she grabbed a sugar sachet and stirred its contents into her drink.

"Melody," she replied.

"That's a beautiful name," he whispered, ignoring her blushing cheeks. "I honestly don't go around picking up damsels in distress, by the way. I'm usually the 'friend-zone' kinda guy in all honesty," Corey added, making her laugh.

"We can be friends if you want?" Melody offered, grinning broadly, and while she somehow knew that neither of them seemed to want that, she couldn't help testing him.

"No way," he replied immediately, only resorting in making her blush even harder. The pair of them then chatted for over an hour, discussing everything, from their favourite movies and music to laughing at just how much they had in common, and their relationship soon cemented even more. When she really did have to head off and catch her train home, Melody struggled with saying goodbye. Their connection had been incredible, and she wasn't quite ready for it to end just yet. Corey seemed to be feeling the same way and sensed her hesitation, smiling across at her.

"I guess this is goodbye," she groaned, looking down at her hands.

"For now, maybe, but I won't let you go that easily. Here, why don't you give me a call and we can meet up for dinner next week?" Corey said, pulling a business card from his pocket and sliding it over to her on the table. Melody grinned and grabbed it, the crisp, thick card and its sharp edges feeling somehow heavy in her hand, and she looked down. The card was dark grey, embossed with just two words in thick black lettering, 'Corey

Black', with his telephone number underneath. This was not a cheap, stock-bought business card that she was used to getting handed by the many businessmen and women she encountered in her role as one of Lord David Pembroke's aides. She had been an assistant to the multi-millionaire for many years now, having learned the full workings of his intricate and very private business life over that time and she was now well versed in his methods and dealings with business partners, earning herself a very respectable wage and some wonderful experience of the hectic industrial world in the process.

"Sure, I'll ring you over the weekend," she promised, checking her watch and standing from the table, aware that she was running out of time. As she tested her ankle, finding the joint almost fully healed, Corey joined her and leaned in close, laying a soft kiss on her cheek. He did not even give her the chance to overthink his closeness, the smell of him and the feel of his lips on her face that burned red beneath them, or the way that his kiss sent butterflies scattering through her abdomen. She swooned, leaning into his strong arms uncontrollably and he held her even closer, just for a moment, before leaning down to whisper into her ear.

"I will look forward to hearing from you, Melody," he said, his voice a hoarse groan. "You'd better ring me," he added before pulling back and stepping away, his hand sliding down her arm to take her hand in his. He gave it a quick squeeze, lingering for just a second longer before forcing himself away. Melody exhaled loudly as she watched him leave, smiling to herself and then having to force her legs to turn and walk in the other direction.

She made her way to the platform and boarded her train for Colchester just in time. The historic Roman town less than an hour away from the capital was her regular weekend respite from the city at her family's home there, and she couldn't wait to get back and tell her sister all about the wonderful Corey Black.

Melody spent her weeknights in London where she stayed in either a small flat or hotel room that was paid for and provided by her gracious boss and corporate tycoon, Lord David Pembroke. He was a kind, giving man despite his incredible prowess in the business world, but he had strict rules regarding his private life and whereabouts, so regularly moved offices, and with that his aides were required to move around the city with him too. Melody would make her way to London Liverpool street train station every Monday morning, suitcase in hand with her clothes and toiletries for the week inside, ready to be collected by one of Lord Pembroke's black fleet cars and then taken to her home for the next four nights where she would deposit her bags and get ready for her working day. Melody would then be escorted to his offices and start getting set up. Laptops and mobile phones their only real necessities, and then they would get to work. Her role was as one of his personal assistants, welcoming his guests and setting up meetings, usually online or via the telephone. She was a very clever young woman, having excelled in her exams at school and finishing university with honours.

Lord Pembroke had told Melody many times that she should accept a promotion from him, that he wanted far more from her, but she was not ready yet. Melody was content to progress at her own speed. She had learned many of his insider trading tips for acquiring other businesses and properties before then making them grow and would be ten-times better off than her business rivals in the future for his teachings. David had disclosed a lot in the last five years, showing her an insider insight on how he expanded his reach in the business world and earned himself vast sums of money in the process. One day, Melody hoped to use some of her experience to further her own business prowess, but for now, she was content to learn and gain proficiency in the hope that she might be able to utilise it in the future.

And so, with all thoughts of her sore ankle long forgotten, Melody made her way home, daydreaming of her handsome saviour and those deep blue eyes that she knew would haunt her for a long time to come and which might already be her undoing. Together, they may just be something special, something that could change history. Melody thought about Corey the entire way home and found herself mesmerised by those eyes, those lips and that way he had held her that spoke of every possibility and also of no promise at all, just the, 'what if?'

One thing Melody was sure of was that she would be seeing Corey again soon. It was more a matter of when than if.

CHAPTER TWO

The next morning, Melody and her younger sister, Callie, made their way into the town centre to go shopping, where they then stopped for a late lunch and a glass of wine outside one of the pubs along the high street. It was a warm summer's day, and they sat basking in the sunshine as they chatted loudly, catching up over their cool drinks and enjoying the easy day. The sounds of the busy town engulfed them as they chatted, people passing by and cars bustling along but it was nothing compared to the noise of the city and Melody truly loved her weekend retreats back home, especially when her sister made time to be with her. She too had a busy schedule thanks to her owning and working full time in a top-class hair salon as its lead stylist and she had already stopped to work her magic on Melody's long auburn hair at least twice that day, insisting she let her cut it. Callie was a shrewd businesswoman, too. Not only did she see to her many clients, but she also trained up her interns herself and was single-handedly running her salon, which was doing incredibly well.

As Melody and Callie gossiped, a group of men wandered past them, each of them chatting loudly too as they joked with one another and made plans for their Saturday night out in the old yet lively town, making both girls look up at them reactively as they did. Melody caught sight of them and took in their cute group of handsome strangers, each of them well-dressed and oozing confidence, but her gaze didn't linger for long on the group as a whole, settling on just the one face she couldn't quite believe was really there, Corey's. He caught her gawking and stared right back at her, seemingly just as shocked to see her there, and he quickly stopped in his tracks, his friends wandering just a few feet further before stopping and turning back to see what he was doing.

"Well, well, well. If it isn't my damsel in distress," Corey said, stepping closer to her with a cheeky grin on his handsome face. "I thought you were going to call me?"

"I was, after the respectable couple of days. Are you stalking me, Mr Black?" Melody asked him, her tone playful, but she couldn't help but wonder what on Earth he was doing there.

"I live here. Perhaps I should ask you the same question?" he replied, summoning his friends back to his side with a wave of his hand.

"Me too. Well, I stay at my family home on the weekends. This is my sister, Callie Buchanan," she replied, waving a hand at her open-mouthed sibling. Melody had told her all about her handsome saviour from the day before, but Callie couldn't help but feel as though she had been mis-sold the actual extent of this alluring man's prowess and sex-appeal. She stood and kissed his cheek, being far from the shy one of the family, and Corey enjoyed her affectionate greeting, but was careful not to seem overly interested. She picked up on his hesitancy and grinned, smiling up at him playfully, clearly pleased that his affections were reserved for Melody alone.

"Wow, I will have to make sure I have a quick word with my big sister for having kept you waiting on that phone call. You'll have to forgive her. What she possesses in brains and business sense, Melody unfortunately lacks in social prowess," Callie told him with a cheeky smirk.

Corey smiled back and gave Melody a quick wink. He then quickly directed Callie towards his friends, eager to talk with her older sister in private.

"It's a pleasure to meet you, Callie. I'd like to introduce you both to my friends," he said, pointing to the group of men with his hand. One of them, a heavy-set man that looked to Melody as if he might be almost seven-feet tall, had a hard stare but a warm smile that seemed forced and insincere, sending her instincts reeling. Melody didn't like him. There was something there that chilled her to the bone, that shook her very core, and she was glad when he made no attempt to chat with her or Callie. Another man, softer looking and with a much kinder face than the first, grinned and reached out his hand to Melody, which she shook courteously and introduced herself. He had dark-brown hair and eyes that seemed wise beyond his years, but was handsome and alluring just like his friend and he soon caught Callie's attention.

"Jonah," he told her, a wide smile on his lips. He then moved over to stand next to Callie, keeping her attention on him while the other two seemingly less interested men chatted behind them, and Corey sat down next to Melody and leaned in, pulling her closer with one hand around her back.

"Do you believe in fate?" he whispered into her ear.

"No," Melody replied, smirking up at him.

"Good, me neither. But, I do believe in happy coincidences," he said, laughing. Corey had a way with words that enticed and allured Melody, drawing her in with each well-spoken syllable, every deep, ominous sound. She watched him, mesmerised while he spoke, utterly enthralled by him, and Melody somehow knew then and there that she was done for.

The two groups spent the rest of the evening together, drinking and enjoying the last few hours of sunshine in the beer garden of the pub. Melody eased a little with the burly man, whom she later found out was called Heath, and even chatted to him for a couple of minutes here and there while the others went to the bar or to the toilets. He seemed quite different than she had first thought, despite his outwardly intimidating demeanour, and although there was still something there that she didn't trust, Melody found herself warming to him a little by the end of the evening.

"Do you really live here in Colchester?" she found herself asking Corey when they had a quiet moment alone later that night, sitting in a small booth by one of the bars they had moved on to with their hands entwined and their eyes locked. He stroked her hands with the tips of his, delicately tracing them across her palms and fingers in an oddly seductive way that made her swoon.

"Honestly, I do," Corey replied, smiling so broadly that his deep blue eyes lit up, hypnotising her. "I love the city, but I can't handle it all the time. My office is in London, so I commute every day, but I spend my evenings and weekends here. I have a flat right next to the station. Want me to show you?" he asked, his smile turning sheepish.

"I would love to, but I need to make sure Callie gets home safely first," Melody replied. She really didn't want to say no, but her protective instincts kicked in rather than be selfish.

"I don't think she wants to go, not back to yours anyway," Corey replied, looking towards the small dance-floor and Melody followed his gaze, spotting her sister and Jonah there. The pair of them were dancing so close to one another it was hard to make out where one of them started and the other one finished. Their lips were locked in a deep, insatiable kiss that proved Corey right.

Within a few minutes Melody had prised apart the enamoured couple and then pulled her sister into the ladies' toilets for the obligatory 'talk'. Callie was twenty-three years old, far from a child and she had gone home with many a suitor on her nights out in town before, but Melody still wanted to make sure that she was okay before she would be happy leaving, with or without her sister in tow.

"I'm going back to Jonah's place. He already asked me," she told Melody, her soft blue eyes alight and excited. "He's so hot, kinda commanding and powerful, but somehow still soft. I think he lives in the same building as Corey, so I won't be far from you," Callie added, making Melody blush at how her sister had already figured out her plans for the rest of the evening. "It's not like you to go home with a guy. You must really like him, Mel?" she pressed when Melody didn't correct her, eager to get as much information as possible from her in their few minutes alone.

"Yeah, there's such a strong connection between us. I can feel it already. It's like I can't say no to him, but I don't want to either," Melody admitted, checking her appearance in the mirror. She looked good, glowing even thanks to the light tan she had picked up after their afternoon in the sunshine. Her dark hair shimmered with its deep red tones and her hazel eyes looked far from sleepy despite their long day out. While applying a light sweep of red lip-gloss Melody watched her sister in the mirror, taking her in for a moment with a smile. Callie's slim shape, medium height, facial features, and hair colour matched hers so perfectly that everyone knew they were sisters with one look. There was one exception, though. They didn't share the same eye colour. She and Melody had found out in her teens that they had different fathers, that Callie's dad, Tim, had raised her, but that their mother had met him when Melody was already one-year-old. Her own father had not made an appearance until she was nearly twenty, and the moment she had looked into his matching green-brown eyes she had known where hers had come from at last.

"Hey, are you listening?" Callie demanded, her hands on her hips. "I said, let's go. I'm ready for bed, if you know what I mean?" she giggled, cocking one eyebrow.

"I always know what you mean," Melody mumbled, laughing as she slid her arm into the crook of her sister's elbow and sauntered out with her to join their dates.

CHAPTER THREE

"Are you tired?" Corey asked Melody as they climbed the stairs to the second floor and walked towards the door of his flat.

"No," she replied, smiling to herself.

"Good, because I couldn't bear it if you said you weren't going to stay with me. I have to be with you tonight Melody," he said, stopping outside the door that she supposed must be his home. He looked down at his hands as he spoke, seeming somewhat shy despite his earlier calm confidence. "Not that I expect anything from you, I just mean I want to be close to you."

"I'm not going anywhere," she promised, stopping beside him and laying a hand on his shoulder. Corey looked up and peered across at her again for a few seconds, basking in her warm smile. He then unlocked the door and ushered Melody inside, unable to hide his grin as he watched her saunter in casually, her earlier social reticence gone now that they were alone again. She stepped over the threshold and took in the dark, manly bachelor-pad and shook her head in mock disapproval.

"This place needs a woman's touch," she told him, taking in the black sofas and grey paint-covered walls. There was just one wall with colour, a feature-wall covered in deep red wallpaper. The pattern on it was bright against the dull hue of the others and it had shelving built into the wall, each one adorned with photographs of Corey with his huge array of friends. There were no personal ones though, only group shots and certainly no intimate poses with other women, which made her smile a little inside.

"No woman, other than you, has ever set foot inside my home," Corey told her, setting his keys and wallet in a large bowl inside the doorway. "I don't make a habit of inviting women home with me."

"I'm happy to hear that," she replied, resting her hip against the sofa casually, but her insides were screaming. She wanted desperately to throw herself at him, to kiss his soft lips all night long, and more.

"Were you really going to call me?" Corey asked, stepping closer.

"No," Melody joked. "You're not my type," she added, a cheeky grin on her face. Corey smirked and stepped closer still, his mouth coming within centimetres of hers, and his hands reached around her back and pulled Melody into him, pinning her body between the leather couch and his own with his powerful frame. She gasped, a breathy, uncontrollable wheeze languidly escaping her lips and couldn't help but bite her lip as she stared at his inviting mouth.

"In that case, I had better let you leave," he whispered, his breath rustling the auburn waves around her cheeks as it delicately fluttered along her jawline.

"I promised I wouldn't," Melody reminded him. "And you begged me to stay."

"Oh yes, well then, I had better be persuasive," Corey replied, capturing her bottom lip with his own and pulling it free from her top teeth. Melody gave in to him, wanting his mouth on hers now much more than any more words or playful banter. She reached up and rested her hands on his shoulders as they kissed, glad he was there to hold her steady, just like at the train station. It started as the kind of kiss she had seen in the movies, delicate and sincere, before soon moving on to the type of kiss she had only dreamed about before. Corey took her breath away, quite literally, and Melody didn't care. She held on tight as he devoured every one of her senses and her mind went blank, utterly lost in the moment, lost in his kiss.

"Very persuasive," she mumbled, as they finally pulled their mouths away from each other. She peered up into his deep blue eyes, feeling fragile and naïve beneath his gaze for some strange reason, sensing a wisdom there that seemed beyond his years. Melody realised she knew very little about Corey Black. He had told her he was twenty-eight years old, just three years older than she was, but had not given much away about his work or his family, his relationship history or his predilections. Melody was inexperienced when it came to having real connections with men and didn't quite know how best to broach the subject with him, but thankfully, he sensed her need for more and took the lead.

"I need to be convincing in my line of work. I don't think I've ever had to be this persuasive though," he replied with a cocky smile that lit up the eyes Melody was still peering lovingly into.

"So, what is it you do then?" she asked, taking his offered hand when he stepped back and then following Corey into the kitchen, where he grabbed a bottle of chilled white wine from the fridge and showed her it, one eyebrow raised. Melody nodded in approval and leaned against the kitchen counter as he grabbed two glasses from a granite coloured cupboard. The grey and black theme continued in here too, and Melody wondered if the whole flat had been decorated in the same way. A couple of red splashes bringing a little flavour to an otherwise cold home.

"In a nut-shell, acquisitions and retrieval. I am based in London most of the time, but travel anywhere I might be needed," he told her, pulling the cork as he spoke.

"So, you're a glorified salesman?" Melody replied, grinning wickedly and Corey looked back at her, a sly glint in his eye as he regarded her for a second, contemplating his response.

"I don't sell, Melody. I buy. Sometimes people don't want to give up their most valuable assets so readily, that's when I go for the kill and make them that offer that they just cannot refuse," he replied.

"Sounds fair enough. We have people that do that for my boss and his associates," she admitted, her business-head on for a moment. Melody genuinely appreciated his directness and couldn't help but admire his business-acumen. "And where is it you work?"

"Black Rose Industries," he replied, pouring the wine into the glasses with his back to her, and Melody's mouth dropped open behind him.

"Corey Black," she mumbled, shaking her head, the realisation smacking her in the face ever so clearly now. "So, Devin and Serena Black are your parents I take it?" she then asked, having heard of the Black family many times before during her business career but never having actually seen any of the private CEO's in person or even in photos. Corey looked back quickly and nodded nonchalantly before turning away again to deposit the remainder of the bottle in the fridge while Melody mulled over her frenzied thoughts.

Black Rose Industries was a multi-billion pound business, owned and run by the Black family without any opposition in their expert territories. They were renowned ruthless moguls, always seeming to know the big business trends way ahead of the curve and finding just the right companies to purchase and sell on, usually for quadruple their original costs. The infamous Blacks were also well-known for their charity donations and multi-media connections, their great-grandparents having owned television and movie companies for generations as well as having musical partners and journalistic input, all of which had been passed down from generation to generation of the Black brood.

They were the ultimate power-family in the business world, yet while Melody and Lord Pembroke's other aide's had often recommended that their boss consider setting up a meeting with one of them in order to advance his own business portfolio, he had consistently refused. Melody had even rendered hopes of possibly moving over to their company once she was ready to advance further up the business ladder, but had never dreamed she would just happen upon one of their board members on a train platform during rush hour, much less that she might be falling for him.

CHAPTER FOUR

"Is that going to be a problem?" Corey eventually asked, wandering over and delivering Melody her now much-needed drink.

"Of course not, but I do think we need to make a deal, here and now, before anything else happens," she replied, taking a long swig of her wine and peering back at him over the rim as her cheeks flushed pink.

"I like deals," Corey said, a smile curling at his lips. "You may proceed with your proposal, Miss Buchanan."

Melody laughed, feeling somewhat more comfortable with this kind of talk, and she made her case as eloquently as she would in her meetings with Lord Pembroke.

"I propose we agree never to talk about our work, except when asked about our day or to discuss our upcoming agendas. It also might be seen as a conflict of interests to discuss our potentially impending relationship with our colleagues, in which case I also propose an orally agreed non-disclosure covenant until such a time comes that we wish to proceed further. Do you agree, Mr Black?" she asked, and Corey's increasingly widening smile then dropped. He regarded her with a determined, powerful look, only serving to alight the fire in her belly again. He stepped closer, his mouth capturing hers again without a word. He then placed his wine glass gently down on the kitchen counter behind her, gripping hers shortly afterwards, and Melody released her fingers from the stem as his tongue delved inside and commanded hers without any hesitation or resistance.

"How's that for an 'orally agreed non-disclosure covenant'?" Corey asked when he eventually pulled away, his smile firmly back in place, but his haughty breath gave away his excitement.

"Oops, I was meant to say, verbally agreed!" Melody cried, giggling to herself, and she couldn't help but blush harder.

"I would've still reacted the same way, no matter what," he promised, stroking her freckled cheek with his forefinger. "But, yes. I do agree. Let's keep whatever this is private for now, and in time we can see where it takes us." Her butterflies returned, and she gazed at him in awe.

Was this really happening? Was she about to embark on a relationship with the illustrious Corey Black? Melody's heart raced at the sheer thought, but the slickening heat between her thighs told her the answer, and it was a resounding yes. The pair of them then grabbed their wine and made their way through to the living room. Corey sliding down onto the large black sofa gracefully and then lifting one arm up, laying it across the back and indicating for Melody to join him.

"Come here," he said, and she did as he asked, nestling herself under his arm and inhaling his mixed scent of cologne and soap that she somehow found intoxicating.

"Do you have any other girlfriends?" she asked quietly, sipping her wine while running her fingers over one of the buttons on his shirt. Melody needed to know. She needed to be sure before she gave herself to Corey if she was one of many women in his life. She knew it was too early to tell where this was going, but it was only fair for him to tell her outright if this was just one of many flings for him.

"No, not right now. But I was in a relationship for a while that ended not long ago. It was a difficult split. We wanted different things," Corey told Melody, seeming genuinely sad about it and he didn't say any more on the subject and she knew without asking that he wasn't keen on reliving his past. "What about you, how many other men should I know about?" he asked, changing the subject, and Melody nearly choked on her drink.

"None," she replied, shaking her head. "Not for a while. My last boyfriend was an arsehole, cheated on me with anything that opened its legs for him. After him, I just threw myself into work," she admitted.

"You're better off without him. Cheaters always get what they deserve in the end, don't you worry," Corey replied, grabbing her glass and placing it on the coffee table in front of them. As he sat back, he pulled Melody close again, cupping her cheeks in his hands and staring down into her eyes. They seemed greener in this dull light and he took a moment to really look, finding warmth and kindness returned in her stare.

"I hope so," she replied, feeling lost in his gaze.

"Will you make love to me, Melody?" Corey then asked, catching her completely off guard but not letting go of her cheeks, keeping her eyes locked on his as he eagerly awaited her reply.

"Yes," she breathed and Corey quickly turned himself to the side, effortlessly pulling her around so that she was then straddling him on the couch. Their lips met, their kisses deepened by his strong arms as they reached around behind Melody's head and pulled her closer. She unbuttoned his shirt, revealing a light tuft of blonde chest-hair that she couldn't help but slide her fingers through for a moment before carrying on, and it wasn't long before his torso was free of its cotton cage.

Corey grabbed the hem of her dress and tugged, pulling it upwards and Melody instinctively raised her arms, allowing the soft material to glide freely up and off, leaving her in her underwear atop him. He pulled himself up, wrapping his arms around her exposed waist, kissing her chest as he reached around and unhooked her bra. Corey then slid that free too and caressed each nipple in turn with his mouth, his hands gliding south where he slid them beneath the hem of her panties and tugged, letting Melody know he wanted them gone too. In one quick move he lifted and tilted her backwards, climbing over Melody on the sofa and pulling down her knickers as he went, making her gasp as his strong hands found her wet opening and caressed her, full of want and need while his mouth still played with her nipples.

"Corey, I want you," she whispered, her voice hoarse. He slid south, his mouth taking care to caress every inch of her exposed flesh, and Melody couldn't help but arch her back up, her body eager to connect with his.

"All in due time, I have an orally binding agreement to finish off down here," he joked, making her giggle excitedly as his mouth then lingered over her swollen nub for a moment, his breath tickling that tender spot between her thighs so delicately.

"I thought we'd already, ah!" Melody screamed, unable to finish her playful response as Corey captured her between his lips and even teeth, his wonderful rhythm sending her body crashing headfirst into an incredible orgasm. She had never experienced anything like it before and literally saw stars for a few seconds as her body continued to pulsate beneath him.

Within minutes, the pair of them had clambered off the sofa and into the bedroom, where Corey discarded the last of his clothes and joined Melody on the bed. She no longer cared about the dark, cold colour scheme or the masculine décor. Melody lay back comfortably on the plump black pillows and stared up into her lover's eyes, watching excitedly as he climbed between her thighs and rested his impressive length on her belly before grabbing a condom from the bedside drawer. She reached down and stroked it, making him gasp, before pulling down the sheath and guiding him inside. Their bodies moved together wonderfully, completely in sync and Melody arched her back as he pulled himself all the way out before sliding in and out slowly, again and again, savouring every moment.

It wasn't too long until he was desperate for more though and he leaned in closer, planting long, intense kisses on her lips while thrusting into her deeply. They came together, their bodies tingling and their eyes locked as each of them reached their high. Melody then slid beneath the covers and enjoyed the musky scent of him on her, not caring one little bit and happily sliding back in his arms once Corey joined her in the bed. They kissed, softly this time and less urgent, but somehow more passionate.

"You are gonna be bad news, Corey Black, I can just tell," she whispered, grinning to herself.

"Funny, I was just thinking the same about you," he replied, kissing her deeply again.

Melody awoke the next morning wrapped in Corey's arms, rested and calm thanks to their lie-in and the safe feeling of being in his embrace. She tried hard not to wake him, but being a light sleeper, Corey's eyes fluttered open as soon as she tried to slide away for a bathroom break.

"Morning gorgeous," he called behind her, stretching out his arms and grinning as he watched her stagger naked into the en-suite. Melody couldn't help but blush. Exposing her body in the morning light soon made her insecurities clamber to the surface. She fixed her tousled hair and wiped away the remnants of the previous day's makeup, opting for a fresh-faced look rather than the panda eyes she had woken up with. After swilling some toothpaste and mouthwash, Melody finally took a good look at herself in the mirror. She couldn't help but smile, the reminiscence of the night before sending both her mind and body reeling with the wonderful memory.

"Everything okay in there?" Corey called from outside the door, grabbing a pair of tracksuit trousers from his drawers and sliding them on.

"Everything's fine, just going for a pee," she called back, shaking her head at her socially inept answer. "What the hell?" she then whispered to her reflection in annoyance.

"I'm going to make coffee, you'd better be in my bed when I get back," he replied authoritatively and she could hear the smile in his tone, uncontrollably blushing again as his words sunk in.

A few minutes later, Corey returned from the kitchen with two homemade lattes in his hands. He placed them on the bedside table and then slid under the soft sheets, grinning to himself as his hands found the still naked woman there waiting for him. Melody had come back in from the bathroom and had stretched out under the sheets in wait for him. She was lying on her stomach with her face buried sleepily in the pillow, gripping it with her hands tightly. One leg lay straight while the other was pulled up at a right angle, opening herself up for him unashamedly. "Hmmm, are you sleepy?" Corey asked.

"No," she replied, letting out a small whimper as his hand stroked her cleft delicately. He shuffled out of his trousers and kicked them to the floor, grabbing a condom as he went and then quickly sheathing himself before climbing over her on the bed. Melody arched her back, inviting Corey inside, and she gasped as he accepted her offer. She pushed back into his heavy thrusts, groaning with pleasure as he slid back and forth behind her and followed his lead when Corey brought her leg down and closed her thighs tightly beneath him. Melody submitted further as he lifted her hips off the bed, gripping her tightly as he rocked her to orgasm over and over again. When they were finally spent, they lay back in one other's arms and basked as each of them caught their breath, the coffee having been completely forgotten.

A loud knock at the door later that afternoon forced the two lovers out of bed at last, the insistent banging surely coming from Melody's little sister, and neither of them was surprised to find Callie on the other side.

"I'm going home now, you coming?" she asked Melody, a knowing smile on her lips as she took in the pair of them and their clear afterglows.

"Well, I urm," Melody mumbled, not wanting to leave yet but not knowing how to say so.

"She can't," Corey said for her, clearly feeling the same way. "Melody promised she wouldn't leave me, and I'm holding her to that. I'll have a car drop you back and she can grab her things. I'll make sure your sister gets to work bright and early tomorrow morning, I promise," he added, making Melody grin broadly.

"It's okay honestly Callie. But, he's right, I'm staying," Melody added, staring pleadingly at her sister, who nodded and shrugged.

"Very well then," Callie replied, winking before turning away and sauntering off to wait for her sister outside.

The burly, mountainous man Heath pulled up in front of the flats a few minutes after Melody had made her way downstairs, the two girls climbing inside the spacious, black car that was clearly very expensive and had had no luxury spared. The interior was bright red leather upholstery, catching Melody's eye, and she couldn't help but grin at her little sister.

"Good afternoon ladies, I'm under strict instructions to have Melody back here within the hour. Where are we headed?" Heath asked them, and Callie gave him their address. She and her big sister then giggled excitedly as he sped away, zigzagging through the traffic with effortless skill and then arriving in half the time it would have normally taken them.

Inside, Melody grabbed her suitcase and packed her work clothes for the week. After a quick farewell to her mother and stepfather, she poked her head around her sister's bedroom door.

"See you next weekend. I hope you had fun last night?" she asked, and even though Callie was already in bed, she still grinned up at her from the pillow.

"Hell yeah," she replied, her eyes glinting wickedly at her big sister.

CHAPTER FIVE

The next morning, Corey woke Melody up with a cup of steaming hot coffee and a warm smile. They had had the most amazing night together again and were both well and truly smitten. Melody had slept soundly in his arms for the second night too, not having even heard him as he had gotten out of bed.

"Morning beautiful," he whispered, laying down beside her on the bed but not daring to climb inside with her, as he was certain they would not be ready to leave on time if he did.

"What un-godly hour is this?" she grumbled, taking the coffee and having a large sip before even peeling her eyes open fully. Corey grinned and leaned up on one elbow to watch her affectionately.

"Five o'clock. Heath will be bringing the car at six. I thought you might like to not have to rush," Corey replied, laughing to himself. Melody finally opened her eyes properly, taking in the already showered and dressed man beside her, and groaned.

"Thanks, aren't you getting the train?" she asked, and he shook his head.

"No, Heath drives me each day. I was meeting him at Liverpool street station on Friday because he had errands to run for me but otherwise we always drive."

"Oh," she replied, surprised but impressed. "And there was me thinking you were one of the little people," she teased, climbing out of bed and shuffling over to the en-suite to shower. By the time she had finished and dressed, Corey had made her breakfast and topped up her coffee cup.

"I hope an omelette's okay?" he asked, an almost shy smile on his handsome face as he placed the plate down before her on the dining table.

"Looks lovely, thanks," Melody replied, taking a large bite of the delicately seasoned, perfectly cooked dish and groaning appreciatively. "Wow, this is amazing," she added, devouring another huge mouthful before he had even joined her at the table.

By seven o'clock, Melody had been safely deposited outside the train station and waited there for her taxi to take her to Lord Pembroke's current office while sipping on a cappuccino from the nearby vendor. Corey had been the perfect gentleman and she couldn't help but think of their weekend together with a lovesick grin on her face. She had never thought she could feel this way, especially so quickly, but she knew she was already falling for him. Melody kept her secret from her colleagues though, just as they had promised each other, and told no-one just why she was so happy as she spent the next five days constantly checking her mobile phone for messages and voicemails from her secret lover. When Friday came around again he and Heath were there to meet her outside the train station to give her a ride back to Colchester for her usual weekend retreat.

"I want you to stay with me," Corey asked Melody as she climbed in. Before she could answer, he kissed her deeply, seemingly having hated being apart from her during the last few days. "I wish you didn't have to be so secretive. I almost called in some favours to have your phone tracked just so that I could be with you again, but I didn't want you thinking I was some kind of stalker," he told her, and Melody couldn't help but laugh.

"My phone is untraceable, remember? One of the downsides of having a paranoid recluse for a boss," she reminded him and rolled her eyes. "Listen, am I gonna have to nip this relationship in the bud now?" Melody then joked. "And there was me thinking I was the one acting like a lovesick teenager." Corey just grinned and pulled her close for another kiss, keeping her by his side and their lips locked for the entire journey back home.

They spent the entire weekend together, barely leaving Corey's bedroom, and once again she rode with him to London the following Monday in order to begin her week of work. They continued to keep their relationship secret and Melody soon felt like she was walking on air thanks to Corey Black and the wonderful way he made her feel every day.

As the weeks passed them by, Corey and Melody soon found themselves spending every weekend together, as well as talking every evening after she clocked-off from work, either on the phone or on their computers via web chats. Melody had never felt so strongly about anyone before and knew she was already well on her way to falling for him. Corey admitted he had the same feeling towards her too, and the pair soon found it harder and harder to keep their business lives from getting involved.

"I'm gonna tell David about us," Melody told him one Sunday morning as she lazed in Corey's strong arms. They had been seeing each other for a few months now and the secrecy was starting to take its toll on her. Melody yearned to be free to see her lover as she chose to and didn't see why Lord Pembroke would be angry about it now that she and Corey had given it some time and knew that their relationship was headed somewhere. "If he fire's me, so be it. I haven't let our relationship affect my work life so far, so it shouldn't be an issue."

"Tread carefully, Mel," Corey replied. "Did you ever think there might be a reason why he doesn't want to deal with Black Rose?" he asked, looking down into her hazel eyes thoughtfully. "I've wondered for a while if perhaps there's bad blood there or something. My father is very cagey when I've asked him about Pembroke before, too."

"Maybe you're right. I'll just wait and see then. I'll tell him when it feels right," she conceded. "Oh, I should be finished earlier tomorrow if you want to stay in the city and meet me for dinner? You could sneak back to my hotel with me? It's not far from the station, so Heath could collect you from there Tuesday morning and take you to Black Rose?" Melody asked him, eager for an extra night together, especially if it meant that they could go out for an actual date.

"Sounds good, I'll take you to a play I've been wanting to go to, it's a dark, sexy immersive production where anything goes," Corey replied, and Melody nodded, thinking to herself that anything with him would be dark and sexy. He mulled it over and then peered over at her questioningly. "Hey, I thought you wouldn't know where you'll be staying until you got there tomorrow though?" he asked.

"Not normally, but we're staying in the same office as last week again. Pembroke's travel guy messed up the booking, but I don't mind. The Hampton Hotel has really good Wi-Fi and the offices are nice. I don't feel so cooped up there as I do in some of the offices we use," Melody replied, snuggling into him.

"That's good. Coffee?" Corey asked, sliding out of bed and pulling on some tracksuit bottoms.

"Always," she replied, pulling the covers tighter around her, the cold creeping in now that her hot lover had left. Corey just laughed and wandered off into the kitchen in search of the drink he had promised her.

***

"I know what you're hiding, Beatrice," Leyla, one of the powerful guardians of the Crimson Brotherhood demanded, her cold stare directed at the trembling white witch before her. She pushed her back into the wall, their faces just inches away from each other's as she continued to stare her down.

"Honestly, I had no idea. We were just following orders. I'm telling you the truth," Beatrice promised, her bright blue eyes peering back up at the demonic woman before her. The usually so commanding and powerful white witch cowered before the infamous Leyla Black, her reputation as a vicious and unyielding assassin proceeding her wherever she went and Beatrice knew not to underestimate her.

"A lie of omission if you ask me," Leyla sniggered, pulling back just slightly, her own deep blue eyes boring into Beatrice's, unfeeling and merciless. "You would be wise not to betray my trust in you now. After all these years of keeping me abreast of the Warriors movements, it would be a shame for me to find out that you have betrayed me over something as small as a simple bounty-hunt?" she demanded, taking in every fearful flinch and hesitant flicker the witch could not hide.

"Not at all. We have been hired to provide a threshold, nothing more. I have no idea what's inside," Beatrice told her, still trembling.

"Hmmm, well then. You had better make sure that the threshold accidentally has a nice, big crack in it, hadn't you? There's something in there that belongs to me, and I want it back. Do I make myself clear?" Leyla told her, a determined look on her beautiful face that told Beatrice that saying no was absolutely out of the question.

"I'll make it happen," the witch promised.

"Tomorrow," Leyla ordered her, holding her stare for a few more seconds before pulling back and wandering away.

CHAPTER SIX

Melody got sorted and headed down to the office the following day, checking her phone one more time in case there was a good morning message from Corey. She assumed he must already be having a busy day as she hadn't heard from him yet, which was unlike her new beau, but had no time to call or text him as she hurried down the handful of floors to make it to the nine o'clock meeting on time.

On her way down in the lift, Melody caught the eye of a woman she had not met before. She was beautiful, probably the most stunning woman Melody had ever seen, and she found herself staring at her for a few moments. As they left the open doors, Melody turned left while the woman turned right, but she flashed her a stunning smile on her way and Melody couldn't help but wonder if she had seen her before, seeming to recognise her face from somewhere.

Around half an hour into the meeting, Lord Pembroke's phone began ringing in his pocket and he immediately grabbed it, not even apologising to the rest of his colleagues for cutting the meeting short and he paced the room while listening intently to the caller on the other end. His eyes widened and Melody saw him taking deep gulps as though his throat was suddenly dry, that or he was trying to stop himself from throwing up his breakfast.

"I'm so sorry," he then muttered forlornly after the call ended, staring Melody directly in the eye. Before she could ask him what he might be sorry for, the wooden doors behind her burst open and a mass of black-hooded figures entered. Each of them dominated the room, both intimidating and creepy. She could not make out any of their faces, but could sense that they were bad news and each of Lord Pembroke's aides' scrambled for the doors, eager to make a run for it. They were quickly intercepted with ease and those that surrendered in defeat were led to one side while those who tried to resist were beaten and forced into submission by the strange and eerie intruders. Melody had fallen to the ground in the craziness, surrounded by feet, and she caught someone's boot on her cheekbone as she fell. She curled up into a ball, being reminded of her fretful time on the floor of the train platform, but was soon grabbed by the hair from behind and forced into a kneeling position.

"Move or I'll smash the other one too," said a voice from behind her and, as though she weighed nothing, Melody was then pulled off her feet and dragged aside to join her colleagues, many of whom were sobbing and begging for mercy, which Melody had the feeling was not an option right now. None of them knew why these people were here, but the way they were all convening around Lord Pembroke told Melody it had everything to do with him, and her stomach dropped as a wave of fear flooded through her.

One of the hooded figures dropped their cowl, but her swollen eye made it hard for Melody to make out the scene before her so she couldn't make out the face yet, her good eye struggling to clear the blur of tears. She could see that Lord Pembroke was sat at his usual seat in the centre of the table again, his hands forcibly positioned on the desk in front of him by a pair of daggers that pierced through his skin and bone, holding him firmly in place while the red-headed figure paced behind him. Melody's vision eventually cleared, and she realised it was the woman she had seen in the elevator. She swallowed hard, remembering how despite being mesmerised and drawn to the woman, something hadn't felt quite right about her. Now she knew why, and fresh tears streamed down her face as she took in her boss's pained grimace.

"Lord Pembroke. David," the woman began, taking the seat beside him. "Did you really think that you could hide forever? You and I made a deal a long time ago, old friend. A deal you have benefitted from for a very long time. Too long. It's time to pay your debts."

"It's not my fault. I told you I would try, but it just didn't happen. We tried surrogates and everything," he pleaded. It was an unusual response, Melody thought, but then again, this was a very unusual situation, after all.

"Excuses, excuses. Do you know what I usually do to humans who make nothing but excuses? I murder their families and make them watch, before I then frame them for the entire thing and relieve them of their beating hearts too, leaving them nothing but a cruel legacy of hatred and loathing. It's very good fun, actually. Perhaps my next visit will be to your pretty wife?" the woman said, clearly enjoying seeing him squirm, and David cried out incoherently in fear and sadness.

"Let's just finish this, Leyla," said a male voice from across the room and a second figure joined her and Pembroke at the table, but he did not lower his own black hood. "I'm bored."

"Just let me have a little more fun, brother. You know how much I love it," Leyla replied, and the second figure shrugged but stayed quiet, seemingly giving his sister a few extra minutes to toy with her prey. "When you pledged your soul to me for riches and power, did I not deliver it?" she asked, and Lord Pembroke nodded. "I gave you twenty years to live the life of the wealthy, successful entrepreneur and you delighted in every second of it, didn't you, David?"

"Yes guardian," he replied, his head bowed.

"And then you asked me for more, and what did I do?"

"You gave me it."

"Yes, I did. And what was the price?"

"The soul of my first-born child," Pembroke replied, sobbing to himself, defeated.

"Exactly, and yet you still have no children, no legacy, no one to carry on the Pembroke name. I would feel sorry for you if I wasn't so fucking furious," she spat.

The small group of men and women still kneeling on the floor then watched eagerly as the woman, Leyla, interrogated him further. Melody stayed as quiet as possible, her head throbbing thanks to the pain in her clearly cracked cheekbone, and she struggled to hear what was being said. It all seemed so strange and she wondered if she might be hearing them wrong, hoping and praying that they might let her and the other aides go soon, but a growing unease in the pit of her stomach told her not to get her hopes up.

"Do you believe in fate?" said the man to Pembroke's right, breaking Melody's pessimistic reverie, and her head immediately jerked up. She knew that voice, and she knew it well. The hooded man noticed her and lifted his head to look in her direction too, pulling the cloak back and then grinning broadly at her.

"Corey," she breathed, bile rising in her throat as she took in the impossible sight before her. "No, it can't be. No," she muttered, shaking her head and panting for breath that didn't seem to want to come.

"Bring her to me," he said, not answering Melody's confused words, and she soon felt strong arms around her again as a mountainous man lifted her effortlessly and half led, half dragged her over and dumped her down into the seat beside Corey at the table. "Thank you Heath," he said as his henchman deposited her beside him.

"You arsehole," Melody groaned, realising that she was not dreaming. This really was a real life nightmare. Corey ignored her words, his wicked smile directed at her while David looked back and forth between the two of them as best he could from his seat alongside the couple.

"Do you want to know how I found you, David?" Corey then asked Lord Pembroke, grabbing his chin and forcing his gaze up to meet his own. "Your gullible little assistant here is to thank for the sorry state you currently find yourself in. Tell him, Melody," he teased, toying with them both.

Corey stood and then pulled, sliding Melody's chair beside David's so they were just inches apart. He then laid one of his hands on each of their shoulders as he continued, delighting in telling their wayward prize all about his retrieval tactics. "Not feeling chatty, Mel? Let me tell him then. She was so starved for male attention that it wasn't long before she was completely at my disposal. It was only thanks to her loyalty and adherence to your paranoid precautions that she didn't spill her guts right from the word go," he laughed. "Stupid little bitch thought I was in love with her, and I played the part well, didn't I?"

"Fuck you," she spat, trembling before him. Leyla watched her with intrigue, staying quiet now so that her brother could continue in their game of cat and mouse, but she never took her eyes off Melody's.

"We did plenty of that, but luckily for me I didn't have to wait too long before something fucked up. Someone made a mistake and as soon as they did, we found our little bounty here, thanks to the information you gave me, Mel." Corey said, laughing while David squirmed in his seat to look at her.

"You did this? How could you betray me? I could have handled it being anyone but you," he asked Melody, his face thunderous, and she gaped at him, open-mouthed.

"Do you think I would just spill all to some guy just because he and I had a bit of fun? You taught me better. I know better than that. Why would I ever betray you?" she insisted, hurt by his harsh words.

"Did you know he was Corey Black?" David cried, making Melody jump. "Did you?"

"Yes, but I never knew about any of this! How could I?"

"I don't care. You betrayed me the second you knew who you were seeing and didn't tell me. This is all your fault, Melody. I'm dead because of you," he bellowed, his words cutting her deep, but she knew in her gut that they were not true. This was all happening because of his actions, not hers. Melody was furious with him and couldn't help the angry tears that rolled down her cheeks.

"How can you say that, after everything we've been through?" she demanded, turning to face him. Corey's sickeningly smiling face still so close to hers, but she ignored him, her pain overshadowing her fury at being used so cunningly by the strange siblings.

Corey watched in wonder as David's features softened slightly as he peered at Melody, his whole demeanour changing, and he couldn't help but wonder what was seemingly so special about their bond.

"Such heartfelt sentiment, don't tell me you're his mistress Melody?" Corey teased, looking from her to David with a sly grin, and she shook her head, sobbing hard.

"Of course," whispered Leyla, joining the conversation again at last while still peering over intently at Melody. "She's not his mistress, you fool. She's his daughter."

"No fucking way?" Corey replied, grabbing her chin and then

staring into Melody's face intently. She tried to pull away from his grasp, but he was too strong, so she just peered up at him and sobbed.

"Just in the eyes, dear brother. She's his, make no doubt about it." Leyla said and Corey burst out laughing in Melody's face, his once handsome features lost to his cruel grin as he stared into her eyes for a moment, forcing her to keep his gaze.

"The lost treasure, under my nose the entire time," he muttered. "Father will be pleased."

"She belongs to me, don't forget," Leyla said, standing and then taking the seat on Melody's other side, turning her chair around so that she now faced her. Leyla's playful smile was back on her beautiful face, her demeanour casual and warm, just like she had been in the elevator.

"Very well. I don't want her, anyway. You are depriving Heath of a conquest though. I had promised him his fun with her when this was all over with," Corey said, but his sister ignored him. Melody's breath caught in her throat, fear making her want to vomit, but she still could not take her eyes off Leyla's. It was as though she was being commanded by her, lured, and seduced or something because it felt as if the entire world around them fell away and the powerful, beautiful woman before her was suddenly all that mattered.

"I didn't know you existed when I made the deal, that's why when I found you I had to keep you secret," David whispered, mumbling to himself and shaking his head as defeated tears fell onto the table before him, but Melody was so entranced and could not respond.

"Your father is going to die today Melody, there's no stopping that. I do, however, want you to join me willingly. I will not kill you. I will let you inherit his businesses and take over as CEO of Pembroke Enterprises, but first you need to give yourself to me. In this situation I would normally strike up a deal, but you've unfortunately forfeited that right thanks to your father's deal that already makes your soul mine. I could force you to do what I want, of course, but that's not the way I like to do things," she said, her mouth sliding over the sounds eloquently and seductively. Melody was utterly transfixed by Leyla, and she nodded in understanding while the fearsome woman continued. "So, to make myself perfectly clear, you have two options. One, join me willingly and have some semblance of a normal life under my guardianship. I will allow you to take over your father's reign, resulting in wealth and a life for yourself under our control, as long as you follow my orders at all times. Or two, you lose everything and Corey will take your soul, anyway. Perhaps he'll even let Heath have his fun with you before putting you out of your misery. What's it gonna be?" Leyla asked, her wicked smile scaring Melody to her core. It was obvious to them all which choice she was going to make, and Melody wanted to come back with a snide reply but thought better of it.

"I'll go with option number one please," she replied, taking Leyla's outstretched hand in hers.

"Good choice. So, you are mine then?" the powerful woman replied, not offering up any information or truths about the free will element of the deal.

"Yes."

Leyla smiled widely and then traced an inverted cross on the inside of Melody's right forearm with her index finger, which burned beneath her touch and then turned black. Leyla then added a couple of extra details to the mark with her fingertip, which Melody could then see turn into red roses that wrapped around the inverted cross on black stems.

"Welcome to the Crimson Brotherhood, Miss Pembroke," Leyla then said, leading her away without giving her so much as a moment to say her goodbyes to her father.

CHAPTER SEVEN

Two weeks had passed since Melody had allowed her soul to be claimed and had then gone willingly with Leyla Black, her new guardian, to the headquarters of the Crimson Brotherhood. In that time, not only had her name been legally changed and she had inherited her father's business and wealth, but she had also been confined to her tiny bedroom almost the entire time. She was in a large dormitory-style building that was at the centre of the huge grounds, nestled in the Yorkshire countryside. Surrounded by guards and under Leyla's watchful eye at all times, Melody truly felt like a prisoner here, but she had endeavoured to try and do everything that Leyla had expected of her since arriving with her following that terrible meeting in London.

She had only been permitted to leave the hamlet once for her father's funeral in London, during which she was not allowed to leave Leyla's side. Pembroke's widow, Janice, had wept openly for her husband the entire time. She'd had no idea of his demonic dealings and while Melody was still angry at him for having been so selfish she still could not bear to tell his widow the truth, opting to let him rest in peace and Janice's memories of him remain pleasant. Melody had already shocked Janice once that day by informing her he'd had a child all these years. A child he had kept a secret from her, and she was not ready for more hatred from the already emotionally wrecked woman.

When the two of them were ushered into a small room by Lord Pembroke's lawyer, Melody hadn't even considered checking with Leyla if she was permitted to go with him, assuming that this was what her guardian would have wanted. The reading of his will would finally make it common knowledge that Melody was his illegitimate child. Everyone would know after today that David had left her his business empire and all of his estate, the only exceptions being his mansion and personal savings, which would go to Janice. She tried to be happy about having been given the chance to go on with her life and head up the vast array of businesses David had accrued in his time, but it was hard to feel excited about a future that was not her own to live. Leyla had made it perfectly clear to Melody already that while she would be the face and the head of the company, all decisions and on-going dealings would be out of her control. Black Rose Industries effectively owned Pembroke's empire now, just as the Crimson Brotherhood owned Melody's soul. She was nothing but their puppet.

When they returned to the small community burrowed in the rolling hills and well out of sight to all the nearby humans, Melody climbed out of the car and started walking towards her room, feeling sad, broken and alone. Everything seemed so very finite now that her father's body was just ashes inside a jar that Janice had taken home with her. Leyla took her arm and walked with her, but then led her past her bedroom door, carrying on down the corridor to another room, where the powerful woman deposited her in a small chair on one side of a huge, dark wooden desk. Leyla sat in the large leather chair on the opposite side and stared across at her.

"You disobeyed my orders today, Melody," she said, calmly and serenely, but the human knew right away that she was in trouble. She shrunk down in the chair, feeling worse than she had a few minutes earlier, but not because of her grief, because of her fear. She tried to think how she had disobeyed Leyla's order, but couldn't think of anything. "You left my side without asking permission," Leyla prompted, and Melody's face dropped.

"I'm so sorry, guardian. I thought you wanted me to go and hear the reading of his will?" she asked, trembling. In just the past couple of weeks, she had already seen the vicious and cold side of Leyla's personality while she was learning the truth about the Crimson Brotherhood, Leyla's demonic parents, and their dark designs for her future. Melody had also been given a humiliating introduction to them by Corey, who now treated her with nothing but loathing and distaste. His own followers actively sniggered at her and whispered about Melody in plain sight, not caring about her hurt feelings, and she hated every single one of them. She was glad that she had chosen to go with Leyla's guardianship, knowing full well that Corey would have made what was left of her life a living Hell if she had chosen him, but she also understood now how pure evil did not always come in its obvious form. The warm, enigmatic woman that sat before her now could be kind, sensitive and caring, but she could turn that off in an instant and had already shown Melody her own darker side. The goddess-like being's unwavering expectations of those she commanded was a constant struggle to live up to, and Melody had already messed up on more than one occasion.

The first time was just hours after she had arrived at the headquarters. She had said Corey's name while talking with Leyla about their past and how used she had felt by him, having been completely lured in by the powerful woman's kind nature and leading questions. As soon as the word had left her mouth, Leyla had struck her across the cheek with such a force that she fell to the floor and her lip swelled to treble the size in mere seconds.

"Lesson number one, do not ever say our names," was all Leyla had said before then leaving her to unpack her things.

The second time, Melody had begun learning about the history of Hell and its heirs. She had discussed the royal family at great length with another of Leyla's followers, a young man named Logan, and he had leaned in, whispering to her.

"What do you think about the heirs all at it?" Logan had asked her, smirking.

"Kinda gross, right?" Melody replied, moving on to learn about their leader's nieces and nephews with him. He hadn't said anything else about it and had then just gone on to tell her about the differences between being a client and being a follower of their powerful guardians.

"A client is a human who has been sought out for one purpose or another, wooed and their contract landed by making them promises and then the client signing the deal that is their hopes and dreams come true in exchange for their soul. They are treated with care, trusted to carry out their required assignments to help further our cause in return for riches and fame," he told her. "A follower is someone who has perhaps had the misfortune to happen upon their demonic guardian at the wrong moment and then been marked. Maybe having found themselves owing favours to the wrong people, or perhaps they are a previous client following on from their completed contract who then effectively becomes a slave before their soul is later procured. Sometimes a follower is simply a person that has already been sold to the Crimson Brotherhood by their parents, such as yourself. A human essentially owns their children's souls and are able to bargain using them as leverage, much to omnipotent orders such as ours' divine happiness," Logan had added. She took it all in, finally understanding her own place in the Crimson Brotherhood and finding herself hating her father in that very moment.

Melody had later been called out to the communal living area, where Leyla stood waiting for her. Logan was hovering to her right, grinning wickedly as she approached.

"I hear you think my family are 'gross' Melody? Care to share your other thoughts with the rest of us? Perhaps you would like to call it a day and go to Hell right now?" Leyla asked, her voice stern and loud, making everyone around them turn and look in her direction. A few other followers even wandered over, eager to see what punishment the foolish girl was going to be given.

"No, mistress, I didn't mean it that way. He's twisted my words," Melody replied, pointing to Logan, desperate to defend herself.

"Silence!" Leyla bellowed, and Melody immediately did as she was told. Corey then teleported to her side, a sneer on his face as he regarded the stupid girl before him and he snapped his fingers, bringing Heath to them. In his warlock henchman's arms stood Callie, Melody's sister, bound and gagged. Her eyes were wide with fear and shock. She had no idea what had actually happened to Melody other than that she had inherited David's business. She knew nothing of how the group of men they had met just a few months before were warlocks and demons, and not that she and Corey had even split up, but she soon caught on that things were far from what they had once seemed.

"Do you believe in fate?" Corey had then asked Callie before teleporting her away with him. A short while later Leyla had then shown her to Corey's bedroom, where she forced Melody to watch him and her sister fucking for hours through a two-way mirror, severing any feelings that might still linger in her heart for him from their past together. Corey knew that they were there. He even winked over at them while plunging deep inside Callie and enjoying making her scream for him while Melody was forced to watch and listen.

"Lesson number two, don't ever talk out of turn again," Leyla had then whispered in her ear.

This time it was different, though. Leyla had an eerie calmness to her now that worried Melody more than ever. She trembled, wringing her hands as she anticipated her guardian's punishment.

"Go to your room. You are not permitted to leave until breakfast tomorrow morning," Leyla told her, and Melody nodded, hoping that she was being let off thanks to her having just said goodbye to her father. She stood and then eagerly made her way back down the hall and into her room, grateful for Leyla's imprisonment rather than another humiliating punishment. She shut the door behind her and turned around to go and get changed, which was when she came face to face with Heath, the huge and violent warlock who had sent shivers down her spine on more than one occasion in her recent past.

Melody quickly turned and pulled open the door again, ready to run away from the scary man, but she stopped herself just before her foot went over the threshold to her room. She realised then that Leyla had purposely given her that order, the command that she stay in her room for the rest of the night, knowing that Heath would be there waiting for her when she got there.

Melody stepped back, knowing that she could not dare defy her mistress again. She then turned back to stare into his cold, black eyes, feeling her will break just a little bit more as she forced herself to follow the command she knew would be a terrifying test of her loyalty to Leyla, but she knew she had to do it.

"Good. Close the door behind you, sweetheart," Heath said,

wandering over to the bed and taking a seat. He patted the spot next to him on top of the duvet, indicating for her to join him, but she hesitated.

"What are you doing here, Heath?" Melody asked. She couldn't help but at least try to find out what her guardian had permitted him to do to her.

"This will all go a lot better if you just do as you're told and don't ask questions," he replied, grinning. "Let's put it this way, I'm allowed to do anything, anywhere, except in that one place Corey laid claim to a while back."

Melody felt as though she might be sick at the sheer thought of Heath touching her at all, let alone in such a vile way and she trembled as she peered back at him.

"Don't you fucking touch me," she replied, knowing that it was a useless threat. He could, and would, do anything he wanted with her. The warlock stood and pushed Melody back over to the doorway, his hands around her neck, and he pulled the door open and held her just millimetres from certain punishment.

"What did you say?" he demanded, smirking at her knowingly. Even though her freedom from him was just centimetres away, Melody knew that her demonic guardian would no doubt have a punishment ten times worse in store for her if she crossed that line, far more so if she bolted.

"Yes," she relinquished, and immediately heard the satisfied growl escape Heath's lips as he pressed her body into his, then pushed her back towards the bed and shut the door behind them.

CHAPTER EIGHT

The next morning, Heath placed an uncharacteristically gentle kiss on Melody's cheek. She groaned and turned her face away, pulling the covers tighter over her bruised body, feeling tender and weak. She was desperate for him to leave and had been awake since sunrise, laying still in the hope he would not want anything else from her until he was required to leave at breakfast time. Heath just laughed and walked away, but not before laying his finger on Melody's temple and muttering a quiet spell, healing her mistreated body instantly.

The pain subsided, and the bruises healed in less than a second, but the memory of their night together remained and would forever haunt her. Melody tried to fight the thoughts of his rough hands against her skin and forceful lips on hers. She had gone along with his every desire the night before but he had still been rough, and she felt disgusting and dirty. Corey had used her up and spat her back out again for both the fun of it and to get his bounty, but this felt one hundred times worse.

Melody sobbed into her pillow and curled up into a ball, a protective position that she knew was useless against these dark beings and their power over her. She knew she would have to get used to the idea, sooner or later, that she had no control, no say at all over her own life, and she would have to learn to follow every order without thinking for herself ever again. Even deviating ever so slightly from Leyla's order had cost Melody her dignity and more last night, and she vowed to herself that she would never let that happen again.

"Good morning, sunshine," Leyla chimed as she joined Melody in her room. "Have fun last night?" she asked her, knowing full well that she had not. Melody sat up in bed, pulling the covers around her naked body and she watched Leyla, feeling angry and betrayed that she had let such harm come to her after her promises at the meeting that day she had chosen to become her follower. She was well aware that Leyla owed her nothing, but she had never considered how much of a worthless plaything she would become under her guardianship. Melody had learned her lesson the hard way, and would make no such mistake again for as long as she lived, but she still couldn't stop that petulant side of herself coming through.

"Yeah, I've never tried anal-sex before. It was great fun," she replied grumpily, but quickly stopped herself from moaning further, afraid of angering her mistress.

"Perhaps you've learned lesson number three, then?" Leyla asked her, and Melody nodded, feeling utterly defeated.

"Yes guardian. I won't ever presume to know what you want from me again. I will ask you or await your instructions," she conceded, forcing herself not to go any further with her grumpy retorts.

"Good, I had hoped you would break sooner rather than later. This punishment, I hope, was the final straw in putting an end to your stubbornness towards my leadership. I have big plans for you Melody and I'm not interested in waiting for you to come around in your own time. Perhaps now you will save your opinions for yourself and always do as I have commanded," she replied, stroking Melody's cheek gently.

"I'm definitely broken all-right, I'll do anything you ask me to do, guardian. Just please don't ask me to let Heath do that ever again?" Melody pleaded, and Leyla smiled at her.

"He'll only be here when you are really naughty, and I didn't let him have every part of you did I?" she asked, her voice high-pitched and irritatingly upbeat as she stared into her hazel eyes for a moment as though she had done Melody a great kindness. "That part of you belongs to me now, only those I allow can have a piece of it."

Melody thought she detected a fleeting look of real affection in her gaze then, as though Leyla had wanted to keep that part of her sacred for some reason but it was quickly gone again so she soon put it down to her own wishful thinking, her own desperation and need for affection making her imagine it. Regardless of what Heath did or didn't do to her, the fact still remained that Leyla's plan had worked. Melody was at her complete command now and was ready to do whatever her mistress told her to.

"Donovan," Leyla called, leading the now freshly cleaned and made-up Melody across the dining room later that morning towards a tall, muscular man with jet-black hair and deep brown eyes. "Melody, this is," Leyla began, but she already knew exactly who this man was and blinked in shock as she held out a trembling hand.

"Donovan Caine, it's nice to meet you," he said in a surprisingly soft tone, taking her outstretched hand to shake. Melody had calmed down now after Leyla's visit and stern words, feeling somehow more relaxed and ready to serve than ever, too afraid to do anything else.

"My pleasure, Mr Caine," she muttered, stammering slightly, but she forced herself to smile.

Donovan smiled down at Melody, his perfect white teeth shining as he grinned, and his chiselled features reminded her a little of Corey and his timeless handsomeness. She quickly pushed those thoughts of her ex-lover away, reminding herself just how awful he had been to her these last few weeks, and she focussed instead on the Adonis before her. Donovan Caine was a welcome distraction. One of the biggest movie stars in all of Great Britain right now, he had worked alongside the biggest starlets in the USA and on home soil, starring in blockbuster hits and rapidly becoming the country's most wanted movie star. The paparazzi followed his every move, his sexy smile always ready to get snapped, and he made no secret of his sexual prowess, seemingly revelling in the attention he would get from women and men alike, but he made a point of never having public relationships. Donovan's exes were never featured in kiss-and-tell interviews, and his perfect name had never been tarnished by scandals or bad publicity. Melody realised now just how and why he had climbed to fame to quickly, the Crimson Brotherhood. He, like many others, including her father, had sold his soul for fame and fortune. He had probably started out as nothing and nobody, and had achieved seemingly overnight success as a movie and television actor. His now seven-figure deals made recent history and his epic physique was undoubtedly the star of many a bored housewife's daydreams while being the envy of their husband's. Melody could not believe that Donovan Caine was stood before her now, so calm, elegant and truly a natural beauty. She couldn't help but swoon, and staring up at him quickly helped to chase away her memories from the night before.

"Pleasure's all mine, believe me," Donovan replied, taking in the woman before him with intrigue and approval. "Guardian, a delight as always," he then added, taking Leyla's hand and placing a soft kiss on the back of it.

"This is the girl I was telling you about," Leyla said, giving her client a knowing look, and he nodded.

"Ah yes, you've outdone yourself guardian," Donovan replied, eyeing Melody curiously and she couldn't help but feel confused and uncomfortable under his scrutiny, feeling as though he were eyeing her up like a proffered prize. "It's lovely to meet you at last, Melody. Our mistress warned me that it might take a while until you were fully, acquiescent, so to speak. I'm happy to hear that it hasn't taken you too long to get used to the Crimson Brotherhood and your place in its slightly stricter world."

"Urm, yeah. This is all very new to me. I think I need some more information though, or permission to follow your lead," Melody replied, completely taken aback. She couldn't understand why Leyla hadn't told her herself that she and Donovan were seemingly going to be paired up. She thought to herself how surely that very point was exactly the reason she had been punished so severely the night before, so that Melody knew now not to take anyone's word but her mistress? Leyla sensed her hesitation and made their excuses, pulling Melody aside for a moment.

"Maybe you aren't ready after all?" she asked her, a fierce tone in her voice as she peered down at Melody icily.

"Of course I am. Look at him, no one would say no. But, I was waiting for you to tell me rather than it coming from him. I thought that was the point you made so eloquently last night?" she snapped, unable to stop herself or take back her snide reply, and Leyla immediately slapped her across the face, hard. She didn't care who watched and Melody fell to the ground clutching her burning cheek as tears stung her eyes and both cheeks glowed red thanks to the combination of the stinging pain and embarrassment at being struck in the middle of a busy brunch like an insolent child. Leyla then walked away without a word while Donovan approached and helped her up. Melody thanked him and noticed that despite his incredible acting ability in front of the cameras, he couldn't seem to hide the satisfied smile on his lips as he took in her rapidly bruising cheekbone.

Donovan shook the wry smile away and grabbed some ice from the drinks tray before wrapping them in a cloth. He then took Melody's hand and led her out towards the field at the back of the mansion, the huge grounds offering them both the chance to be alone and to take in the beautiful gardens all around while she held the offered ice-pack to her burning cheek.

"I'm sorry Donovan. I'm trying my best. I understand if you aren't interested," she mumbled, hating feeling so defeatist.

"I've made my decision already. I think I made it the second I saw you," he said, stopping and looking down at the quiet girl with an almost shy smile. "Our mistress was right, as usual, you're perfect for me."

"Donovan, I don't know what to say," she whispered, taken aback by his wonderful words.

"Just say you'll be mine and I'll do the rest," he promised, leaning down to kiss her unharmed cheek and Melody couldn't help but blush and swoon.

"I'm all yours, Mr Caine," she replied, making his smile widen.

Leyla and Corey watched the two of them from afar, the powerful guardians seeing the strong connection that had already seemed to come to life between them first-hand.

"Well done," Corey said, his tone cold and flat, just like his expression.

"Thank you, brother. I had hoped I was right about her. Even our parents have decreed that they be together after watching her progress over the last few weeks. I think there's more going on here than even we know about," Leyla replied, still watching her two followers thoughtfully.

"Business will be booming for Pembroke Enterprises once Caine is on board and their relationship is public. She will bring in many souls for us," Corey said, clearly seeing things from only the business standpoint.

"Yes, but I can't help but think it might be more than that. I wonder if perhaps I have inadvertently stumbled upon Donovan's soulmate with he. He has never responded this way to a woman in all his life and given his dark past that can mean only one thing, Melody Pembroke is more than what she seems," Leyla replied, her eyes on the clearly already enamoured couple before them.

"I think you're overthinking things, dear sister. She's nothing more than a plaything, don't you think I would have noticed if there was more to her than that?" he asked, and Leyla just shrugged, suspecting that he didn't want to admit that as well as not noticing what was right under his nose that he might have been wrong about what Melody was capable of as well.

"I'd like for us to meet for the first 'official' time somewhere public, like a function or party hosted by a mutual friend somewhere, for the cameras' sake," Donovan told Melody a while later after she had calmed down from Leyla's punishment and he had explained his arrangement with their guardian to her a little better. He too was her follower, marked and owned by Leyla however, Donovan was a client of hers rather than a puppet like Melody was. Leyla served him in many ways that would further the Crimson Brotherhood's reach and power over the industries surrounding him and his line of work in return for his continued service and, of course, his soul at the end of it all.

Melody had watched him intently, her hazel eyes peering up into his dark ones as he spoke, and he enchanted her. Donovan Caine was a truly beautiful man. His arms were covered in dark, gothic tattoo sleeves depicting fallen angels and a beautiful woman atop a throne made up of human skulls that she couldn't help but wonder might be his interpretation of the Dark Queen. She had previously seen his torso in magazines so knew that his chest and back were covered too, with dark wings that spread across his shoulders and a huge skull on his chest. Today, though, he looked effortlessly relaxed in his grey suit trousers and black shirt he wore open at the neck, the sleeves of which were rolled up, showing off his impressive forearms. Donovan had seemed relaxed with her, talking and moving with Melody like a genuine gentleman. He soon made her buzz with the hope that he was telling the truth about being pleased with her as Leyla's choice for whatever plans they might have for her as his new conquest, however he hadn't been completely forthcoming with those plans as yet.

"I'm sure our mistress can arrange something suitable. Have you had any dealings with my father's movie studios?" Melody asked, trying to think of a place where they could feasibly meet each other under the eyes of their peers.

"You mean, your movie studio," Donovan corrected her, but gave Melody's hand a gentle, supportive squeeze. She nodded and shrugged.

"It's all still very new. I can't even begin to think of it all as mine," she told him, opening up a little. Melody twisted a lock of her auburn hair around her finger absentmindedly as she spoke, her thoughts turning to her father and her heart hurting a little at the memory of his funeral just the day before. Donovan reached across and slid his hand up her forearm, pulling the curl free before taking her small hand in his.

"You'll get used to it. The Crimson Brotherhood love to take whatever they want, but in return, the things they have given me far outweigh anything I have to offer," he replied, tapping his chest thoughtfully, seemingly indicating his soul.

"Don't you worry about the afterlife? Surely we will just become demonic playthings bound for eternal pain and suffering?" she asked him, careful not to talk too loudly about her concerns.

"Yeah, but I know I'm bound for Hell no matter what. I might as well live it up while I've got the chance. I'll owe what I owe when I get to the other side."

"That's one way to think about it," Melody conceded. She could understand his thinking, and even found herself agreeing with him. She might as well enjoy herself. After all, her father had not given her the choice of whether to sell her soul or not, but Leyla had still chosen to give her riches and potentially a hot, movie star boyfriend, so she hoped that this life of servitude wasn't actually turning out too badly in the long-run. If only she could just close her mind to the terrible lessons she had needed to learn so far. Donovan smiled, a broad, happy grin that Melody couldn't help but find infectious, and she immediately perked up again, grinning back across at him, their hands still entwined.

"Now that I think about it, there was a script I liked from Pembroke Studios. How about we set up a sit-down in a few weeks and we can have an official meeting to discuss it? We will hit it off immediately, of course, and then I will take you to a dinner or something just the two of us a short while afterwards?" Donovan asked her, and Melody blushed.

"Why, Mr Caine, are you asking me out on a date?" she teased, making him laugh.

"Yeah, I guess I am," Donovan replied, the look on his face telling Melody that he hadn't done so in a very long time.

Leyla later told Melody that her suspicions were right and that Donovan had sold his soul for riches and fame, but that Leyla had also agreed to give him more. To give him a trophy wife to have on his arm and to pose for the paparazzi with on the red carpet at his movie premiers. He wanted a beautiful, self-reliant woman who had a strong will yet who could be persuaded to adapt to his, as she put it, 'alternative lifestyle,' but she refused to tell Melody any more. Donovan's request had clearly needed much thought, but Leyla confided in her she had gone to him straight after Melody had joined her following and offered him her new follower, the multi-millionaire heiress with a strong business acumen and just the right qualities he was looking for in a woman.

"You're not obviously good looking, but you have pretty eyes and with a decent makeup artist on hand and a proper haircut, you'll do nicely," Leyla added, leading her back to her bedroom.

"Thanks. I bet there was a compliment in there somewhere," Melody joked, getting a rare laugh from her powerful guardian.

"You did well today, after your momentary lapse in etiquette, but I'll let that slide. We'll put it down to your girl boner over Donovan," Leyla teased and Melody laughed loudly.

"A girl boner?" she cried, shaking her head.

Leyla continued to laugh with her, the two of them acting like real friends for a change and Melody almost forgot what her mistress had put her through the last few weeks, especially the night before in order to achieve her acceptance of this dark world so quickly. It was almost as though Leyla had known that Donovan's affections were a time-sensitive issue and she wanted Melody to be the one he chose, but of course she would never presume to understand her strange and scary guardian's motives, she had grossly mistaken her actions before and had vowed to herself that she would never do it again.

CHAPTER NINE

Melody stood staring out at the lake a few weeks later. She was still confined to the Crimson Brotherhood's headquarters but now that she had gotten used to it she found it to be a surprisingly nice, homely place that was so large she actually found she had plenty of space in which to be alone thanks to the impressive grounds. The sunset looked beautiful against the roaming Yorkshire hills and autumn sky, and she wandered down to the wooden dock thoughtfully. Donovan had been in touch and had set up a meeting with her and some of her associates at Pembroke Studios to discuss the script. Many of her colleagues had either now been forced into service of the Brotherhood or had been replaced by those already initiated, but they all still had their parts to play in order to make it all seem real to those outside of their orders' command to continue the Crimson Brotherhood's reach and sway. They had a brunch meeting arranged for the next morning and she found herself excited to see Donovan again, his impressive body and warm smile playing on her mind, and Melody couldn't help but think that a future with him by her side, even playing the part of the trophy wife, was not all too bad.

"Fancy a swim?" said a voice she knew all too well from behind her, and Melody froze in surprise and fear. Strong arms wrapped around her from behind and soft lips found her cheek, laying uncharacteristically gentle kisses on her jaw.

"No thank you guardian, I ought to be heading back," she replied, remembering her enforced manners despite her loathing of her ex. She then started trembling as Corey began nibbling on her earlobe, trailing kisses along her neck as he held her there, not letting Melody leave.

"I've missed you," he whispered, his kisses making their way across her jaw again, and she laughed uncontrollably.

"Liar."

"It's true. The taste of your sweet pussy still lingers on my lips, Mel. I want you," Corey told her, turning Melody around to face him and then planting a deep, intense kiss on her lips.

"I don't care what you want. I don't belong to you," she replied, desperately trying to get away from his grip and intense gaze.

"As if I give a shit about what you want or to whom you belong," he whispered and then teleported her away without another word.

Corey threw Melody down onto his huge bed, the bed she had watched him in with her sister just a few weeks before, and she shook her head, climbing up off it and making her way over to the door.

"No, I'm not your girlfriend anymore, or your follower. I don't even like you, you disgust me," she said, trembling with fear as she spoke, but she knew she couldn't let him have his wicked way with her tonight.

Corey stepped closer and pinned Melody to the wall behind with his powerful body, staring down into her hazel eyes as he took in the strong-willed girl before him. He regarded her for a moment, his deep blue eyes seeming dark in the dim light, and he stroked her cheek with his hand, brushing the stray locks of hair behind her ear.

"I hated you back then. I hated the fact that I had to give part of myself to some foolish human girl in order to get what was rightfully ours all along. I used you, Melody. I pretended to love you, to feel and all the while I was just having my cake and eating it too," Corey admitted, confirming her suspicions at last.

"Then why do this now?" she asked, her voice faltering as she peered up at him.

"Because somehow the thought of you and Donovan together stirs something inside of me. You are mine. You were mine before I let Leyla have you and you were still mine when I wouldn't let Heath have all of you," he replied, and Melody shuddered at the memory. She pushed him away from her with a groan. Her feeble arms did nothing against his rock-hard body, but Corey stepped backwards anyway, giving her some room to breathe.

"How did you become such a cold, vicious monster? What made you this way?" she asked.

"Not what, who. I told you before about my last girlfriend, you remember? She tore my heart out, ripped it into a thousand pieces and then burned it in the ashes of our relationship to make sure that I could never love again. I do not love you. I never did and never will Melody, but I do want to fuck you. I want to make you scream so loud that the whole headquarters can hear you. I need to feel you come so hard that you fall to pieces thanks to my touch and cannot sit down for a week," he replied, grinning sexily at her and Melody's core tensed wonderfully at the sheer thought, betraying her head and heart with every tight throb.

"No. I belong to your sister. You don't touch me again until she tells me to let you. I've learnt that lesson already, as well you know," she told him, walking over to the door. Melody wanted nothing more than to leave Corey there, to have him watch her walk out and to slam the door in his face. She got a kick out of the thought of leaving him unsatisfied and alone.

"Leyla's standing behind that mirror. She wants to watch us," Corey replied, pointing at the same mirror Melody and Leyla had watched him through not long before, so she knew it was possible. "Why don't you ask her yourself?" he added, sensing that she was intrigued.

Melody paused and took her hand off of the door handle. She looked back at him and Corey shrugged nonchalantly, his calm, sexy prowess making her wonder if he might be telling her the truth. She wandered over to the mirror, staring at her reflection, unable to actually see whether her guardian was on the other side or not.

"Mistress?" she whispered, her eyes searching for any sound or sign of movement behind her reflected image. The lights then turned off, engulfing Melody in complete darkness. She gasped and wrapped her arms around herself, feeling fearful and regretting the way she had just spoken to Corey. Despite their past, he was still a member of the Black family and a guardian in the Crimson Brotherhood alongside his siblings. Melody knew she should have never spoken to him that way and found herself shaking hard thanks to the adrenaline and fear that rushed through her now.

"I don't want her to see," whispered Corey's voice in her ear, and she could sense that he was standing just inches away from her still trembling body. He laughed, a breathy, soft snigger and then turned Melody to face him. She could still see nothing as he lifted her by the thighs before moving back over to the bed, where he wrapped them around himself, his lips finding hers in the darkness. He then laid her down and pulled off her clothes, peeling each layer slowly as though he were unwrapping a much anticipated present, taking time to kiss and touch her as he went.

Melody couldn't see a thing in the pitch-black darkness, but Corey didn't seem to have any trouble at all and he commanded her body in a way she hated him for, wishing she could push him away and say no. But another part of her desperately wanted the pleasure that she knew he was more than capable of delivering her, and she gave in. When his mouth then devoured her aching cleft, Melody called out incoherently and writhed on the bed, gripping the sheets beneath her in her hands as he circled her swollen clit with his tongue and delved his fingers inside her wet opening.

"Still so sweet," he murmured, the vibrations from his voice making her shudder beneath him. He sucked her nub gently for a few more minutes, moving slowly inside of her and then as Melody neared her release, he quickened his pace, sensing her closeness. As she came, he clamped down hard with his lips, heightening her sensitivity and delivering Melody to her second climax within seconds. He then climbed over her in the darkness, pulling off his own clothing as she panted and trembled beneath him, this time from her wonderful pulsating waves of pleasure instead of her fear. Corey then pushed himself inside of her, lifting her hips to meet his and thrusting inside of his conquest hard. Melody cried out with pleasure as he lifted her legs and placed them over his shoulders, opening her up to him further, and he didn't hold back. She still couldn't see a thing, but the powerful strokes of him inside her after so long made Melody's every wonderful sense feel heightened, and she allowed herself a rare moment to enjoy it.

After he had reached his own release, Corey pulled her close and embraced her tightly, their bodies still so hot, but he didn't care.

"That was fun. Now get the fuck out of here," he then told her, sliding off the bed and then flicking on the lights before handing Melody her clothes with a wicked grin.

She knew she should feel hurt, angry, and used, but now more than ever Melody knew for sure that she no longer cared for her ex and she just laughed off his taunt. He smirked at her, ready for the tears or the begging, but he didn't get it. Melody just grinned back at him and quickly got herself dressed.

"With pleasure," she replied as she opened the door and wandered out without even a backwards glance.

"Have fun?" Leyla asked her as Melody made her way inside her room and got undressed for a shower. She had teleported in just after Melody had returned, a knowing smile on her lips.

"Yes mistress, it was quite fun I will admit," she replied, looking over at her guardian playfully, but she was still worried she might be punished for accepting Corey's attentions. "Am I in trouble?" she asked, wanting to check. She removed the last of her clothing, her adrenaline and hormones still making her buzz, but she was eager to wash Corey's smell off of her, hating him as much as ever.

"Not at all. When any member of the Black family asks for you to do something, it is your duty as a member of the Crimson Brotherhood to do as they have requested. Anyone else and I would have interfered right from the beginning, but not with him," Leyla replied, eyeing Melody's naked body as she grabbed a towel and wandered into the en-suite.

"Thank you guardian, I wasn't sure you'd be okay with it. After all, you did say that I was to be with Donovan?" she asked, and Leyla joined her in the small bathroom while Melody began washing her own sweat and smell of her lover from her still sensitive body.

"Like I said, anyone else, absolutely not. And anyway, you still have a lot to learn when it comes to Mr Caine. Things between the two of you are to move slowly and you are absolutely forbidden from having sex before you are married, as per my father's orders," she told her over the sound of the running water. Melody poked her head through the gap in the curtain, a confused look on her face.

"I don't understand. I thought that was not one of your laws?" she asked.

"It's not," Leyla replied, her face stern. "But it is one of your orders, so do not question it again, Melody."

"I won't, I'm sorry," she immediately conceded before getting on with her shower in silence.

Leyla stayed with Melody as she dried off and got herself ready for bed, Melody feeling so at ease with her guardian now that she no longer worried about being naked before her. The terrible lessons she had been taught since that day in David Pembroke's final meeting had already changed her. Melody knew it to her core. She was no longer the timid girl she once was, her confident nature having finally surfaced while her clever, self-preserving prowess had also taken the front-seat and she somehow felt completely at ease with being given orders to follow now. Melody had come to realise though that she had been following orders her entire life. Her father had come back into her life when she was a teenager, giving his long-lost daughter money for her future and also the financial backing to go to university, but only if she did everything he asked her to, including never telling another soul that she was his child. She now knew why.

When Melody had finished her schooling, David had wanted her to work for him, demanded it even. And, while he had made her go through the internship program and interview process like anyone else in order to maintain her cover, he had groomed Melody to be the perfect candidate and none of his aides ever noticed his preferential treatment towards her. They only ever talked closely in private, or on David's secure telephone line, and Melody realised now that he had always intended for her to inherit his business, but perhaps not quite so soon. David Pembroke had been given everything he had ever dreamed of, but he had sold his own soul plus, albeit unknowingly, that of his only child, in order to acquire those things. Thinking of him now, Melody knew she could not be angry with her father. If anything, she pitied him.

'I will never be like you, but then again, I will never get to choose who I become thanks to your selfish choices,' she thought to herself as she climbed into bed, almost having forgotten that Leyla was still hovering.

"Did you enjoy it in his arms, Melody? His mouth on yours as he made you come?" Leyla asked, stepping forward and taking a seat on the bed beside her. Melody gasped, shocked by her questions and she stared at her wide-eyed.

"I hate him. I wanted to walk away and leave him there frustrated and alone," she answered.

"But you didn't, why?"

"Because I hoped he was telling the truth. I liked the thought of you watching," Melody told her, being brazen, but she didn't care. Despite everything she had been through at her hands, there was a real bond between her and Leyla, and she loved it.

"I was watching," the guardian admitted, a sly grin curling at her lips.

"Even in the dark?" Melody asked, looking coy.

"Yes, especially then. Corey knows I can see better in darkness. My senses are keener, second to none, Melody."

"Then why?"

"Because it is I who owns you, and I own every inch. Despite what my brother might think, I allowed tonight to happen because I knew you could do with the release. I control everything that happens to you, and I decide everything you do. Even if you don't realise it yourself at the time."

"Then why don't you order me to be with you instead? If you asked me to kiss you, I'd do it in a heartbeat," Melody said, feeling butterflies in her stomach at the sheer thought.

"Because, for one, I don't ever get involved with my followers. They all fall for me Melody, it comes with the territory, so I never trust it when foolish girls want me to kiss them." Leyla said, chastising her a little with her snide comment. "And two, do you think I would ever have to order someone to kiss me? They beg for it, Mel. They would have to worship me like a goddess before I'd even consider something as small as a kiss. Don't forget who you are talking to," Leyla told her, and Melody cringed at her forwardness.

"I'm sorry mistress, I wasn't being presumptuous, I just," she started, but Leyla stopped her.

"You're forgiven. Now, go to bed. You have a big day tomorrow."

CHAPTER TEN

The next morning, Melody was rudely awoken by a small, grumpy yet beautiful woman, who shook her awake and then barked orders at her.

"Get up. Wear this. Sit down," she said, pointing to some clothes that had been laid out and then a small chair in the centre of the room. Melody yawned loudly but did as the woman had told her, sliding into a stunning but sophisticated black suit dress and then taking the seat.

She sat for a short while, being poked and prodded by the woman, who fiddled and fussed with her hair and makeup before finally stepping back and looking at Melody thoughtfully.

"Yes, you'll do," she then said.

"Well done Meri, perfect as usual," said Leyla as she joined them, and the woman performed a small bow before heading back out the door.

Melody stood and checked herself out in the mirror, finding her reflection far from the scruffy image she thought she would see after only being out of bed for twenty minutes. Her auburn hair had been tied up in a delicate knot on top of her head, the sides having been pulled up and pinned in place to create a classic, beautiful look that framed her oval face perfectly. Her makeup was stunning, seemingly natural, but the light touches of dark brown on her eyelids accentuated her hazel eyes effortlessly.

"Whoa, Meri really knows her stuff," she murmured as she took herself in.

"She sure does. I have asked her to be your assistant, so from now on expect to wake up to her happy face each morning," Leyla replied, laughing as Melody rolled her eyes.

"Who needs an alarm clock? Get up! Wear this! Sit down!" Melody joked, imitating the woman, but she was also grateful for her help, knowing that it would have taken her hours to make herself look this good.

"Donovan will be pleased," Leyla said with a sly grin, ushering her towards the door with her.

They ate breakfast alone in the large hall that catered for all live-in members of the order, Leyla running through some more details with Melody regarding their working arrangements.

"So, no more moving around the offices. As you can gather, there is no longer any need for secrecy. We have procured you the top five floors of the building next door to Black Rose's premises in London, and you are now in complete control of Pembroke Enterprises. There's no board of directors, no shareholders for you to answer to, but you will be surrounded at all times by your aides, all of whom are fellow members of the Crimson Brotherhood. Your working relationship with Black Rose will not be common knowledge, but you will not make any decisions without coming to me first. I know you understand that concept at last, don't you?" Leyla asked, one eyebrow cocked.

"Absolutely," Melody agreed, not having to be warned twice.

"Good, here are your things," Leyla added, producing a large plastic wallet and handing it to her. Inside were Melody's new passport, driving licence, bankcards and even a replacement birth certificate, all in her new name – Miss Melody Pembroke. There were also deeds and official documents proving her ownership of both the company, a house in an area of London named Primrose Hill and the business premises Leyla had just told her about plus a new mobile phone, a final link to the real world outside these dark walls.

"Wow, this suddenly all feels very real," she admitted, looking up at Leyla with a scared look.

"That's because it is. Your new life awaits you, Melody, but there will be a certain amount of trust involved. Trust that you need to earn before you can go it alone," Leyla told her. "You are never to be without a member of the Crimson Brotherhood by your side, and you will continue to live here at first until you are ready to move into your new home in London. Meri will then live with you. She is to become your full-time assistant and will report back to me on your progress. I will only see you when necessary, but I will stop by to check in on you from time to time as well, just to make sure you're following my orders and being a good girl," she added, smiling playfully.

"Wow. Okay, but will I really need a live-in nanny?" Melody joked, and Leyla nodded firmly.

"Yes, she will be everything you need her to be Melody, so do not joke. You may even find Meri to be the one being who might save your life one day, or save you from a beating. She is a succubus demon Melody, have you ever heard of one before?" Leyla asked her, and she nodded confusedly.

"I thought they are demons that make men have sex with them?" Melody asked her.

"They used to be, but times change and so must our kind. Many succubae work in the movie industry, or even in the escort business. They are beautiful, smart women whose job it is to seduce men, but they have many means with which to do it. Meri does enjoy the company of her conquests, of course, but she has moved away from her old life. She joined the Crimson Brotherhood many years ago and has used her talents for our benefit ever since. Her abilities lie in her hands and Meri delights in using them to produce seductive works of art, as such. Take your styling this morning, effortless yet stunning. She is also cunning, strong, fast, and intuitive. You will benefit profoundly from having her around Melody. Not everyone is so lucky."

"Whoa, that's so cool, my own demonic assistant. You should get her to make you look pretty sometime," Melody joked, jumping up from her seat and running over to the coffee machine before Leyla could retaliate. The powerful woman just watched her with a smile as Melody filled two mugs and brought them over.

"It's a good thing you appeased me with caffeine, otherwise you'd be across my knee right now," she told her, a playful threat, but Melody couldn't help but wonder if she would ever actually do it.

Leyla escorted Melody down the corridor inside one of Pembroke Studios' many wings a short while later, steering her in the direction of the casting office. Inside were many people Melody had never met before—script writers, producers, and the director of the movie that they were pitching to Donovan, whom she was told would be arriving any second. She chatted with the team quietly for a minute, playing her executive role well and she soon felt comfortable, her business-head back on and she felt at ease back in this persona she had always played so well. Luckily, Leyla and her other siblings were so reclusive that no one in the business world knew what they looked like, so it didn't matter that she accompanied Melody today. She had reminded her not to say her name just in case, but Melody already knew never to make that mistake again.

When Donovan entered, the entire room fell silent, basking in the ominous man's sexy, haughty presence, and everyone peered up at him in awe. He had with him an entourage of assistants, his own producers and writers, along with a lawyer, briefcase in hand, who took a seat to await the impending contract that may soon need negotiating.

"Mr Caine, it is a pleasure to meet you. My name is Melody Pembroke," she said when she had her chance to greet him, offering him her hand to shake. He eyed her with a warm, sexy smile and shook it.

"I'm sure it is, Miss Pembroke," he joked, and she couldn't help but grin.

She then introduced him to the team, each of them taking a seat around the large round table while they discussed the project and hashed-out the finer details. By the end of the day, the negotiations were done, and both parties were satisfied, so the contract was made up and signed.

"Here's to a wonderful partnership," Donovan whispered to Melody as he kissed her cheek, passing her a glass of champagne to celebrate their deal.

"A movie about making a deal with the devil. How poignant," she replied, clinking glasses with him before taking a long swig of the bubbly drink.

"Miss Pembroke, I'm afraid you have a plane to catch, so we need to go. The car is waiting," said a voice beside her. It was Leyla, and she was eyeing her sternly.

"Of course, thank you for reminding me, Lisa. Mr Caine, will I see you again in a few weeks when re-writes commence?" she asked, handing him one of her posh new business cards.

"Sure, I'll call," he answered, stashing the card in his pocket and watching her as she left, never taking his eyes off his new project as she said her goodbyes to the teams.

"Well done, but you seemed to forget that it was meant to be the first time you two met. The air was buzzing thanks to your connection, so I decided it was time to get you out of there. All the others will just think you two seemed to hit it off quickly rather than anything more," Leyla told her as she and Melody climbed into the waiting car. Heath turned around to look at them both, a disgusting smile on his lips as he took a lingering glance at Melody and her stunning new look.

"Where to?" he asked, still not taking his eyes off her.

"The airport. We need to catch a flight somewhere," Leyla replied, looking across at Melody. "You have offices in Barcelona, Venice, and Frankfurt. We can jump on a plane to any of those in the next hour and make out that you had business to attend to there," she added, looking at the flight timetables on her mobile phone.

"Venice sounds good?" Melody answered, and after a quick nod from Leyla and a couple of taps on her handset, they were booked in. "Are you coming with me?" she then asked, surprised.

"Yes, there are a few things I need to tell you about your beloved movie star Melody and it would be better if we had some privacy," Leyla answered, her gaze flicking over to their driver and Melody nodded, unsure what truths she needed to learn about him but she was hopeful that they weren't going to be too awful.

CHAPTER ELEVEN

Leyla and Melody sat atop the rooftop bar later that evening, basking in the glorious end of summer sunshine, dressed in billowing skirts and skimpy tops. The Italian sun was still intense and wonderful, reminding Leyla somewhat of her real home, Hell.

A waiter deposited two glasses of dark red wine before them and she took a long, appreciative sip. It had been a long time since she had taken a break from her usually so hectic schedule and taking some time off was nice, despite it being a last-minute tactic she had needed to use in order to keep up the pretence of Melody and Donovan's long courtship.

"You look beautiful, just basking in the sunshine," Melody told her mistress, meaning every word. "When was the last time you took a break?"

"Thank you, it's been far too long since I just sat and enjoyed the sun on my skin. As you might have already guessed, I'm kind of a workaholic," she replied, taking another swig of her wine with a smile.

"I don't believe that for a second," Melody replied, jumping as the new phone in her bag began to chime loudly. She grabbed it and stared at the screen for a moment, reading and re-reading the text message Donovan had just sent her a few times. Leyla grabbed the phone out of her hands, reading the words aloud.

"So, today I met a beautiful, talented, and alluring business woman whom I couldn't help but undress with my mind the entire time. I think I even signed on to star in a movie where I only get naked once, which goes against everything I stand for so I am endeavouring to amend it so that I get to show off my impressive body and gargantuan cock at least three times, not that there's a certain Chief Executive I'm trying to impress or anything," she said, laughing.

"Hmm, gargantuan cock?" Melody mused, looking dreamy for a moment as she imagined Donovan naked.

"It's not quite that big, don't get your hopes up, Mel," she told her, laughing when Melody pouted in annoyance.

"Ah well, I'm not allowed to partake anyway, am I?" she asked, reminding Leyla that she still had some things to tell her about the gorgeous man, and she knew it was time.

"There is a good reason you are not to be with him in that way yet, Melody. Why you cannot give yourself to him too soon," she began, putting the phone away so that she had Melody's full attention. "Donovan is a very passionate, overwhelming lover and many a powerful woman has fallen to pieces after he has walked away from them. Although he has asked me for a wife, I cannot guarantee that he will stay interested after he has had you. Donovan is a man who enjoys power and the control of the conquest, but he often loses interest once the prize is his. I do not want that to happen to you, Melody. Even my parents recognise the necessity to enforce the rules here," Leyla told her, and Melody's smile dropped, but she could understand it.

"There's more," she continued, not letting her speak until all the cards were on the table. "Donovan Caine is more than just a womaniser Mel, he is a powerful lover in every sense of the word. His tastes have grown darker and more violent over the years and he now expects full control and submission from his concubines. He is currently forbidden from picking up lovers in the conventional way because we have had to pay off women in the past that he took things too far with. Their silence did not come cheap and so now he may only fuck those who have been paid large sums of money to do so. Those who have expertise in the area and are willing to take what he has to offer, those who sign a contract beforehand not to sue him or tell anyone what he has done to them."

"Whoa, fucking hell. So what, he beats the shit out of them while they have sex or something?" Melody asked, and Leyla nodded. "Why couldn't I just find a nice, normal guy?" she added, her mind racing with her interpretation of the so sexy man's sordid preferences in the bedroom. "He can't have always been like this, do you think he could ever have a real relationship?" she asked, hating the idea of having not only an arranged marriage but also one that could never progress to a real one thanks to the lack of sexual contact.

"He is a nice, normal guy, Melody. He just has a side to him he cannot control, nor does he even want to. The gratification he gets from those violent encounters not only serves to quench that thirst within but also to calm him when it comes to everyday life. It is not a disease, nor is it something that he needs curing of. You will just need to find your way, but that will take some time. Time that we are giving you between now and your wedding, which will only go ahead once my father is satisfied that you can handle him. You two do seem to have a connection already though. Perhaps in time you could tame his needs a little, but if you move too soon, he will destroy you, Melody. He will make what Heath did to you a fond memory. Put it that way," Leyla told her with a grim look, and Melody had to try hard to swallow the lump in her throat. "Lots of our members pair up to help further their careers, but do not have real relationships with one another when the cameras are off and the doors are closed. Prominent and very famous homosexuals have been marrying one another for centuries to maintain their 'normal' cover," she added, but the explanation still didn't help to put Melody at ease.

"So, I'm destined to be in either a violent or sexless marriage with only my ex who hates me to keep me company and the disgusting warlock on hand to teach me a lesson when I've been bad? Sounds like a fucking amazing life you've planned for me. I know you don't owe me a thing, that I'm nothing but a puppet for you and your family to command, but it still feels shit," Melody replied, downing her wine and walking away, tears streaming down her cheeks as she walked as quickly as possible back to her room, desperate to be alone.

When she reached her room, Melody flung herself on the bed, sobbing into her pillow. She soon felt a hand on her shoulder, but she wasn't interested in talking it over just yet.

"Please leave me alone. I just need to be by myself right now," she said, hoping that Leyla would give her some privacy, but instead, she felt the bed dip as her companion sat down on the bed behind her.

"No chance," whispered Corey, who grinned down at her when Melody turned over onto her back to look up at him in surprise.

"What are you doing here?" she demanded, wiping her eyes.

"I wanted to come and see if you were okay," he replied, looking down at her with a concerned expression.

"Fucking liar," she replied, but laughed when Corey couldn't help but grin broadly at her.

"Can't blame a guy for trying."

"Can tell him to go fuck himself though," she replied, realising now that their mutual dislike of one another had turned into a somehow playful back and forth that they shared openly. No more pretence, no more fake romance, and Melody much preferred knowing where she stood with the powerful, dangerous man.

"Okay, I was feeling horny and figured I'd come and see if you were feeling the same way, too? I never thought watching you walk away from me last night would leave me wanting you so much more. I'm just glad we don't have to pretend anymore," he told her, sliding down her skirt and panties as he did so, and Melody didn't stop him.

"What if I say no?" she teased, opening her legs wide and showing off her ready body, her tears now long forgotten.

"I'll be persuasive," he replied, sliding down his trousers and joining Melody on the bed. Corey immediately plunged himself inside her wet and ready opening, groaning as her muscles tightened around him instantly.

"It seems you've persuaded me this time, Mr Black," Melody said, groaning as he slid in and out, hard and fast.

"I always do," he replied, grinning wickedly down at her as she came undone beneath him.

Melody dozed lightly on the bed a couple of hours later, grateful that Corey had visited her to take her mind off of the terrible truths Leyla had told her, but now she just wanted him to go away again. They'd had their fun, but now she was ready to apologise to her guardian, knowing that she had been wrong to storm off.

"I think it's time for you to go, don't you?" she asked, laying on her front on the bed while Corey lay beside her messing around with his mobile phone. He then discarded his handset, turning to face her on his side.

"Did she tell you about him, what he does to women?" Corey asked, and Melody nodded. "You know he'll have to take many masochistic lovers over your marriage while you remain unloved and never getting fucked?" he added, enjoying toying with her emotions. He just could not help himself.

"Yep, thanks for reminding me. I guess it looks like I'll be a trophy wife who'll have to endure his numerous affairs or sit back while he pays women to let him beat the shit out of them, all the while hoping that he never turns that side of himself on me," she replied, her face forlorn.

"Being submissive to a dominant lover is not just about his needs. Yes, there's the pain, but it's also about the control, the trust and, more importantly, the pleasure. I can teach you how to submit," he offered, sliding his hand down Melody's naked back.

"That would require me to trust you, which I can never do again. Maybe I should just learn to take a beating," she replied, burying her face in the pillow to hide the tears that stung her eyes at the sheer thought.

"I could teach you that, too," Corey whispered as he climbed over her and lifted Melody's hips off the bed and she instinctively bent her knees, pushing her thighs closed. Corey grinned, stroking her soft skin as she arched her back and tilted her hips up invitingly. He slid himself inside her again, thrusting hard as she moaned beneath him. He pushed her knees together tighter, enjoying his power over her more than ever. Corey then reached over and grabbed her robe from the hook beside the bed, slipping the tie from its loops. "We'll see, shall we?" he asked her, pulling Melody's hands around behind her back and quickly tying them together in an unyielding knot, his hard-on still pressed deep within her clenched cleft. She tried to wriggle free, testing the knot, and he quickly slapped her bum cheek, hard. So hard that she cried out and he couldn't help but smile.

"Please don't hurt me," she begged, breathing heavily. The pleasure from his penetrating hardness and the pain from his slap combined in a far stranger, more satisfying way than she would ever have realised before, and Melody knew she wanted more.

"Do as you're told and I won't have to. Face down, arse up Mel, or else I give you a matching handprint on the other cheek," he ordered, and she quickly righted her posture. Corey grabbed the knot between her wrists, using it as an anchor as he fucked her hard, sliding himself all the way out before thrusting his long cock inside her again and pressing himself into her g-spot.

"Fuck," Melody cried as an orgasm claimed her. She trembled and bucked thanks to the forceful sensations, but Corey carried on. His hands slid from the knot and grabbed her hips hard as he continued his thrusts. He then slid his right thumb slowly across her bum cheek, down to her clit for a few circular sweeps and then up towards her behind, stroking her tight bud in the centre gently. Melody immediately squirmed, not wanting him to push her into doing it that way. "No," she begged, crying out as another slap singed her other bum cheek.

"Tell me what he did, and how it felt," Corey demanded, his fingertip still circling the tight opening gently. "Tell me," he said again, pressing himself inside her harder.

"He forced me down and shoved it in. He wasn't gentle, and he didn't care. Does that make you happy, you bastard?" she shouted, tears streaming down her cheeks.

"No, you know it doesn't. Did he make you come?"

"Yes," she admitted, ashamed to say so.

"Show me," Corey said, sliding himself out of her and pulling open her bum cheeks. "Trust me Mel, relax. I'll be slow, I won't hurt you."

For some reason she hated herself for, Melody instinctively followed his command, relaxing her body and unclenching her muscles as he slid the tip inside, moving slowly as he pushed more of his hard length inside her tight back opening. He slowly moved in and out, feeling her relax more and more with each thrust before she could eventually take all of him, her body welcoming and ready.

"Corey," she groaned, coming for him again as he continued his pursuit of her, desperate for her submission and getting it. He slid his hand down to her clit again, stroking it as she climaxed and delivering her with an almost instantaneous second orgasm as he shuddered with his own release.

Corey then untied her and slid himself out of Melody's still throbbing body, the two of them falling into an exhausted heap on the bed alongside each other. She trembled, trying to fight her emotions and failing miserably, but he just held her.

Neither spoke as they rested, both of them staring at the ceiling both shocked and turned on by what had just happened between them. Melody had never thought she would trust Corey again, let alone trust him enough to let him tie her up and have his way with her so forcefully. He had given her a wonderful insight into the world of the submissive and dominative relationship, and while she knew Donovan was one hundred steps ahead of her on that road, she had to admit she had thoroughly enjoyed her taster. Corey then stood and began getting dressed, watching her as Melody wrapped the robe around herself and pulled the tie closed with blushing cheeks as she wound the satin rope closed.

"Well done. Lesson two continues tomorrow," he told her, and Melody looked up at him wide-eyed. He laughed and shrugged. "Worth a try," he added.

He stepped forward and Melody thought for a moment he was going to give her a kiss goodbye, hating that she secretly wanted it. Instead, Corey lifted his hand to her cheek, taking it in his palm and staring down into her eyes for a second before he pulled it back and swung it over to meet her face again with such force that she fell backwards onto the bed. Melody's hand immediately came up to hold her burning cheek as she screamed in pain, cursing him under her breath.

"Don't ever say my name again, even when you're coming," he scalded her before teleporting away, a sick, satisfied smile on his gorgeous face.

CHAPTER TWELVE

Melody stayed in her room alone for the rest of the night, she had a long, hot bath and while she was angry, as usual, at Corey, she also couldn't help but remember their time together with a stupid grin on her face.

Leyla brought her breakfast the next morning, eyeing her still red cheek but she said nothing. Melody was sure that she somehow knew what had gone on between her and Corey anyway, so she didn't bother explaining.

"Our flight is at nine o'clock tonight," Leyla reminded Melody, who wolfed down her croissant and coffee in seconds, famished thanks to having not eaten since dinnertime the day before.

"Can we go on a gondola before we leave?" Melody asked, having forced away her unease. She was grinning excitedly at her mistress and Leyla couldn't help but say yes, completely enthralled by her eagerness. They spent the day riding around on the fantastic waterways and taking in the views of the breath-taking city, stopping for coffee and shopping while chatting away as though their hard conversation the day before hadn't happened.

"I really do like you sometimes, by the way," Melody told Leyla later that afternoon as they devoured pizza and shared a bottle of expensive wine.

"There's a compliment in there somewhere," Leyla replied, grinning over at her.

"I know me and your brother are having some kind of strange, kinky fun, but I still hate him. I just wanted you to know. I guess I just like those moments when he stops being such a monster and makes me feel good about myself for a change. It's fucked up I know, but in this crazy little world I'm in it makes sense to find my happiness somewhere, even if it is with someone I hate," Melody told her, admitting to her guardian, and to herself, how she was feeling at last.

She was lost, sometimes feeling so alone that she wanted nothing more than to just fade away. But there had been just a few moments where she had truly felt alive in the last few weeks, most of which had involved Leyla, but she had already warned Melody not to think of her that way. Many of the other times had strangely enough been with the man who had not only broken her heart, but had then gone on to treat her like nothing but a piece of dirt on his shoe afterwards. "Maybe girls really do like bad boys after all," she added, musing aloud as Leyla watched her with intrigue.

"I've got nothing against fucked up little pleasures Melody. I'm the epitome of self-sabotage and loathing, while strangely also wanting nothing more than to be loved and happy. I think we can all be guilty of being a little fucked up," Leyla replied, opening up a little, too.

The two women boarded their plane later that evening and headed back to London, where Heath met them and drove the pair to Melody's new home close to the centre of the city without ever saying a word. Melody just hoped that he might have been ordered to stop his disgusting advances by one of the Black family members.

They pulled up outside a beautiful white-brick house, three stories tall, classically decorated and with a perfectly kept lawn at the front. On the driveway sat a bright red sports car, and Melody couldn't help but stare at it all in wonderment.

"Welcome home," Leyla said, opening the car door and taking her hand. Heath left them both there, Leyla having ordered him away, and the two of them made their way inside. Melody had to root around in her bag for the key Leyla had given her, and then she also had to punch in the security code when inside the vast hallway, but was grateful for the increased security. Once inside, she flicked on the lights and gaped, taking in the beautiful open-plan house. A large living room was to her left, more than big enough for the three huge leather sofas it housed, along with a couple of storage units and a large television. Towards the back was the kitchen, equally as large and beautifully decorated to imitate an old diner with booths and candy coloured work surfaces from centuries before that were an eclectic taste, but very stylish and comfortable.

Leyla then gave Melody the full tour, showing her the study that would be her office while at home and then up the two separate flights of stairs that led to three large bedrooms on each of the top floors, all with their own en-suite. The master bedroom was an enormous size, and even had a walk-in wardrobe full of suits, dresses and other expensive items of clothing that had already been procured for Melody to wear in her role as the millionaire heiress and chief executive. She took it all in without a word before finally taking a seat on the chaise at the end of her ginormous bed.

"This is too much. How can I possibly live here all alone?" she asked Leyla, who joined her, taking her hand.

"You won't be alone. Remember my orders? We will stay here tonight just because I wanted to show you, but then we will go back to headquarters for a while. After that you'll have Meri here at all times, and of course Donovan when the time comes," she told her, smiling warmly.

"I can't tell whether being exposed as David's daughter that day was a blessing or a curse. I feel so confused, my emotions are all over the place and I don't know where my life is headed. How do I know who to trust, what to believe in?" she asked her mistress, hoping she would not be angry at her openness.

"How many times do I need to remind you, Mel? I'm the only one you can trust, the only one you need. I've decided I'm putting a stop to Corey's visits. You belong to me and I'm within my rights to demand he ceases his advances, unless you ask him for them of course. You and Donovan will be together as planned. It won't be perfect, but it'll be a good match and you'll find your way together. That much I do know," Leyla promised, kissing her cheek lightly in an unusual display of affection from her normally so distant mistress.

CHAPTER THIRTEEN

"Okay, so let's go over the plan one more time," Melody said down the phone in her hand, Donovan's raspy tones filling her ear as he laughed but agreed. A couple more months had passed and plans had been put in place to begin filming, thanks to Leyla's clever planning, excellent contacts and meticulous knowledge of the human world of show business. "So, there's me, standing at the bar and you wander up all like, 'hello, Miss Pembroke, how are you? Nice to see you again,' and I'm playing it cool but agree to let you buy me a drink. We get chatting, hit it off, and voila! We'll officially announce that we're dating after the movie has finished shooting, but we'll leak photos of us sneaking a kiss and snuggling under the moonlight here and there. Sound good?" she asked, double-checking that her new beau was happy with the plan.

"Sounds wonderful. I'll be every inch the cool, suave, sophisticated gentleman while you swoon and fall utterly under my spell. I'm very glad we're filming on location in Hawaii. That island is so small we just cannot help but bump into each other while you're there, plus you'll be all scantily clad in bikinis and short dresses," he replied, seemingly more than happy with Leyla's plan so far and Melody couldn't help but laugh.

"I can't wait. I'll see you in the airport lounge in the morning," Melody said, snuggling down to get ready to sleep once she finished the call. She was still staying at the Crimson Brotherhood's headquarters under the watchful eye of Leyla and her cronies, much to her annoyance, but Melody didn't dare grumble about it in fear of the punishment she knew she would receive for her foolishness. She couldn't bear it if her mistress sent Heath to her room to teach her a lesson again. Despite their closeness and her improved obedience, Melody still knew never to take anything for granted in his terrifying new world of hers.

"Ten hours and counting," Donovan murmured, sounding sleepy too, and after a mumbled farewell they hung up and Melody turned out the light and fell fast asleep.

"Wake up, get dressed," ordered Meri, as usual, shocking Melody awake. She was beginning to get used to these abrupt wakeup calls now, but she still found herself groaning every time the stern woman disturbed her slumber. While Melody yawned and stretched, Meri worked her magic. She was ready within fifteen minutes and followed Leyla out to the awaiting car, coffee and bagel in hand to have on the go. Once they were away from the Crimson Brotherhood headquarters, the group teleported away, arriving in the specially prepared area of the airport that had been used by the demonic travellers for many years. Melody's phone buzzed in her pocket as she sat down and began reading the paper, finishing off her breakfast as she perused the business pages absentmindedly.

She fished out her handset and read the text message, grinning to herself as she did so.

'I'll be there in five, just need to push through the paparazzi first x,' it read, and she checked the clock, glad that he would arrive in plenty of time before the flight was due to leave. They heard the commotion before Donovan reached their private lounge, the flashes of cameras and cheers from the media dazzling them all for a moment before the burly man stepped around the doorway and waved his adoring public goodbye, his huge bodyguard shutting the door behind them.

"Good morning, guardian," he said, bowing to Leyla in respect.

"Good morning Donovan, good to have you here on time for a change," she replied, smiling at him and patting him on one muscular shoulder. The three of them had just a few minutes alone before the other team members would come to join them, so Leyla graciously led her disciple over to his future wife so that they could greet one another in private.

Melody stood up from her plastic chair, taking in the stunning man before her, the butterflies in her stomach going crazy as she peered into his dark-brown, mesmerising eyes.

"You got fat," she joked, running her hands over his impressive pecks and abs. He had bulked up tremendously since she had last seen him, Donovan's biceps easily three or four times the size of hers now.

"I think you'll find it's muscle, cheeky bitch," he teased, and she giggled timidly as she peered up at him, his incredible body so close that she could smell his musty cologne.

"My bad," she admitted, grinning at him as he grabbed her hands and pulled her arms tightly around his waist, wrapping his own bear-like arms around her shoulders as he too took a long sniff of her hair and kissed her forehead.

"How am I going to endure the next twenty hours on a plane surrounded by people who want me to work when all I will be able to think about is you?" Donovan asked her rhetorically, pulling away and righting himself just in time for the large group of their colleagues to join them.

Melody quickly made herself look busy, fiddling with her paper while Donovan greeted the team, working his magic on them all, who were quickly star-struck and eagerly followed his lead through the remainder of the terminal towards their private jet.

The flight was indeed long and excruciating. Sitting at the huge desk in the centre of the plane, Melody and Donovan's eyes met over their scripts numerous times, stirring both of their senses and eventually Leyla led her away, insisting that she needed to catch up on some phone calls while the time difference was still on their side. Melody did as she was told, knowing that her mistress was right and she then kept herself busy for the rest of the journey, refusing to rest in order to be tired enough to sleep through her jet-lag when she got to the other side.

The small island they had chosen was beautiful, a truly stunning backdrop for the sultry, sensuous tale of a young, handsome, and talented wrestler who makes a deal with the devil to stay young forever. Donovan's character was every woman's dream, and Melody found herself interested to see him in action on set once everything was ready to get going. She caught herself watching with a smile as he rehearsed with the leading lady and joked with her while showing off his impressive body without any insecurity, and rightly so. The actress didn't have to pretend that she was attracted to him, her advances were obvious before the cameras were even rolling and Melody forced herself to look away, choosing to trust that Leyla had told her the truth about only specific, professional women being his sexual outlet rather than random hook-ups.

After a couple of quiet days on the island, Leyla being sure to keep Donovan busy with his training and Melody hectic with her business from back home, she finally allowed the pair of them to go out for drinks with the team. Melody waited at the bar, knowing that this was the chance for them to hit it off in public that they had both been waiting for, and it wasn't long until he wandered over and ordered himself a drink.

"And one for Miss Pembroke, please," he added to the bartender, smiling over at her. She accepted the fruity cocktail and the pair of them chatted loudly, ensuring they were overheard laughing together, discussing their shared interests and debating long into the evening.

"Well, Mr Caine. I have to admit it was a nice surprise to have learned we have so much in common. I look forward to getting to know you better while we are here," she said, accepting a kiss on the cheek and then bidding him goodnight. Donovan grinned at her, his perfect features even more stunning thanks to his recently sun-kissed skin.

"The feeling is entirely mutual, Miss Pembroke," he replied before following his burly assistant, Coby, to his room to call it a night as well.

Early the next morning, Melody went for a walk along the quiet beach with Leyla, the pair of them chatting naturally as they went. During times like this, Melody genuinely felt as though the two of them had become real friends, and she enjoyed the powerful woman's company very much, finding herself accidentally forgetting just how dangerous her true nature could be. They stopped after a while and stood in the warm shallows together, the crystal clear water lapping gently at their feet, and Leyla took Melody's hand in hers.

"Are you happy, Melody?" she asked, finding herself interested in this human's life far more than she had ever been in any of her followers before, but she still refused to admit that there was a strong connection there.

"Yes guardian, I am. Thank you for doing as you promised and not letting your brother come to my bed. Being left alone at last has truly helped me clear my head and I trust in your plans for me. I believe now that despite the hardships we will have to work through soon, Donovan and I can at least give this relationship a try. I will follow your lead, I will do anything you ask of me." Melody replied, smiling over at her, their hands still entwined.

"Good, then how about you kiss me?" Leyla replied, catching Melody off guard and she turned to face her, looking around to check that no one was watching. Without hesitating for another second, she leaned forward and took the powerful goddess-like woman's mouth in hers, their lips touching softly at first, but then deeper and more powerful. Leyla pulled Melody closer and pressed her body into hers, their mouths locked while their tongues explored one another's fervently. Melody swooned, completely taken aback by it, but also hot and horny thanks to the powerful woman's touch and delicious taste. When Leyla finally pulled away, she was left feeling weak, excited and enthralled by the mesmerising woman before her and panted as she steadied her feet in the wet sand. "Hmm, yeah, I get it now," Leyla then whispered, staring into Melody's eyes thoughtfully, but she said no more, grinning over at her as she wobbled on her weak legs.

Without another word, Leyla took her hand again and led Melody along the beaches edge, neither one of them talking this time as they soaked up the morning sunshine. After a few minutes of contented silence, Melody noticed a figure running towards them in the sand. It was Donovan out for his morning training session. He slowed his pace when he saw them and pulled the headphones from his ears as he neared, grinning broadly at the two blushing women, but he just took their red cheeks as nothing more than a sign of the morning warmth.

"Hello ladies," he said, planting soft kisses on first Leyla's, then Melody's cheeks. He looked fantastic, wearing only a pair of shorts and running trainers, so showing off his gloriously muscular and tattooed torso and he grinned, noticing Melody's eyes on him as she took him in with a satisfied smile.

"Good morning Donovan, where's your guard?" Leyla demanded, but then they saw Coby as he came clambering over the sand dune behind him, trailing after Donovan thanks to his inferior speed. "You disappoint me, Coby," she said, clearly furious for him letting Donovan speed ahead like he had. "You'd best train harder and ensure you keep up with your charge here in future, otherwise I'll see to it that you're replaced," she threatened and he bowed, clearly embarrassed.

"I'm so sorry guardian, how might I atone?" Coby asked and Leyla smiled widely.

"Have you ever practiced Kung Fu?" she then asked him with a smirk, discarding her sandals, and Donovan grinned, taking Melody's hand in his and pulling her aside.

"This should be good," he told her, and the pair of them then watched as Leyla and her unfortunate adversary readied themselves for a fight. The incredible guardian took down Donovan's assistant in less than four moves, but made him try again over and over until he was eventually spent and could not get up again. "What I'd give to go a few rounds with her, so strong, so powerful," Donovan added, watching Leyla with an envious look, admiring and respecting her powerful prowess with an almost seductive gaze. Melody also detected that dominant side of him behind that stare. He wanted to beat her and to own her, it was clear to see. Despite knowing that he was dangerous, she couldn't help but want him more, desperate to have him stare at her in that way, and Melody's core throbbed at the sheer thought of his powerful body commanding hers. In that moment, she would've given anything for him to look at her that way. Melody would've even happily taken a beating from him, finding herself horny as hell and desperate to relieve the sexual tension that twisted at her gut.

"One day I'll let you try Donnie, and then I'll teach you what it's like to be someone's bitch," Leyla told him, having overhead him despite him having spoken so quietly, and even Melody couldn't help but laugh.

"And I would welcome the chance to be your bitch, for I could never envision myself as anyone else's," he promised, submitting to her so clearly that even Melody swooned before their mistress too, their kiss still so fresh in her mind.

Shooting for the movie soon commenced, the cast and crew working hard despite the heat, and Melody was impressed with Donovan's on-screen prowess. He truly was a gifted actor, and she began to see past the burly exterior, sensing the emotional connection he felt to his character. Their own connection to one another grew effortlessly as the time passed too, until after just a couple of weeks, they were ready to 'accidentally-on-purpose' get caught stealing a kiss late one night behind a palm tree. Coby poised from afar, his camera at the ready and zoomed in to the spot he knew the couple would soon retreat to. It wasn't long before they snuck away from the group and readied themselves for their first kiss.

"Why didn't we practice this before?" Melody asked him, trembling as she peered up into his almost black eyes in the darkness.

"Because it has to be real. It has to be our actual first kiss caught on camera. For us to keep forever as well as for the papers," he said, pulling Melody closer and stroking a stray lock of sun-stained auburn hair behind her ear. "You truly are captivating. I want you to be mine Melody."

"I'm all yours. I want you to own every part of me, Donovan," she whispered, tilting her face up to meet his gaze, and he grinned widely at her promise before placing a delicate kiss on her lips. She was surprised by his softness, yet she gave in to his firm hold on her and leaned into his embrace, naturally deepening their kiss. Within seconds, his tongue was delving deeply inside her ready mouth, his hands caressing her arms and then her face as he devoured her senses and then pressed himself harder into her, pinning Melody against the tree behind. He then lifted her legs up around his waist, pressing his impressive hard-on into her thigh as they kissed, forgetting all about their photographer a couple of hundred metres away.

Donovan actually let out a deep growl when he finally forced himself to let go and pulled away, his body full of need, desperate for his release, and Melody stared across at him, feeling eager for her own satisfaction too. He took a few more steps away, forcing himself to retreat before he took her the way he really wanted—hard and heavy. This woman meant more to him than that, though, so he used every ounce of willpower to pull back.

Melody panted as she watched him. Donovan's dark expression pained, and she couldn't help wanting to leave him with a lasting memory of this night. She lifted her dress, slipping down her panties, which she then kicked over to him and then opened her legs as he picked them up and gave the thin lace a satisfied sniff. She then placed one foot against the tree behind her and moved her bent knee to the side, showing her forbidden treasure off to him brazenly as he watched. Melody bit her bottom lip as she slid her hand down, rubbing on her throbbing nub as he watched, wide-eyed and enthralled by her as she pleasured herself right in front of him.

Melody closed her eyes as she came, unashamedly crying out for him, but her voice was muted by the crashing waves behind her. When she finally opened them again, she found Donovan on his knees a few feet away, Leyla's hands around his neck to stop him from coming any closer to Melody, but she hadn't taken him away or stopped him from watching her enticing and sensuous show. In fact they were both watching her with dark, dangerous stares, Donovan's eyes full of desire and need for her. Melody then dropped her skirt, covering herself again, and she wandered away without a word, not stopping until she reached her bedroom, locking the door behind her and then falling onto the bed with a satisfied sigh.

"Well, if he didn't want you before, he most certainly does now," Leyla told her as she teleported to her room a few minutes later, shaking her head at Melody, but she didn't punish her for pushing the boundaries. As far as Leyla could tell, her brazen, intimate show had worked in putting Melody above all others when it came to his affections.

And of course, Melody loved the idea that he wanted her so very much that he had needed to be restrained. Even thinking of Leyla's hands around Donovan's throat made her wet and sensitive, throbbing in her core and eager for her release all over again.

Leyla teleported away as Melody began to fall asleep, but within seconds she jerked awake, sensing someone else in the room with her and she looked up groggily, trying to see through the darkness.

"Boo!" whispered Corey in her ear, sliding under the sheet with her, and Melody couldn't help but jump, shocked to find him here when he had already been told to stay away. Without a care for his new orders, he slid his hands up her bare legs, gasping when he felt how wet she was beneath her shorts.

"No," she groaned, but couldn't help herself, lifting her hips to meet his soft hands.

"One more for old time's sake?" Corey insisted, sliding down her clothes and leaning over her beneath the thin bed sheet, ready to plunge inside when she gave him the word, that one little word he so desperately needed. She wanted to say no, to tell him exactly where to put that stiff staff that rested precariously close to her core, but her own need got the better of her.

"Yes," she breathed, moaning loudly as he slid inside her and gave her those much-needed releases over and over, only stopping when the sun began to rise and she was finally spent.

CHAPTER FOURTEEN

A couple of days later, the news hit the headlines about the playboy movie star and the millionaire heiress's on-set romance, their chosen photographs from Coby's various shots having been sold to the tabloids under a pseudonym. Their passionate pictures quickly made the front page of every magazine and newspaper in both the United Kingdom and globally, thanks to Donovan's vast fan-base. The most-used photo was a stunning and clearly unmasked portrayal of just a split-second before their first intense kiss, and Melody had to agree that Donovan had been right. Seeing their real passion forever immortalised via the camera was wonderful and she couldn't help but check the news pages online to read the fans and critics comments on their relationship. The Crimson Brotherhood, while powerful and global, did not reach every business or even every country across the globe, so there were still those who accused Melody for possibly having abused her power in the movie industry to win his affections.

One critique caught her eye, making Melody's blood boil, and she read it over a few times, seething more every time and Leyla reminded her that for those in the public eye, they never could please everybody and that she would have to get used to it.

The article read: 'I cannot help but find it suspicious that the woman who not only interviewed and approved Donovan Caine for his newest role, has now miraculously appeared on set for the duration of the recording, and has been found locking lips with the star himself. I might go as far as asking if she might have abused her power, but of course, there will never be any proof of that, so we are forced to take these images as evidence of their budding romance. Time will tell if you ask me, give it six months and if they are still together, then I'll eat my words,' and Melody vowed to make that one journalist in particular regret his harsh comments. She was determined to prove him wrong.

After a few more weeks, the on-location part of the movie wrapped and the cast and crew celebrated in style with a party and drinks at one of the largest and most prestigious hotels in Honolulu. They partied for hours, Leyla keeping a watchful eye over the besotted couple while Coby ensured that the paparazzi were positioned perfectly to capture the small, tender moments between the careful and well-prepared lovers. A gentle touching of hands, Melody wiping sauce from Donovan's mouth after he had devoured a canapé, and their eyes locking over a champagne toast was all they would be getting tonight, but it was more than enough to showcase their connection.

Additionally, the next morning, Leyla orchestrated the perfect stolen moment to add to their exposé. She teleported into Donovan's room with Melody, her hair and makeup done perfectly. She quickly changed into one of Donovan's t-shirts and tracksuit bottoms, making it look as if she had spent the night with him in his hotel room. Her own room was directly opposite his, and so timing was everything.

As Melody opened the door, she checked the corridor was clear and stepped out unseen. For now. Donovan grabbed her for a deep, fervent kiss, his fantastic body on show as he wore just a pair of tracksuit trousers to purposely give the impression that he too had just pulled on some clothes after leaving his bed with his lover to say goodbye. By the time they had pulled away from their passionate embrace, the corridor was full of paparazzi, shouting and snapping their photographs as Melody shrieked and fumbled with her key before throwing herself inside her room, playing the embarrassed shy girl while Donovan simply smirked at the cameras and winked, waving them goodbye as he stepped back into his room and closed his door behind him.

Their pictures circulated within minutes, their names hitting the top online keyword searches almost instantly, and even Melody had to admit, they looked fantastic together. When they boarded their plane the next day, Melody was no longer the nobody who had wandered through the airport unnoticed with a coffee and bagel in hand like before. She held onto Donovan's hand and he pulled her protectively through the crowd, the pair of them smiling for the camera's while also pretending to shy away from the attention they were getting.

Their welcome in London the next day was much the same. The pair posed for the cameras and even agreed to a brief interview while they made their way through the busy terminal.

"Melody and I are very excited to explore our relationship further now that we are home. The sun, sea, and sand might have helped me man up and take charge of my feelings towards this beautiful woman, but I can assure you, I had certainly noticed her well before we even set off. I played it cool, of course, hoping that she might notice me and then one night something between us finally blossomed," he told them, grinning broadly, his warmth and gentle nature seemingly genuine as he held her close.

Coby then arrived and ushered the pair of them into the waiting car. Once inside, Donovan dropped the façade though, and turned to Melody. He stared into her hazel eyes while his hand pulled through his black hair roughly, his expression almost threatening.

"I need to have you soon, Mel. I feel like I'm going to explode if I can't be with you. This pretence is killing me. Please tell me you'll ask Leyla to let me have you?" he almost begged, but she was scared by his forcefulness.

"It's not her order, Donovan, it's her parents'," Melody reminded him and he nodded, but was clearly unsatisfied by that answer. She couldn't help but start to feel scared of him, the dark urges in him bubbling only barely below the surface of his stoic face, so she pulled her phone out of her pocket and quickly dialled their mistress. "I need you to please have someone ready for him when we get there," she asked, and Leyla quickly agreed, sensing his pent-up urges through their bond. "Thank you guardian." Melody responded, saying nothing more as she stashed her mobile phone back in her pocket.

Donovan didn't even put it together that she had just called ahead to make sure that a lover was waiting for him back at headquarters to fulfil his dark needs with, still believing that she had no idea about his violent urges and sadistic tastes in the bedroom.

"You'd better move away Melody," he told her, physically pushing her aside with his strong hand and she could sense his rage building inside of him. He looked at her as though he were almost ready to tear her apart and Melody cowered before him, knowing full well that Donovan would eat her alive if she did anything to tip him over that delicate precipice right now. She did as he asked and slid over as far as she could while he stared out the window and Coby floored it, driving through the winding roads to the mansion at his fastest speed yet.

Donovan flung himself out of the car forcefully and without a word to Melody when they arrived at the Crimson Brotherhood's headquarters, quickly following Coby to his chambers, where she knew an outlet for his sexual frustrations awaited his intimidating attention. Leyla climbed into the car when he had gone and moved towards Melody slowly, and the poor woman hadn't realised she had stayed frozen in her seat just like a scared doe who had just endured a car ride with a tiger. She was trembling in fear thanks to having just witnessed the powerful change in the warm, gentle man who had not long before held her tight and kissed her softly, making Melody see for the first time just how careful she needed to be with him.

"It's as if he's two different people," she eventually muttered, looking into Leyla's beautiful blue eyes.

"He kind of is. He is the normal, human man with wants and needs like any other, but he is also a dominant sadist, Mel. It is more than a fetish. It is an overwhelming urge to have complete and total power over another person. He wants to fuck, yes. But, he also wants to hurt people. He wants to make them scream and beg him for more. He wants to own their pleasure, and their pain. That night on the beach, he was about to drop his pants and fuck you against that tree, a perfectly wonderful experience for any other lovers. However, he might have hurt you, and then he would've felt guilty about it, only making him want to hurt you more in order to deal with that guilt. It is a vicious and shameful spiral Melody, one that can only be curbed with taking out that need on willing lovers. Ones who do not judge him and ideally ones that enjoy the pain he inflicts, those that are just as full of dark urges as he is and they want what he will give them. Do you understand?" Leyla asked, not holding back this time in her explanation. She needed Melody to know, to trust her instincts and never push him to the brink of his need again.

"What starts out as passion can quickly turn to poison where he is concerned. Tread carefully and never take his affections for granted," said another voice as a woman joined them in the car. She was beautiful, truly stunning, with coppery red hair and icy blue eyes, just like her daughter's.

Melody immediately fell to her knees before one of the Crimson Brotherhood's powerful leaders, Serena Black. She greeted her daughter and then laid a gentle hand on Melody's shoulder, drawing her gaze back up to hers.

"I'm sorry. I didn't mean to make him snap," Melody said, her face still pale as she climbed back up into her seat.

"It wasn't you. None of this is you. This is him. His dark need and you must learn how to be part of it. You need to see it," Serena told her, climbing back out of the car. Melody nodded and then followed the omnipotent mother and daughter team out of the car and towards the house. The three of them then teleported to a small room situated behind the mirror in Donovan's room, much like she had seen behind Corey's, and she wondered for a second if all the bedrooms had mirrors like this.

Melody then gasped and stifled a gag as she looked through the grey-tinted window at the awful scene before her. Donovan stood naked over the huddled figure of a dark-haired woman. She too was naked, her body severely beaten and beginning to bruise already. She whimpered as he leaned down and cupped her face with his huge hands, staring at her with cold, almost dead-like eyes.

"It's okay, Mel. I love you," he said, stroking the blood-soaked hair out of her eyes. He then leaned over her from behind and plunged his hard cock into her with such force that she cried out. He twisted her hair around his hand and pulled, gripping it tight as he continued to thrust into her from behind so hard that she shuffled forwards on the floor beneath her uncontrollably. He came quickly the first time, pulling his huge cock out of her and then forcing her to drink his release down, slapping the woman hard across the face for wasting just a drop. The trio watched as he continued fucking his partner over and over again until he was finally satisfied.

She then lay on the bed for a few moments in silence before a witch came in and gave her a healing potion. Her wounds and bruises disappeared almost instantly and then the woman climbed up from the bed and ran her fingertip down Donovan's sweat-dusted chest.

"Thanks gorgeous, you really are a fucking animal aren't you?" she said, clearly having got what she had wanted from their experience too, and Melody felt like she might be sick. Donovan ignored the woman, having seemingly zoned out completely, and she left without another word.

"If you want to go to him, it's safest while he's sated and vulnerable so now's a good time," Serena told her, teleporting Melody outside his door with her. "Tread carefully. Don't let him dominate you, otherwise you'll mean nothing more to him than that woman who just left. Make him see you as more, treat you as more, and there may be a life there for the two of you yet," she told her, giving Melody some sound advice, and she vowed to try her best to have that between them. This could not be their life forever. Melody knew she had to force him to disassociate his feelings towards those women from his affection for her. It was the only way to bring him some balance.

Melody nodded and stood at the door, thinking over what she wanted to say to him as Serena teleported away, leaving her alone in the hallway. After a few moments, she knocked on the door and went inside, finding Donovan lying in the same position on the bed where she had seen him before. He hadn't moved an inch, his breathing slow and steady, but he wasn't asleep. He was staring up at the ceiling as though in a daze. Melody glanced at the mirror, knowing that their mistress was still watching from the other side, but she was grateful for her presence and welcomed her watchful eyes on them.

"Donovan," she whispered, unsure how to approach him. She didn't want to sit down on the blood-stained bed, still feeling sick thanks to the memory that played in her mind of him and that woman together, the woman she was very aware he had called, 'Mel'. She opted to wait for him to come back to himself in his own time rather than keep on trying to rouse him, so stepped back and climbed up onto his chest of drawers. Melody folded her legs underneath her and she watched him for almost an hour. Donovan was neither awake nor asleep as his disturbed mind processed his time with the woman who had both satisfied and curbed those awful needs, for now. He eventually sat up, rubbing his eyes as he looked around at the trashed room with a sigh and stretched as though having just woken up from a nap.

"What the fuck?" he asked as he caught sight of Melody sitting opposite him in the chaos, watching him with a still scared look. "Mel, you shouldn't be here. I can explain," he started, but she held up her hand to quieten him.

"I know what you are, what you need. I've known since just after we first met," she told him, her voice calm and steady despite her frenzied thoughts. "Don't be ashamed Donovan, I don't even want you to be sorry. I just want you to know that you will never, ever do that to me. Is that understood?" she demanded, standing and wandering over towards him.

She was tiny and slight in comparison to his huge frame, but Donovan watched her, taken aback by her dominance. "I just asked you a question, Donovan," she said sternly, stroking his dirty cheek with her hand and climbing on his lap, kissing him deeply. She peered down into his eyes, her confident, powerful prowess not faltering for even a moment now, and she realised then what he needed from himself and from her. He needed to be dominant with those other women, but he needed to be told no when it came to real life, and she wondered if Donovan had ever loved another person enough to listen to them when they told him no. His actions told her he hadn't respected another woman other than Leyla in his entire life, and it was her job to give him everything he desired in return for his soul and continued service, so of course she wouldn't deny him his violent, masochistic lovers when he wanted them to attend to his every dark need.

Melody knew then that it wasn't that she must learn to be submissive to him. She needed to learn to dominate him. His dark urges could be fed, could be quenched when needed, but between those times, she would take the lead and ensure that he never treated her that way. If she tread carefully, cleverly now, Melody realised she could become the only one he would let tell him what to do. Melody knew that she could never abuse that trust, that power, and in just the few seconds that passed between them in that intense gaze, they both knew it. There was no going back now. Her body and soul made him a promise there and then, and Donovan somehow sensed it and accepted their unspoken agreement, visibly relaxing beneath her.

"I will never do that to you Melody, I promise. You are the only woman I've wanted to make love to in my whole life. I will never, ever hurt you," he replied, his hands running through her hair as he took in her determined, decisive expression and he admired it. She could see it in his eyes.

In a sudden, uncontrollable moment of rawness, Donovan then wrapped his arms around her tightly, burying his head in her bosom. Melody felt his tears slide down onto her chest as he wept, and she couldn't help but sob too as she felt the emotions consume him so powerfully. He seemed so small, so fragile, but he didn't fight it.

Donovan Caine finally let his hard demeanour drop thanks to having Melody's arms around him, her love and support that seeped into him and the trust he felt towards her, allowing him the much-needed release at last.

When Donovan finally stopped and peered up at her, seeming his usual self again, Melody smiled down at him.

"What am I going to do with you?" she whispered, running her hands through his dirty hair. She didn't care that he was filthy, covered in sweat, tears and even blood. Melody knew that he needed her and she was not going anywhere.

"Just love me. I'll do the rest," he answered, kissing her deeply. Melody leaned into him and then took one of his huge hands, her own need urging her on now too, and slid it down over her breasts and hips, coming to a stop between her legs.

"I'll do more than just that," she replied. Donovan reacted instantly, knowing what she wanted, and his fingers stroked their way inside her with ease. Melody then rode back and forth on him while pushing them deeper, keeping in control the entire time, her own release the only goal now. He gasped loudly when she came for him, delighting in the feel of her body as it tensed around his fingers before she then lifted off and wandered over to the doorway.

"Wash her stink off and then we'll go and speak to our guardian, together. I need to be your wife sooner rather than later, Donovan Caine. I need to have you, it's time for you to be mine," she said, smiling across at him and he nodded.

"Of course. And, I'm already yours, angel," he replied, submitting to her without hesitation or question.

CHAPTER FIFTEEN

Melody wandered back to her room, a content smile on her face as she went through hers and Donovan's change in dynamic in her mind. She was still scared of his strength, knowing that he could overpower her with ease and still treat her the way she had seen him do to the woman who had serviced his urges so professionally earlier on, but she knew that she would have to learn to trust him not to. Time and hard work would be the only way, but she knew they could both only wait so long before they would need to spend the night together. It had been just a few months and Melody was already growing frustrated. The foreplay would only satisfy them for so long and she was not willing to be with anyone else to satisfy that need in the meantime. Regardless of the fact that she knew Donovan would need to be with other women during the course of their relationship, that was out of necessity, and so she would allow him to do that without ever making him feel like it was cheating. She, on the other hand, had no excuse and vowed to herself that she would never willingly cheat on him. Melody was also very aware that her choices were not her own anymore, and so filed away that little loophole in her mind to stop herself from feeling guilty if she was being punished or was ordered into someone else's bed in the future by her powerful mistress.

She got showered and changed before heading back out of her room in search of both her guardian and her movie star. As she left the bedroom, Melody found someone else waiting for her in the corridor. Corey stood leaning against the wall opposite her bedroom door, one leg bent and his foot placed casually against the brickwork behind him while his hands tapped impatiently on his raised knee.

"You kept me waiting," he said, taking in the woman before him with a sneer.

"I didn't realise you were expecting me, guardian?" Melody asked. Her earlier confidence shattered by Corey's presence. He embodied everything that was so wrong with her well thought-out plans for her and

Donovan.

"I didn't know either until I found myself outside your room," Corey replied, stepping forward and pinning her against the door behind her with his powerful body.

"I'm not yours to command," Melody reminded him, gasping for breath in his tight hold. He grinned down at her before reaching his hands up to her chin and tilting her face up towards his. Corey planted a soft, delicate kiss on her lips and then trailed his kisses down to her ear.

"I'm forbidden from asking you to fuck me," he whispered matter-of-factly. "But, not from saying yes when you beg me to fuck you, don't forget."

"I'll never do that again," she whimpered, trying her best to stay strong while intoxicated by his scent, powerful words and incredible body that still pressed into hers so forcefully.

"We'll see. Give it a few more months and you'll be begging me to scratch your itch, Mel. I might even see to it that yours and Donovan's marriage is put on indefinite hiatus," he threatened, and she pushed his shoulders hard with her hands. He humoured her and stepped back slightly, regarding her with a sly grin, enjoying the fact that he had clearly hit a nerve.

"You wouldn't? You don't even want me. Why would you fuck with my life when I'm nothing but a toy to you?" Melody demanded, unable to hide her anger.

"Because sometimes while playing the game, the King wants the pawns to be happy and live in peace without moving them on to certain defeat. Other times, he wants to fuck with them and sacrifice their measly lives in order to empower himself. Sometimes, though, he is just a fucked-up bastard who enjoys messing with his playthings for nothing more than the sheer fun of it. Maybe that's the most satisfying part of the game, the control?" he mused, his eyes dark as he toyed with her. Melody understood the chess references, but couldn't help herself from messing with him in return, not thinking about the consequences for doing so.

"But you're not a King, Corey," she replied, grinning wickedly. "You never will be either, will you? You're nothing but a spoiled little rich boy who enjoys his misery so much that he wants everyone else to be a part of it alongside him." she said, her voice full of hatred and loathing.

Corey's eyes then turned black as he regarded her for a moment. The air buzzing around him ominously and Melody's smile dropped, but she held her ground. She anticipated the usual slap across the face from him, but this time it was a full-blown punch to the gut that sent her flying through the air, and she landed hard on the ground a few feet away. Melody's breath wouldn't come to her as she lay there desperately tying to catch it, knowing that she was badly winded. Black spots filled her eyes as she continued to gasp, eventually taking a much-needed breath, but her head still spun.

Corey then stood and towered over her, glaring angrily, his god-like prowess scaring the hell out of her. He leaned down and straddled her, gripping Melody's throat with his strong hands, the muscle giving way beneath his tremendous force immediately. Her silent pleas left her trembling lips as he choked her, the life quickly draining from her, and Melody soon began to drift away.

"I will never let you go Mel, don't you see that? Even if I don't want you anymore, I still don't want anyone else to have you. Get used to being my bitch," he growled in her ear, the last words she heard before losing consciousness.

"Get the fuck off her," cried Donovan, rounding the corner and finding the powerful guardian choking the life out of the woman beneath him, his woman, Melody. He threw himself at him, forcing Corey to release her throat and then knocking him back onto the ground. Donovan leaned over Melody protectively, checking for a pulse while Corey shook off the surprising blow and steadied himself, his sights now set on the foolish boy before him. Donovan's head was still lowered over Melody, his tears falling down onto her as he trembled in panic, fearing that she might be dead, and he never anticipated the blows that were then rained down on him from his powerful adversary's fists.

He cried out as punch after punch, kick after kick, pummelled him, all the while forming a protective barrier around Melody's limp body.

"Enough!" shouted a voice somewhere close by, Leyla's voice, and after delivering a few more blows, Corey finally stopped and walked away, roaring with rage and devastating everything else in his path. He punched a huge hole through Melody's bedroom door as he stormed past his sister, his face contorted with rage.

"They both deserved it," he told her, and Leyla took her brother's face in her hands, staring into his blue eyes intensely.

"I didn't say that they didn't deserve it. I just said they'd had enough," she told him, calmly and quietly. Corey took a deep breath and then wandered away, his anger still consuming him, but he no longer lashed out and teleported away to visit another of his lovers, needing the release Melody had refused him.

When Melody finally awoke, she shook uncontrollably, suddenly remembering Corey's reaction to her foolish words. Her neck throbbed, and she remembered his hands around her throat with a shudder. Melody tried to swallow, nearly screaming in agony as her swollen muscles moved so painfully and she heaved, the wrenching of her stomach only serving as a reminder to the other blow she had received to the gut, the bruising to her chest and ribs adding to her suffering.

When she finally sat up and took in her strange surroundings, Melody trembled in fear even more, seeing the crumpled heap of the man she had been so excited to call hers just a short while earlier laying beside her on the cold ground. Donovan was black and blue with bruises, unconscious and almost unrecognisable thanks to the terrible blows she could only assume must have come from Corey, too. She didn't remember even seeing Donovan in the hallway with them, but guessed that he must have appeared after she had already slipped away and, judging by his wounds, perhaps had even tried to fight Corey.

"Donovan," she whispered, her voice barely making its way through her crushed larynx but he didn't rouse anyway, still completely out of it, and Melody sat back on the hard floor, looking around her, trying to make sense of where they were. It was a cold, empty room. The walls and floor were completely tiled with black granite and a dim bulb lit up the dingy space. There were no windows, just one door that was locked when Melody tried it, and there was a bucket in the corner, presumably for them to use as a toilet. She gagged again, trying to make sense of it all but soon gave up. Her pain overwhelmed her and so she curled up in a ball next to Donovan and tried her best to fall asleep, the sobs still coming but she didn't fight them.

"Fuck, Mel. Wake up," she heard a voice say, groaning as she stirred, but as she blinked awake Melody was pleased to see the relief on Donovan's face, however battered and bruised he was. He lifted her into a sitting position, wincing and groaning too as he moved his sore limbs, but he pushed on through the pain, focussing on her rather than on himself.

"I'm okay," she managed to say, her voice just a hoarse whisper but he could hear her fine thanks to the silence that surrounded them. He cupped her face with his palms, looking deep into her eyes as he checked her over.

"Shit, how did this happen?" Donovan asked, lifting her shirt to check the huge bruise that swept across her chest, pushing gently to check that her ribs weren't broken. She winced and tears ran down her cheeks uncontrollably.

"I'm such a fucking idiot," she whispered, running her hands over his split lip and broken nose. Without another word, Donovan pulled Melody into his lap, where he cradled her protectively and held on so tight that it was as though he was fearful that she may be ripped away again without a moment's notice. They sat together silently, taking care of one another without words or even any more painful movements, but they both knew that the other one was there for them. Melody somehow fell asleep again after a while, giving in to her body's need to rest as she succumbed to his embrace and so did her huge protector, each of them praying that they would make it through this in one piece.

CHAPTER SIXTEEN

Melody and Donovan stayed in that tiny room alone together for three weeks, being fed just once a day by a hooded warlock who wouldn't even look at the pair of them when he delivered them a measly portion of food each and discarded the waste from their makeshift toilet. Melody hated having to use the bucket in front of Donovan, but their humiliation soon dissipated as time went on and each of them were soon too weak, both physically and mentally, to care about such trivial things. They lay in silence together most of the days, their hands held tightly or their bodies lying curled together on the hard floor, but neither was strong enough to pursue conversation let alone anything sexual while alone together.

Both of their wounds had now healed. Donovan's nose was a little crooked thanks to it not having been properly set, but he otherwise only had superficial wounds. Melody's swelling and bruising had gone down, but her voice still faltered when she spoke and was huskier now than it had been before, making her wonder if it might never go back to sounding the same as it had been.

The pair of them were weak thanks to their injuries and lack of food, dirty thanks to neither of them having showered in weeks, and both were still so very scared. The worry of their continued punishment still hung over their heads and they hated that they had been told nothing about where they were or how long they were to stay there. The tiny amount of food only barely gave Donovan and Melody enough to survive on and the pair of them continued to just sit or lie while wrapped in one another's arms, both of them silent, broken and afraid. Melody was glad she wasn't alone. Lying in Donovan's embrace was the only thing keeping her from going insane, even though they were both still too exhausted to talk nowadays. When the light overhead would turn off she would mouth a silent plea to their guardian, somehow convinced that Leyla was watching them. That she might even be in there with them in the pitch-black darkness, remembering her comment before about her preferring the dark.

When the door finally opened and Heath wandered inside, his

disgusting smirk back in place, they both just found themselves staring up at him in shock. Without a word, he grabbed Melody by her greasy, matted hair and dragged her out by it, her hoarse screams silenced by the slap he then delivered to her cheek. Donovan jumped to his feet and tried to follow them, but the door swung closed in his face before his weak body could reach it.

Melody was then quickly teleported away and delivered to her room, where a potion sat on her bedside with a note next to it. She read it and paled, falling to her knees weakly and weeping silently into her hands. It read:

'Drink this, get showered and dressed. Your trial begins in one hour.'

Six hooded figures sat before her as Melody was led into a small chamber somewhere towards the back of the mansion that she had never been in before. The potion had healed the last of her injuries and rid her body of any sign of the beating she had taken at Corey's hands, but she was still incredibly skinny, feeling weak and she cowered before them, trembling uncontrollably. One of the figures stood and lowered their hood. It was Leyla, and she regarded Melody with clear distaste now, far from the friendly affection she had last seen in her.

"Melody Pembroke, how do you plead?" she asked, fixing her with a stern look.

"I'm sorry guardian, I don't know what my charges are," Melody replied, looking down at the floor and away from Leyla's contemptuous gaze.

"You are charged with continually disrespecting your guardian and other high-ranking members of the Crimson Brotherhood. You are accused today of abusing the trust the Brotherhood has placed in you and flaunting the rules to suit your own agenda," said the figure to her right. He, too, stood and lowered his hood, taking his sister's hand in his. Corey smirked at Melody, clearly revelling in her fear.

"It wasn't like that. I did everything you asked of me," she replied, feeling woozy thanks to her malnourished body being flooded with adrenaline.

"Did you, or did you not, purposely antagonise another guardian in a blatant attempt to goad and anger him?" Leyla asked Melody, knowing that she meant how she had spoken to Corey that day in the corridor, and she nodded.

"Yes, mistress, I did," she admitted, and Corey's smile widened, relishing in her clearly broken will.

Donovan was then pulled into the room by Heath's aggressive lead. He joined her before the council table, his body now healed as well and he stood tall, but she could tell that he was still weak, too.

"And what of you, Mr Caine? Did you seriously attack a guardian?" Leyla bellowed, clearly angry with them both. Melody wanted to scream at her, to remind her just why Donovan had forced himself between her and Corey, but she stayed quiet, knowing she had to be careful now or else force them both to endure more punishments.

"Yes mistress, I did," he replied, saying nothing more, and she wondered if he was thinking the same as she was, that no matter what reason or excuses they might have, none of the council members that were sat before them now cared and they would go forever unheard.

"Well then, that settles it. Your insolence has not only brought shame to you both, but has proven to be a great humiliation to me, forever tarnishing my reputation as a guardian. I wash my hands of you both. Corey, you may decide their punishments," Leyla said, taking her seat again and glaring at the two of them angrily. She hated they had been so rash, but knew that she was in no position to intervene now. Any favouritism towards her followers was a sign of weakness, and she would never let a couple of idiotic and selfish humans affect her position in the Brotherhood. Leyla closed herself off to Melody completely now. Off to any emotion or affection she had ever felt for her and the powerful guardian's cold, hard stare gave away her bitterness. Melody was no longer her friend, or anything more, despite knowing she had felt that spark between them. They were nothing more than a guardian and follower, and never would be again.

"Donovan, you are to be on lockdown. You will return to the cold, dark cell for another few weeks, alone this time. Heath and Coby will then accompany you for the rest of your work commitments, and you are otherwise confined to your bedroom until further notice. Absolutely no female visitors," Corey told him, and Donovan bowed but said nothing. He did begin trembling though as he contemplated the terrible stretch of time alone in that cell before him and Melody wanted nothing more than to comfort him but knew better than to even try and show any affection right now.

"And Melody," Corey said, grinning at her wickedly. "Firstly, your espousal to Mr Caine has now been put on permanent hold," he told her, walking around the table to stand before the still trembling woman, eyeing Melody with a look of dark satisfaction that made her want to vomit. "You are to be accompanied by Meridiana and my coven at all times from now on, to keep you in check as well as ensuring that you and Donnie do not see each other in secret," he told her, and Melody nodded in understanding. She hated he had gotten his way, that he had indeed managed to get her marriage put on hiatus, but she knew better than to answer back, so just stared at the floor.

Corey then paused, leading her to believe that his sentence had been delivered, but then he fixed her with a stern stare and terrifying grin. "Oh, and one more thing. You are mine now," he added, taking her right hand in his and summoning Leyla's mark to the surface of her forearm. He fixed her with a contemptuous look, actually laughing as a few tears then fell down her sullen cheeks, and she shook her head in fearful surprise. Corey ignored her. He then stroked his finger over the black cross and its red roses, altering the image to add thorns to the stems and a serpent that wrapped around the rose bush over the inverted cross. Melody now bore his mark rather than Leyla's. She belonged to Corey and knew that there was nothing she could do about it.

Her breath left her in a rush and she struggled to catch it again, sobbing violently as a barrage of tears fell down her cheeks while her new guardian continued to hold on to her hands, his powerful grip the only thing still keeping her standing. Melody continued to shake her head, truly regretting every word of her foolish taunts in the hallway and wobbled, struggling to stay upright on her weak legs.

No concern was given to the stupid girl and Donovan was then quickly led away by his warlock watchers without a word. He too sobbed loudly but was ignored and the council members stood and filed away, seemingly satisfied by Corey's sentencing.

"I'm sorry, I'm so sorry. Please," Melody begged once they were alone, falling to her knees before him, and Corey stroked his hand down to her chin, lifting her gaze to meet his. He grinned down at his new pet wickedly and stroked her cheek with his thumb.

"You will be sorry Mel, trust me," he told her, and she squirmed away from his touch. "Now, let's get you out of these clothes," Corey added as he teleported her to his room.

CHAPTER SEVENTEEN

Far away from the Crimson Brotherhood headquarters in the home of another of Leyla's clients, a young woman named Laurie stood cowering in the doorway of a double garage, hidden in the shadows as much as she possibly could. She had to try desperately hard to calm her hurried breathing, to slow her loud gasps, and she closed her eyes, trying to listen hard for her pursuer, hoping she would know if he was nearby. She stood as still as possible for a few moments, concentrating hard.

"Gotcha," a deep voice whispered from beside her, and Laurie's eyes snapped open instantly. He grabbed her arm and she tried to run but then felt his hand slam across her left cheek with such force that she fell to the ground and hit both her knees hard on the unyielding concrete floor, grabbing at her stinging cheek as he towered over her and began unbuckling his jeans.

"No," she tried to protest, squirming away as he pinned her down, but it was no use. Xander was far too strong and it was only seconds before he had ripped off her knickers and was inside her on the cold hard ground. She climbed up onto her hands and knees as he thrust hard inside her wet opening, coming almost instantly as he gripped her tightly and delved deeper than she had ever thought she could take, her body completely at his command, but that was just how she liked it. Laurie pushed back into his thrusts, groaning as he ravished every inch of her body and commanded every one of her senses, building her delicious climax until she screamed his name and begged for more.

When they were both spent, Xander scooped her up in his arms and carried Laurie to the guest bedroom. She snuggled into his embrace and smiled, breathing in his manly, sweaty smell for a while, before falling into a deep, relaxed sleep. When she woke the next morning, Xander was smiling down at her, his thumb rubbing gently over the slight bump he had left on her cheekbone, but there was no bruising, so both he and Laurie knew it wouldn't be too bad. She had taken worse from him during their vehement and sometimes furiously intense role-plays, and she didn't care about it one little bit. He leaned in and kissed her, softly at first and then deeper, more passionately before he climbed over and nestled himself between her legs.

"Feeling good?" he asked, growing hard and ready for her again as he began trailing kisses down to her breasts and stomach. Laurie looked down at her gorgeous lover, her forbidden treasure, and smiled contentedly. Xander was not hers to love and yet she couldn't help it. She loved him with every inch of herself and delighted in the fact that he wanted to play dark, naughty games with her just as much as she did with him. She squirmed beneath him, drawing his gorgeous dark-brown eyes upwards to meet hers, a satisfied smile curling at her lips, and she nodded, opening her legs wider in invitation.

Xander made love to Laurie for as long as possible before being forced to send her home again, but this time their intimate few hours was nothing like what they'd had the night before. A far different dynamic ensued, and she relished in this time together just as much. He kissed her deeply and pressed his long cock into that tender little nook inside of her that tensed around him wonderfully every time, making her gush and climax for him before she fell back on the bed, deliciously exhausted, and he quickly did the same.

"Amelia will be home soon," he then told her, rising from the bed to take a quick shower and Laurie knew it was his way of asking her to leave. By the time he had cleaned up and wrapped himself in a soft, expensive towel, Laurie was already dressed and ready to go. She needed to get in a shower too, and still smelled of sweat and sex, but she didn't care. She had no one to hide it from and would give herself a thoroughly deserved soak when she got home.

"Until next time," she whispered into his ear before delicately tracing her tongue over his earlobe and strutting down the hall and out the front door, taking in the huge mansion with its private driveway and stunning grounds as she went, captivated as always by the beauty of this huge house that Xander shared with his wealthy wife.

Amelia Burns was a very well-known television presenter. She worked in London for a few days each week covering news stories and events for the nationwide television channels and earning a vast wealth in the process. Amelia was a national treasure, her contracts were worth hundreds of thousands of pounds and wherever she went, her adoring public welcomed her with open arms. Xander and Amelia had now been married for ten years, and they had started out working hard, on the breadline yet happy until one night six years ago when Xander had been introduced to the mesmerising and brilliant demonic temptress Leyla Black at a party in London. A party hosted by a mutual friend, or rather, loyal follower who had agreed to procure more souls for his mistress in order to prolong his period of grace under her guardianship. She had soon offered to make Xander's dreams come true, in return for his soul and a life of servitude, of course, and the selfish man hadn't needed much persuasion before he had said yes. Xander had joined the Crimson Brotherhood immediately and every one of his dreams came true thanks to their influence. He followed their orders and pledged his soul to the Brotherhood's leaders, participating in dark ceremonies and strange initiations without ever looking back at his old life again despite his wife having no idea about any of his cloak and dagger private life.

Things had changed even more when Laurie had quite literally bumped into Xander during a night out with their groups of friends. He had stood on her little toe while waiting in line for pizza, breaking it instantly. After then taking her to the hospital and spending the entire night with Laurie to make sure that she was okay, he was already in love. Their connection had been instant and although he was honest about his marriage, she just could not keep away. They then found themselves in bed together the very next night as his wife's image played across her television screen while she read the ten o'clock news, her voice muted but her eyes boring into Laurie's as her husband expertly caressed every inch of her body. But she loved it, she loved him already as though some divine intervention had brought the pair of them together.

"Amelia's gone for four days this time," Xander told Laurie as she stepped out of the car a couple of days later, looking sexy and seductive in her tight black tube dress and stiletto's, her dark-brown hair pulled high in a long ponytail and her fingernails sharpened to a point and painted bright red.

"Good," was all she replied, stepping up on her tiptoes to kiss him before following her lover inside. The pair of them chatted for a while, eating dinner together and discussing their week like any other couple, yet all the while their upcoming evening together was looming, driving them both wild in anticipation.

"Do you have anything in mind for me tonight Laurie?" Xander asked once the maid had left for the evening and they were finally alone. The staff of the house all knew that she was his mistress. Most of them had caught the two at it at some point over the last couple of years and although they were positive that Amelia didn't know about them, they had to trust that the staff wouldn't ever tell her. Xander had always been sure to give them extra allowances and bonus cheque's here and there too, anything to secure their silence even more.

"Yes," she replied, picking up a handful of grapes and slowly eating one at a time. Xander was on the edge of his seat. He had never played the dark and intimate games he now played with Laurie before meeting her. Amelia was more of a 'missionary position with the odd switch to doggy-style' kind of woman. They had always had a good sex life during their marriage, but her busy schedule left him frustrated and her too tired most nights when she actually was home. Laurie was a welcome outlet for all of that energy, and the intense games she like to play had him wrapped around her little finger. Laurie loved to be dominated, to both be forced into submission and to willingly give him it, depending on her mood, and while it might seem to any outsiders that she was the weaker of the two, she was the one who told her lover how, when, where and what he was to say and do to her, very much the actual dominant of the two but they both loved that intense dynamic they willingly shared.

"I've been a very naughty girl Xander, I need to be punished," she whispered, a cunning smile curling at her red lips. Without another word he led her out to the bedroom where he pulled Laurie over his lap and lifted her dress. He knew without her asking that she was ready for a spanking and he delivered each slap effectively before rubbing the tingling skin to soothe it and moving on, stopping only when her cheeks were bright pink and she was almost ready to explode thanks to her delight of both pain and pleasure.

Xander and Laurie then fucked for hours before finally slowing their pace and making love. The games were over and this was the only time their real emotion was allowed to show. She wrapped her legs around him and stared up into his eyes as he pressed himself deeper inside of her, peering back.

"I love you," Xander whispered as he watched her unravel beneath him, kissing her tender lips as she pulsated around him.

"I love you, too," she replied, gripping him tighter and pulling him close as he too reached his climactic release.

Sometime before dawn, Laurie woke thanks to a cold shiver than persisted in running up and down her spine. Before she even opened her eyes, she could already somehow tell that they were being watched. Two hooded figures stood over them, one on either side of the bed, and the one closest to Xander reached her hand down to rouse him from his slumber. He jumped awake and looked around, blinking to clear his blurred eyes and grabbing Laurie's hand to check that she was still there.

"A word please, Xander," said the figure, lowering her hood and as she did so revealing the long, red braided hair that fell behind her and the piercing blue eyes that they could both make out in the shadows.

"Of course, guardian," Xander replied, standing and pulling on his pyjama bottoms. Laurie made a noise in protest to his leaving her, but was too scared to speak and he just shushed her without any explanation. She couldn't understand what was happening or why Xander seemed okay with all of this. She was scared to her core and did not like the way these hooded figures made her feel. He knew but left her side anyway, unable to refuse his sinister mistress.

"Xander, you have lived a very good life under my guardianship, would you agree?" Leyla asked him once they were alone in the living room. He sat opposite from her on the huge sofa, nodding profusely as he tried to determine why she was here.

"Yes, mistress," he whispered.

"I'm glad you feel that your time served has been well spent, but I'm here to inform you that your period in the Crimson Brotherhood has come to an end. I am here to collect the soul you have promised me," she said, speaking calmly and serenely while he sat trembling before her.

"No guardian, please. I have more I can offer you," he begged, jumping out of his seat and kneeling before Leyla. "I will do anything you ask."

"You are lazy Xander. You were once a struggling doctor, working yourself to the bone at that hospital, but you loved every second of it because you were living your dream. You then decided that a life of hard work was not for you, so you asked for riches but yet you didn't want to work for them yourself. You wanted fame but didn't care to put in the effort to achieve it and you wanted freedom without having to answer to anyone for it. I gave you all of those things. Your loving wife is ambitious enough for the two of you, she shares her wealth without question and she never enquires what you do while she is off working herself to the bone to keep you in the life to which you have become accustomed. You have been granted this life for many years as thanks to selling me your soul, plus you promised me your first-born child's soul too, a child that has yet to make its way into this world, I might add," she said, her face uncaring to his pleading look and submissive pose. "For that promised soul I gave you Laurie. I used powerful magic to find and call your soulmate to your side Xander, and I would hate to have to involve her in our affairs any further," she added, a sinister smile creeping into her beautiful face as a blood-curdling scream emanated from the bedroom behind them.

Xander flinched and bowed lower to his fierce mistress, while his ears could not block out the sound of his lover being clearly punished for his mistakes in the other room. He could hear the slaps that were being delivered to her gorgeous face and body as clear as anything his ears had heard before and could not force the sound away, no matter how desperately he wanted to cover his head and scream for them to stop.

"Please don't hurt her," he whispered, his face contorted with fear.

"Perhaps, if she were to pledge her soul to me as well, and the two of you also agree to carry out further undertakings I require some help with, I could offer you another ten years of happiness in return for such signs of your loyalty?" Leyla offered, the silence between them being filled with the sound of Laurie's sobs from the other room while Heath's deep voice laughed gruffly.

"I'll do anything you ask. Just please make him stop," Xander replied, his face mashed into a scared and worried guise.

"You don't even know what it is yet," she told him, her smile widening.

"I don't care, I'll do it. Yes guardian, I accept."

In the bedroom, Laurie lay curled into a balled heap on the floor, sobbing uncontrollably, following the still hooded man's ruthless, strong hands on her. He had reached down and grabbed her by her hair almost as soon as Xander and the woman had left, flipping her onto her belly and then leaning over her on the bed.

"I hear you like it rough Laurie, that you like to play rape," he had whispered, running his hands over her scantily clad body and tracing one finger over her naked bum to her inner thighs.

"No! Get off me, please," she had cried, not wanting it for real. She had never fantasised about it actually happening to her. It was always under her control.

"I'm going to show you what it's really like," the man had then promised, throwing her onto the floor and slapping her across the face again and again until she fell down at last and stopped her pleas. He then towered over her and lifted Laurie into his arms, placing her back on the messed up sheets and stepping back, removing his cloak and unbuttoning his jeans.

"Not this time, Heath," commanded Leyla as she opened the door and re-entered with a very pale Xander in tow.

"Fucks sake," he grumbled, doing his jeans back up and pulling on his hood again as Xander moved to the bed to pull Laurie into a protective embrace.

"Mark her, heal her, and wipe her memory. Then come back to headquarters," she commanded, before turning to Xander. "I'll be back to take you up on that promised favour soon," she told him and then disappeared, having teleported away without another word to the trembling man before her.

Heath did as she asked, reaching out to touch the frightened woman's temple and then he whispered a strange spell in a language neither she nor Xander had ever heard before and she quickly stilled. Laurie nodded and agreed to his request, offering him her wrist, which he marked with Leyla's symbol, and then she fell asleep again in an instant. Her body was healed and her mind cleared of her ordeal, as per Leyla's orders. After all, the message was for Xander, not her, and he would never be allowed to forget his promises to the Brotherhood or the cost of them, but his mistress needn't suffer, they weren't all evil.

When Laurie woke the next morning Xander was peering down at her, fear in his eyes and while she couldn't understand it, somehow she knew that she too was terrified to her core, she just didn't know what she was so scared of. The last thing she remembered was falling asleep in his arms the night before.

CHAPTER EIGHTEEN

"You look so beautiful when I've just fucked your brains out. I might almost say you're perfect," Corey said, running his hands up and down Melody's naked back thoughtfully, and she couldn't help but laugh gruffly.

"That must mean I am perfect, then. After all, you've fucked my brains out every day for months now. Maybe one day you'll just admit how much you love me," she replied jokingly, burying her face into the pillow to mask her groan when he slapped her bum cheek and then she wriggled away and wandered into the en-suite.

"I do, honest," he called after her, grinning wickedly.

"Liar," she mumbled as she locked the door behind her and climbed in the shower, eager to clean the smell of him away. Despite her enjoying their passion, she hated Corey even still. She had fully recovered from her time in dirty confinement with Donovan in that awful cell quickly thanks to the witches and their potions, but had been at the behest of Corey's every desire ever since that day. Melody had no other choice in the matter, and her new guardian had been exploiting his control as much as he possibly could. When she came back out, her master was lying on the bed with his head in a magazine, a recent copy of 'Business Weekly' with his own gorgeous image displayed across the front of it. He looked fantastic on the cover, dressed all in black, but his shirt was ripped open and underneath it he wore a t-shirt with the letter 'B' emblazoned on it to imitate that of an old superhero. The cover had the headline, 'billionaire bad boy finally ready to settle down,' and he read aloud the article as Melody joined him on the bed.

"The past couple of years have seen a huge change in this country's business world. Melody Pembroke, the illegitimate yet capable heiress to her father's fortune, has not only brought about a welcome change to our economic growth but also empowered other family-run businesses to follow the same acumen. The reclusive Black family has also changed hands, the youngest member of the dynasty, Corey, having inherited the throne atop the Black Rose Industries tower with just as much ease and even more growth to his family's legacy. The famously feuding companies recently revealed another twist in their tale when the two moguls announced they were officially an item at last week's masquerade ball hosted by the notorious bad-boy Black to commemorate his takeover. Ever since Pembroke's sudden split from movie star boyfriend Donovan Caine six-months ago, she has remained quiet, almost reclusive herself, but now we know why. Black, it seems, was a good friend of hers for years, but they had kept it quiet because of their family's feuds. In an exclusive interview with us recently, Corey revealed how he didn't just aid Melody in getting over the breakup with Caine after the star was found cheating on her with her assistant Lisa, but that he also helped mend her broken heart. During those difficult days, Corey revealed he fell in love with Melody, the notorious bad-boy changing his ways at long last thanks to his first ever deep and meaningful connection. While he was once a mutual friend of both parties, he had chosen to step away from his destructive movie star pal and follow his heart instead. Us here at 'Business Weekly' not only applauds his kindness, but we also wish them the best for their future, both personally and industrially. We actively support their relationship and look forward to hearing more in the future on how he swooped in to rescue his damsel in distress and win her heart."

"Don't make me sick," Melody replied, but laughed when he shot her his best shocked look. "You look like an idiot on the cover as well. What does the 'B' stand for?"

"Black, bad-boy, big-dick, take your pick, sweetheart. And anyway, I thought you just said something about being in love with me?" he cried, feigning hurt feelings.

"Nope."

"Well, you love to hate me then?" Corey teased.

"Not even that much," Melody replied. "I hate to admit how much I love to hate you," she added, enjoying that they could be so playful with each other at times now.

"I'll take that," he replied, a cunning smile on his face. "Sometimes I crave your hatred more than I desire your love. I want your rage more than your affection, Melody. I guess it's true what they say, a leopard cannot change his spots."

Melody knew that he was hoping she would bite, that she would continue on and come back with some witty remark after another that he could punish her for. But she bit her tongue, not giving in, knowing better than to let her once so quick outbursts flow any more. The last few months had been really hard on her. Losing Donovan had hurt more than she could ever reveal to her new master but she had worked herself through the emotions and grief she felt for him, and the relationship she had accepted she could no longer have with the man she was so deeply connected to. Corey had been his usual, mean self but had put her through an extra layer of his torturous, cold-hearted nature at first, punishing Melody hard and he made no secret of the fact that he had enjoyed every moment of it. His control had been relentless, his affection destructive, and she had learned to become subservient to him very quickly or else suffer even more.

They had now moved into her London home together, a so seemingly normal progression for other couples, but she didn't feel comfortable being with him on their own. At least in the small hamlet in Yorkshire she was surrounded by other beings and fellow followers at all times, and having them close by had brought her comfort, despite knowing that even if she screamed at the top of her lungs for help, none of them would ever have come to intervene. Corey's dealings with his marked followers were his business alone. Even Leyla didn't bother to look at the poor woman any more. She no longer seemed to care or notice Melody's suffering and actively avoided her when they were at the headquarters, removing Donovan from her presence whenever they had all been there together for the regular brunches and meetings of the dark order too.

The day Corey had marked Melody was an awful memory, but it was nearly a year ago now and time, along with her sheer stubbornness, had numbed that pain at last. He had softened just a little over that time, allowing Melody some supervised time to work with Leyla and Donovan eventually. Neither had bothered to try and talk privately with her as they put together hers and Donovan's breakup to publicly shame the movie star for supposedly cheating on her six months ago, but the world soon forgave him. Donovan's new movie had been a huge hit, and he was a bigger star than ever now, still accompanied everywhere by his paparazzi. He had recently signed on to do a sequel with Melody's studio, a public signal that the two of them were now over their breakup. The pair of them had not been allowed a single moment alone since their days in the cold, filthy room so had never been able to process their terrible memories together but they had both kept living, carried on breathing, and trying their hardest to make amends for their misdemeanours in the hope that their harsh punishments would someday be over. As a client, Donovan's life had returned to normal months ago, his punishment a proverbial slap on the wrist compared to what Melody had endured thanks to Corey's new ownership of her but there was nothing either of them could do other than stay away from one another just as Corey had commanded, making sure not to get her in any more trouble.

Corey had then recently decided to openly be seen to be in a relationship with Melody, their companies having become powerful associates in the capital and monopolising every business sector between them, only adding to their combined wealth and power. Their pairing had worked out wonderfully, and they had played the 'star-crossed-lovers' routine well at a recent ball hosted by the powerful mogul. Corey had staged the whole night, Melody being dressed in a skimpy outfit and heels that were so high that she could barely walk. The pair were known to be friends, having publicly conquered their business rivalries, and he had then purposely had Melody tripped over while dancing close to her in the bustling crowd, catching the flailing woman in his arms and staring into her hazel eyes in an elaborate display of affection and warmth. He had later told their colleagues that he was overcome with his need to come clean in that moment and had publicly revealed their relationship, having then planted a deep and meaningful kiss on the beautiful woman's lips while everyone watched on in shock and awe.

Meri knocked and entered their bedroom, curling tongs and makeup bag at the ready, and she quickly got to work, making Melody look presentable for her business trip to Venice. She was looking forward to having a few days to herself, having promised Corey numerous times over the past year that she would forever remain loyal to him now, and she had proven it to him over and over again. Melody had given all of herself to him in that time and had never fought his advances ever again. Their time together had been a combination of incredible lovemaking, hard lessons, and tests from her unfeeling master, and she never wanted to relive those lessons again. Corey didn't love her, and she knew he never would, but Melody didn't care. She didn't love him either. As awful as the truth was, Melody was happier knowing where they both stood with one another and she had just carried on regardless, glad to be alive and taken care of by her dark and dangerous lover no matter the forced submission that came with the territory.

The masquerade ball had been fun. After their big reveal he had openly adored her, his hand never leaving the small of her back and he spoke unashamedly to their business associates about his supposed love for her and their amazing relationship. It had made Melody feel good, wanted, and loved, even if it was all just for show.

She left for the airport without even a kiss goodbye and enjoyed the peace and quiet of the private lounge and the flight, opting to read a book rather than work on the plane, and within a few hours she had checked into her waterside hotel and changed for her dinner meeting. Meri took her across the city to a stunning veranda restaurant bathed in the orange glow of the setting sun and she stared out at the water in awe, not noticing that the restaurant was empty apart from her.

"It's beautiful," she whispered to herself, remembering her time with Leyla in this same city with a smile and basking in the last of the day's warmth, when a strong hand wrapped around her throat from behind.

"It'll do," whispered Corey into her ear. "We are being watched, so make it believable, Mel," he added before she turned to face him and did her best to fake a huge smile and fling herself into his arms.

"What are you doing here?" she squealed, forcing her voice out loudly to seem excited, but underneath she was seething that the couple of days by herself he had promised had turned into just a few hours. Corey just grinned and climbed down on one knee, pulling a small black box from his pocket and lifting it up for her to see. Melody gulped and gasped, feeling as though she might faint.

"I love you more than I can ever say. More than I can ever show. Melody Pembroke, will you be mine?" he asked, one eyebrow cocked. She wanted to scream at him and run away, to beg anyone who would listen for help, but she knew it was useless. Melody forced herself to smile and looked down at the gorgeous man who she wished would just love her the way he had once pretended to all that time ago when they had first begun seeing each other. She didn't care that he was faking it back then, she would do anything to have that Corey back again.

"Corey Black you bad boy," she replied, relishing in making him wait for her yes and enjoying breaking the rules by saying his name. He had needed to relinquish that order in public so that she was free to speak to him just as any normal couple would do but she knew he hated it. Melody knew the rules. She understood that when she agreed to marry him she well and truly did belong to him, forever, but that she also had no other choice but to play along in his game. "Yes, I'm yours Corey, now and forevermore."

He slid the impressive diamond onto her finger and pulled Melody off her feet into his arms, kissing her deeply while the restaurant staff clapped loudly for them and the paparazzi snapped away from across the water.

CHAPTER NINETEEN

Corey and Melody were married in secret the next morning, their dark ministers performing the ritual in Venice's Satanic church while just Corey's mother and father witnessed. Melody had never met Devin before but didn't even get the opportunity to talk with him. He and Serena teleported away as soon as the ceremony was over rather than them stay to celebrate their son's union, and he hadn't so much as uttered one word to their new daughter-in-law.

"I feel like the saddest bride in all the world," she mumbled to herself as she peered at her reflection in the bathroom mirror, her empty eyes giving away her depression and the sense of all-consuming loneliness she could only barely hide.

"Just think of all those poor girls forced into arranged marriages with fat, ugly men, with dicks the size of hotdogs. At least you've got a hot, bad-boy husband with a cock to rival a horse's and the power to deliver you with orgasm after orgasm for the rest of your life," Corey said as she made her way into the bedroom, clearly having been listening in.

"And an ego to match," she replied, slipping out of her thin dress and joining him in the bed. "Where do you want me?" she asked, leaning up on her elbow to look into his deep blue eyes. Melody was so used to just doing everything he wanted her to now that she no longer thought for herself or tried to guess what Corey wanted. It was easier to just let him order her around. After all, she was his, ready and awaiting his commands at all times, and it was strange when he hesitated for a moment. Corey took Melody's hand and placed it over his heart, looking back into her hazel eyes for a moment, his expression almost soft.

"I wish I could have you in here, Melody. I really wish I could. I know we joke and we fight and I've hurt you, a lot. But you're honestly the closest to anything real I've ever had. I thought I was just having fun, but realised I was never strong enough to stay away before, let alone how truly addicted to you I seem to have become," he told her, stroking her face and she felt as though she might cry, the numbness inside she had grown so used to suddenly panging with life, with hope.

"Why do you always have to play with me? I'd forgive you for anything, but don't you dare make me love you, Corey. Don't you fucking dare," Melody replied, climbing on top of him and kissing him deeply in an attempt to distract them both from his rare, heartfelt words.

"We both know I'd ruin it well before you even started to love me Melody. That's the beauty of what I am, and the truth of everything I'm not. Now, lay back, wife, I need to taste your sweet pussy," he demanded, quickly switching back to his playful self again as he flipped her beneath him and dived under the covers. She laid her head back on the pillow and opened her legs, his mouth quickly commanding her clit, and she writhed beneath him, her body ready as always to love him, even if the rest of her was still fighting it.

Corey groaned as she came for him, speeding up to bring her a second throb and then he plunged his hard cock as deep as he could in her still tensing cleft. Melody threw her head back and gripped the pillow beneath her tightly, lifting her thighs to meet his thrusts and welcoming the barrage of kisses he delivered to her neck, breasts, face, and then lips, devouring every one of her senses. When he finally reached his end Melody was utterly spent, trembling as she came down for the tremendous highs her husband had delivered over and over again with a satisfied smile. Instinctively, Corey held her tight, wrapping his arms around her as she drifted off to sleep.

"You're gonna be bad news, Mrs Black, I can tell," he whispered in her ear, but Melody didn't hear him. She was already fast asleep in his arms.

The next morning, Melody awoke from a restful sleep to find Corey gone. They were still in Venice, staying in a stunning suite with far too many rooms for them to use for just the two of them, and the place looked amazing in the fresh dawn light. After wandering around sleepily, she eventually found him on the small balcony, sipping on a milky coffee as he worked at his laptop.

"Morning," she said, sitting down in the chair opposite him and covering her bare legs with her shirt as best she could against the early morning chill. Melody then reached over and stole the half-full coffee from the saucer beside her husband and grinned as she finished it.

"Cheeky bitch, I bet you think you'll get away with murder now that you're my wife?" he asked, but his tone was thankfully playful.

"Strangely, I think you'd be okay with murder," she replied, one eyebrow raised. "I realised something, though. I said your name last night and you didn't punish me. Should I expect a slap at some point this morning?" she asked cautiously, and he immediately looked over his laptop screen at her.

"You're my wife now, Mel. Of course, you are permitted to say my name," he replied, as if she should have known that already, and Melody nodded. All he'd need was an eye-roll at that moment to really belittle her, but she held back a snide retort that was bursting to be set free and just smiled sweetly.

"Oh, that's good to know. Just your name, I take it, not anyone else in your family?"

"Absolutely not. My father's already not happy with you, so you'd better not anger him further," Corey told her, getting back to work and her mouth dropped open in shock.

"Hang on a second. What do you mean he's not happy with me?" she blurted out.

"You fucked up Mel. He and my mother wanted you to be with Donovan. They had it all perfectly planned out, but then you went and made me want you. It's also your fault that I even had the opportunity to take you from Leyla, ergo it's your fault that their plans were scuppered," he said, shrugging as though he didn't care, and maybe even believed that all of this was in fact Melody's fault and not his.

"I knew he wasn't impressed yesterday at the ceremony. It's not my doing though, it's yours. You arse," she grumbled.

"Yeah, but I'm their golden boy. I can do no wrong," he replied, laughing at her unease. "I've found him a new project to work on though, so don't worry. He'll soon forget about your misdemeanours. And, when we give them some grandchildren soon, they'll definitely forgive you," he added, laughing harder as his words sunk in and she grimaced.

"I can't, Corey, no," she whispered, her eyes widening as her stomach dropped at the sheer thought.

"Well, you're not getting any younger sweetheart, we'll need at least three or four kids so that'll take up the better part of your thirties," he replied, and she squirmed in her seat, shaking her head. Melody hated defying him, but there was just no way that she could concede in this matter. Not yet, maybe not ever.

"No, I said no," she shouted, standing and going to storm off, but Corey grabbed her, yanking Melody down onto his lap and pulling her into his strong arms.

"Hey, I'm not getting any younger either, you know. You do realise I'm nearly seventy?" he asked, instantly relieving the tense atmosphere, and she pulled back to look into his eyes, grinning broadly.

"That's why you're such a miserable old bastard then," she teased, and kissed him before he could answer with a witty comeback. When she had calmed down completely, Corey let go of Melody and she padded into the bedroom to get dressed, almost bumping straight into Heath as he teleported into the living area of their suite with a disgusting grin.

"Forgive me, Mrs Black. I'll be more careful in future," he said, eyeing her half-naked body for a second before Corey snapped his fingers, letting the deviant warlock know he had been caught.

"Make sure you do, Heath. I'd hate to have a disagreement with you after all these years of loyal service," he told him, his eyes darkening uncontrollably for just a moment and his most devoted servant bowed before him apologetically. Corey then stepped forward and took the envelope from Heath's hands, eyeing its contents with a smile.

"Everything is ready master, the announcement is good to go, we just need to know your choice," Heath told him, rising and then teleporting away when Corey gave him an approving nod.

Melody joined him in the living area again a few minutes later, fully dressed, and she scanned the room for Heath, grateful that he had gone again.

"I have something to show you," Corey told her. He sat on the couch and patted the spot beside him, ushering for his wife to join him there. She did what he wanted, as usual, and waited for him to slide the contents out from the large envelope. Corey grinned as he handed her a thick stack of photographs, all of them featuring the pair of them in loving embraces, locking eyes across a crowded room or even in the throes of passion.

"Who took these?" she asked angrily, but Corey shushed her. Melody continued through the pile, finding another envelope at the bottom of the small heap with the previous day's date handwritten on the front of it. Inside were the most beautiful pictures she had ever seen, close-up shots of her eyes and lips as she smiled and basked in the sun, wearing her black wedding gown, roses in hand. The little stack of wedding photos was truly stunning, well taken, and captivating. The last handful were of the two of them together, husband and wife, looking happy and in love.

"We don't even look like we're pretending," she whispered, taking in the beautiful shots in amazement.

"I think in that moment we weren't," Corey replied, taking the photograph from her and pulling his mobile phone from his pocket. He quickly dialled Heath and read him the serial number from the back of the photo before hanging up and taking the pictures out of Melody's hands. He placed them on the table in front of them and then lifted her up into his arms. He carried her into the bedroom and almost threw her onto the bed, his most primal, instinctual need to be inside of her taking over.

CHAPTER TWENTY

The news of their marriage broke while Corey and Melody were busy in the bedroom together. Neither one of them heard the barrage of phone calls and text messages they seemed to be getting on their mobile's in the other room while they kept each other far too busy in their bed. Corey pulled Melody close, shuddering his release before sitting back and taking a good look at his wife with a satisfied smile. Her hands were bound above her head using the tie from her robe, her body at his complete command and despite her fears, she somehow had learned to trust him. Melody peered back at Corey with a shy smile, sliding her trembling legs closed to hide her body from him. He still couldn't quite believe she was his. Despite everything he had put her through, Melody still revelled in his affection and did all that he asked of her. There would always be a part of him that held her in such high regard, despite his constant insistence that he didn't love her. Corey wrenched open his wife's legs and ran his hands up her thighs, stroking her clit and making her come for him one more time before he could even contemplate releasing her from the knot above her head.

"Not until I say we're finished," he muttered, watching as Melody unravelled beneath his touch, her release exploding out of her core and her hips bucking while he rubbed her for a few more seconds.

"Anything you say," she replied, enjoying as his eyes washed over every inch of her exposed skin appreciatively.

"That's more like it," he said, leaning up to untie her wrists. He stood and wandered into the en-suite for a shower while Melody rested on the bed for a minute, wonderfully exhausted and rubbing the warmth back into her wrists. "Come on!" Corey shouted from the steamy room and she jumped up off the bed, quickly joining him before she knew the dripping wet, god-like being would come to get her. She had learned that lesson before.

When the pair finally emerged from the bedroom, dressed and ready for the promised evening out Corey had insisted she be prepared for, he finally allowed her a moment to check her mobile phone. Melody shrieked when she realised she had over one hundred missed calls and text messages.

"What did you do?" she asked him, one eyebrow cocked.

"I married you, of course," he teased. "I just made it public this morning."

"Of course you did," she replied. "I'm gonna have to ring my mum before we head out if that's okay?" she added, and he nodded. Melody dialled her mother's number and listened while she was chastised and then congratulated before being handed to her sister for pretty much the same speech. Callie's recollection of her night with Corey had been wiped from her memory, thankfully, and so she was truly happy for them, remembering nothing but the connection she had once known them to have before and after her few months with Donovan. Melody sometimes wished her own memories had been wiped, too. She had even begged Corey to do it before, but he had refused, of course. He wanted her to remember everything, to live with the constant fear that he might put her through those terrible things all over again in order to keep her subservient.

Melody surfed the Internet as she chatted with Callie, finding the photograph she had picked out earlier of her and Corey on almost every business and celebrity website proclaiming their news to the world. When she had finally said her goodbyes, her husband stood waiting for her, hand outstretched, and she took it.

She followed him out of the room and down to the lobby, where they were ushered into a waiting gondola and then made their way down the narrow waterways while the paparazzi ran along beside them, desperate to get snaps of the happy couple and capture their swift progression from intended to being husband and wife. Melody waved as they sped away, snuggling into Corey as they rounded the corner, and then they made their way across the city to a quiet corner of a bustling restaurant that served local delicacies and exquisite wine. Their date was actually rather fun, and she enjoyed having the playful Corey with her that night, him seemingly gentle and kinder with her now that she was his wife, and Melody hoped things would stay this way.

They returned to London a few days later, neither of them able to get away for longer, so a proper honeymoon would have to wait. She still found herself smiling naturally and feeling wonderful, uncontrollably walking on air despite constantly telling herself not to trust it for even a second.

Meri came to see her at the house in Primrose Hill a few weeks later, hurrying Melody out of bed as usual and giving her instructions on her attire and style for the day, before going over her schedule with her. Meri had fast become all that Leyla had once promised her to be. She did absolutely everything for Melody, and she knew she would be absolutely lost without her. Corey had already left for the day, not telling her where he was going or what he was doing, as usual. Melody didn't care though, and part of her never wanted him to disclose the details regarding the poor souls he was either acquiring or retrieving during his working day.

"Shooting begins on Donovan's movie today. As chief executive, you are expected to be there, Melody," Meri told her as she served coffee and the trembling woman nodded.

"We'll be fine. I know I haven't seen Donovan in months, but all in all, we still parted on good terms, despite what the papers might think. Will we head straight there this morning and then come back in time for the gala this evening?" she replied, and Meri nodded.

A very nervous Melody arrived at Pembroke Studios a few hours later, her demonic assistant and Corey's coven of watchers in tow. All of them had taken on the roles of her aides thanks to her husband's still so constant watch and tight control over her. At her masters' request, Melody had recently had the studios completely refurbished too, the entire building having been doubled in size and renovated throughout in order to increase their already high revenue. Each of the vast areas was now capable of shooting numerous projects at any given time, and had already started getting booked up by other movie producers and television show companies. Most of them were already beholden to the Crimson Brotherhood in one way or another, and had them to thank for their successes so far, but Corey also delighted in using Melody as his puppet in those meetings that involved new potential clients and aspiring moviemakers or actors. Being there again reminded Melody of her recent past and the things Corey had made her do for him thanks to her influence over her clients and associates under Pembroke Enterprise's vast reach. She had hated every second of it, but knew that she had no other choice. Melody acted as his spokeswoman as she delivered the spiel regarding budgets and overheads, acting as though she wasn't sure whether they were a worthwhile investment before then luring them in and offering them everything they desired. Plus, there was the added assurance that their projects would be a success if they signed on the dotted line in blood and paid with their souls. She desperately wanted to tell each poor fool to refuse her offer and run away every time. She desired nothing more than to turn down every ambitious soul who darkened her doorstep, but she didn't dare.

Another memory flooded her mind as she sat at her desk, looking at the seat opposite her where her guests would sit and beg for the opportunity to have her studios' backing and network connectivity. Even her sister Callie had come to her a few weeks ago asking for financial support to pursue her acting career, and this time Melody had quickly told her no despite her responsibility to the Crimson Brotherhood to at least look into her request. There was absolutely no way that she would ever drag her family into this terrible life she now led and she soon persuaded Callie to stop being so foolish and concentrate on more achievable dreams. She hated to quash her sister's ambition but she couldn't stand it if she had made that deal. Callie hadn't spoken to her for weeks afterwards, hurt and angered that her rich sister wouldn't help, but Melody didn't care. All she wanted was for Callie to be safe, so it was worth having the cold-shoulder for.

Melody had not been punished for denying her master her sister's soul until days afterwards. She had hoped that Corey was unaware of her doings, but had constantly worried that he might find out and still punish her for it, which in some ways was worse. At times, she fretted so much that she considered just spilling the beans in order to get it over with. When the day had finally come that he acted, being Corey's wife didn't save her from a sound beating thanks to her selfless actions. He hadn't said a word as they went to bed one night, but then randomly let her sleep in the following morning, laughing when Melody jumped out of bed in a panic to get to work.

"It's fine," he had said, laughing as he slid out of bed and took her hands in his. "I rang in sick for you, you're gonna be out for the rest of the week."

"Why?" she had then asked, wondering what he wanted her to do that would take up the next three days of her time and her stomach had dropped thanks to the dread that then filled her. Corey gripped her hands tighter, sensing her urge to turn and run, but they both knew that it would be pointless.

"Because, my dear wife, I'm going to fuck you and then beat you, and then fuck you again, over and over for the next few days. I won't be soft, and I won't be gentle. If you dare make a sound the entire time, I'll make it last an extra day for every word that escapes your lips. Do you understand?" Corey had asked, a vile, sinister smile crossing his face that made him look so ugly that Melody had then felt sick to her stomach. She had just nodded, knowing that his evil game had already begun, and that she had to let him have her, let him hurt her again and again until he was finally satisfied that she had learned that terrible lesson.

"Donovan Caine and his sadistic side's got nothing on me sweetheart, I hope your sister's soul was worth it," he had whispered in Melody's ear a few days later when he was finally through with his terrible punishment and Melody had just sobbed harder, staying silent despite him pressing himself into her battered and bruised body. When Corey finally healed her and teleported away, she had screamed into her pillow until her voice was gone, hating her husband more than she had ever hated anyone before.

CHAPTER TWENTY-ONE

"Mrs Black, so wonderful to see you," Donovan said when the pair of them finally saw one another later that afternoon at the studio. It was the first time in months, and they made a point of shaking hands while everyone looked on, watching the pair of them with intrigue. "Look at you, you're positively radiant. Marriage becomes you," he added, kissing her cheek lightly.

"Thank you Donovan, you've bulked up since the last time I saw you. Ready for round two?" she asked, and Donovan nodded, taking a seat beside her at the huge desk as they chatted some more. Eyes and ears were still on them but they didn't care. They both knew that they'd be under the scrutiny of both the Crimson Brotherhood's members and their unmarked human colleagues during this first sighting of them together since their split, and neither seemed willing to give the onlookers anything to report about. The pair quickly found themselves comfortable in each other's presence and so at ease, their terrible history having formed a strong bond between them on top of their chemistry that Melody honestly felt she needed in this awful world she now lived in. She had accepted that her and Donovan would never be together, and moved on, but the numb hole inside of her, the cold, empty void that would never be filled with love or respect from her husband somehow felt a little less empty when Donovan was around. Melody let herself enjoy the way he made her feel. He was her friend. They had terrible, dark secrets and they would both keep them forever, but they also had a genuine affection for each other that despite the awful last year was still there and neither one of them fought it.

Donovan's assistant soon brought over the final script to look over and the star's notes, along with a coffee and a protein bar for her boss. Melody noticed a small glint in the girl's eye as she attended him, but also the shift in his demeanour as he gave the young woman her orders. He was her Dom, Melody could tell right away.

"Are you, being careful?" she whispered, keeping her eyes down and quickly scanning the paperwork before her while he almost choked on his coffee.

"How did you know?" Donovan replied, completely taken aback.

"This is me you're talking to," she replied, and he eventually shrugged, silently agreeing that Melody truly was the only person who might know his real self and see it so clearly despite his careful guise. He seemed to accept that they still had a close bond too, the only true connection he had ever had with another person, and yet he knew that holding out for her was useless. And so, Donovan had accepted Leyla's gift of a submissive assistant to curb his dark needs. He liked asserting his control over the girl and had assumed his role as the dominant with ease. Donovan had never shown this new partner the submissive side of himself that he had once shown Melody. He had never shown anyone, and wondered if he ever would again. Despite the two of them having only been together a short amount of time and never actually having made love, Melody knew that she was still the only person who had ever seen that raw, powerless man who had held her in his arms that day after he had scratched his dark itch with that masochistic woman Leyla had procured for him. She was also the only one who had seen him break down, watched the ever so strong man crumble, and seen him laid bare during their disgusting incarceration together in the depths of the Crimson Brotherhood mansion while they awaited their trial. Melody understood Donovan, and he knew her, inside and out. No one could ever take that away from her and Melody kept that little warmth in her heart for him locked away, knowing that at times she needed to remember that someone, somewhere, actually cared for her.

"Yes, we're both being careful. I'm in control but I haven't done the really hard stuff in a long time Mel, not since that day," he said, and she knew he was thinking of the same moment as she was, the day he had sprung from the car to pursue an anonymous lover to beat rather than lash out at her. "I don't have those urges as strongly anymore, but I still need the control. She's a great sub, she does everything I ask of her and it's exactly what I need right now," Donovan admitted, looking down at his script, not wanting to look into her eyes. "How about you? Are you doing okay with your loved-up and happy new role as the doting wife and subservient lover?" he asked quietly, and the way he had asked it was not lost on Melody. She was playing a role, and they both knew it, but just to be safe, she answered with a lie, but he knew the truth, anyway.

"Corey and I are really very happy and in love, he's everything I want and need," she whispered and he could do nothing but offer her an understanding, warm smile in return.

"You'd make a great actress Melody," he mumbled, hanging his head sadly.

***

"Action!" shouted the director, and shooting officially commenced on Donovan's new movie a couple of hours later. Melody watched the actors for a while, purposely busying herself when Donovan removed most of his clothes for one of the sex-scenes in case of watchful eyes, but otherwise the day was a success and she returned home with Meri later that afternoon.

"Well, well, well. If it isn't my darling wife," shouted Corey from the bedroom as she came inside the doorway and pulled off her high-heeled shoes, rubbing her toes to get the blood flowing back into them. She climbed the stairs quickly, always knowing not to keep her master waiting for her, and then rounded the doorway to their bedroom while unbuttoning her jacket. Corey was laid on the bed with his laptop propped up on his knees, flicking through some documents and he ignored her at first. She pulled off her jewellery and placed the expensive adornments in their boxes, all the while sensing the tension reverberating off him, but she didn't dare ask what was going on.

Melody slid off her dress and underwear, standing naked at the end of the bed while Corey continued to type and click, his eyes never leaving the screen. After a few minutes, she figured he must not want her in that way, so moved over to the hook beside the bed to grab her robe, and that was when she caught his eyes on her at last.

"Did you have a good day, darling?" he asked, his voice cold. "Did you enjoy spending time with your old friend?"

"I was pleasant, and I was professional. As per your instructions, darling," Melody couldn't help but reply, her tone vicious too. Corey turned the screen and showed her a photograph of her and Donovan sat at the table in the studio office, chatting and drinking coffee, their eyes locked in nothing more than a friendly gaze, but she could tell that he still was not happy about it.

"Too. Fucking. Friendly," he told her, his voice so stern and commanding that Melody trembled in fear and nodded in defeat. "I've decided we aren't going to the gala tonight," he added as he turned the laptop back around and began typing again.

"But, I'm the new ambassador. I've got a speech to do and everything," she begged. "Corey, I did nothing wrong today, there's no need to punish me. This is for the business, not for me," she added, trying to get him to change his mind for that aspect if not for her.

"Turn around and face the corner, Melody. You'll stay there until I release you, is that understood?" he ordered, and she nodded, shuffling over to stand in the darkest corner of their room, his new favourite place to send her during his heartless punishments.

Melody was just hopeful that he would release her in time for the gala to start. Corey was toying with her and asserting his control, as usual.

She locked her knees and closed her eyes, readying herself for her stint while forcing her mind to settle and focus on anything other than the aches in her legs that quickly began to sweep up and down them. She was also well aware that she had just spent the best part of the last eight hours on her feet and they were quickly starting to hurt too. Being forced to stand still in a corner for what she assumed would be around two hours would be tough, but she focussed hard, not letting him win, and righted her stance for the long and painful couple of hours ahead of her.

CHAPTER TWENTY-TWO

"Mr and Mrs Black, how sublime to see you," said another businessman who kissed Melody's cheek and fawned over her stunning dress. She smiled sweetly and chatted to him, Corey playing the ultimate gentleman and devoted husband so perfectly that no one had any reason to think otherwise. This man had to have been the fortieth person she had spoken with that night. All the while, her feet and legs were aching terribly, shaking beneath her dress in her incredibly high and uncomfortable heels. Corey had only just about released her from her punishment in time for Meri to put the finishing touches to her hair and makeup before he then teleported them to the gala. Melody had recently become a patron for a prestigious and highly profitable war foundation named 'Help with Honour' and these galas were only held twice a year, but this was her first one. It was important that she make a good impression, so she had endeavoured to leave only when she had greeted and spoken with everyone who wished to have a moment with her. She also had a speech to deliver and was grateful when she was ushered away for a few precious moments away from Corey's controlling embrace.

Melody took the stage, standing tall and beautiful while elegant and poised as she smiled warmly down at the attendees and pulled the microphone up to her lips.

"Thank you all for being so welcoming to my husband and I, and for making us feel as though we can be an integral part of this very important foundation. Together, I know that we can help make a real difference in those people's lives that need it the most. The foundation-," Melody began, reading from her auto-cue, but then the words began to blur before her eyes and she felt woozy.

Melody blinked hard, trying to refocus, but suddenly felt as though the floor fell away beneath her and she slipped to the ground in a crumpled heap, completely out cold. Everyone around her ran to her aid, no one more so than her seemingly doting husband, who knew full well she had fainted thanks to sheer exhaustion, yet lifted her into his arms and leaned in to speak into his burly bodyguard's ear.

"Heath, bring the car around. We might have to go and check on the baby," he whispered, but it was loud enough for just those close enough to hear. He then deposited Melody on a nearby sofa and then gave her a glass of water as she came to, fawning over her and stroking her cheek gently while pulling off her high heels.

"Corey, I," she tried to say, still swaying despite now being sat down.

"Shhh, it's okay darling. Let's just get you home to rest," he replied, lifting her to her feet and helping Melody to walk, a protective arm around her, and he made their excuses as he led her towards the door. The crowd had now dispersed, but the whispers had already begun, the women unable to hide the gossip they had just overheard. By the time the two of them had finished making their apologies and left with Heath, the rumours were already circulating about her alleged pregnancy.

"You fucking bastard!" Melody bellowed, having checked her laptop the next morning while resting her still weak body in bed. She had decided to work from home and was glad that she had now, thanks to the flood of calls from her friends and family back in Colchester as well as emails and interview requests from a variety of business and family magazines from across the globe. Corey poked his head around the bedroom door and laughed, joining her on the bed as he, too, flicked through the news on his tablet computer.

"There's no such thing as bad publicity, Mel," he replied, grinning. "I saw an opportunity, and I took it, simple. Now you'll have to give me a baby," he added.

"Fuck you," she replied, her blood boiling.

"If you insist," Corey replied, closing her laptop and pulling her over to him on the bed, grinning wickedly at her.

In the weeks that followed, Melody found the barrage of questions and concerned looks infuriating. She went for an interview with a business newspaper a month after her unfortunate moment of weakness to discuss the foundation, but was instead asked so many personal questions that she had cut the interview short, going on the record as officially having had a 'false alarm'.

"We will have a family eventually, I have no doubt. But this time we just hadn't gotten the dates quite right and my darling husband thought it must have been the reason why I fainted that night. I was late, but found out a few days ago that I am not expecting. I can't wait to be a mother, but right now I'm happy focussing on my career," she told the disappointed reporters. Melody then left the building and made her way across the city, Meri talking furiously on the mobile phone next to her.

"Yes, we can confirm that Mrs Black is not pregnant," she said over and over again to the various callers. Melody couldn't help but smile to herself as she sat back in the leather seat and closed her eyes, enjoying her moment of victory for a while before finally letting the dread set in as they neared the house.

She was in the middle of a videoconference at her home office when Corey stormed in later that afternoon, his eyes dark and his expression fierce. He knew that her associates in Germany were watching her and so he stood over her behind the screen, still as stone, his cold eyes on her while she finished the conference and said her goodbyes, hiding her fear from them as best she could. Melody then slid her laptop closed and flinched as her husband finally moved over to her, coming around to her side of the desk and turning her to face him.

Corey fell to his knees before her, his hands on her thighs, his body language suddenly sad and almost soft, and Melody was taken aback by his seemingly hurt feelings.

"Why do you do this to me, Mel?" he asked, peering up at her as he rubbed his hands against her bare skin.

"Because I told you no, and last I checked, you have to adhere to those rules, even if you don't follow any others," she replied, sliding her hands over his. Corey then climbed up and reached a hand up over her belly thoughtfully.

"I wasn't talking about that, I'll put a baby in there eventually don't you worry," he replied coldly, running his hands higher up her body to her face and he stood, leaning over her with his face just inches from hers. "We both know that I always get what I want sooner or later, Melody. I had hoped you might have learned that by now," Corey added. His expression had now turned from pained to enraged in less than a second, and she tried to pull back from his grasp.

"What do you mean then?" she whispered, biting her lip to stop it from trembling as she took in his hard gaze again, him having switched back to his stern look so quickly.

"What I mean is," he began, stroking her cheek softly and pulling her lip out from between her teeth. "Sometimes I think you were sent to test me, to be my undoing. I even thought for a while that you might be starting to make me go all soft and gooey inside," he said, rubbing her cheek with his finger again delicately while peering down into her hazel eyes solemnly. "But as time goes on, I realise that you aren't testing me, you're inspiring me. I have always enjoyed my job, all the fucking with and hurting people, but never in the ways I have enjoyed it with you. I used you, I messed with your life and I forced you to do everything I could possibly imagine to fuck you up, and yet you just keep on pushing me. It's like you can't stop yourself. You're my muse Melody, my dark and twisted source of sheer fucking inspiration, and when I look at you, I just keep coming up with more and more ways to hurt you. To break you. And I love it," Corey replied, reaching behind her head and grabbing her hair tightly before he yanked her head back and took her mouth in his by force. Melody trembled, hating his sinister view of her, and she winced as he pulled her hair tighter in his balled fist, pulling at her sensitive scalp harshly.

"Run," he then whispered, letting go and stepping back a few feet. "I'll give you two minutes and then I'm coming to get you. The sooner I find you the worse it'll be, so I suggest you find a good hiding spot," Corey said, his face thunderous, but he also seemed excited by his terrible game of cat and mouse.

Melody kicked off her shoes and bolted, not hesitating for even a second. She could only think of one place, the one hideout she had kept in mind for over a year should she ever need to try and hide in this vast house. She made her way to the top floor and then climbed into the small cupboard in one of the spare room's en-suite bathrooms. The unit was deceptively deep, and she had purposely made up a wall of towels inside to cover the cupboard's true depth. She climbed in, closed the door behind her and then rebuilt the stack of towels before sitting back and closing her eyes as she rested her head on her knees. Melody listened hard, slowing her panicked breaths as the excruciating minutes passed.

After many hours in the tight hole, she eventually emerged, the numbness in her legs getting the better of her, and Melody immediately regretted it. The game was not over. Corey had changed the rules though and she couldn't help but wonder if he had only told her to run because he wanted to know if she had a hiding spot already picked out should she ever need one. If her suspicions were right she had now given away her only advantage.

She stumbled forward on her knees, but the entire house was now bathed in pitch-black darkness and she struggled to find the staircase, stepping down carefully as she went and still listening hard for any sign of her husband. She eventually noticed a little bit of flickering light coming from the living room and moved towards it hesitantly. Melody rounded the arched doorway, finding her guardian sitting on one of the huge sofas while watching television, seemingly so relaxed and calm.

"Oh, there you are," Corey said, a huge grin lighting up his face in the darkness. "Your lover is on, look," he added, beckoning her over to join him on the sofa. Melody took a tentative step towards her now so composed husband and she wondered for a second if maybe she had misheard him earlier.

Melody trembled as she sat down beside him, her eyes on the screen as Donovan's movie played before them, but she just could not concentrate on the scenes in front of her.

"Corey, please. Just do it, I can't bear waiting," she begged, flinching as he wrapped an arm around her back and pulled her over for what would seem like just an ordinary cuddle for any other couple.

"Do what, darling?" he teased, and she could hear the smile in his voice as he toyed with her. Corey then reached over and grabbed her chin, pulling Melody's face up to his, and he planted a soft kiss on her still trembling lips while his hand slithered down to her throat. "This?" he then asked, gripping her neck tight. Corey then suddenly stood, lifting Melody off the sofa with him and then throwing her across the room using no effort at all. She flew a few feet in the air and then slammed into the huge television, smashing the screen before then tumbling to the floor in a heap, and the huge set then fell on top of her. Melody screamed and cried out as she clambered free, her left arm and side throbbing painfully, and she knew she must have broken bones.

"I'm so sorry, it's all my fault and I will never make a fool out of you again. Please, I'm sorry," Melody muttered as she stumbled towards him, falling to her knees before her guardian.

"No, you won't, I'll make sure of it," he agreed, reaching down to stroke her bruised face before delivering one more slap across her cheek and then walking off towards the hallway. "Hurry up and get to bed, I'm not finished with you yet," Corey added on his way and his broken wife could do nothing but follow him, despite being so broken and battered that she could barely stand.

CHAPTER TWENTY-THREE

More weeks quickly passed and his punishments steadily grew worse. Corey hadn't been kidding when he had called Melody his muse and she felt so very lost and alone in their marriage, despite being constantly accompanied by her husband's employees.

Tears ran down Melody's cheeks uncontrollably as Corey pinned her to the wall one night, his tall, strong frame pressing her so hard into the cold brick from behind that she could barely breathe.

"You're late," he demanded, his voice a deep growl. "You know I don't like to be kept waiting."

"I'm sorry," she breathed, trying to push him backwards ever so slightly so she could take a much-needed breath, but it was pointless. "Ask Meri, she'll tell you."

"It's true master. The final scene took longer than anticipated and we didn't leave the studio until over an hour later than we should have. I rang ahead and told you, remember?" the demonic woman told him, knowing that he was already well aware of the change in his wife's itinerary.

"Yes, of course, my bad," Corey said as he released Melody and stepped back. "You're excused," he added, not even looking at Meri as she nodded and walked up the stairs to her room. Melody smoothed her dress and caught her breath before turning to face Corey. Her hatred for him was growing every time he did something like that, and she knew he was doing it because she still hadn't caved about the baby issue.

"Take off your clothes," he ordered, and Melody wobbled on her heels for a moment, feeling faint again after another long day at the studio.

"Please Corey, I've barely eaten and we have the wrap party tonight. Can I just grab something to eat and then I'm all yours?" she asked, stepping forward to kiss his lips as softly as she could, fighting the urge to bite down and give him something to actually complain about, but she knew better than to push him. He had been unusually mean lately, chastising her about every little thing she might have done wrong and punishing her regardless of her pleas and explanations. He kissed her back, sliding off her jacket as he did so and then unzipping the suit dress she wore, sending them both tumbling to the ground.

Corey stepped back and took a good look at her. Melody had gotten skinny over the last few months thanks to her gruelling work schedule and his demands on her spare time. They were showing now, and she looked utterly exhausted.

"Do not disobey me, Melody. Go and stand in the corner," he said, his voice uncaring, and she did as she was told, sobbing as she faced the living room wall and trembling with the cold chill that had just swept down her spine.

A short while later, Melody felt warm hands grasp her back and lead her away from the corner, bending each leg to remove her heels and then pulling a warm robe around her shoulders. She had her still tear-stained face buried in her hands, having clammed up as she had huddled in the dark corner, and when she finally looked up, she was surprised to find Leyla standing before her.

"No, he won't be happy that I came out of the corner," Melody mumbled, trying to pull away but the powerful woman shushed her, stroking her face as she sat down on the sofa and pulled her into a deep, protective embrace. Melody trembled in Leyla's powerful arms, her tears dry, but the sobs still pulsated from her as she huddled in the protective arms that were wrapped around her for the first time in what felt like forever. Melody leaned into Leyla's hold and let herself feel cared for and safe for a few moments, having almost forgotten what it felt like.

"Corey's making you dinner, he's even cooking it himself," Leyla told her as she rubbed Melody's cold arms and legs with the warm, fluffy robe a few minutes later. "He'll never tell you just how much you mean to him, Mel. He'll never admit that he loves you, but there is a part of him that cares, however well he hides it. I think we're all hoping you'll fix him," she added, but Melody just shook her head.

"He doesn't know how to love, and he doesn't care enough to figure it out. Sometimes I just want to grab the people around me who are not part of this world and beg them to save me, make them see the truth. Living this terrible life is destroying me slowly one awful day at a time," Melody whispered into Leyla's tight hold, an almost silent admission that her old mistress heard clearly despite her friend's hushed tone.

"I know," was all she could say in response.

Corey soon came in and deposited three plates piled high with pasta and sauce before uncorking a bottle of wine and ushering them both to join him. He watched with intrigue and a little hint of malice he just could not hide as Leyla unwrapped her arms from around his wife and checked that she was okay. Even his big sister had an affection for Melody that she didn't bother to mask, and unlike him, she was not afraid to show it.

"Always a pleasure sis, what brings you around?" he asked as he poured the wine into three awaiting glasses.

"I just thought I'd stop by and see how you both were. And, well, I've been thinking about a client of mine who is having a dilemma. You know how if you gave away a naughty puppy to the pound, and then their new owners were mistreating it, wouldn't you find it hard not to step in and give them a kick up the arse every now and then?" Leyla replied, smirking at her brother as she led the still trembling Melody over to the table with her. Corey sneered, taking a long swig of his wine as he stared angrily at his sister.

"Maybe, but then again, what if the puppy was naughty and coddled before and then was even worse in their new home, always testing the new owner's patience? Sometimes punishment is the only way to make the foolish little thing learn," he replied and Melody just stayed quiet as she tucked in to the delicious meal before her, desperate to quell the deep rumbles in her stomach after so long without a proper meal.

"You can't choose to have a clever, independent puppy and then chastise it when it rebels against your dictatorial reign. Sometimes you need to just let it be who it is, to let time and experience help the puppy find its own way," Leyla replied, tucking in and giving her brother a thumbs-up for the delicious meal.

"Yeah, but sometimes that clever, independent puppy can choose to be a real bitch and you just get a kick out of delivering it with a really good punishment," he told her, grinning over at Melody who still had her eyes on her dinner.

The conversation soon moved on, Leyla and Corey catching up while Melody stayed silent. She ate the whole plateful and relaxed in her chair, finally warming up thanks to the nourishment and weight off her feet. She even let herself enjoy the wine, grateful for the rest and for Corey's attention being off of her while Leyla chatted away animatedly about her new clients. Melody almost got the feeling that Leyla was keeping him occupied and that she had stayed late on purpose for her benefit, but she would never get her hopes up.

Melody showered and changed after her plate was cleared and she had been allowed to leave the table, feeling much better after having eaten something, and she then made her way downstairs once Meri had finished making her look fabulous for the wrap party. She was wearing a dress that had cost more than her little sports car that was forever parked out front but she was forbidden to drive, and she felt amazing. The extravagant purchase was well worth it.

Corey's eyes lit up as she descended the stairs, her floating skirt billowing around her ankles, but she managed to still walk gracefully and poised, enjoying the look in his eyes as he admired his wife.

"Not bad for a naughty little bitch, is it?" she asked when she reached him, and he shrugged, immediately switching back to his playful demeanour.

"You'll do."

The wrap party was a blast, everyone was in high spirits and the champagne flowed while the stars, writers, crew, and executives all mingled effortlessly and enjoyed their night. Corey left Melody to talk with some of the actors she had gotten on well with during the shooting for both movies, and she welcomed the time away from under his constant watch. She grabbed another glass of wine and chatted even louder, making no excuses for her exuberant attitude and relaxed demeanour.

"I'll take a glass of your finest red wine," Corey asked the bartender, nodding appreciatively when the slight man produced a bottle of an expensive vintage wine from beneath the bar.

"Mr Caine bought this especially for you sir, he instructed me to give you this if you ordered red wine. He said nothing but the best for you and Mrs Black," the man said, his eyes darting to Corey's left and he turned to follow the line of sight. Donovan was making his way over to them and grinned at Corey. They were, after all, supposed to be old friends in the eyes of the public, so the two men shook hands and Corey graciously accepted the wine from the bartender.

"Well aren't you just kissing my arse wonderfully tonight Donnie, I hope I don't puke into my lovely wine," Corey said, clinking glasses and smiling across at him as they spoke, ensuring their cover was well maintained. Both men smiled warmly, looking at each other like nothing but old friends despite their harsh words, and none of the crowd around them had any idea just how much hatred and anger there was between the two of them.

"I am humbled by your presence, as always, guardian. Thank you for coming, I hope you enjoy the movie," Donovan replied, being careful to talk respectfully to Corey, his memories still very fresh in his mind of their awful punishments thanks to him, and he knew never to let his formality slip again.

"I'm sure I'll be far too busy fucking my wife's brains out to ever find the time to sit and watch it, I'm afraid." Corey replied, smiling broadly and patting Donovan on the shoulder, maintaining their fake easiness with one another. "You know how amazing she is in bed, or wait, no you don't do you?" he then teased.

"I have to say I preferred her back when she had a little bit more meat on her bones and happiness in her eyes, but each to their own. And I tell you what, seeing as you're so busy, I'll just send you the DVD," Donovan conceded, his fake smile not fading from his handsome face as he responded carefully, not wasting the opportunity to speak up about Melody's skinny body and obvious unhappiness. Corey sneered but carried on, eager to gain the upper hand again.

"Yes, you do that. Oh, and by the way, do you remember that time I beat the shit out of you for standing up to me? That was fun, wasn't it? I'd quite like to do that again sometime. I enjoyed it very much," Corey whispered, his fake smile and friendly demeanour never faltering despite his harsh words.

"I'm sure you did. I, however, had a far different level of enjoyment from that day and will have to regretfully decline."

"I seem to remember almost choking the life out of my dear wife first, though. Did you enjoy seeing me do that to her, Donnie? I bet it turned you on, didn't it?" Corey pressed, goading him, but Donovan refused to let his words get to him.

"Maybe just a little," he joked, laughing loudly as though the two of them were casually reminiscing.

"Sure it did, I bet you'd get a right hard-on if you saw some of things I do to her now, the things she lets me put her through over and over again. That poor woman, how could you ever have let her be mine Donnie. How could you let her down so profoundly? Did you know that I was fucking her while she was seeing you?" Corey then asked, a sinister glint in his eye.

"No guardian, I did not. And, I don't need to know the sordid details of your fucked up bedroom antics, thank you very much," Donovan answered, clearly struggling with Corey's awful words now.

"Suit yourself. I do have one good story to tell you before I let you go back to your party though, old friend. You remember the night of your first kiss under that palm tree? Of course you do," he said, laughing gruffly. "Well, I teleported into her hotel room after she left you and fucked her brains out until the sun rose the next morning. She was so wet, so turned on from the little show she had given you, Donnie. Melody was like an animal, insatiable and her cunt so sweet I couldn't help but take every bit of that passion you had stirred in her for myself. I guess you could call yourself her fluffer for me. She was putty in my hands, just like she is now, and of course that's all thanks to you as well, isn't it?" Corey said, speaking slowly and eloquently, his words cruel and cutting.

He felt Donovan's energy shift and readied himself, knowing what was about to happen, and he had to stop himself from smiling as Donovan balled up his hand and punched him right in the mouth, splitting his lip instantly. Corey played up to the shocked audience around them, but couldn't resist in then throwing a carefully placed retaliatory punch to Donovan's nose in return, breaking it instantly and he fell to the ground.

Everyone around the pair of them stood staring at the two men in shock. Coby quickly attended to his boss and he led him away while Corey sat down on the bar stool and dabbed at his lip with a napkin, watching as Melody ran through the crowd towards him. Her eyes were wide, but she forced her fearful expression away and instead replaced it with her best look of concern that she could muster.

She grabbed another paper towel and fussed at her husband as the crowd began to disperse and talk amongst themselves again, all the while eavesdropping on the two of them, so she remained cautious.

"What happened? Meri just grabbed me saying you and Donovan had had a punch-up?" she asked, looking into his deep blue eyes pleadingly.

"He was being rude about you, Mel, making jokes at your expense. I think he's had too much to drink, but no one gets to talk about you that way, especially not him. Not after what he put you through," he said, but purposely stopped short for a dramatic pause. "When I asked him to stop, he punched me, so I hit him back," Corey added, wincing as she checked his swelling lip.

"You need to get this checked out, it's split pretty bad," she muttered, knowing that they would have to leave the party early now, and she wondered if that was why he had goaded Donovan. Melody was also well aware that he could just heal himself too, playing up the injury on purpose for the crowd.

"Just kiss it better for me, darling. I'll be fine," Corey replied, stroking her beautiful face. She didn't hesitate for even a moment and she did as he asked, laying a gentle kiss over his swollen lip and he pulled her closer, deepening it slightly. Melody could taste his blood in her mouth and grabbed a tissue to spit it into once she pulled away, but instead Corey handed her his glass of wine to wash it down with.

"All better now," he said as she cleansed her palette of the metallic taste, grinning as he watched her lick the last tiny drop of blood from her own lip and then take another sip of the delectable wine.

"I'm keeping this," she said, taking his hand and leading him through the crowd towards the bathroom where she then dabbed at his lip some more with a tissue and he finally used his powers to make it look a little better than it had before.

"See, we don't have to go home yet," he told her, grinning happily down at his prize. "Go and have fun darling, why don't you grab yourself another drink?"

She took advantage of his good mood and decided she would do just that. Without even replying to him Melody then finished the last of the wine and handed Corey the empty glass before wandering back through the crowd towards her friends and their still flowing champagne, while some of the young executives walked over to chat with Corey, eager to hear the story of his showdown with Donovan.

CHAPTER TWENTY-FOUR

Back at home later that night, Melody drunkenly fell inside the doorway and flopped down on the couch. She began to remove her shoes while giggling loudly to herself as Corey punched in the security code inside the doorway.

"I've never seen you drunk before, I like it," he said, standing over her as she fiddled with the clasp on her heel and fell backwards into the soft leather, sticking her leg up for him to undo the catch, Melody's drunken hands having been unsuccessful. He laughed but removed the shoe for her, tossing it over his shoulder with a cheeky grin before sliding his hands down her leg and pulling off her stockings, one at a time, and then her knickers were sent flying too. Corey then lifted up the drunken woman and turned her over onto her stomach, unbuttoning each of the delicate satin buttons at the back of her dress while she unpinned her hair, the auburn curls falling down beside her on the soft couch. Corey groaned appreciatively as he shuffled Melody out of the dress and laid her on her back again, exposing her tiny, perfect body. He then climbed over her, grinning as she unbuttoned his shirt and tossed it aside before moving on to his trousers.

"Are you going to punish him?" Melody suddenly asked, peering up at Corey in the dim light. He looked beautiful, his handsome face so rugged and mesmerising that she found herself swooning over him, hating the way the alcohol had dulled her hateful numbness towards her evil husband. Melody continued to watch him as he contemplated his response, but Corey didn't say a word. He just leaned down and stared into her eyes, seemingly reading her for a moment, and she felt uncomfortable beneath his scrutinising gaze, unsure what he was playing at. Corey then grinned and slid the last of his clothes off, his smile never faltering.

"No, I won't punish him because he gave me exactly what I wanted," he eventually answered, pulling her up to meet him.

"What's that?" Melody asked, staring up into her husband's eyes while her head swam, feeling woozy thanks to the copious amounts of alcohol running through her system.

"You," he replied, kissing her, and the pair of them fell back onto the sofa. After a few minutes, he leaned up on his elbows over her, staring into Melody's hazel eyes again and she frowned.

"What?" she demanded. "Why are you staring at me like that?"

"Because I have a very important question to ask you and you will not answer until you say the one word I want to hear, and that one word alone. Will you give me a baby, Melody?" Corey asked, his voice determined and stern, powerful, almost like an order. Everything inside of her wanted to say no, as usual, but for some reason her entire mind, body, and soul was overcome with another urge, an urge to say the one word she had refused to give him so many times before and she struggled to fight it.

"Yes," Melody replied, trying to clamp her hand over her mouth to stop the sound from forcing itself out of her lips, but it was already too late. She shook her head, trying to take back the word, but she was powerless. Corey lifted her hips and slid forward, his satisfied smile never leaving his lips as he plunged inside of her, soon filling his wife with his dark seed as she unravelled beneath him again and again thanks to his powerful thrusts.

The next morning, Melody awoke and immediately regretted the amount of alcohol she had consumed the night before. She groaned and buried her head in the pillow, trying to block out the sunlight that was streaming in as she dozed back off for a little while.

Corey woke her an hour later, bringing his wife toast and coffee in an unusual display of kindness, and Melody instantly eyed him suspiciously.

"Who are you and what have you done with my husband?" she asked, grabbing the toast and devouring it in just a few mouthfuls. He laughed, pulling her into his arms as Corey slid beneath the covers with her and held her close.

"You are more beautiful to me than anything else in this entire world, Melody Black. Do you know that?" Corey asked, still holding her tightly, and she whimpered, unsure why he was saying nice things to her. Melody didn't trust him when he was being nice and she was feeling too fragile to hide her fear.

"What did I do wrong? I feel like shit this morning already, thanks to all those drinks last night. Can't that just be my punishment?" she asked, feeling the toast churning in her stomach as the fear of her husband's unusually affectionate words filled her body with dread.

"You've done nothing wrong Mel, I just wanted to tell you how beautiful you are. I'll be sure to give you more compliments in the future. I don't want you freaking out every time I say you look nice," he joked, pulling back to look at her and after a few seconds he began to feel her relax.

"Oh, okay. Thanks," Melody replied, still uneasy, but she lay back in his arms without questioning him again. Her memory of the night before was hazy, but she remembered Corey and Donovan's altercation by the bar, hoping that he would not be waking up in that awful cell this morning thanks to his outburst, but she didn't dare ask.

The pair of them then relaxed together for a while before Corey slid his hands down Melody's back, cupping her bum cheek as he pressed his hard-on into her hip to show his wife that he was ready for her. Instinctively she submitted, leaning back to let him climb over her in the bed.

"Where do you want me?" she asked, opening her legs. Instead of climbing into her inviting space, he suddenly grabbed Melody and lifted her up in his arms, throwing her over his shoulder as he marched out of the room.

"Everywhere," he replied, ignoring the wriggling woman on his shoulder and the surprised squeals he received in response to his unexpected move. "We'll start with the kitchen." Corey said with a wicked grin as he took her downstairs and pinned Melody against the kitchen counter, their bodies moving against each other's so effortlessly, so passionately, and he kissed her with an urgency she had never felt from him before. Melody gave in to his obsessive need, finally letting herself enjoy the side of him she was never usually graced with, the side of him that seemed to actually like her and enjoy her company. She didn't dare let herself believe he might love her, knowing far better than that, but Melody still let herself enjoy the numerous orgasms and intense loving waves that were rolling off her suddenly very impassioned husband.

After two more days of endless lovemaking, Melody finally laid a hand on Corey's chest, her eyes staring up into his while her knees trembled beneath her. She had been straddling him for a while on her high-backed leather office chair, riding him while Corey had watched her with a satisfied smile.

"I can't carry on, I need a break," she whispered, lifting herself off his lap before climbing up and lying back onto her desk, Corey still sitting in her chair in front of her glistening body.

"I suppose we can stop for a bit," he murmured, running his hands up her trembling thighs before stroking a hand across her stomach thoughtfully. She watched him, confused for a moment, but then the memory of her drunken acquiescent moment flooded her mind and she sat up, staring at him angrily.

"You absolute bastard!" Melody screamed, storming out of the room and slamming the door behind her. She ran up the stairs and flung open the bedroom door, anger and pure hatred fuelling her onwards. She had intended to pack a bag and leave him at last but Corey had teleported into their room before she even reached it, grabbing Melody and pulling her into his arms as she tried in vain to fight his hold.

"Took you long enough to remember," he whispered into her ear, laughing gruffly as she attempted to squirm away again.

"I hate you," she replied, falling weakly into his firm grasp, her exhausted body giving way beneath her and she couldn't fight him.

"I know," Corey replied, not caring that she meant it.

CHAPTER TWENTY-FIVE

Melody clambered out of bed and ran for the bathroom, groaning as she emptied the contents of her stomach for the third time that morning.

"Surely there's nothing else left!" she cried, brushing her teeth again to get rid of the taste of bile before heading back out and climbing back under the sheets with her grinning husband. A week had passed since she had said yes, and the last few days had seen Melody spend longer by a toilet than she had in her office.

"It's just your hormones, it'll calm down soon," Corey told her, running his hand over her belly gently. She had to admit, he had been gentler and kinder since the night of the wrap party, and she enjoyed having his nicer side around for a while.

Corey held her close and breathed her in. Melody smelled different to him somehow, as though her body had changed already thanks to his child that he knew was growing inside of her. His parents had summoned him as soon as they felt the change in the air too, congratulating him, and Devin had given his son a genuine smile and a pat on the back at last.

"And here was me thinking you'd never settle down. Granted, you chose someone who I expressly forbade you from seeing," he had said, grinning down at his youngest boy with nothing but affection and warmth. "But, I suppose that's all part of the fun, isn't it?"

"Absolutely. Part of me wonders if that was your plan all along, Dad," Corey had replied, but he got nothing but a shrug in response from his powerful master. "I know what she is by the way," Corey had then told him, admitting his findings to his father, and Devin just nodded.

"Then make sure you keep her close, and that she gives you many more children before she's had enough of you," he had added, seemingly knowing that being a terrible husband might ultimately land him with a short marriage. He then hugged his son goodbye, as did Serena, before sending Corey back to London to be with his wife.

Melody woke from her nap with a long stretch, feeling better and more energetic than she had in days. She immediately hopped out of bed and wandered the house in search of her husband, always mindful that he might want her for something before allowing her any time to herself. Corey was nowhere to be found, but even stranger was the fact that she seemed to be completely alone in the house. Not even Meri was lurking somewhere close by like she usually would have been, and at first Melody felt odd, unsure what to do with herself.

She decided on coffee, so prepped the huge machine in the kitchen, flicking the switches until she found the right setting for her much-desired latte. She also clicked on the small but state-of-the-art radio that sat on the kitchen counter, pressing on all the buttons until she finally found a station she liked before taking a seat at the counter and browsing through a magazine. Cheesy pop songs played one after another and she couldn't help but turn up the volume and bop in her chair. The vibrant tunes were speaking to her and she soon found herself dancing around in the kitchen in a rare happy mood as she began making herself some food. With the posh coffee-machine blinking at her it was ready, Melody reached up to grab a mug from the cupboard, having to go up onto her tiptoes to reach the tall latte glasses, when a deep voice behind her startled her and she nearly dropped the glass in her hands.

"I'll have one please, if you're making them?" the man said from the doorway, a man Melody had never seen before, yet she somehow instinctively knew who he was from Corey's description of his family from many conversations ago. She fell to her knees before the Black Prince of Hell, Blake, and bowed, the coffee glass still in her hands, and he placed a gentle palm on her shoulder.

"I'm sorry. I didn't mean to startle you. And, you most certainly do not have to bow before me, Melody. You're family. We greet each other like this," Blake said as she stood, giving her a swift kiss on the cheek and she blushed, feeling so small and insignificant under his powerful gaze. She couldn't help but stare at him, his incredible prowess and intimidating demeanour filling the room around them, but he was also warm and looked her over with a genuinely affectionate contemplation.

"I may be married to your cousin, your Majesty, but I am his property, not his equal. I hate to say it so bluntly, but he has always made sure that I know my place. I am not worthy of calling myself your family. It wouldn't feel right if I didn't greet you in the way I have always been ordered to," Melody replied, looking down at their feet, feeling sad and a little shocked that she had been so honest. Blake took her chin in his hand, lifting her gaze to meet his as he took her in for a moment. She had no idea that he could read her mind and so just stood awkwardly for a few moments, waiting for his reply.

"You're a strong woman, Melody, I can tell. And I bet that's what he loves about you. I have a hunch you've poked and prodded at that temper of his far more times than you'd care to admit, but that you've also taken your punishments with grace and humility. However, something tells me you still did it again and again, regardless?" Blake asked her, taking Melody's breath away, and she nodded.

"I have been known to push his buttons on purpose in the past, but I'm learning to stop. He doesn't let me get away with any of it and I just can't take the punishments anymore," she replied, shocking herself further that she was being so open with the god-like being before her.

"Don't. Submissive little, 'yes women,' don't get anywhere in this life, or the next Melody. Don't ever lose that independent spark inside of you, it's everything you are and everything you have to give, and it's perfect. Let it grow and he'll respect you more for it. You'll find your way with him as time goes on," Blake told her, and she couldn't help but swoon under his intense gaze.

This dark and dangerous man was an infamous force of darkness, but at the same time Melody couldn't help but stare up at him with admiration and even lust, feeling utterly lured in by his powerful prowess. Blake still stood ever so close to her, his hand on her chin keeping her gaze on his incredible green eyes, and Melody let herself enjoy their moment, knowing that their few seconds of closeness was more to do with his pity than his admiration.

"You after a fight, Rose, 'cos I'm game?" called Corey from the doorway, watching as Blake let go of his wife's chin and released her from his consuming gaze. He walked towards Corey and the two of them eyed each other seriously for a moment, before suddenly breaking out in huge smiles and wrapping their arms around one another affectionately.

"You could try, but I don't think you want the embarrassment of getting your arse whooped in front of your lovely wife," Blake told him, grinning broadly at his cousin.

"She'd probably get a kick out of it," Corey replied, laughing when Melody nodded in agreement. She was watching them eagerly, tucking into a sandwich she had grabbed from the fridge as she waited.

"You'd better take care of this one Corey, there's something very special about her," Blake added, winking at Melody. "Who would've thought it, you and I both settling down after all these years of being bad-boys?"

"So you and that girl really are serious then? It's Tilly, isn't it?" Corey asked, taking over the coffee prep that Melody had now seemingly completely forgotten about, and Blake nodded.

"Yeah, it hasn't been easy don't get me wrong. I didn't want her to break down my walls. I didn't want to feel or to love, or for her to love me. I pushed her away every chance I got, but a good woman has a habit of leaving their mark on you," Blake replied, and neither Corey or Melody missed the point he was making so clearly to them about their fraught relationship too.

"Don't make me puke," Corey joked in response, ever the playful one rather than talk about his feelings. "We have a love-hate relationship. She loves to hate me and I would hate to love her, isn't that right Mel?"

"Something like that," she agreed without even looking at him, finishing off her food and then depositing her plate in the sink. Blake watched her as she cleaned up the mess Corey had made at the coffee machine and then finished making the lattes without a word, serving him without even realising it before handing the pair of men steaming hot, milky brews with a smile before grabbing her own and heading towards the doorway to leave them to talk.

"Before you go, there's a party at the penthouse tonight that you're both invited to. An orgy that my mother is hosting," Blake said, taking a long swig of the hot brew and Melody's eyes opened in shock. She looked over at Corey, but couldn't read his reaction to Blake's invitation.

"Your mother will be there?" she asked, completely taken aback at the prospect of the Devil herself being on Earth that night.

"Yep, and she won't be happy if you don't come along," Blake added, and his cousin nodded in understanding. Blake had seemingly teleported over to see them especially to invite the pair along to their gathering, and even Melody could tell that you didn't turn down a personal request to attend a party hosted by Cate Rose.

"Sure, but we won't be taking part," Corey replied, taking a sip of his latte.

"No, I wouldn't hear of it, not given Melody's delicate condition," Blake agreed, looking down at her belly and she blushed, shocked that he could know already. "I assume you'll make a formal announcement soon, but you might want to come along early tonight to inform my mother in person?"

"Of course," Corey replied, knowing that it was expected of him to speak with his Queen regarding this new development and he nodded to his powerful cousin.

"Great, see you later then. Thanks for the coffee, Melody. I look forward to seeing you again," Blake said, kissing her cheek again before teleporting away.

She hovered in the doorway, wondering if she should join Corey at the counter to drink her coffee with him, but his cold, angry voice quickly stopped her.

"You'd better get the fuck out of my sight Mel, before I do something we'll both regret," he said, sipping on his drink as though he were calm and collected, yet she could tell he was far from it. She turned on her heel and quickly made her way to her office, where she sat trembling in her seat, hoping that he didn't decide to follow her.

CHAPTER TWENTY-SIX

After he had calmed down and they had changed, Corey teleported Melody into the London penthouse. That was a permanent base for all things relating to the royal family of Hell and their omnipotent leader, Cate Rose, the Devil. They had arrived early as per Blake's request, and Corey stood waiting for an audience with his aunt while Meri kept Melody busy with fixing her hair and makeup for the upcoming party, each of them assuming that the Queen would only choose to greet her nephew personally.

Corey couldn't help but think of his extended family, envious as ever of their higher power, but he was also pleased to be invited back to the penthouse again after such a long time. Blake and his sister Luna regularly came to Earth with the full moon to have their fun or see to any business matters that required their attention, but Corey hadn't seen his cousins properly in years. Corey's parents had moved to Earth permanently almost seventy years previously to pursue their own form of leadership atop the business ladder, and that was when the Crimson Brotherhood was conceived. The pair of them, and their three children, were not bound by the moon like their Queen and her offspring, so were free to live on Earth for as long as it was worth doing so. The business, Black Rose Industries, had been around for over a hundred years already and had supposedly been passed down from generation to generation of Black children, however they had just kept it going between them, each one having their turn at running it before handing over the reigns just like Devin had done with Corey only a few months before.

Their secret society had also been tremendously successful and had expanded over the years thanks to the many humans who wanted riches and fame, and they were more than ready to sell their souls in order to get them. Corey hadn't lied to Melody all that time ago when he told her he was in, 'acquisitions and retrieval.' His role had always been to procure the souls for their family's use, but also to repossess any who didn't deliver on their promises, such as the likes of the late David Pembroke. Leyla was their lead bounty-huntress. She was a formidable and truly powerful being who had contacts and informants all over this world as well as in those realms both above and below, but she kept her more sinister skills reserved for those who truly deserved it. Those who kept her waiting or had made her have to go and find them.

Their older brother, Braeden, was very different from his two younger siblings. He was just as powerful and extremely clever, but he was the merciful, thoughtful one who devoured entire libraries of books in pursuit of knowledge rather than souls, and was fluent in every language he could find. He had spoken of love to Corey many times since meeting his own wife, an ancient demon named Bastet, but Corey had always refused to let his brother's words sink in, not caring to hear of such nonsense. He and his cousin Blake were very alike in that way, and they had made each other feel better knowing that they were not alone in their cold natures. Despite his resistance, though, the last couple of years had changed him, and Corey had always known that Melody was to thank for it. There was more to their bond than just his ownership of her, but he just could never say it, or let himself even feel it.

He and Blake had turned into very different beings now and although his powerful cousin had learned to let down his walls, to love and to trust, Corey just could not do the same. He envied that Blake had finally changed his dark ways for the woman he loved, lowering his walls that they had all assumed were set to surround the cold-hearted Prince for eternity. And all thanks to this girl. While the story of his and Tilly's powerful union was wonderful, Corey still couldn't understand it. As he stood there, deep in thought, he zoned out, lost in his memories and the mixed emotions he couldn't help but feel as he mulled over his time with Melody. He wanted to understand and let himself feel real love and affection for her, but it was just so hard and it wasn't in his nature to care enough about anything to make an effort to change.

"Just because she isn't the perfect pawn in your games, doesn't mean she's out to hurt you," whispered a voice in Corey's ear and he turned to embrace the voice's owner, his aunt and Dark Queen, Cate. He kissed her cheek and smiled warmly into the stunning face of his almighty mistress. She looked truly beautiful, elegantly dressed in black, as always, and with her graceful prowess so effortlessly present. He was drawn to her, to her power and to the darkness inside so strongly that he felt the familiar all-consuming urge to fall to her feet and beg to attend her. Corey worshipped Cate and served her with every breath he took and with every soul he claimed. His affection for his Queen was the only love he had never fought to suppress, just as any other demonic servant did not ever deny their leader their love, respect, loyalty, and unwavering service.

"But she has every reason to hurt me. How do I know she won't just destroy me as soon as I let her in, like the last time I let myself love another?" he asked, peering up at his Queen solemnly, all joking aside now. Her green eyes bore into his as she continued to read him, a warm, gentle smile on her lips despite knowing how awful he had been with his poor wife.

"She isn't to blame for your past, Corey Black. You and your sister promised her the world, in one way or another and on many an occasion, might I add, and yet you've done nothing but fuck her life up. You're the one who has destroyed her, but she has yet to try and murder you in your sleep. I'd take that as reason alone if I were you," Cate told him, smiling tenderly but maintaining her serious expression. "You took everything from her and then slowly gave it back again in one twisted little game after another, and she still holds you in her arms and kisses you goodnight. That woman still basks in your smile and yearns for your approval and affection, yet she constantly has to remind herself not to fall in love with you because she knows it will be the end of her if she did. If you don't want to look after her properly, let her go Corey, or else drop this façade and step up," Cate told him, kissing his cheek one more time before letting him go, her sights set on greeting Melody. The intimidating Queen placed a kiss on her cheek too.

"Your Majesty," Melody said with a surprised look, bowing to the Dark Queen and Cate instantly stopped her, peering into her eyes, reading her for a moment. Corey watched on with fearful intrigue, wondering what nuggets of truth their mistress was plucking from her mind. Melody trembled before the omnipotent woman's gaze but stood firm, feeling somehow stronger than ever in her presence, and she enjoyed Cate's company very much.

"Well done for putting up with my nephew, Melody. I think you might just be stronger than any other woman that has walked this path before you. There are many ways in which you have been tried, tested, punished, and broken over your short life, but yet you still stand tall and you are a good person, worthy of so much more than you've been given. You might hide your pain behind your sweet smile for now, but it won't be like that forever, I promise. One of these days, you might just find yourself with the power and control while your husband stares at you in awe. Make no mistake about that," Cate said, peering across at her earnestly. "I know how it feels to be a powerful lover's plaything. I know how powerless you must be feeling, how trapped and afraid, but trust me, it will get better. To be desired is every woman's dream, but when that desire turns to obsession, the consequences are never good. I cannot tell if he loves you, or if he even can love, but I do know that you have been the object of his obsessive cravings since the day you connected so naturally with Donovan Caine. Knowing that you belonged to someone new set Corey off in a passionate fixation that has now overtaken both of your lives. Only time will tell if you'll get out of this in one piece Melody, but I absolutely believe that you can if you just stay strong."

"Thank you, your Majesty. I cannot even begin to know where to find that strength, but I guess that's the point. Maybe I'll find it just when I need it the most," Melody mused aloud, smiling affectionately at her Queen.

"I'm sure you will. Oh, and congratulations by the way," Cate added quietly, ensuring they weren't overheard, her hand trailing down from Melody's cheek between her breasts and down to her stomach where it lingered for a moment. Melody gasped, the strange sensations she received from Cate's powerful touch making her feel woozy but wonderful and she couldn't help but smile, basking in the Queen's tingling touch, kind stare, and encouraging words.

Cate then said her goodbyes to them both and made her way across the room and out to the terrace. She would remain out there until it was time to make her entrance later that evening, and both Corey and Melody watched her with open mouths and awed expressions as she left. The two of them couldn't help but keep their eyes on her until Cate was out of sight, mesmerised and lured in by her so completely that even Corey had to shake it off, taking Melody's hand and leading her towards one of the guest bedrooms so that they could be alone.

"What did you show her, Melody? She can read your mind. What did she find out from you? I need to know what she found there, and what she said to you," he barked when they were inside the large bedroom, his voice stern and he was clearly worried. She wrenched her hand free and glared at him.

"That's between me and her. And, she could've only read the truth in my mind, Corey, of course. If you're ashamed of what she found, then that's your problem, isn't it?" Melody snapped, watching as he paced the room before her.

"How can I change when all you do is antagonise me?" he demanded, standing just inches away from her, and Melody placed her hands on his chest.

"No Corey, it's not me. I was never the problem and we both know it. You need to stop it, stop being so paranoid, and stop being so mean," she told him, suddenly feeling so calm and strong. Melody stood tall and proud, feeling somehow powerful despite knowing that she was pushing her luck, as usual. Cate's words had stirred her resolve, and she couldn't help but exert a little of her new-found prowess over her husband.

"I can't. I'll never be good enough. I have to force you, otherwise I know you'll reject me," he admitted, taking a deep breath.

"I don't want you to be good enough. I just want you to be mine. I need to know that you belong to me, just as I belong to you. I want to be your equal. I can't keep walking this road alone under your harsh scrutiny, Corey. I've lived my entire life in the shadow of powerful men, in constant servitude, but somehow I'm still not good enough? I remember every single awful thing you ever did to me, every scar that I feel but do not bear, thanks to your potions and spells that heal them. I can't ever forgive you." Melody breathed a deep sigh. "But, I do love you," she said, finally saying the words she never thought she would say to the man who had put her through so much.

"I cannot love. I'm not capable of it, let alone worthy. I'd have to break you one hundred times before I could love you even once. I've failed you every chance I've had to love you," he said, sliding to his knees and peering up at her with a forlorn expression.

"I know. I won't fail you now Corey. I'll save you, but you need to save me too," Melody said, falling to her knees in front of him, the sobs forcing themselves out of her like vicious throbs that forced her to feel, that made her love. "Fuck you Corey Black, you did the one thing I asked you never to do, you made me love you."

When they had both calmed down, Corey and Melody left the guest room and joined the party in the main living room. The place was now packed with demons and their followers, many of who stopped to chat with them for a few minutes, eager to have a royal ear. Corey kept Melody close the entire time, but she stayed quiet, letting him do the talking while she people-watched with a warm smile. Being there was so different from being at their usual business functions and star-studded parties. Melody's attention was normally highly sought after at those, her associates dying to have some time with her. At the penthouse, she was just another human. Yes she was Corey's wife, but he was the royal star. He was the powerful entity, and she was just his follower.

A little later, Melody caught sight of Blake and a beautiful blonde woman walking through the crowd together, his arms around her protectively and his entire body language effectively screaming out his feelings for her to everyone around them. The Black Prince wasn't ashamed to love her. He wanted everyone to know it, and Melody found herself envying the stunning girl. Her heart burned, beating hard in her chest with fear and anxiety over what was to come in her future alongside Corey. Melody saw nothing but an unloved existence before her and yet she would remain held captive in his obsessive embrace until she was no longer of use or in his favour. The sheer thought of what came after that was enough to make the recent past seem like a little slice of Heaven in comparison.

The Queen soon entered and made a short speech, but it wasn't long before those who wanted to partake in the orgy were stripping off and waiting patiently for their chance to start their passion-fuelled party. Melody kept her clothes on, knowing that she and Corey were not going to join in, but she couldn't help but watch, her eyes drawn first to the Queen and her once human husband, a demon named Harry. They were making love to one another atop the soft throne, their bodies out of reach to any of the participants thanks to the thin veil that surrounded them, adding to the sense that they were truly a forbidden prize to behold but not to touch. Their passion was so real, unmasked and free. Melody had been told the history. She knew now how Cate was once married to Lucifer and she had taken the throne before then marrying Harry some years later. It was plain to see just how powerful they were together. How that lowly demon empowered the almighty Queen just by being beside her, loving and caring for her so strongly that she could do nothing but flourish thanks to him. Melody wanted that so much, and in that moment, she even let herself think back to the look on Donovan's face when they were both so sure that they could do just that for one another. If only they had been allowed to try.

Melody then watched, enthralled, as Blake led his lover on to the bed, his fantastic body on show and her slight frame seeming so small when wrapped in his loving arms. She could see that Tilly must have been injured. She had thick plaster casts on each wrist, but she didn't seem to care about them one bit, nor did they hold the lovers back at all. Melody wondered to herself why she hadn't been healed like had always been done with her wounds, but didn't think to ask Corey.

Her concentration was quickly drawn to the lovers themselves as they dominated their area of the large bed. Blake and Tilly's passion was consuming. Their love unbound, and Melody watched them for a long while, not caring that Corey was watching her as she did so. Even when the rest of the participants climbed on to the bed along with the royal beings and their lovers, Melody still could not take her eyes off Tilly. She was mesmerised, intrigued, and even a little turned-on by the sight of them. She stared at Blake's gorgeous face as he watched his lover come undone for him, delighting in the taste, touch, and pleasure of her company as if he was content to live in her embrace for all eternity, as though he was ready to worship at her feet rather than ever demand she worship at his.

"Home," Corey whispered in her ear when the intense thrum of the crowd started to grow darker and thicker with its sexual tension. Melody could sense the sudden change too, the shift from an alluring thrum to all-out sexual frenzy and she took his hand without a word.

The pair of them teleported back home and she immediately changed out of her tight black dress into a floating nightdress that felt good against her already tender and slightly swollen belly.

Melody was quiet and thoughtful, their intense evening playing on her mind as she went through her night-time wash routine. She was still no further in knowing where she stood with her so gorgeous and sexy yet distant and controlling husband. Even in that powerful and open moment in the penthouse, he had still not told her he loved her, and Melody suspected that he never would.

A few mornings later as she hugged the toilet seat and emptied the contents of her stomach, Melody sobbed as silently as she could, weeping tears of pure sadness. She was filled with an overwhelming desire to run away, to find a way out of this marriage, out of this deal she had made with the Crimson Brotherhood. She wracked her brains thinking how she might do it, but came up empty every time.

When she finally emerged from the en-suite, Corey lay on the bed reading a magazine with a photograph of the two of them on the front cover from the night of the wrap party.

"Mr and Mrs Black certainly stole the show at the recent wrap party for Pembroke studios' newest movie, Dark Destiny two, starring none other than Melody Pembroke-Black's ex-boyfriend, Donovan Caine." he began, adding, "I hate you decided to use a double-barrelled name by the way," and Melody just smirked, knowing that his displeasure was exactly why she had decided to double up her surname. It was essential in her official capacity anyway to ensure that the Pembroke name was handed down to their children along with her empire, so they both knew that he had no choice but to allow it. She fixed her hair and cleansed her face as he continued, staying quiet while he carried on reading out the article.

"After reports that it had been a hard split for Melody and Donovan last year, all those working with them on this project have been pleasantly surprised by the gentle and warm connection the two seemingly still share, far from the bitterness many assumed would ensue once they were working together again. You might even have called it the perfect breakup, but nothing is ever quite so simple and something, or should we say someone, always cracks eventually. This time, though, rather than it being the woman scorned who had broken the perfect cover, it was Donovan Caine himself. The usually so cool and calm bad-boy seemingly had one too many drinks at the wrap party and was overheard making rude comments about his ex-girlfriend to none other than Melody's new husband and their mutual friend, Corey Black. Sources tell us that Black repeatedly asked him to stop, but that Caine continued to get wound up at seeing his ex so happy with her new beau and he then punched Corey in the mouth. Anyone else might have wilted under the mammoth man's attack, but Black reportedly retaliated with a single punch to Donovan's nose, breaking it and flooring him instantly. Now, while we all do love a bad-boy but certainly do not condone bar side punch-ups, we here at 'Entertainment and Style' magazine whole-heartedly agree that Donovan crossed the line and deserved to be put back in his place. Good on you, Corey Black, for standing up to him and defending your lovely wife. We all wish we could find someone like you."

"Oh my, your ego's probably bigger than your epic cock right now, my darling," Melody joked when Corey had finished reading the article aloud, and he couldn't help but laugh at her but nodded in agreement, shrugging nonchalantly. "You've already shown me that article, by the way," she added, slumping onto the bed beside him and burying her face in the pillow groggily.

"I know, but I like this one so very much. Me, the hero, who would've ever guessed?" Corey replied, stroking his hand down her back as she lay exhausted beside him.

"If only they knew the truth," she mumbled and Corey slapped her bum cheek, hard enough for the sound to reverberate around their huge bedroom but not hard enough to hurt her and she wriggled away from his touch, giggling as she squirmed.

He had been making an extra special effort with her recently, desperate to show her he had meant what he had said in the penthouse. Corey was well aware that she needed more than that though. She deserved better, but he just couldn't give her it. He couldn't let her win. That side of him just could not back down. He was too stubborn and afraid of letting go of his control in fear of getting hurt. And yet, Corey was also well aware that in doing so he was pushing her away with every day that passed and he still hadn't changed his awful ways.

CHAPTER TWENTY-SEVEN

Leyla wandered the corridors of the Crimson Brotherhood for hours, her mind in turmoil and her body unwilling to rest, so she had endeavoured to walk it off. It was no use though. She needed to unwind properly and there was only one way she truly knew how, hunting. She checked her files, scanning for anything, anyone she could use to curb this need inside of her and one name suddenly sprang to mind, Kris Brooks. She had given him strength, wealth, fame and the captain's spot in the England football team, everything he had ever wanted from her almost ten years ago in return for his soul. She was a little early in claiming her prize, but the formidable woman didn't care.

Leyla teleported to the sports star's driveway and then watched him for hours through the windows of their huge home. His wife was a stunning beauty, all of which was bought for her by her vain husband. She was just as ugly on the inside as he was, cold and crueller than almost any human Leyla had ever seen. Josie Brooks had made a habit of luring young women into bed with them, setting up threesome's with the desperate girls and then not letting the women touch her husband as they fooled around, tying them up and gagging them while she had her depraved fun and Kris just sat back and watched. Their warlock handler had needed to use far too many memory-cleansing potions over the years, and Leyla was glad that she could finally say goodbye to their contract.

She waited until they were asleep and then teleported into their room, making her way through the pitch-black darkness with utter ease and a sinister smile. Her features were contorted, her face a dark, evil version of her usual self and she traced a delicate finger over Josie's forehead, waking her instantly but she was also magically frozen in place, unable to move as she stared up into the shadows, desperate to understand what was going on. Her body then began to move uncontrollably, as though she were nothing but a real-life puppet, and she had no idea who was pulling the strings.

She stood and walked around to Kris's bedside, standing over him in the body that was somehow no longer her own that then grabbed a pillow and smothered her husband with it, pressing hard over his panic-stricken face. Josie's strength was somehow tenfold now, her body pressing down on him with such force that he could not fight it, could not fight her. Although Kris writhed and tried to pull himself free, it was no use, and he quickly succumbed to his dark fate.

Josie then lifted the pillow and climbed back into bed, snuggling up to her husband's lifeless body and falling back into a deep sleep.

Leyla grinned, lowering her hands that had magically been controlling the poor woman like a marionette, and she walked out from where she had been hiding in the shadows. Within seconds she was gone again, knowing that Mrs Brooks would wake up in the morning, remembering nothing but a terrible dream in which she had suffocated her husband with her pillow, only to find that it was all very real and then she would rot in jail for a murder she didn't technically commit.

This tiny act of vengeful murder only did a little to curb Leyla's dark needs, but she sat back at her desk and plotted more, plotted the demise of those who had wronged her and grinned to herself as she imagined their faces when she brought the axe down at last.

"Soon," she whispered to herself, flicking through her files again in search of her next victim to quench the seemingly insatiable thirst that had now risen inside of her.

***

By half way through her pregnancy, Corey began growing paranoid about his wife and their unborn child's safety. He started taking Melody along with him on all of his overseas business trips to collect his clients souls or to hunt down those who had tried to flee their contracts. In those times, she was completely secluded, sheltered from his dark doings and surrounded, as always, by her magical entourage. They were extra vigilant with her safety and Melody would be expected to stay hidden while Corey carried out his business and completed the retrieval process as per his sinister job-role requirements. In just the last few weeks, she had travelled the world alongside him and yet had never seen the outside of her hotel room during any of those times. One day she finally exploded in rage and screamed the place down, throwing a hissy fit the likes Corey had never seen before. Melody's hormones and anger combined with her stressful workload back home that she was struggling to keep on top of sent her reeling. Her few days of being dragged away with Corey were incredibly unwelcome and she couldn't keep her mouth closed, despite knowing that he would be angered by her outburst.

Corey just laughed, seeming to almost find her rage endearing, and stepped over to her, grinning broadly as Melody scowled at him angrily.

"Your foolish attempts to sway my decisions or make me relinquish my hold on you are truly embarrassing Melody," he said, slapping her across the face as hard as ever before, having given up on trying to be kinder to his wife. He was still being careful to send her flying into the arms of his warlock Heath rather than into a heap on the floor. He didn't want to put the baby in harm's way after all. She clambered free of the horrible man's arms and forced herself to stand again, holding Corey's gaze and not letting the tears fall that stung at her eyes.

"What's the point of all the entourage and hired goons to keep me safe when you still persist in knocking me about every time I voice my opinion?" Melody asked, trembling but not letting her voice falter as she called him out on his behaviour.

"Oh dear, Melody. Is that what you think they are here for?" Corey asked, closing the gap between them and stroking her still sore cheek with his finger. "For the smallest part, they are around to keep you safe from harm, as well as to keep an eye on what you do and with whom you are associating. But mostly, they are around to make sure that my baby is safe. You just happen to be part of the package," Corey added, smirking evilly at her.

"Ah yes, your baby. I'm well aware just how little I am worth to you in this equation. Perhaps I will be lucky and the baby will be born full of loathing for you thanks to how riddled I am with hatred all the time, and also thanks to the stress you consistently put me under. It's a wonder he or she has even survived this long inside my broken body," Melody spat.

"Keep on talking like that and one of these days, I might just unchain my heart from yours and I will finally be free of you, Melody. Then you can sit and dwell on your terrible past with only your hatred to keep you company, for you can guarantee our child will forever be by my side, not yours," he threatened, stepping closer and staring her down. Melody tried in vain to stifle her sobs, hating that he had all the power and knowing that he was telling the truth, that he could easily take the baby away from her if he wanted.

"Is there even an ounce of compassion or love inside of you, Corey? Is there a tiny part of you that wants me to be happy and cared for in all of this?" she whispered, feeling herself falling to pieces beneath his cold stare.

"Of course there is. I just keep that guy locked away because he's weak and makes me sick. He comes out every now and then and you know that, you've seen him? I even let him issue just one other order to your protection team, for purely selfish reasons, of course. Do you want to know what else they are here to do?" Corey replied, looking down into her hazel eyes with an almost gentle expression on his face now.

"What?" Melody asked. She couldn't help herself, even though she knew that she more than likely would hate his answer.

"They are on-hand to make sure that no one tries to take you away, not as in kidnapping or hurting you, that's obvious," he said, grabbing her cheeks and pulling Melody's face upwards so that she could not help but peer up into his deep blue eyes. "They are also here to make sure that no one tries to save you from me."

"No one would be so foolish as to try, and I would never be so stupid enough to ask. There's no one left in this world or the others that care enough to want to see me be free of you, Corey. I'm just trying my best to survive you," she replied, and for the most part, she believed every word of it.

The next morning the pair of them teleported to the city of Cairo, Egypt, where Melody looked out at the ancient monuments from her prestigious prison of five-star luxury at Corey's chosen hotel but was forbidden, as ever, from leaving the safety of their threshold. For some reason and regardless of the risks, Corey and Heath came back to their suite in the dead of night with their prize bound, gagged, beaten, and broken. Rather than shelter Melody from the sight of the poor man who had tried to defy his guardian and get out of his terrible contract, her husband took the opportunity to teach Melody another cruel lesson. Corey not only woke her up but then also made his wife watch as he and his henchmen tortured the poor man some more.

"Please stop. I don't want to see it, Corey. You know I am loyal to you, how much I have given to you. I thought we had both finished these lessons by now?" Melody begged, unable to look into her husband's eyes as she pleaded with him. The poor man before her gazed over at the gentle woman and his desperate stare silently pleaded for her mercy and help, but she knew she was in no position to offer him any such respite.

"I want you to see what happens when people try to run from me, Melody. I'm still not sure if I can ever trust you not to try and escape me, or take away my child. You'll watch this over and over again until I know for sure that you understand the implications for doing so," Corey replied, laying a gentle hand over her stomach as he spoke, rubbing the bump. He then grabbed her chin with his other hand, forcing her eyes down onto the crumpled heap of human before her. "If you tried to run now, I'd beat every part of you except this. Afterwards, I'll make sure you never have a thought of your own, let alone ever try to run from me again. You can't ever escape me, you cannot kill me, and you can never overpower me. Sometimes I just like to remind you of that."

"There's no need Corey, I would never risk running from you or trying to rid myself of your claim over me. I learned that lesson a long time ago and have proven my loyalty over and over again since then," Melody replied, trembling as she spoke. "Every inch of me belongs to you. I will never run, fight, or try to overpower you. Why would I fight a battle we both know I would lose without you even breaking a sweat?" she added, submitting to him in a way she had always told herself she would never do, but her fear drove her onwards.

Corey just smirked, his sinister grin turning her stomach, and he then led Melody closer to the man who cowered before his master and pleaded for mercy.

"Kill him," Corey muttered, handing Melody a dagger. Her eyes opened wide, and she shook her head, unwilling to blacken her soul by committing murder.

"No, I won't do it, Corey. You cannot make me." she told him, aware that her free will was the only thing stopping him from forcing her.

"Death is his only salvation, the only merciful act he can have right now is a pain-free passing, and I will not deliver him that. Without your mercy, Melody, this man will die long and slow, torturous and lengthy. You choose."

"I won't do it," Melody told him and Corey shook his head, clearly disappointed in her. He snatched the dagger, stepped forward and plunged the blade deep into the man's gut, and then grabbed Melody by her hair, forcing her down onto her knees so that she straddled him while he slowly began to bleed out beneath her. Her trousers were quickly soaked in the claret liquid seeping out of the poor man and she watched for what seemed like hours as the life drained out of him, this lesson as clear and concise as any other her fearsome husband had taught her over their time together.

"You see?" Corey asked as the final light behind the man's eyes flickered out and he stopped writhing, stopped breathing and his heart ceased its beating. "Humans are nothing, I'd tear you limb from limb if you betrayed me Melody. Make no mistake about that. And next time, the blade might just be in the hands of our child instead of me and they might just have been taught to take human life as easily as you might snub out the life of a spider that dared make its web in your doorway. Next time I tell you to do something, fuck the free will, you do it," he warned and Melody could not help but tremble in fear at his awful words, knowing at last what terrible plans he had for their child's future.

"Never," she whispered, watching as death finished claiming the man beneath her.

"Petulant as always, but will you remain so until the end, my love? Your father was the same way, until I slit his throat, of course."

CHAPTER TWENTY-EIGHT

Melody wandered the quiet halls of Pembroke Studios in search of the bathroom again. She kept getting turned around and had completely lost her bearings in this new area of the rapidly expanding set.

"For fuck's sake," she grumbled as she rounded a corner and then bumped straight into her new assistant, Laurie.

"Hey, there you are," Laurie cried, stopping and laying a hand on her now heavily pregnant boss's shoulder. "I was getting worried about you."

"I couldn't find the bathroom. This baby is making both my brain fry and my bladder weak. Thank goodness I've just got a few weeks left," Melody groaned, running her hand over her now protruding belly with a sigh. She was feeling incredibly heavy and knew that she should really be taking it easy, but she couldn't help but come in to work, especially when the director had asked for her specifically. She had gone in to find that he simply wanted to discuss his next project in private before pitching it to the producers, unsure of the gritty crime he wanted to transition into and whether it had a place in the current movie-scene.

"I'm not sure there's a market right now, but trends are always changing and I think if it's a good script it'll speak for itself," Melody had told him, relaxing in the small office with Dustin Golding, the director she had now worked with many times and considered a good egg as far as other members of the Crimson Brotherhood were concerned. He had then thanked her and left, their meeting over quickly, and Melody had been glad of it.

Laurie watched Melody with an affectionate gaze, genuinely having been a good assistant to her over the past couple of months since Meri had been taking a break from her duties. Meri had interviewed the replacement candidates herself and had chosen the human woman over other demonic applicants because she had passed every test the demon had given her with ease and had a natural calmness that seemed to rub off on the now so highly-strung pregnant boss during her trial period. Melody had to agree with Meri's choice. Laurie had been more than capable so far and had settled into her life with relative ease. She too was a follower of the Crimson Brotherhood, one of Leyla's souls, and she provided Melody with a tiny link to her old guardian too, which she liked.

"So, how about I take you to the loo and then we'll grab some lunch before heading home?" Laurie asked, reminding Melody of the pressing that was happening on her bladder right now and she immediately agreed. It was eerily quiet in the usually so busy studios. She had never been in on a Sunday before and Melody missed the bustling, busy feel it was usually teeming with. When they finally found their way back to the canteen, Laurie brought her over some coffee and a sandwich, and Melody quickly set about devouring the lot.

"Hmm, the coffee tastes funny today?" she said, watching as her assistant took a sip and shook her head.

"Nope, tastes fine to me," Laurie said and Melody shrugged, wondering if the spicy mayo in her ham sandwich had affected her tastebuds.

Half an hour later when they were finished eating and ready to head off, Melody stood and brushed the crumbs from her sandwich off her belly, thinking to herself that Corey would be pleased that they would make it home sooner than she had anticipated, already planning out her evening in her head, hoping that he would be in a good mood and they could spend some time relaxing together. While neither had changed their ways, and despite the terrible lessons he persisted in teaching her, the two of them had still grown closer during her pregnancy and had even been acting genuinely affectionate and more caring to one another. He hadn't hurt her badly since before the baby had been conceived, and had even stopped playing his nasty games to upset her in the last few weeks, much to Melody's happiness. Her heart was now full of love for her precious little bundle inside of her, and although she had never spoken to Corey of her feelings for him since that night at the penthouse, she knew that some of that heart now belonged to him too.

A sharp, tensing pain shot through her a few seconds later, nearly flooring Melody, and she had to grip the back of the chair next to her for support. Laurie rushed to her side, rubbing her back gently and peering up into her eyes with worry.

"Shit, I think that was a contraction," Melody mumbled. "We need to get me back home," she added, but her attempt to step forward was thwarted by another sudden rush of pain that claimed her entire body. She shuddered and fell to her knees, the intense throb sending her head spinning and her body weak. "Whoa, that was very close together," she groaned, panicking.

"It's happening," Laurie said, and Melody hadn't even realised that she had grabbed her phone, but was glad that she had seemingly called ahead for help. "You need to come with me now, Mel. It is very important that you listen to me, trust me and do exactly as I say."

"What? I need to get home. Corey needs to take care of me," she replied, shaking her head.

"Absolutely not. Corey is not going anywhere near this baby. Trust me," she said, her expression solemn when Melody eyed her cautiously and her water broke all over the hard floor.

Leyla then appeared at her side and took Melody's hand in hers, teleporting her away with her to a dark room where she then laid her down on a bed covered in towels and blankets, everything seemingly prepared for her impending arrival. Melody went to speak, but was silenced by a tremendous burst of pain that shot down her legs and made her heart pound in her ears, her body falling back limply on the bed. She screamed loudly thanks to the immense pain, feeling sure that these contractions were too strong. There had been absolutely no build up to them and it felt as though they had gone from zero to one hundred per cent in mere minutes. Leyla shushed her and then removed her clothing before checking between Melody's legs, nodding at a man behind her who moved forward and took control, urging Melody to push with her next contraction. And then her baby was born within seconds. She went white with shock, her human body not ready for the incredibly fast labouring process, and then she started to shake as the realisation began to dawn on her.

The man wrapped her tiny baby up in the blanket while Leyla cut the cord, watching as Laurie tended to their patient, helping her calm down and breathe through the still immense pain. Leyla soon passed the precious bundle to Melody, who took her baby with tears in her eyes, and then uncontrollable, powerful sobs forced their way out of her. It had all happened so fast and she was so confused, not able to understand where they were or why Leyla had intervened.

"It's a girl," she said, stroking the baby's head and smiling across at her, and Melody couldn't help but smile back, so happy and whole at last. The baby's tiny eyes were closed, the precious bundle already seeming at ease despite her quick release into the real world, and Melody couldn't take her eyes off of her. Dark eyelashes rested on her chubby, rosy cheeks and she sucked at her thumb as she snuggled into her mother's embrace. Melody could see that she had blonde hair, the soft fluffiness barely visible in the darkness, and she couldn't wait to see it as it grew longer, wondering to herself whether her little angel would have curls like her or straight hair like Corey's.

After a few minutes, the placenta was delivered and the man that was assisting them set about cleaning up the mess on the bed while Leyla sat down next to Melody and stroked her face gently, her own head bowed as she steadied her thoughts.

"Why couldn't Corey be here? What's going on?" Melody asked her after the awkward silence, cradling the sleeping baby in her arms protectively. The tiny bundle stirred and turned her head, looking for milk, and Melody pulled open her shirt and began feeding her without hesitation or self-consciousness about her body. The baby latched on without any fuss and began drawing small mouthfuls while her mother gasped. "Feels weird," she laughed, looking back at the quiet guardian beside her.

"I hate him Mel, I hate everything about him and everything he's done. I won't let Corey hurt you anymore," Leyla finally promised, her beautiful face so very sad.

"What don't I know?" Melody demanded.

"So much Mel. I don't even know where to start. I lured you here with Dustin's help today, and then Laurie gave you a potion to start your labour. I'm sorry we had to do it this way. I know the pain must have been unbearable, but it was the only way to get you away from Corey without him being suspicious. I know you want to think that he's changed, that deep down beneath that horrid exterior he loves you, but it's all lies Mel, it's all his games. He's used you from the moment he first met you on that platform. He fucked you up as often as he could and he messed with every bit of happiness you ever felt. Corey has been the perfect husband the last few weeks, am I right?" Leyla asked, and Melody nodded, her face pale and her afterbirth pains forgotten. Leyla bit her finger and then reached forward and placed a drop on Melody's tongue, healing her instantly, but she still felt sick. "It's all because he's playing another game Mel, another awful game and you're the only piece on the board he wants to use, you're the only piece he ever wants now and despite him making you feel like a Queen, you're still just the pawn. Does that make sense?"

"Kind of," she sighed. "So, what was he planning Leyla, please just tell me," Melody replied, instinctively holding her daughter closer to her.

"He was going to have the baby taken away when it was born and then replaced with another human one. Your baby was then going to be taken to Hell, where it would be taught only how he wanted it to be. Corey wants to control your child Mel, he wants for her to be just like him and for you to just keep on popping them out for as long as your body could bear it. Almost like his own personal following of half dark, half-light beings," Leyla said, and Melody peered down at her lovely little baby and her heart broke. Tears fell down her cheeks, and she curled into a protective ball around her tiny angel.

"How can I protect her, I'm powerless to stop him?" she asked in a sorrowful whisper.

"I will keep you both safe. I will keep you hidden. But, you will have to call upon something inside of you first, a power you don't even know you have. I can teach you, just like I had always wanted, like we had always planned. That's the real reason my father was disappointed that Corey had decided to have you for himself rather than follow the plan for you and Donovan to be together. You two are soulmates Melody, that's the simplest word for it. You and Donovan were destined for one another before you were even born and my father wanted you two to meet for a very good reason," Leyla told her, tailing off thoughtfully, as though not sure how to say the next part.

"What reason?" Melody asked, stroking her daughter's cheek as she finished her feed and fell asleep again so peacefully.

"Because you are the direct descendent of an angel, the purest line of direct blood-relative humans we have known, and not through the many generations like most of the ones we've found, but through your father. David Pembroke was the son of the angel Camael, Melody. A hidden gem we procured and owned for many years until the Warriors of Light found him and tried to hide him from us. We got David to agree to not only sell us his soul, but that of his eldest child in the hope that we could have you both in our command, but about twenty years ago he found out about his true heritage and tried to get out of his deal. That's why Corey used you to find him, and then when we found out you were his child, I quickly claimed you as mine, but Corey soon set about making you his trophy. He knew you weren't his, that you were destined to be with Donovan, but that just made him want you more."

"Whoa, so all this time he's known this about me, that I'm part angel? And he made me have a baby with him, made me trust him and then he was gonna steal her away thinking I wouldn't notice?" Melody cried, growing angry at the sheer thought of her husband's terrible actions, and his even crueller plans. "He truly is the worst person I've ever known."

"No, I am, but I never meant to be," said a voice from the shadows and then Donovan appeared, smiling warmly at her before stepping closer and laying a gentle hand on her arm. "She's beautiful, just like her mother," he added, laying a soft kiss on Melody's forehead.

"Thank you, it's good to see you Donovan," Melody said, peering up at him longingly. "And, how are you the worst?" she added, frowning. She finally understood their strong, natural chemistry and was glad he still cared enough to be here, that any of them cared enough to save her.

"Because I fought back. I knew what he was doing. I knew I shouldn't ever have let him push me, but I just couldn't help myself. I'm everything I ever told you I was Mel, everything you saw me to be in that bedroom. I won't deny that I have made huge mistakes when it has come to keeping you safe. I'm sorry. At that trial, I knew he had won. I was broken and beaten. I thought I had lost you forever, but after our punishment was over, Leyla told me about our fated bond. She warned me that Corey would do anything to keep a tight hold on you, that he would delight in my demise, so was no doubt going to try and push me into doing something foolish, and I let him get to me. Then my mistress came to me with a plan to win you back. We were going to kidnap you with the help of Laurie and Xander here," he said, looking over his shoulder at the man who had delivered the baby and he waved awkwardly. "But then you got pregnant, and he heightened your security so much that there was no chance. We kept trying to put together the perfect time, place and reason for you to come alone or with just your undercover new assistant away from his gaze, but he never let down that secure bubble around you, until today."

"I've endured years of pure torture thanks to him. I know you had to bide your time but I hate it that it took you this long. I despise him so much," Melody said, trying to hide her sorrow, but she failed miserably.

"We all do, Mel. You have no idea how many times we wanted to charge in and take you away, but he would've seen that coming a mile off and so we had to wait. He has no idea that Leyla has done this to him, or that you know about your angelic heritage. We have the element of surprise now," Donovan replied, and Melody nodded in understanding. "As far as he's aware, I have no idea about you either, or about my own heritage," he added, and Melody looked at him confused. "Oh yeah, that's the reason we're meant for each other, you are the direct descendent of the angel Camael, and I am the son of Lilith's half demon lovechild," Donovan told her, and Melody couldn't help but gape at him, dumbstruck by his admission.

"You're what?" she mumbled, and Donovan laughed.

"Lilith is a level one demon. She had a hard time accepting the changeover in Hell's leaders when the old King was overthrown by the Dark Queen. She was sent back to Earth, and that's when she hooked up with a human for a while, went off the rails a little bit by all accounts. You might call them her rebellious years. Demons don't normally have accidental pregnancies, but somehow it happened to her, and that's when my mother was born," he told her, smiling and shrugging when Melody gazed up at him in shock.

"Whoa, so do you have demonic powers?" she asked him, realising that a lot of his darker urges made sense to her now.

"No. Her daughter, my mother, renounced Lilith and ran away to a nunnery, where a white priest got her pregnant at the age of sixteen. Fucking pervert. I was shipped off to an orphanage because she died giving birth to me and he didn't want his wife to find out about us. My guardian here sorted him out for me when I joined the Crimson Brotherhood. My very first request was not for fame or fortune, it was for revenge and she gave me it," he told her, looking down at Leyla thoughtfully.

"Oh, Donovan, I had no idea," Melody said, her face full of sorrow for him and his dark past.

"It's okay, I was just a young man then and I'm a very different person now, apart from my obvious rage issues, but somehow having you around helped that go away little by little."

"Your partnership would have been the joining of light and darkness this world needs, but Corey didn't care about any of that. He just saw you as a coveted prize and after having been with you before we got to Pembroke, he thought he had some kind of claim on you," Leyla chimed in, shaking her head in disgust. "What's done is done. We can only try and move on from here, but we need to keep you both hidden until I can take care of my brother, in whatever way I'll have to. Your baby still has Corey's darkness in her as well as your light, but she can be corrupted either way. You will have to nurture and protect her lightness, find a balance for her just like my aunt did with my cousin of half light and dark," Leyla said, but tailed off rather than tell her too much about her young cousin Lottie's story of seclusion and fear.

"So what now?" Melody asked a short while later, cradling the now washed, dressed and snugly wrapped newborn that was hungry again, so suckling on her other breast. "I won't run away. I can't leave my life behind. I owe it to my father to carry on his legacy, but, how can I go back to Corey?" she added, knowing that being with him was absolutely not an option.

"I could go with you, or I'll ask our aunt to help," Leyla replied. Melody could tell that she was thinking hard about how to proceed, but she also knew that there was only one option. She had to go alone.

"I tell you what, you think of something while I go back and confront him. I can't let him win again, not this time. Can Astrid stay here with you until we can figure it out? That's what I'm calling her, by the way. She'll be my little star in the sky, my beacon of hope, the divine strength I need so much. I'll tell Corey she was taken away by angels or something?" Melody asked, looking at Leyla with a pleading gaze, hoping that she would understand that no matter how hard it would be for her to go back there she just had to. She had to defeat him herself, even if that meant being away from her baby in order to do it.

"I'll go back with you, we'll say we were kidnapped by white witches and taken to a church where you delivered and then the baby was taken away," Laurie agreed, clearly liking this plan very much.

"That's a good plan, actually. Corey will be so fixated on the witches that he won't suspect us. He wouldn't even think to question me or our family. He'll believe it was down to Camael. We will need you to go back a bit battered and bruised, though I'm afraid, but I think you could get away with that story. Donovan and I will stay here with Astrid. We won't let her out of our sight for even a second Melody, I promise," Leyla told them, and they all agreed.

As hard as it was to say goodbye, Melody placed her tiny baby in her aunt's arms and kissed her softly. She couldn't help her tears from falling, but she didn't fight them. Her love for her daughter was too strong and she would spend the rest of her life doing whatever it took to keep her safe.

"One more thing," came a voice from the shadows, making them all jump, and then Harry stepped out of the darkness with an apologetic smile. He held his hands up to show he meant no harm and approached the group slowly. "It's okay. The Dark Queen has sent you a gift, Melody. She wants you to succeed. Corey's dark actions go against everything she and Lottie have set up and he needs to be stopped," he said, handing Melody a small vial. There was a note with it and she took the two items from the demon with a gracious smile, opening the card and reading the handwritten message inside.

'Drink this potion and not only will your strength and stamina increase, but your enemies will feel the pain they inflict on you tenfold. Be careful, be clever, and do not underestimate my nephew for a second.

So mote it be,

Cate x'

Without hesitating Melody drank the potion and forced herself to swallow the thick, foul tasting drink in one gulp before Harry smiled and wished her good luck. With a kind stroke of Astrid's cheek, he then teleported away. Melody didn't feel any different following the potion, but hoped that Cate's words were true and she was glad to have the almighty Dark Queen on her side despite her own family's involvement.

"Who wants to slap me around a bit then?" Melody asked, looking at Donovan with one eyebrow cocked and a wicked grin on her face. "Just the face, a couple of slaps will do," she added, not wanting to take too much, but he shook his head profusely.

"No way, I told you before and I meant every word," he replied, looking shocked that she had even offered him first refusal. Leyla stood up, handing Astrid to him as she rolled her shoulders and eyed Melody with a cheeky smile, pretending to limber up in readiness to deliver a thorough beating.

"Pussy," she said to Donovan, shaking her head in mock disgust, and she stepped closer, taking Melody's cheek in her hand. "This might hurt a little, but I'll be as gentle as I can, I promise," she told her. In one quick move, Leyla pulled her hand back and slapped Melody hard across the face. She swore, stumbled and grabbed her red-hot cheek, taking a second to right herself, but then she was shocked to see Leyla on her knees before her, gripping her own cheek with a painful scowl.

"What the?" she started, but then couldn't help but laugh as she realised the full meaning of Cate's promise with that potion. "Your enemies will feel the pain they inflict on you tenfold," she said, helping Leyla up as she rubbed at her face for a few seconds before it finally calmed down, her healing powers kicking in.

"Well, Corey's gonna get the shock of his life next time he decides to give you a wallop," Leyla told her, and Melody grinned widely, forgetting the sting in her cheek now.

"I'll make sure to really rile him up then, I might just tell him what I really think and let him go for it," she replied before stepping back and letting Leyla deliver a couple of blows to Laurie's cheeks too, ensuring she had extra bruises to add to the story of her trying to protect Melody from their captors.

CHAPTER TWENTY-NINE

Melody lay in the back seat of the car, curled up in a tight ball as she sobbed loudly and cried into her hands. Laurie drove as fast as she could through the London streets, the sun rising on the horizon behind them as she finally pulled into the huge garage of Melody and Corey's home. She clambered out, falling to her knees as she exited the car, going to the backseat and then shaking Melody to try and rouse her.

"Please Melody, please get up. You're home now, you're safe," she begged, rubbing her boss's shoulder worriedly, but then was thrown back as Corey flung her out of the way and climbed into the car, where he lifted his wife into his arms.

"Where have you been?" he cried, clearly worried, but then he noticed her now flat stomach. "Where's the baby, Melody?" he asked her as he carried her inside, his eyes wide and scared but she couldn't answer, her emotionally painful wails and sobs forcing their way out of her, making it impossible to speak. "Where's my baby?" he asked again, growing angry and by the time he placed her down onto the sofa, he was shaking with rage. "Where is my fucking baby, Melody?" Corey bellowed, shocking her back to reality, and she shook her head, climbing up on her knees on the soft leather and cowering before him.

"They took her away," she mumbled, rubbing at her face to wipe away her seemingly never-ending stream of tears.

"Who took her away, what the hell happened to you? I need answers Mel, or so fucking help me I'll torture everyone in my path until I get them, starting with you," Corey promised, his threat full of pain and rage, yet she knew he would do it. Melody wanted to wait as long as possible to show him her new power thanks to the Dark Queen's potion, wanting to enjoy it when his inflicted pain was then returned ten times as bad to himself and so she calmed down, ready to tell him their cleverly constructed lies.

"Angels," she whispered, staring up at him as Laurie came in and started locking all the doors and windows of the house in a mad panic. Corey ignored the woman, his eyes on his wife as he took in the one word that had spoken volumes to him. "I went into labour and then they just appeared, witches, hundreds of them. They took us away and I couldn't stop her from coming, the baby. Next thing she was gone," she whimpered, looking skywards and he knew exactly what she meant.

"You did this, didn't you?" he asked her, taking her wrists in his hands and holding them out so that she couldn't hide her face behind them again. "Did you call to them? Did you ask them to take her away from me?" Corey cried, his pain and anguish clear on his face.

"I had no idea what I really was until they told me, but you knew, didn't you? I should never have heard about my heritage from them Corey, you should've told me all along. I would never take your child away from you. What heartless monster would ever take a baby from their loving parents' arms?" Melody asked, and a glimmer of hard truth flitted across his eyes. She knew he was wondering if she somehow knew his plan, but then shook it off, clearly thinking that there was no way she could know.

"I'm sorry Mel, I just can't believe it. How could she just be gone?" he whispered, falling to his knees and then pulling her into his arms, stroking her bruised cheek with his finger. "Did they hurt you?"

"They healed me after the birth, but then we had to fight a couple of witches to get away. I don't think they cared once they had their prize. I was not who they had come for," she said, sobbing into his tight grip.

"What are we gonna do?" Corey muttered, rocking as he held his still trembling wife in his arms.

"What can we do? We'll need to try and find a way to get to her, but in the meantime we have to think of a cover story, or else do you know any other babies that we can use as a stand-in?" she asked, knowing full well that the human baby he was planning on switching theirs with was no doubt due any day now.

"I'll see what I can do, we'll tell everyone you're in labour now but having the baby at home. I'm sure I can find one of my followers who would be willing to let us borrow their baby for the public appearances and stuff," he replied, so calm and seemingly genuine that she might almost have believed him if she didn't know the terrible truth, that he'd had one lined up to take their baby's place all along.

"I'll do everything I can to fix this Melody, I promise," Devin told her a few days later, wrapping a protective arm around his daughter-in-law and eyeing her earnestly. She nodded, leaning into his embrace uncontrollably despite their previous estranged relationship, but she knew now exactly why he hadn't been happy with her before. Melody also wondered to herself whether he knew the truth now, if they all did, but so far no one had let on that they knew a thing about Leyla's actions, and so she maintained her cover, just in case.

The baby that would be imitating hers was with its real mother back in the main house of the Crimson Brotherhood's little hamlet, ready to travel with them to London and begin their deception to the well-wishers and onlookers. Melody didn't care for the child one little bit and was not looking forward to having to snuggle and coo over the stand-in but she forced herself to get on board. Everything she did was for Astrid, and Melody was not going to blow their cover, no matter how broken she felt inside.

Devin had called an emergency meeting to discuss their options, so he, Braeden, Melody, Corey and Serena were now gathered in a small, private annex room towards the back of the huge main house.

"We're just waiting on Leyla and then we can begin," Serena said, smiling warmly at them all and they closed the doors, ensuring they had privacy. Melody tried not to look confused, wondering to herself why her old mistress had not sent her apologies already, when Leyla suddenly appeared beside her. She hugged Melody tightly, staring down into her eyes warmly as she took her in.

"I just can't believe this has happened to you Mel, to you both," she said, looking over at her sour faced brother. "We will figure out a way to find her. There has to be something we can do?"

"I think we should send someone up there to get her," replied Corey. "But dad says it's not a good idea."

"No, I said it wasn't a good idea you going up there. Not that you'd be able to, no matter what you tried. Your soul is well and truly blackened beyond repair, my son," Devin said, eyeing him darkly.

"What if Melody tried?" Leyla asked, and Devin thought about it for a moment, tapping his chin as he pondered.

"Perhaps, but she might need to cross over, though. Would you allow that, Corey?" Devin asked, clearly meaning that she would have to die, and Melody sat and peered at her husband with intrigue, eager to hear his response. After a moment's thought, he answered, his face calm and solemn, but she didn't believe his seemingly heartfelt words for a second.

"I'm sure Melody would agree that we have to do whatever it takes to get our baby back. If sacrificing herself is the only option, then I am behind her all the way," he said. Melody smiled but said nothing, feeling sure that her spiteful words could not be hidden if she opened her mouth right now and thinking that it would suit him perfectly if she was to kill herself. She then might somehow deliver their baby to him before taking her place as a worthless soul in either Heaven or Hell, she was still not entirely sure where she would end up. Either way, she knew they wouldn't actually be doing it. Her daughter was still on Earth after all, which Leyla knew all too well, so there would be no point.

"She would have to die in a righteous way. Suicide or anything sinful is completely out of the question. I will think about it some more and try to find another way. You are not to act until I give the order, understood?" Devin asked them, and they both nodded. They all chatted some more, going over the story with Melody again while each of them asked questions and they brainstormed their ideas. Eventually Devin released them from their meeting, seeing the weariness in Melody's eyes, and they dispersed.

"Oh Mel, I'm sure that wherever your sweet little girl is, she's healthy and happy. You'll have her in your arms soon, I have no doubt," Leyla told her when they stood to one side together after the meeting was over. Melody focussed on the two words, happy and healthy, hoping that they were Leyla's way of giving her a little update on her precious child. Astrid was now just four days old and Melody already couldn't sleep knowing that her daughter was not with her, only adding to her cover of the distraught childless mother. Thankfully, Corey had left her well alone since she had returned to him at their London home without their baby.

Melody played her part well, as did Leyla, and neither one slipped up for even a second while they were under the watchful eyes of their family. Leyla hugged her again and then teleported away without another word. Melody then made her way across the room towards Corey, who stood chatting with Heath and Logan, two more beings she truly hated with all her bitter heart.

"I'm going for a walk to the lake. I want to be alone," she told him, no affection in her voice as she regarded her husband, and Corey just nodded and carried on his conversation as though he couldn't care less what she was doing or if she wanted company. Melody walked slowly, taking her time, and she ended up spending over an hour walking along the water's edge as her mind buzzed with all the craziness from the last few days.

The sun set and the stars began to shine overhead as she wandered back towards the main house. Melody looked up and found the brightest one, her hand over her heart.

"Soon, my little star, soon," she whispered into the breeze as tears rolled down her cheeks.

.

CHAPTER THIRTY

A few weeks later, no developments or decisions had been made that would work to find their lost daughter, and Melody wandered the studios in one of her many ways she used to stay busy and keep herself out of the house, and away from Corey's gaze. Not wanting to spend any time with him unless absolutely necessary, Melody hadn't stopped working, and was glad for the distraction working gave her rather than sit around pining for Astrid. She was with one of the new designers, Lena, chatting and wandering around the set with her, discussing the props and scenery for the movie they were due to start shooting in the spring. She had come back to work as a much needed distraction from everything at home, blaming it on her being a workaholic and none of the humans around her disbelieved her story at all.

"We'll be using a lot of special effects, but will also need a vast woodland and a beach scene," she told the woman, who jotted down her notes furiously.

"Excuse me, might I borrow Mrs Pembroke-Black for a moment?" a soft voice asked, and Melody turned to find Laurie standing behind the pair of them, her warm smile wide.

"Sure. We will continue this tomorrow. I look forward to seeing your sketches for the two sets we already discussed," Melody replied, following Laurie out the studio and towards her office.

"Everything's prepared for your conference call, sorry for disturbing you," Laurie said, wandering away with a sly smile as Melody let herself in to her large office and then shut the door behind her, being sure to lock it.

"What did I say about keeping me waiting?" said a voice from behind her as a powerful torso pinned Melody to the door. She gasped and laughed, pushing back with her hips to move the strong man away before turning and planting a deep, wanting kiss on his lips. Melody peered up into her lover's eyes and grinned broadly at him.

"Donovan, I told you to wait here patiently for me, and for you to think carefully about what you've done while I was away," she replied, pushing him backwards so that his muscular arse perched against the huge wooden desk and he grinned. "Next time you're late, I may just handcuff you to the chair and let the cleaners find you."

"I will not ever be tardy again, boss. I did think about it. I thought long and hard," he replied, drawing out each word as he peered up at the woman he loved so very much.

"Good, because I would hate to have to punish you now that we've finally figured this whole thing out," Melody replied, lifting one leg and placing her foot on the door behind her, twisting her knee sideways and opening her legs, showing off her lack of underwear brazenly in the dim light.

"Mmmmm, what will your husband say?" Donovan asked, falling to his knees before her and shuffling forwards, licking his lips anticipatively before trailing kisses up her bare thighs to her already throbbing nub.

"I don't give a shit. All I care about is the three of us being together at last," she replied, her head falling back against the hard wooden door as her paramour devoured her body and her senses with his perfect lips.

"I can't wait to see his face when you tell him," Donovan said later, pulling on his suit jacket as Melody climbed into the underwear she had stashed in a drawer and then checked her reflection in the mirror. The pair of them had finally been able to sneak some time alone together while busy at the studio over the past couple of weeks and things had quickly progressed from them being star-crossed-lovers to beginning a full-blown affair.

Astrid was currently being cared for by Leyla in the small cabin Melody had delivered her in. Donovan would stay there at night to take over while Leyla went about her work in order not to have her absences noticed. The beautiful baby was now almost six weeks old, and Melody missed her so much that it hurt. She had still not seen her since that day, surviving on photographs Donovan would take on his mobile phone and listening to his stories of her progress, but it was all worth it. She was working hard to maintain her cover with Corey for the time being while plans were being finalised for his demise, and while she hated being apart from Astrid, she knew she had to do what was right by her tiny baby now so that they would be together soon.

Melody had also been careful not to let Corey touch her since the angels had supposedly stolen their baby, whether sexual or otherwise, and the pair of them had quickly returned to their mutual hatred for one another. Corey seemingly even respected her need to be alone, believing that it was because of her grief, and she let him. He truly trusted and seemed to believe the story she had fed him about the angels, and so far his father had not told him otherwise so she hoped either he didn't know the truth or that he was on her side just as Cate had been when she had sent Harry with the potion.

Donovan finished getting ready and sat down on the small sofa, watching as Melody applied her makeup and fixed her dress. She was so confident, so powerful now, thanks to having learned the truth about herself and about him. The pair of them were stronger than ever, and he looked forward to building a life with her when Corey was finally out of the picture. He just had to be patient.

"I can't wait either, but I've decided you're the one doing the big reveal Donovan. It will be the ultimate kick in the teeth." She grinned, a wicked, cunning smile that showed him just how much she was looking forward to seeing Corey crumble. "I'll see you there. Don't keep me waiting," Melody told him with a wink, relishing in her dominative prowess over her dark lover, and he bowed in response. The pair of them had found that they had been right with their approach to their relationship before. She had to be the one to take the lead, and it was the perfect dynamic. Melody had to make the decisions and be strong for them both. In return, Donovan would trust in her and do everything she asked of him, making them both stronger. In just the last few weeks, she had reached a more steadfast, powerful place in her life that even Corey could not seem to shake. She and Donovan both understood now how amazing it felt to be in the arms of their soulmate at last, and they would do anything to protect it, to protect each other. Pain and violence were not even in their equation, all thoughts of sadism now completely gone from Donovan's once fragile mind and urge-ridden body.

Thinking about it now, Melody was convinced that Corey was readying himself to lose her anyway, for her to follow through on her promises and go to Heaven in order to retrieve their daughter, and she let him think that she too was mentally preparing herself for that fate. It was easier if he let her go, and stopped trying to own her or control her. Corey had never loved her, Melody knew that now, and she also didn't care anymore.

Later that evening, Melody made her way into a party she had organised as a way of congratulating her employees on a successful year. She went straight over to the bar area where she greeted her husband with a kiss to his cheek and then ordered the pair of them a drink, eager as ever to maintain their public profile of the perfect marriage.

"Where have you been?" Corey asked, leaning in to speak privately in her ear, and she faked a smile up at him.

"The studios, I had a meeting with Lena and then a conference call," she replied, and he seemed satisfied, bored as usual by her work commitments so he didn't question her further. She soon left his side to go off in search of a friendly face in the sea of colleagues. She knew every one of their faces and names, but none of them knew her, not the real Melody Pembroke-Black, and they probably never would. She chose a spot beside a loud group of women simply for the perfect view it gave her of her husband at the bar and then watched as her lover made his way towards him.

"Mr Black, what a nice surprise," Donovan said, reaching a hand out to his powerful foe with a forced smile. He was bigger than ever, his muscles bulging beneath his suit jacket, and Melody couldn't help but appreciate the view for a moment.

"Donovan, good to see you. I trust rehab went well?" Corey asked loudly, ordering the starlet a glass of lemonade in an attempt to shake him. Donovan took the cool glass and had a long sip, grinning appreciatively across at Corey as they stared at each other in the bustling hall. He played along, pretending to have gotten sober since their fight, and Donovan didn't care at all that Corey was clearly itching for another one. Donovan had a secret to tell, and a very big one at that, so he delighted in his own game as he negotiated his way around, informing his adversary just what he had been up to during his recent past.

"Wonderfully, thank you for the concern. It's been far too long mate, do you know I had a lot of time to think and I cannot help but reminisce on old times." He paused for a sip of his drink before turning his dark brown eyes into daggers that bore into the powerful guardian's without a hint of fear despite their awful history. "Like that time your wife looked me in the eye and told me she needed to be mine sooner rather than later? She needed to have me so very much, for me to be hers. I was willing to do anything she wanted of me back then, and I still am," Donovan whispered, patting Corey on the back and acting like old friends who were rekindling their friendship. Corey's face contorted into an angry scowl that he tried to turn into a sinister smile, but he was too irritated.

"Well, I wasn't there until about an hour later, if you'll remember? I'll just have to take your word for it, but make sure you be careful, Donovan. I wouldn't want anything to happen to you now that you're finally getting your act together," Corey warned, his expression fierce.

"Absolutely, and your wife is to thank for that, as a matter of fact. It's a funny story, really." He sniggered, leaning closer so that he could whisper. "Do you remember the time she disappeared and your baby was stolen by angels?" Donovan asked him in a whisper, and Corey's eyes darkened.

"Yes," he whispered back icily, unable to hide his rage now. Donovan continued before his powerful adversary's anger got the better of him and put a hold on his cleverly thought out conversation.

"Well, what if I told you she lied? What if I told you she hid the baby from you, and that I've been taking care of your precious little girl all this time? That I've been bonding with her, nurturing her?" he said, grinning wickedly.

"I will kill you where you stand Donovan, I don't care who's watching," Corey replied, his voice full of malice and pain, but he couldn't help but wonder if his words were true.

"Oh, then I'd also better not mention the fact that less than an hour ago I was fucking your wife's brains out, had I? That I can still taste her sweet pussy on my lips and how she came for me over and over," Donovan told him, seeing and feeling the venomous rage bubbling over underneath Corey's calm guise. Melody joined them just at that moment, stepping between the two from her place in the swarm. The move would be seen by the others in the crowd all around them as an attempt to come between the rivals of old and to keep the peace. She had cleverly stepped in at just the right time, knowing that Donovan had delivered the terrible blow to her husband's ego, and she readied herself for his response, placing a hand on his chest and peering up at him earnestly.

"Mel, please tell me this piece of shit is lying?" Corey asked, and she shook her head slowly, never taking her eyes off his.

"Oh dear, it seems the cat is out of the bag darling, my bad," she whispered, stepping back slightly into Donovan's personal space. He grinned, placing his hand on her shoulder before then running one finger down the arm at her side to her hand, relishing in Corey's furious gaze as he watched them interact with such a delicate touch.

"Oh Melody, I think you must like being beaten, tortured and violated after all, because you know that's what is awaiting you, don't you? I've waited a very long time to give you the beating you deserve, and now I get to punish you both, again. I'm gonna enjoy this," Corey whispered in her ear, grabbing her arm and dragging Melody over towards the doorway in an attempt to take her somewhere private to teleport from.

"Please Corey, I can't live like this. I am sorry, please don't hurt me again. I'll be a good wife, I promise," she whimpered, a little too loudly as they passed the various onlookers who watched them in shock. They soon began whispering furiously before the pair of them had even left the room. All eyes then fell on Donovan and he ran his hands through his black hair, playing his role as the tormented hero perfectly.

"Everyone go back to your party, turn the other cheek just like always," he then blurted out, encouraging everyone's minds to wander about the real relationship they had thought was going on atop the two empires. Whispers were quickly rife, all those around them suspecting that things might not be as perfect as they had once thought.

CHAPTER THIRTY-ONE

Melody couldn't help the maniacal laugh that escaped her lips as they reached the empty corridor and she twisted out of Corey's grip, turning to face him with more hatred in her eyes than he had ever seen in them before.

"Maybe my aunt was right. I should've just let you go a long time ago, Mel. I'm glad I didn't. I'm glad I get to fuck you up in every way I can imagine all over again. I get to make you my bitch at last and by the time I'm done with you, you'll beg for death and I won't give it to you until you bring me my daughter," he told her, grabbing Melody's hand and teleporting her away with him just as Donovan came through the doors behind them.

"You wish," she muttered as they arrived in their bedroom and Corey flung her on the bed. He removed his suit jacket, rolling his shoulders as if readying himself to deliver her the biggest beating ever. Melody just sat still, watching him calmly from her perch on the edge of the bed.

"You women are all the fucking same, aren't you? No matter whether I'm the perfect boyfriend or the domineering husband, you still insist on torturing me," Corey cried.

"I don't know who that girl was who broke your heart, but one of these days I'm gonna find her and thank her. Being with you has been the worst few years of my entire life, but it ends now and I will never let you control me again, Corey. I'll never stop fighting and I will never back down ever again. You'd better watch your back, because one of these days I'm coming for you," Melody replied, her voice a terse, heartfelt threat, and Corey's eyes burned black as his dark power bubbled inside. After a few seconds he stepped forward and laid his left hand on her cheek, stroking her beautiful face gently for a moment before gripping her hair. He then brought back his other hand, sending it flying towards her face with such force she was almost knocked unconscious and the pain reverberated around in her skull.

Corey lifted her to a standing position using the hand that was still fisted in her hair and then flung his wife across the room, stepping forward to retrieve his broken puppet just as the potion Cate had given Melody began to work its magic on him. He fell to his knees and grabbed his head, screaming in agony as a violent wave of pain hit him. Corey just about steadied his pounding skull when a second wave of pain flowed through his back, mirroring the injury to Melody's battered body that lay slumped in the corner of their bedroom.

"What did you do to me?" he bellowed, recovering far quicker than Melody thanks to his incredible dark powers and he turned his wife over onto her back, slapping her cheek to revive her and he winced as the pain stung at his own too. Melody groaned as she came to, staring up at Corey with a scared expression but she could see that it was working, he was in pain thanks to her new power and she was willing to bear the brunt of his rage if it meant that he too would suffer. She laughed up at him, her tears falling uncontrollably down her cheeks, but she ignored them and egged him on, ready to take more.

"I didn't do anything to you, but I have changed, Corey. You will feel every ounce of pain you give me tenfold, so go ahead, give me your best shot, or are you too much of a pussy to take it?" she asked him, not even flinching as a second slap silenced her. Corey straddled her on the floor and quickly let his fury overpower him. His hands gripped her neck tightly, and he pressed down, coughing himself as he squeezed Melody's windpipe and held on as she drifted in and out of consciousness for a few moments.

"I can take whatever pain you think you can give me, Melody, but what can you endure? How much can you survive?" Corey asked, contempt clear in his voice. "Or will death be your last insolent move, dear wife? In either case, I'll see you in Hell."

Melody drifted away at last, passing out thanks to Corey's hands that still pressed down around her throat. This time, though, she was very aware that she felt light, free of pain and was seemingly ascending, her soul aching for its release from her broken body. She blacked out somewhere shortly after that, her heart pounding in her ears as a light hold seemed to carry her away.

Melody came to on her knees inside a white pentagram. She jumped and looked around her, seeing nothing but white, and her panic instantly set in. A young, beautiful woman with dark brown hair and piercing green eyes then came towards her, kneeling down to join Melody and laying a warm, soft hand on her shoulder as she smiled across at her.

"Do I know you? Where am I?" Melody asked. She was sure that this woman looked somehow familiar, but couldn't have guessed the answer.

"You and I have never met, but you know my family. You are my family. My name is Lottie. I am an angel and Cate Rose is my mother. Your grandfather, Camael is my boyfriend. Do you see Melody? Do you understand how we are all interwoven, linked, and all part of one another's fate? Astrid is part of that too. I will send you back to her when my cousin has been dealt with, but for now you need to stay here," Lottie told her, eyeing Melody with genuine affection and love.

The angel was truly the image of her mother and Melody knew it was Cate she was thinking of when she had recognised something in Lottie. She had heard her name being mentioned before and knew that this must be Cate's child of half light and darkness, that the stories were true and she had ascended to become an angel. The very idea brought Melody so much hope for her own child, and for herself, as she was sure her own soul must have been blackened by her time with Corey. Surely the lightness she had within could not possibly be a match for the dark bitterness and hate he had given her. Lottie watched Melody with a smile, her emerald eyes boring into hers as she read her thoughts, and she exuded a calm, loving sense that seemed to seep into Melody, helping her deal with her terrible ordeal and memories that were swamping her mind.

"So, I'm not dead?" Melody finally asked her after a few minutes, peering back at Lottie with a worried stare, feeling utterly shocked and afraid, alone and weak.

"No, you are very much alive, we just brought you here for safe-keeping," Lottie replied, wrapping her arms around the trembling woman and hugging her tight, tighter than she had ever been held before and Melody fell to pieces in her arms. She shook violently and sobbed as tears forced themselves out of her body and she finally let go of all the hate and fear, fraught with emotion and pain she had kept bottled up for so long.

Regardless of anything else, though, she also felt an overwhelming sense of freedom. Corey finally knew the truths that they had kept hidden from him. She knew that his time of reckoning had finally come and Melody found peace in her revenge. Being the ones to have delivered him his fate was wonderful and although she knew she shouldn't be happy that his demise had come, she couldn't help it. Melody also still felt terrified, fearful of the repercussions of her actions and that small flicker of happiness soon melted away as fear for hers and Astrid's futures took its place.

"I'm so alone, I'm so scared," she whimpered into Lottie's chest, and the angel didn't let go of her for even a second. "How can I take care of her when I can't even take care of myself? I couldn't stop him doing all those things to me and sometimes I even liked it in some sick, perverted way. At times I think I even loved him."

"We all mess up Melody, but you know now who you are and what your life can be, thanks to Donovan and Leyla having taken you from Corey's darkness and leading you into the light. Those two dark beings showed you who you really were. They showed you love, care, compassion and warmth in a way that no other being has ever done for you before, and they will continue to do so even after you return to them safe and sound. I believed all along that you would find your way Melody, we both believed," Lottie said, pulling back at last as another pair of strong arms wrapped around Melody from behind in the bright room.

"Don't be afraid, don't ever be afraid again, Melody. Be brave, be ready to love and be strong," Camael told her, his expression shocked as his granddaughter turned and cradled herself in his arms, sensing their bond on an instinctual level. Melody felt as though time had stood still for them, his powerful embrace the only thing she needed in all the world to feel whole again. Even Lottie could sense her lover's light seeping into his lost relative, Melody's body lapping up his shared essence willingly, and Lottie watched as it empowered her and strengthened the angelic human's body and soul. Lottie then reached out and took Camael's hand in hers, grinning at him as she came to realise now just how much both he and Melody had suffered all this time. The powerful angel knew how to hide his guilt at having lost sight of his child and grandchild all those years ago so well that she had never noticed it until now.

"We're here now. You can trust us," Lottie said, taking Melody's right arm and covering Corey's black mark of ownership with her palm. After a few seconds, she pulled her hand away and stumbled back, shaking off whatever powerful backlash she had had to endure thanks to her incredible spell and Melody stared down at her now un-branded arm in shock.

"You're free," Camael told Melody, his arms still wrapped around her tightly and he leaned over to pull Lottie into his arms too, their circle of love and trust feeding off one another's power and they stayed like that for what felt like forever.

CHAPTER THIRTY-TWO

"Leyla? What are we doing here?" Corey asked, his voice hoarse and battered body still frail and weak as he took in his surroundings. The backlash of his vicious choking methods on Melody had truly been his undoing, tenfold hadn't seemed like much when it had been a slap but almost killing Melody had taken his own body and soul far beyond anything he would have ever imagined. Even hours later he was still weak.

He looked around again, his stomach in knots as he took in the cell they were in, and the heat and stifling pressure that told him they were in Hell. The dingy room was basically just a hollowed out piece of rock somewhere in the depths of the castle, far away from the lavish splendour he was used to. His neighbours were most likely other traitors to Cate's balance, but once that door was sealed, Corey knew that there was no sound to be heard, no interacting with fellow inmates. The torture of being alone with your thoughts for so long was enough to drive a person mad. Powerful demons like Corey wouldn't rot or wither, they would just sit and stew. He hoped it wouldn't be long, just a couple of years as a slap on the wrist, but the look on Leyla's face told him otherwise.

"This is your punishment. You have been tried and sentenced to one hundred years in this dungeon, Corey. You have done nothing to embrace our new balanced worlds, constantly flaunted your power over your poor wife, and you even planned to take away her child. Who do you think you are?" Leyla demanded, staring down at her brother with sheer disgust and hatred on her face.

"Leyla, don't you see? I just wanted to further our bloodline. The child would be better off embracing the darkness, it's who we are no matter what our aunt wants."

"No, you're the one who doesn't see Corey. You fucked things up for all of us. I've had to come back here now too as apparently I cannot be trusted either. I have to prove my loyalty to our Queen through service and unwavering submission now, but it's worth it knowing that Melody and Donovan can raise that baby in a loving, caring home without any input from you. You're my brother Corey and I love you, but I will never let you out of this cage until I know you can be trusted," Leyla told him before teleporting away, sealing the door behind her and leaving her brother in his misery for a century of solitary confinement. Corey screamed out to her, to anyone who might hear with his grainy breath. He bellowed his pleas and promises from within his small cage, but it was no good. He lay back on the bed and stared up at the ceiling, his blood boiling with venomous rage as he began plotting the demise of all who had wronged him, including his sister.

***

"Thank you both for coming. I know that you've been through a lot. I am sorry it took so long to remove him from the situation, but I hope you can understand why I had to give Corey the benefit of the doubt all this time?" Devin asked Melody as she and Donovan joined him in his private office a few weeks later.

"Even the Queen and the Black Prince tried to warn him off that road he had chosen to go down. I didn't see how bad he was at the time. I guess I gave him too many chances as well. I believed in that side of him that seemed to want to change and care for me and Astrid in the way we needed. He could've turned it around any time but he chose not to," Melody replied, her eyes sad as she thought about everything she had been through at his hands, but she quickly pushed it aside, refusing to let thoughts of Corey upset her.

"I know. He and his unrelenting darkness have no place in our new balance. His punishment is unavoidable. I just hope that in time he will learn the error of his ways. I'm sorry that he hurt you Melody, I'm sorry for everything," Devin said, watching her with a sad expression.

"I'm not going to say that it's okay Devin, because it isn't. But, I'm moving on with my life now and no matter what he did, the fact still remains that I have my daughter to take care of and a family to honour," Melody replied, instinctively looking skywards and Devin nodded. He looked pale, thin and so very sad that her heart truly felt for him, but there was no messing around now. She would not allow any of them to subdue her true self ever again.

"I understand. And, I'm glad to hear that you met Lottie at last," he said and Melody smiled. "I guess you already realised that she is the Queen's youngest daughter, a child of light and darkness just like Astrid. She and the High Council of Angels have now begun a new regime across all of our worlds, a new balance. There will always be good and evil, light and dark, but now neither side is permitted to force the other's hand and we all need to adapt to maintain that balance. Corey has now been imprisoned for one hundred years and after that time, if he still has not changed his ways, the

Queen will repeat his sentence. He will never be allowed to hurt you or your family, I guarantee it."

"Thank you. It seems I have a fair few powerful beings watching over me and Astrid now. I like knowing that she will be safe," Melody admitted, smiling as Donovan took her hand in his. The last few weeks had been wonderful. Having both Astrid and Donovan back in her life where they belonged had brought Melody such happiness that she could not even begin to tell her father-in-law about.

"As do I, and I want you to know that I never knew of his plans for when she was born. He must have known I wouldn't approve, so he never told me or Serena his terrible choices for her upbringing," Devin told her, his handsome face barely hiding his disappointment. "So, now on to bigger, better and brighter things. I can sense that you are no longer marked as Corey's follower thanks to our dear angelic mistress, and therefore you are no longer a member of the Crimson Brotherhood. While every urge inside of me wishes to make you a deal in return for your continued service, or else threaten to take everything away that you have been afforded so far, I am not going to do that, not to you," he added, leaning forward as he spoke.

"I wish to provide for my grandchild as much as I can. I want her to know that she is loved by us all and that she is safe here. And, as it happens, I am now down not only Corey as a guardian but also Leyla. She too has been summoned to remain in Hell for as long as it takes for her to gain the Dark Queen's trust again. She has admitted to her dark sins and accepted her punishment with grace and humility. So, how would the pair of you like to become guardians in their places?" Devin then asked, staring at the two of them intently. A moment of stunned silence passed between the three of them as both Melody and Donovan mulled over Devin's proposal. There was a big part of her that wanted nothing to do with the Crimson Brotherhood at all, but then again if she was in a position of power within the order rather than a pawn on the lower rung like before, that would give her a much greater control over her own life, Astrid's upbringing, and the future of her business empire.

"What would our roles be? Please, could you give me more details on our responsibilities?" Melody eventually asked, intrigued and ready to negotiate, her business head back on as she regarded her powerful leader.

"You would take over from Leyla, Melody, but not in her bounty-huntress areas of expertise, of course. You will take on her clients and maintain their deals, deliver on her promises as well as ensuring that they behave. The continuation of our dealings is key to our continuation, but we will never resort to sinister methods ever again. You will be a guardian who is not only a light being but who also respects our new balance, our fresh world, and the new commandments that will come along with that. You will also act as a go-between for our side and the Warriors of Light, an order similar to ours run by angels and white witches. You will be the buffer Melody, the spokeswoman, to the other side. You will continue to head up Pembroke Enterprises, but I would also like you to take over the running of Black Rose," Devin said, laying out all of his cards on the table without any fear of overwhelming her. He knew she might still say no, and understood her reasons not to accept, however he hoped that Melody would see sense and stay with them.

"Whoa, I don't think I could do all of it. I have a child to raise too, don't forget?" she replied, thinking it all over and mentally calculating how many hours she would have to put in.

"You can take a backseat from both companies, employ chief executives if necessary, but you would be the public face and the deciding vote for both empires. We will tell everyone that you and Corey have divorced, and that he has moved abroad, leaving you in charge while he goes and 'finds himself'. We can even leak rehab stories to the press if you like. You would be free to live and work between here and London and I will personally see to it that yours and Donovan's schedules allow for you to be together as much as possible," he told her, looking over at Donovan now to make him his offer while Melody thought about hers for a few minutes.

"Donovan, I would like for you to take over from Corey, acquisitions and retrieval, but again, no longer anything sinister. You will use the darkness you already possess to learn the skills required and become a formidable bounty-hunter where necessary, but you will also negotiate contracts and maintain your own list of clients, just as Melody will do," Devin told him, and he nodded in understanding but said nothing.

Devin could tell that they were close to accepting, that this future was a far better one than either of them had even considered they would have now that their guardians were gone. Despite Lottie having taken away her mark, each of their own deals were still playing out and they were both beholden to the Crimson Brotherhood in one way or another, especially Donovan. He only had a couple of years until his time on Earth was up and he would transition into the role of follower rather than client. "You will no longer be obligated by your own deals, either of you. As guardians, you will be given amnesty for your past and granted magical powers, including teleportation and immortality," Devin added, as though reading their minds, sweetening the deal. Melody looked at Donovan, both of their eyes wide as they considered the possibility of a long and free life together.

Donovan had already told her he was willing to be a father to Astrid, their bond already incredibly strong, and Melody knew he would be a wonderful partner and father to the future family they both wanted together too. Thanks to the terrible events of the last few years, Donovan's darker nature and urges had taken a complete turn. He neither wanted to hurt or dominate Melody now, quite the opposite, and he allowed for her to be the one in control, submitting to her entirely, whether alone or in the company of others. Melody was the calming influence he had needed all along, the light in his darkness that had completely set him free. She was the one who needed to have her voice heard now, to have the deciding vote, and her soulmate was more than willing to oblige, relishing in her new-found confidence and reaping the rewards for her unbridled happiness. Neither said a word, but their eyes seemed full of promise as they stared at one another, a silent back and forth of understanding and love passing through their intense gaze.

"I accept," Melody said, grinning at Devin, and he couldn't help but smile back broadly.

"Me too," Donovan added, leaning forward to shake Devin's outstretched hand.

"Wonderful. We will perform the ceremony after brunch on Sunday. Tilly is coming to complete her initiation task and then we will all get together to welcome her and induct you both as official guardians for the Crimson Brotherhood. In the meantime, take the next few days together and enjoy being with your family," Devin said, a weight having been lifted off his shoulders. A weight put there by his youngest child's foolish ways but he was so glad to finally be able to right some of Corey's wrong's and looked forward to the future with his granddaughter close by.

CHAPTER THIRTY-THREE

"Give me everything you've got, Caine. I want it rough," Melody groaned as she climbed up on all fours before her lover and leaned back into his rock-hard abs. Despite her hatred for her ex-husband, Corey had taught her just how she wanted her lover to be. She knew how hard and how far she liked to be taken when it came to being in the bedroom with someone she trusted not to hurt her. Melody didn't care who had taught her these lessons, it was Donovan who was now reaping the rewards.

His powerful urges soon surfaced, but he knew how to control them now thanks to her teachings and he played along with her command, her order, gripping Melody's hips in his strong hands and pulling her back even further to meet his hard length as he slid himself inside of her and thrust. He slammed into Melody just a few times before she cried out and her first orgasm claimed her. Donovan allowed her a few seconds to come down from her high, pushing into her as Melody's core throbbed around him and he too groaned in appreciation of her beautiful body. He held her tight, rocking back and forth whilst nestled deep within her inviting cleft, and she screamed his name and came for him again.

Donovan then flipped Melody onto her back, lifting her calves up over his muscular shoulders and thrusting into her again while she shuddered and relished in her wonderful aftershocks. His mouth trailed hard kisses up and down her legs, Donovan's lip curling as he tasted her salty flesh, and Melody soon felt his teeth skim her soft skin as he lost himself in the moment. He had an urge to own her, to claim her, and Donovan knew that a bite would do just the job. His mouth opened a little more, but she quickly assumed the dominant role and stopped him before he could go any further.

"Stop it, Donovan, look at me," she said sternly, giving her lover the constant guidance and support he still so desperately craved before lowering her legs and pulling his powerful torso closer with her strong thighs. "Now, make love to me. Soft and slow."

Melody had seen his expression change in that intense moment, just a flicker of dark urge, but she had quashed it immediately, knowing instinctively when his inner demons would surface. Donovan followed her lead, leaning down to kiss her deeply as he rode her slowly and then came.

"Yes angel, yes," he groaned as he unravelled, his eyes on hers as she led him so lovingly into her enraptured state with her, kissing her lover and holding him tightly while Donovan let go of all his fear and pent up anger, giving himself to her entirely.

The pair of them lay wrapped in each other's arms later, watching as the sun rose in the sky outside and Donovan traced his fingers in tiny circles across Melody's naked back. She smiled and soon found herself peering down at his impressive body art. No matter how many times she had gazed upon his tattooed body, she was mesmerised by the stunning artwork every time, as though seeing it anew. His depicted scenes of angels and demons were somehow the perfect portrayal of their story, however, he had gotten these tattoos years before they had even met. The stunning woman atop a dark throne on one arm was indeed Cate. The likeness was uncanny. On his other bicep was a white angel with her arms and wings wrapped around her demonic lover in a heart-wrenching scene of powerful love surviving against all odds.

"Do you think this is you and me?" Melody asked, tracing her finger over the huge muscle with that scene painted on him. They really were part of him, as though this ink truly belonged on his body in such a way that plain skin there would be the foreign presence rather than the art.

"Yes, I used to stare at that one for hours, hoping that one day I would find my angel who could love me despite my darkness, but I never thought it could ever happen. I found out recently that the artist who designed and tattooed me is a prophet, makes sense now." He grinned and kissed Melody's forehead. "You've fixed parts of me that have been broken since I was a little boy. I only knew loneliness, fear, greed and self-loathing until there was you. Even then I still let those deviant urges rule me, but not anymore and never again Mel. I love you so much, and with every beat of my heart, I love you more," Donovan told her, his dark eyes alight and happy.

"Don't," she whispered, burying her face in his shoulder. "I'm not ready to be loved just yet, not that much anyway," Melody said, still feeling as though those emotions were a forbidden urge, just as forbidden as Donovan's dark ones. She still worried that Corey might appear at any moment and punish them both for her betrayal and wondered if she would ever feel truly free of him. But she also knew that she had to trust that her dark in-laws and leaders would do as they had promised and keep them safe from him. In the meantime, she knew it would just take her a little time to learn and to trust again.

"Never. I know he made you feel unlovable, but I'm going to spend the rest of my life proving how wrong he was. You are the centre of my entire universe, my night and my day. You will never hear me say that I hate you, and I will never hurt you. I would die before I ever let anyone hurt you again, I love you Melody and I am going to tell you so at least ten times every day for the rest of your life," Donovan promised, taking her beautiful face in his hands and then kissing her passionately.

"I can't wait to be your wife, Donovan Caine. No matter how wicked or deviant you can be, you'll always be beautiful to me," she whispered, grinning up at him like a lovesick little girl.

"The feeling is entirely mutual, Miss Pembroke," he replied, refusing, as ever, to acknowledge her soon to be absolved marriage to Corey.

***

When they were getting ready to go to the Crimson Brotherhood's headquarters the following Sunday for brunch, Melody still felt uneasy, especially at having Astrid come along with them. Laurie had stayed on to work with her and had been given the role as Astrid's nanny, and Melody trusted her completely thanks to their history and close bond. She also was mindful of the fact that she was soon due to inherit Laurie's contract from Leyla, cementing her power over her assistant, but she promised herself that she would never abuse that control. It would just help her to put her trust in Laurie a little easier.

Melody wasn't looking forward to going to the headquarters with everyone there though, and she couldn't help but feel as if Astrid should be far away from the many poisonous people who still lived inside those walls. She wanted nothing more than to refuse Devin's invitation but at the same time a big part of her wanted them, especially the likes of Heath and Logan, to see for themselves that she, Leyla and Donovan had taken down the terrible tyrant Corey Black at last. She wanted to walk through the hall with her head held high and have everyone see how strong she now was and how commanding. Cate's words to her that day at the penthouse resonated inside of her and she knew that her Dark Queen had been right.

Now that they were no longer accompanied by a demonic guardian, they could not teleport, but neither Melody or Donovan cared at the moment, knowing that they were about to be transformed forever later that afternoon and could then do all of those things themselves. They had left their home in London on the Saturday and then made their way to the beautiful Yorkshire town of Harrogate, where they would await collection to head the rest of the way to the Crimson Brotherhood's headquarters with an escort the following morning.

Donovan had sensed her fear before they even arrived, and so when Sunday morning came, he wrapped their precious child up in a baby carrier that he strapped protectively across his torso, her tiny head poking out and watching the world go by now that she was more inquisitive. Melody loved how Donovan cared so much for Astrid. Her tiny face would light up when he cooed at her and he too would show her a dazzling smile full of pure happiness and love in return. He had also helped Melody to bond with Astrid once she had her back again, having struggled after missing out on the first few weeks of her life. But, he had pushed her and supported Melody every step of the way, taking charge at times but also knowing when to take a step back and let their bond develop naturally.

Donovan looked every inch the handsome, doting stepfather and neither he nor Melody had then shied away from the paparazzi that had already snapped at them. The photos of the couple setting off from the house together had already begun circulating online, but neither of them cared. He had moved into her huge house with her weeks ago and the papers had gone crazy, desperate for their story, but neither one had personally revealed anything to the press yet. They both still needed some time to let the dust settle before they could be strong enough to let others publicly piece together their fraught story.

Despite being used to teleporting, the two lovebirds had actually enjoyed the long journey together the day before and had then woken up refreshed and relaxed in their hotel that morning. They had then gone for a long walk through the beautiful gardens in the bright morning sunshine together as a family. Donovan was dressed casually, his baggy, ripped jeans and biker jacket showing off his impressive muscles while Melody wore tight, skinny black jeans, a checked shirt and leather jacket, both of them stylishly effortless yet as beautiful a couple as anyone had ever seen. They looked amazing together and exuded an air of tenderness and pure love that everyone could see clearly. Added to that, the cheerful, smiling baby who rested happily against his chest and their perfect family portrait became clear. The world had come to accept Melody and Donovan as an item again, and had acknowledged their pain despite neither of them ever telling a soul the truth about what had happened that night after the fundraiser. The rumours were rife though, the eavesdropped conversation between Corey and the two of them that night having been passed around like Chinese whispers, however the fact remained and was now quite clear to all the gossipers – Corey Black had been a controlling, manipulative husband who had driven a deliberate wedge between Melody and Donovan back when they were dating in order to have her for himself. Over time, she had become a forced submissive to his controlling nature, but eventually Donovan had seen Corey for who he truly was and had fought for her. The true hero, it seemed, had lived in the shadows all along, but was now free to get the girl and live happily ever after. They really were happier than ever now too thanks to their freedom and the acceptance of them as an item by those closest to each of them. Melody's family were told the watered-down version of her story and

Donovan's closest friends the same, but all agreed that the couple radiated a happy, carefree feel to them now that the love of their soulmate was finally theirs.

Jonah had performed a mirage spell shortly after the party to make himself look like Corey, and he had let himself get photographed as he moved out of both their home and the country months ago. Jonah had gone a step further and posed for shots of him, as Corey, going off to rehab a few days later, adding to the cover story of his breakdown and Melody had been grateful to him for helping her.

She had then ensured that their publicists had run with the story of how Donovan had swooped in to save the day and protect his one-true-love, needing him to be the hero in everyone's eyes, not just hers and Astrid's. Since then they had remained quiet, reclusive even, and Melody had worked from home in order to maintain some privacy while the dust settled. This outing was Melody, Donovan, and Astrid's first public appearance as a family and although she was tense, Melody still loved every second of it. Donovan's hand never let go of hers, and just that link helped them both hold their heads high. The paparazzi were thrilled to finally catch a glimpse of the three of them, especially baby Astrid who had been hidden away for months alongside her mother and stepfather, and they could all see the change in Melody now, not just in her physical appearance but in her entire demeanour.

As they walked along the cobbled streets and stopped at a café for a cup of tea together in the sunshine, Melody's smile was wider and more genuine than ever before. Nothing could break them ever again. She had complete faith now that her life was finally headed in the right direction and she had already begun planning out her future with Donovan by her side.

He watched her, relishing in her bright smile and basking in her laugh, two things he hadn't seen in her for a long time but just recently had found their way back to her again. Donovan was madly, devastatingly in love with Melody. There was no doubt about it. But, he was in love with all of her, the good and the bad, the broken and the mended. Despite her developments, he could see that she was still struggling. She had finally told him every single thing that Corey had done to her over their time together and the pair of them had wept for what felt like days as Melody finally let go and offloaded her awful past. She was strong now, stronger than even she realised herself, but she could still be that scared girl again in a heartbeat and he hated it. Donovan had seen it for himself just a few days before, when Melody had been making them coffee in the kitchen. He had slammed his hand down beside her to squash a bug, the loud and sudden forcefulness of his blow to the counter top sending her into a panic attack the likes he hadn't seen her have in weeks, and Melody had fallen to her knees instinctually in submission. Donovan had joined her on the floor, wrapping her up in his bear-like grip until she came back to herself, her body still trembling even then, and it had been hours before she was back to normal again.

Melody, Donovan, and Astrid arrived at the hamlet later that morning of the brunch. The three of them made their way inside, instantly greeted by Devin and Serena, who cooed over Astrid but didn't try to lift her out of Donovan's hold, understanding their need to keep her close. At six months old, Astrid had already developed her own little personality and had a happy smile that only those close to her ever received. She already seemed to know to be wary of strangers and so never warmed to people straight away. She looked like a real mixture of her parents, with Corey's blond hair and Melody's hazel eyes, she even had the tiny dimples in her cheeks that Melody had as a young child and the tiny streaks of red from her father that had now begun to show in her already curling locks.

"Welcome back," Serena said, giving her granddaughter a kiss on her tiny forehead before hugging Melody and kissing her cheek affectionately.

"Thank you for having us, and for everything you've both done to ensure our safety," Melody replied, being carefully courteous because she was aware that while Corey most certainly deserved his punishment, he was still their child and it would be hard for them both to keep being reminded of his misgivings.

Laurie arrived soon after them and Donovan finally handed over their little bundle, who was now fast asleep in his strong arms, to their most trusted assistant. He and Melody were then led into a small office towards the back of the huge main mansion and they sat down opposite their omnipotent leaders. Devin leaned forward and spoke first, eloquently and calmly.

"So, as you are both aware, the balance of power has been altered, leaders changed and our worlds united at last thanks to the Dark Queen and her angelic daughter. The time of reckoning has been and gone, the wars have been fought and won. Now, while that's great for Heaven and Hell, it is left to us to ensure that our Earthly realm is led in a way that will reflect that balance. It is a realm that Serena and myself have inhabited permanently for over fifty years and we have built an empire over that time, a following all of our own whilst serving the Dark Queen. Over the years, we have procured many souls for many uses—servitude, power in various industries, command over armies, control of countries and sometimes for just the sheer thrill of having a well-known tyrant or dictator of ours in the history books. We do this for power, control, and command, for what else is there in this life or the next to strive for?" Devin asked, his speech sending Melody's mind into overdrive as she thought about all the humans she had worked with over the last few years that served the Crimson Brotherhood and their dark deals. She had never considered how it was they had come to be so very powerful, such a dominant force in the human world and yet the humans still had no real idea that they even existed. "Conspiracy theories have always been rife when it comes to us and our cause, but they only add to our orders' intrigue and has even made humans seek us out in the hopes we would deliver them their dreams. Most of the time we do, if they are worthy and have something decent to offer us, and other times we recruit them as followers instead, a concept which I know you are well aware of now," Devin continued, looking at Melody and she nodded.

"As I told you before, today the demon Tilly will be coming here. She wishes to join our order as a demonic client and so has been given an inductive task to complete in order to prove her loyalty. You are not to speak to her of her task, for she believes it to be secret, but after it is all over we can sit down with her and you can officially meet at last," he added.

"She's a demon now?" Melody asked, taken aback by Devin's explanation of her.

"Yes, Blake turned her. I understand the two of you met a while ago?" Devin asked, and Melody nodded. "She was almost killed by a white witch before the treaty was formed and so was turned directly into a demon rather than the Black Prince let her die. Tilly is now a level one demon, and she has come to the Crimson Brotherhood to ask for our help. In return she has agreed to join us and carry out whatever tasks we ask of her." Devin told them and his powerful wife sat forward to speak up at last.

"Demons, angels, warlocks, and witches on either side may ask for our help, just as humans do, and we are sworn to give it to them. But only as long as they pledge themselves to the Crimson Brotherhood in return for our support. Tilly has agreed to join us, but she is not anyone's follower or client, she is a demonic ally and therefore her account will be taken by myself, Devin or Braeden, no one else is to be involved unless we ask for your assistance. Even as guardians, the two of you will only be privy to the information we allow, otherwise it is not your place to ask questions," Serena added.

"Understood, your Majesties. We will only carry out the duties we spoke of a few days ago and anything you come to us with, we just want to be happy and be together," Donovan told them, settling the matte. Both their powerful leaders seemed satisfied.

"Excellent, speaking of, your marriage to Corey has now been dissolved, Melody. You are free to do as you wish, marry who you wish," Devin told her, having looked at Donovan when he said the word 'marry'. "I will only ask one favour of you. Would you keep Astrid's surname as Black, for our legacy? We will never intervene in her life, or ask you for anything when it comes to our granddaughter, but we do want you to know that you can trust us to take care of her if you feel ready to let her out of your sight anytime, it would be our pleasure to babysit or look after her so that you two can have some time alone. We want to be part of her life Melody, but we will leave that up to you and promise never to push you," Devin added, and Melody couldn't help but catch the sad look that swept across both his and Serena's faces as he said it. She knew that they could be trusted, but she just wanted to wait until they had finally made her a guardian before relinquishing her tight bubble around her little girl.

"We know that we can trust you both. I promise we will let you have her to stay when everything calms down," Melody replied, feeling ready to move the conversation on.

"I'd like that," Serena whispered, taking her husband's hand in hers. She was a truly beautiful woman. Her accent reminded Melody of an old American movie star she had seen on television once with her deep colloquial British tones combined with Americanisms that she couldn't seem to lose despite her many years away from that home. "We will proceed with your rituals this evening after everything with Tilly has been arranged. There are many matters at hand, many things at play right now and you'll forgive us for not being too forthcoming at first, but in time, you will learn and advance higher within our order. No one will treat you with disrespect again. No one will ever harm you and you will each have the power to both help and to punish those who require your attention."

"Sounds good to me. I'll be starting with Heath if that's okay?" Donovan asked, a dark glint in his eye that was a clear look of revenge.

"I'm afraid that while he assisted both of our children, he is the chief warlock of Leyla's coven, so no, you cannot punish him," Devin replied, his serious face then breaking out into a wicked grin. "But she can," he added, pointing at Melody, and she couldn't help but smile broadly back at him.

"Of course, I'm inheriting what was once hers, so that includes her coven, I assume?" Melody asked, and Devin nodded.

"Absolutely, and with that comes the responsibility of keeping them in line, in check. Heath has been a deviant and disgusting part of Leyla's team for far too long. You will have the opportunity soon to punish him however you see fit."

CHAPTER THIRTY-FOUR

Later at the brunch, Melody and Donovan chatted happily with other members of the Crimson Brotherhood while enjoying the elegant food and good company. The two of them were congratulated on their relationship and wished well by everyone they spoke with, adding to their trust of the Brotherhood and its members at long last.

"Ms Pembroke, Mr Caine. It's a pleasure to meet you, my name is Maximilian Dante and I would like to introduce my companion," one of the members, an American who had teleported over especially for the brunch said, bowing graciously as though he already knew they were due to become guardians soon. Melody recognised his guest immediately but waited for the demon to give them her name, as was the custom.

"Tilly Mayfair," said the demon to his right, smiling and shaking each of their hands as they greeted one another. "It's wonderful to meet you both."

"It's a pleasure to chat with you at last Tilly, and congratulations on your transition," Melody replied, taken in by the stunning demon. She still felt that niggle of envy in her gut at knowing that Blake had not only changed his bad-boy ways for her but that he had also sired her in order for them to be together for all eternity. She had known from the start that Corey would never do that for her, but it still stung a little. "I saw you and your fiancé at the penthouse a little over a year ago, but unfortunately, we didn't have the chance to speak with each other. You were, how should I say it, otherwise engaged."

"Yes, I remember that night fondly," Tilly joked, smiling widely as she reminisced. "Blake told me that he had invited you and Corey. I'm sorry I didn't get the chance to say hello."

"Don't be. It was a pleasure to be there, and he was very welcoming, as was the Dark Queen. It was just a shame that we weren't in a position to join in at the time, as I was in rather a delicate way," Melody said, a cunning smile on her lips.

"I'll be sure to invite you along again in future then, especially now that you and your soulmate have connected at last. I was very sorry to learn of the full extent of Corey's overbearing ways. It's good to see that you are strong and happy again. You deserve it," replied her demonic companion, her smile genuine, and Melody really did feel as though they could be friends somewhere down the line. "I understand you have also met Lottie? She and I grew very close before she went to Heaven. I miss her terribly," Tilly added and Melody grinned widely, thinking of the beautiful angel who had given her so much in just the short time she had spent with her and Camael in Heaven.

"I bet you do, she's the most beautiful thing I've ever seen. She took Corey's mark away and stole me away when he almost killed me. I'll be forever grateful for her and Camael," Melody replied, a tear in her eye and Tilly smiled warmly back at her before they both forced themselves to move the conversation on before they broke down. The small group chatted for a little while longer before Tilly was pulled away to chat with more of the Brotherhood's members, all of whom very eager to have her ear. She had become infamous as both Blake's human lover who had thawed his cold heart and won him forever and as the first royal-blooded demon.

Melody suspected that the Dark Queen had great plans for this woman and didn't envy her that sense of servitude she assumed might come with the territory as Blake's powerful follower, vowing to herself to try and become Tilly's friend in the future. She would no doubt need an understanding shoulder to cry on eventually and unfortunately Melody was well versed in these dark beings and their sinister designs, so she knew she could prove herself to be a much-needed comrade as time went on.

Later that evening, after everyone else had gone home and Tilly had reportedly completed her initiation task, Melody and Donovan were summoned to Devin and Serena's private chambers. They made their way down the hall, hand in hand, and neither spoke as they let the realisation sink in of what was about to happen. Melody stopped just outside the door and planted a deep, passionate kiss on Donovan's lips.

"What was that for?" he asked, stroking his hands up to her face and taking her cheeks in his palms.

"I just wanted one more kiss while we are still just you and I, humans who are disturbingly flawed but who love each other and will do anything to protect that," she replied, wrapping her hands around his waist.

"By the end of tonight, we will have changed, yes. But not in any way that will affect or alter the way we think or feel about one another. This progression is going to give us the life we both truly deserve Mel, by taking this guardianship, I am protecting our love and our future. Imagine it, we will not die and become demonic playthings. We will not grow old and miss out on our daughter's long life. Meeting you was where my life truly began and it just so happens that the end is luckily getting further and further away," he replied, grinning broadly and she nodded, calm and ready again after her momentary lapse in courage.

"Then what are we waiting for? Let's get in there," she replied, taking his hand again and following his lead.

Inside the small room, two pentagrams had been drawn on the floor, one in black and one in white. Neither Donovan nor Melody needed to ask which one they were to stand in and took their places while waiting for whatever ritual they needed to complete to start.

Devin and Serena appeared, each of them accompanied by a powerful being. Serena held onto Camael's arm, chatting quietly as she led him towards Melody and he joined her inside the white pentagram. Her grandfather kissed her cheek affectionately and held her close, his light power seeping into her again just like it had in Heaven, and Melody smiled up at him, welcoming his shared essence. Devin led the other attendee over to Donovan, who greeted his grandmother, the demon Lilith, with a kiss on her cheek and a broad smile as she, too, joined him inside the black pentagram and held his hand.

"This is the first time I have actually laid eyes on you, my dear boy," Lilith said, peering up into his eyes with an unusually soft expression. "I'll make sure it's not the last," she promised. Donovan seemed too choked up to respond. He just nodded and pursed his lips, taking a moment to look upon the face of his only family with a tender, loving gaze.

"Thank you both for coming," Devin said, addressing both the demon and angel as the four of them turned towards him, awaiting their next instructions. "In order for your two descendants to transition into our order as powerful guardians, they not only need guidance and knowledge but also power and ancient wisdom that comes from an offering that only powerful entities can provide. It must come from family. The primeval laws will only allow the sharing of essence to empower a human but not turn them if it is a willing family member who carries out the ritual. As Melody and Donovan's kin, are you both willing to share some of your essence with your relatives in order to empower them both with light and darkness?"

"Yes," both Camael and Lilith replied, each of them holding out their wrists to Serena. She approached and slit Camael's arm first, pushing the bloody forearm into Melody's mouth, and she drank down his offered blood for a few minutes before Serena then pulled it away again. Camael then rubbed his arm with his fingertips, healing the wound instantly and he then held onto his woozy granddaughter while Serena moved sideways and did the same to Lilith. Melody watched as Donovan drank his grandmother's blood too, her eyes drawn to his as he did so and she saw his dark nature rise from deep within. She sensed it come to blacken his eyes but then he commanded it, controlled it and by the time Lilith's wrist was withdrawn he was back to his usual self again.

"Turn to face each other in the pentagram," Devin told them, and all did as they were told. "You have each been chosen to receive a great gift of almighty power. You will be forever connected to your omnipotent kindred and will be a vessel for their forces on Earth. Do you promise you will harness their offering and use it to help ensure a balance to our worlds?" he asked, looking between the pair of them.

"Yes," both Melody and Donovan answered, even though neither looked away from their powerful grandparents' gaze.

"Good. Your family have shared their essence willingly, and a bond connects you for eternity from here onwards. Now, seal your union with a kiss." He ordered them. Without hesitation, Melody lifted up onto her tiptoes and planted a tender kiss on Camael's lips, sensing as his given power seemed to explode within her and reverberate around her entire being. He held her tight, not letting her go until the transition was complete. By the time she pulled away she felt amazing, full of light power and strong. Melody looked up into his eyes and smiled.

"Thank you," she whispered, sensing his love and warmth towards her through a new and very potent bond.

"You are very welcome," Camael replied, taking her forearm and then sliding the tip of his index finger across it delicately in the same way Leyla had once done, this time drawing a cross with a star behind it which glowed gold against her pale skin. "This is your mark Melody, the symbol of your guardianship that you will share with your followers and clients from now onwards. You are not beholden to any deal, nor is there any claim on your soul. Congratulations," he told her, grinning and laughing when she then wrapped her arms around him tightly.

Lilith did the same to Donovan, delicately tracing a new inverted cross on his forearm, which came up red before she added a black rose to it, indicating his new symbol of guardianship, too. He smiled and thanked her, finding his voice at last, and she kissed his cheek affectionately.

"Well done, both of you. Welcome to the Crimson Brotherhood, guardians Caine and Pembroke. Say goodbye to your grandparent's for now, we have many matters to discuss and powers to teach you," Devin told them and, after hugging Lilith and Camael goodbye, both Donovan and Melody stepped out of their pentagrams and took each other's hands. Their light and dark powers ignited between them as their skin touched, delivering each of them with an intense, primeval spark. It was an overwhelming force of balance, power, love and trust that sent a throb straight to Melody's core. She basked in that wonderful glow for a moment before finally peering up at Donovan excitedly.

"Whoa, so opposites really do attract," he whispered, grinning down at his lover.

During the next few days, Melody and Donovan quickly learned all about their new higher powers and how to use them. Neither would age naturally nor die now that they possessed more light or dark power than humanity inside of them, so while they were not full angels or demons, they were as close to being so as any human could be. They could use their powers to alter their ages as necessary over the years before either going into temporary hiding like Devin and Serena had, or by changing their appearance and adopting another family alias in order to remain in the public eye later on. Their incredible strengths now added to their prowess, too. Donovan finally knew what he was trying to fight against with Corey all those times and he shook his head after a training session with Coby one morning, laughing to himself.

"I never stood a chance before, did I?" he asked the demonic being who was once his guard but who was now his assistant.

"No, but it was funny watching you imagine taking him or Leyla on. Either one would have eaten you for breakfast," Coby joked, putting ten more kilograms on Donovan's already heavy weights bar. "Remember that day on the beach when she repeatedly kicked my arse without even breaking a sweat? Talk about embarrassing, but you would've been down after the first blow, mate."

"Are you two gonna get over your bruised egos and get ready? We need to be at the studio in half an hour," Melody chimed in from across the room, her hair and makeup having been expertly done by her re-instated assistant Meri. She looked beautiful, calm and powerful now thanks to her transformation, in far more ways than just physically. They were due to go back to London and begin their transition back into their old lives as CEO and movie star, starting with a meeting to discuss Donovan's newest movie contract, and she was well aware that they were already running late.

Donovan did a few more lifts and then stood from the bench, grinning over at Melody and then teleporting behind her, gathering her up in his strong arms. She wriggled herself free and ran away, laughing. They had been practising their teleportation techniques religiously and were both fast learners, their powers flowing easily to assist from within them when either called upon it and her strength now perfectly matched his despite their vast differences in shape and size.

"You can run angel, it's okay. I don't mind catching you," he groaned, his wicked grin so sexy and alluring.

"No way. We have somewhere to be, and I will not let you distract me. Even if those biceps are driving me crazy," she teased, teleporting away before he could grab her again.

The happy pair arrived at the studios just in time for their morning meeting to begin, having teleported directly into her office. Melody shot Donovan her best scowl, but he just laughed it off, throwing her over his shoulder as though she weighed nothing, and then deposited her on the huge desk.

"Just give me five more minutes. They can wait," he pleaded, sliding his hands up her thighs and cupping her mound. Melody gave in, as always, but eyed him with the dominant stare she was now so used to engaging when it came to their sexual moments together. Whether tender or wild, Donovan still needed to be led, and he watched her, eagerly awaiting her instructions.

"You have precisely five minutes. Tell me what you want to do to me," she whispered, biting her lip as she peered up at him.

"Well, firstly these panties would need to go," Donovan replied, pushing them aside with his finger, delicately tracing the tip around her already throbbing nub as he did, and Melody groaned.

"Yes, what else?"

"Then I need to touch you, but the place I need to feel is so deep inside that I can only get there by doing this," he told her, sliding two fingers deep inside her wet opening and pressing down on her g-spot. "Ah yes, there it is," Donovan added, falling to his knees before her, and Melody laid her thighs on his shoulders as he continued to rub her.

"What else?"

"I need to taste this," Donovan said, planting a tender kiss against her clit before parting his lips and pulling it into his hot mouth. Melody gasped as he sucked, rubbing his tongue around her throbbing nerve ending for a few moments and bringing her quickly to the edge of her climax thanks to the wonderful combination of his mouth and his fingers working expertly in sync.

"Very good, and what comes next?" she breathed, already beginning to unravel.

"You," he groaned, pressing down harder with his tongue, and he gripped Melody's thigh tightly with his free hand as she exploded in orgasm beneath him.

CHAPTER THIRTY-FIVE

Present day

Down in Hell, Cate sat back and let the memories Tilly had finally shown her following her meeting with Devin and Serena wash over her again. She could understand the need for one almighty power to take control of the Earth, but she could still not get her head around her sibling's methods in which to gain that power.

The dust had settled now between Heaven and Hell thanks to Lottie's reign as mistress of the High Council of Angels having begun. However, while they were united and at peace for the first time in centuries, Earth still remained an unclaimed buffer between the two worlds thanks to the various beings who occupied it, and the two powerful orders of light and darkness who maintained control over the realm.

Tilly's strange admission regarding Devin's plans for Lucifer had unsettled Cate though, and no matter what happened to the earthly dominion she still held so dear, she knew she had to act upon the information her soon to be daughter-in-law had given her in that terrible dungeon. Devin needed to be interrogated and the reasons for his actions laid out openly for her before Cate could settle her mind. Her faith in her extended family had been broken and the powerful Queen needed him to open his mind up in order for her to regain that trust. Blake had not spoken to her since she had tortured his fiancé, and quite rightly so. Cate knew he understood her reasons though and once Tilly roused from her pain induced slumber, she too would inform him that his mother had had to do it, that she had even given Cate permission to do whatever it took to unlock the secrets Devin and Serena had hidden away in her mind.

She teleported up to the Crimson Brotherhood's headquarters with the next full moon and requested a private meeting with her sibling, eager to have the details from his own mouth. He agreed and led her to his office, watching Cate with a fearful look, a look she had not seen on his face in over one hundred years, and it only served to unsettle her more. She and Devin then sat staring at one another over his desk, the powerful Queen eyeing him thoughtfully.

"So, I thought it was about time we had a little sit down, just you and I. This is your one opportunity to tell me all the things you have tried to hide from me and explain your reasons why," Cate said, letting him know she was now onto him and his secretive methods to try and hide his dealings from his ruler.

"My Queen, I," he began, desperate for a moment to explain himself, but she just raised her hand, silencing him instantly and he watched her intently, letting his sibling carry on.

"I will give you the chance to reveal all before I deliver my verdict, for I am eager to hear just how you can justify your actions against my reign and me. Anyone else would have already been punished beyond belief thanks to what I have already discovered Devin. Poor Tilly is still recovering from her ordeal thanks to you and your secretiveness. Her spilt blood is on your hands and you should be the one to explain it to Blake," Cate told her sired sibling, staring across at him with black eyes and a forceful expression. He could tell that she was furious with him and his methods of trying to find a way to get to their master, and he knew that he would have to tell her the truth now despite how hard it would be for him to reveal his misgivings to his omnipotent sibling.

"Please hear me out," he said again, but quietened thanks to her cold stare.

"Open your mind to me Devin, stop trying to hide the truth and then this will all go a lot smoother," she told him, sensing his hesitation at opening up to her and it just served to anger her more.

He shook his head, taking Cate's hand in his and peering up into her eyes earnestly.

"Not yet, I'll give you everything but I need to explain myself first, just please give me time to tell you and then I'll show you?" he implored and even though Cate was desperate to know just what he had been up to without her knowledge, she couldn't help but be intrigued by his fear. Cate enjoyed watching him squirm, and despite her love for Devin, she leaned in close and couldn't help but whisper a sinister promise into his ear.

"You have my attention Devin, but I will have your soul if I am displeased with your explanation, so you'd better make it good," she whispered, holding his hand tighter and then teleporting him back to Hell with her in order to interrogate her sibling properly.

They arrived in her chambers within seconds, having teleported directly into one of her antechambers that led to many private rooms off of her and Harry's bedroom. Tilly lay asleep in a bed nearby, her body and mind still a mess because of the terrible time she had endured thanks to Cate's recent interrogation tactics. It had worked though and the Dark Queen had gotten everything she had wanted from the still young demon, but she knew that there was much more to the story and now the only one who could give her it was Devin, who now looked down at the demon wide-eyed and Cate was sure she even noticed a chill run down his spine as he contemplated his admissions.

Cate led Devin through to her private office, the doors and windows of which had been magically sealed so that the Dark Queen could always be sure that whatever was said inside these walls was completely private. She sat down in her huge, black chair that was ornately carved with demons and roses, adding to her scary guise as she watched her sibling for a moment.

"So, I understand you want our sire's angelic essence for yourself?" Cate asked as Devin took a seat opposite her. He nodded and peered across at his sibling, taking a deep breath and then beginning his tale of darkness and light.

"Yes, I want it for myself, to empower me. I have discovered over the years that if an angel or demon willingly gives up some of their essence to their direct descendant, they can be empowered with it, effectively turning them into a being of half-light and half-darkness. I have done it recently with Melody and Donovan. Camael and Lilith gave them some of their power and they now embody that given force with ease and natural prowess. I have tried it in the past, but it didn't work. The essence has to come from their kin. You have this realm, and Lottie commands Heaven. I just want what is rightfully mine, what you promised me many years ago when you asked me to live on Earth indefinitely. I want more power. I want to command the Earth and all those who live there. You know I would never abuse my position, that I would rule with respect to the balance of our worlds and never show bias to one side or the other, especially if I am transformed into a half being," Devin said, trying to watch Cate's face for any sign of her response to his words.

"That's all very well Devin, but yet you have not taught your children to live this way you speak of. Why did you allow Corey to take possession of that poor girl and go against your orders? He should have been stopped long before things got so bad, I should never have had to step in," Cate replied, making Devin jump.

"I didn't realise you had to intervene? I'm so sorry, my only weakness is my children, and I have no excuse for his behaviour. I guess I just hoped that Corey would see sense in his own time, that Melody might heal his cold heart, just like Tilly has with Blake. I know now just how wrong I was, how much I failed him. I have given her the existence she deserves, the power she should have always had, and a life ahead of her she can look forward to. What else can I do?" Devin asked her, burying his face in his hands.

"You're right, you've done everything you can to right the wrongs done to that girl. She will be protected forever and so will her child. You are lucky she has such a forgiving nature, otherwise you can guarantee that you would have never laid eyes on that child even once. Don't ever let her come to harm again, is that understood?" Cate asked.

Her eyes were back to their usual shade of green but were speckled with black spots as she thought about the poor young girl who had been forced into the servitude of her kin's order, only to have her life chewed up and spat out again by its powerful leaders. Cate knew Melody was in a happy, safe place now, and she was determined to keep her there.

"Yes, my Queen," he replied, wringing his hands.

"So, on to our other business. Time to reveal all Devin," she reminded him and Devin stared down at his hands, unable to meet his omnipotent sibling's gaze.

"Okay," he whispered, taking a deep breath. "Well. You remember when Tilly was stabbed, and the witch gave her a message to give to you from Uriel? Well, that message actually came from me."

CHAPTER THIRTY-SIX

"What?" Cate bellowed, standing and slamming her powerful hands down onto the table between them, staring at her sibling angrily and visibly shaking. Devin held up his hands and cowered before her, pleading thoughts flowing from him openly as he shrunk back in his seat.

"Please, you promised you'd hear me out," he reminded her, and Cate took her seat, her eyes never leaving his.

"You have precisely one minute to appease this desire I have to rip your lungs from your chest and watch you squirm in misery Devin. How exactly did you put together the attempted murder of Blake's follower?" she asked.

"I digress, I'm sorry," Devin admitted, bowing his head. "The threat was still Uriel's, but there was a deal in place that affected the way that he did it. Deals I had struck with the angel many years ago in order to get what we both wanted." He cringed. "When I began acquiring light beings as members of the Crimson Brotherhood, the angels soon caught on that I was working outside of our usual remit. The archangel Michael sent his coven to retrieve me and I was taken to an astral plane to discuss just why I was tracking down descendants of angels and acquiring their souls. I revealed all, my plans for my own future and my desire for a balanced power, and luckily I appeased them. During the sit-down, Uriel made an appearance. He questioned me at length about Lottie and you, what you were doing, and how she was. I only told him what was necessary but his curiosity on her was far from quenched, he wanted her, wanted to own and command his child as a force for both light and darkness on Earth. While I didn't want that for Lottie, I saw it as an opportunity to get what I desired." Devin told her. He was well aware that his minute was over, but Cate seemed satisfied with his explanation so far, and so he continued, still staring down at his hands as he spoke.

"I made him a deal, as is my nature to do so. I offered to give him Lottie in return for him delivering me Lucifer. I knew you would never just hand over our master if I asked you to, you've made it perfectly clear over the years that he is yours and yours alone to punish for eternity for his terrible actions. I just wanted to see if you would release him. I never intended to give Lottie to Uriel, never. In all honesty, I just wanted you to slip up, to unwittingly reveal our master's location and then I would do the rest, so I had ears on you as much as possible, hoping and praying to get something from you, but you never did."

"You should give me more credit than that," Cate whispered, still eyeing him dangerously, and he conceded, nodding and shrinking back even more before her almighty frame.

"I do, and I knew back then that it would not be so easy, but I was feeling desperate. You have no idea how it feels to have once been given everything by our powerful master, only to have it ripped away again and then having been seemingly forgotten by all those who I placed in such high regard. You and Lucifer were both so happy to just leave me to it up on Earth, and I was expected to get on with things. After a while I began to resent you and everything you had been given. Don't get me wrong, I know you've had it bad. I'm no fool. I truly believe that you deserve your throne, but I think I deserve one too," he said, finally meeting her gaze.

His mistress watched him for a few moments, mulling over the information she had just been given and the jealous reasons behind them. Part of her wanted to give Devin everything he had asked for. She agreed with him for the most part, but just could not get over the way he had gone about it all.

Before too long, her decision was made.

Devin would get what he desired, but at a price. She stood and walked over to him, and then reached down to stroke his face gently.

In a flash, she kicked the chair from underneath him and Devin fell down onto the hard floor, sprawling on his back in shock and she then climbed over him and sat down. She straddled her sibling and pinned him to the ground with barely an ounce of her immense strength before leaning down so that her face was just centimetres away from his. Cate's breath fluttered over his lips as she spoke. Her eyes were jet-black again and were almost lifeless thanks to the intense effervescence of power within her.

"Do you remember when we were younger, Devin? How much we loved one another? I do. I remember how we made love for days and you worshipped my body while I worshipped yours too," she said, her hands stroking his cheeks gently. Devin stayed silent and in shock at her passionate words. However, he sensed her rage and desperately hoped that Cate would calm down.

"I'll always love you. I never stopped," he whispered.

"You may say that, Devin, but your actions say otherwise. You need to show me how much you love me," she replied, her hands finding his shirt, which Cate then ripped from his body in one quick tug. Devin gasped, taken aback by her advances, but he didn't stop her. Despite being terrified, he couldn't help but be turned on by Cate's incredible prowess and he stayed silent, finding himself desperately hoping that her next move would take her hands further south. "Do you want me, Devin? Do you want to be with me again?" Cate whispered, her lips still so close to his, and he groaned.

"Yes. I want you so much, just like we used to," he replied, his heart pounding in his ears.

"You'd cheat on your wife for me? You'd let me cheat on Harry with you?" she asked, panting and grinding into his already bulging hard-on.

"I will give you anything you want. I will do anything you desire, my Queen," Devin replied, watching as Cate sat upright atop him and grinned.

"Anything?"

"Yes," he said, desperate to have her again, but then he stopped dead when he realised what he had just done. He had just given his omnipotent sibling permission to do anything she desired to him, and he knew full well just what she was capable of, and so cringed. She then laughed at the top of her lungs, a sinister, depraved laugh that sent shivers down his spine.

"I was hoping you'd say that," Cate replied. "It's time you stopped with the bullshit, Devin. If you want Lucifer, there's only one way to get to him." She then reached down and scraped her fingernails swiftly across Devin's chest, drawing blood instantly. He cried out, lifting his hands to try and stop her as Cate then began raining down forceful blows to her sibling's chest. Her hands then gripped his wrists and pinned them to the floor on either side of his head.

"Please, I don't wanna die," he mumbled, the deep gashes on his chest making him wince as he spoke.

"You aren't going to die, but you've gotta get pretty close before I can open the prison. You told me I could do anything I wanted to you. This is what I want. Now, hold still," Cate replied, her creepy smile returning to her face and Devin did as he was ordered, pulling his hands behind his head and interlocking his fingers. He closed his eyes and readied himself, hoping that she would go easy on him, but then again, he knew how angry she was and so resigned himself to the fact that this was going to hurt a lot.

Cate let herself go. All the anger, pain and betrayal she felt pouring out of her via her forceful hands. Devin cried out and even sobbed as she punched, scratched, and tore at him ferociously. She ripped flesh and broke bones before finally coming to a stop, her hands wrapped around her sibling's beating heart. His eyes flew open, silent pleas begging her not to crush it, and Cate just laughed again before sliding down over him, the locket that she wore at all times falling forward.

She grabbed it with her free hand.

"I hope you're ready for the horrors that await you in his awful new home. Lucifer is in this locket, Devin. I imprisoned him inside and now he's all yours. I am going to put you in there with him, and you will not be permitted to leave until he is dead. Should you fail or reconsider your decision to kill him, so be it. But, you will never be released unless I am free of him," Cate told him, holding up the locket for Devin to see.

"I understand," he said, staring up at his sibling and eyeing the ornate locket she wore every day. He had seen that same pendant around her neck so many times before and had never considered that it might be their master's final resting place on show to everyone around her, yet no one ever had a clue. Cate smiled as she read his now open thoughts, enjoying her deception, and she then wrenched her hand out of Devin's chest cavity, taking with it his beating heart.

He gasped and sputtered, fear filling his eyes, and Cate watched him for a few seconds, basking in his dread. She then shoved his heart back in, watching as his body quickly healed again, but he was far too weak to speak or even hold her gaze.

"There we go, now you are ready," she whispered softly, stroking her bloody hand down Devin's cheek in an oddly affectionate way. He stirred but didn't say anything, his weak body completely at his Dark Queen's command. She then held the locket over his freshly repaired heart and closed her eyes.

"By the power of light and dark, I take command over your mind, body and soul, Devin. You are mine to command and shall never be free from this prison until I, and I alone, release you," she said, over and over again, until his limp form began to shudder beneath her. Within minutes, he was pulled inside the locket, the magical doorway opening ever so slightly to let him inside, and then the locket was sealed shut again.

Cate then let out a shrill scream, offloading the remainder of her torment in one blood-curdling moment of pure, desperate fury. She stared down at the now empty space beneath her, the floor that was covered in blood, along with her clothes and hands.

"Don't let me down Devin," she whispered, holding the locket tightly in her bloody palm before heading off to get cleaned up and to see to her children and husband. Despite everything that she had just done, Cate shook off her anxiety and forced her calm mask to fall back in perfect place. They had a wedding to plan and a white warlock to try and turn, and she was looking forward to taking the next step in making her family whole again, while Devin did her a macabre favour and took care of the devil on her shoulder, just like Lottie had taken care of the angel that had been on the opposite one.

***

"Master?" Devin said, his body curled in a protective ball as he looked at the filthy cell around him. He expected to find a weak, feeble old man, but instead his blood ran cold and his vision eluded him as shadows seemed to attack his senses and render him powerless. All he saw were the black eyes and fearsome face that then pounced at him from within the darkness, Lucifer's deranged sights set on nothing but the death of his oldest son. During his long imprisonment and the torturous punishments inflicted on him by his daughter, Lucifer had turned into nothing but a wretched shell of the powerful being he once was. He was now full of nothing but hatred and malefic intent, and while Cate was the real object of his depraved, murderous fantasies, Devin would have to do for now.

"Your master is long gone, Devin, but there's one way you can make me strong again. You can give me back the power I once gave you," came Lucifer's hoarse voice as he closed in on him.

"Funny, that's exactly the reason why I'm here too," he replied, readying himself for the fight that was no doubt about to ensue.

The end.

About the author

LM Morgan started her writing career putting together short stories and fan fiction, usually involving her favourite movie characters caught up in steamy situations and wrote her first full-length novel in 2013. A self-confessed computer geek, LM enjoys both the writing and editing side of her journey, and regularly seeks out the next big gadget on her wish list.

She spends her days with her hubby, looking after her two young children and their cocker spaniel Milo, as well as making the most of her free time by going to concerts with her friends, or else listening to rock music at home while writing (a trend many readers may have picked up on in her stories.)

Like many authors, LM Morgan has a regular playlist of tracks she enjoys listening to while writing, featuring the likes of Slipknot, Stone Sour, Papa Roach, Five Finger Death Punch, and Shinedown. If you'd like to listen along with her, you can find her playlist on Spotify under 'writing dark romance'.

LM Morgan also loves hearing from her fans, and you can connect with her via www.lmauthor.com

If you enjoyed this book, please take a moment to share your thoughts by leaving a review to help promote her work.

LM Morgan's novels include:

The Black Rose series:
When Darkness Falls: A Short Prequel to the Black Rose series
Embracing the Darkness: book 1 in the Black Rose series
A Slave to the Darkness: book 2 in the Black Rose series
Forever Darkness: book 3 in the Black Rose series
Destined for Darkness: book 4 in the Black Rose series
A Light in the Darkness: book 5 in the Black Rose series
Don't Pity the Dead, Pity the Immortal: Novella #1
Two Worlds, One War: Novella #2
Taming Ashton: Novella #3

And her contemporary romance novels:
Forever Lost (gangster/crime)
Forever Loved (gangster/crime follow on from Forever Lost)
Rough Love (MC crime/mystery story. Can be read as a stand-alone)
Ensnared – A dark romance
Tommy's Girl parts one and two (dark psychological thriller)
Dark Nights and White Lights: A collection of short stories, flash fiction and poems
Tommy's Girl parts one and two (dark psychological thriller)

LM also writes YA Science Fiction under the alias LC Morgans, with her new novels:
Humankind: Book 1 in the Invasion Days series
Autonomy: Book 2 in the Invasion Days series
Resonant: Book 3 in the Invasion Days series
Hereafter: Book 4 in the Invasion Day series
Renegades: Book 5 in the Invasion Day series

LM also writes dark vampire fantasy under the alias Eden Wildblood, with her new novels:
The Beginning: Book 1 in the Blood Slave series
Round Two: Book 2 in the Blood Slave series
Made of Scars: Book 3 in the Blood Slave series
Even in Death: Book 4 in the Blood Slave series
Tortured Souls: Book 5 in the Blood Slave series

Printed in Great Britain
by Amazon

32251628R00207